SWORD-SWORN

SWORD-SWORN

A Novel of Tiger and Del

JENNIFER ROBERSON

DAW BOOKS, INC.

DONALD A. WOLLHEIM, FOUNDER

375 Hudson Street, New York, NY 10014

ELIZABETH R. WOLLHEIM
SHEILA E. GILBERT
PUBLISHERS

www.dawbooks.com

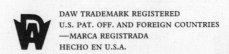

DAW TRADEMARK REGISTERED
U.S. PAT. OFF. AND FOREIGN COUNTRIES
—MARCA REGISTRADA
HECHO EN U.S.A.

PRINTED IN THE U.S.A.

For
Shera Roberson
March 5, 1928–April 9, 1999

In 1998, I finished a historical novel just at the end of the year. My next task was to begin this one. I took a couple of months off to recharge the batteries and planned to get started in early '99.

But that March, my mother was diagnosed with cancer. As the only child of a long-divorced woman, I became primary caregiver; within ten days of the diagnosis, I became executor.

Some authors work through their grief. But I found myself caught in the midst of a tremendous sea-change: my mother, dead; plus the responsibilities of packing up, closing down, and preparing for market the house I grew up in, while also doing the same with my own home as I prepared to move to another locale along with ten dogs and three cats. Frankly, writing a book became incidental.

Life has settled down now. I have returned to writing full time. But I must pay tribute to my mother, who was the classic "guiding force" behind my love of books; who read to me nightly as I fell asleep; who critiqued my early attempts at fiction; who never once failed to support my efforts; who took such joy in my publication. From the time I was fourteen and writing my first novel until a few days before she died, she encouraged me always to chase my dreams.

Mom, you never got to read the most recent of my works.
But I know you are a part of those books,
as you will be a part of everything I write.
God speed.

SWORD-SWORN

PROLOGUE

THE SAND was very fine and very pale, like Del's hair. As her skin had been once; but first the Southron sun, followed by that of the sea voyage and its salt-laden wind—and our visit to the isle of Skandi—had collaborated insidiously to gild her to a delicate creamy peach. She was still too fair, too Northern, to withstand the concerted glare of this sun for any length of time without burning bright red, but definitely not as fair as she'd been when we first met.

Oh. That's right. I was talking about the sand.

Anyway, it was very fine, and very pale, and I had worked carefully to smooth it with a good-sized peeling of the skinny, tall, frond- and beard-bedecked palm tree overlooking the beach, the ocean beyond, the ship I'd hired in Skandi—and then I had ruined all that meticulous smoothness by drawing in it.

A circle.

A *circle*.

I had thought never to enter one again.

But I smoothed the sand, and I drew the circle, and then I stepped across the line into the center. The center *precisely*.

Thunder did not crash. Rain did not fall. Lightning did not split the sky asunder. The gods, if any truly existed, either didn't care that I had once again entered a circle, or else they were off gallivanting around someone else's patch of the world.

"Hah," I muttered, indulging myself with a smirk.

"Hah, what?" she asked, from somewhere behind me.

I didn't turn. "I have done the undoable."

"Ah."

"And nothing has smited me."

"Smitten."

"Nothing has *smitten* me."

"Yet."

Now I did turn. She stood hipshot in the sand, with legs reaching all the way up to her neck. They were mostly bare, those legs; she habitually wore, when circumstances did not prohibit, a sleeveless, high-necked leather tunic that hit her about mid-thigh. In the South she also wore a loose burnous over the leather tunic, so as to shield her flesh from the bite of the sun, but we were not in the South. We were on an island cooled by balmy ocean breezes, and she had left off most of such mundane accou-trements as clothing that covered her body.

I did say she had legs up to her neck. Don't let that suggest there wasn't a body in between. Oh, yes. There was.

"Lo, I am smitten," I announced in tones of vast masculine appreciation.

Once she might have hit me, or come up with a devastating reprimand. But she knew I was joking. Well, not entirely—I *do* appreciate every supple, sinuous inch of her—but that apprecia-tion has been tempered by her, well, *temper*, out of unmitigated lust into mere gentlemanly admiration.

Mostly.

Del arched one pale brow. "Are you practicing languages and their tenses?"

"What?"

"Smite, smote, smitten."

I grinned at her. "I don't need to practice. I speak them all now."

The arch in the brow flattened. Del still wasn't sure how to take jokes about my new status. Hoolies, joking about it was all I *could* do, since I didn't understand much about the new status myself.

Del decided to ignore it. "So. A circle."

I felt that was entirely self-evident and thus regarded her in fulsomely patient silence.

Her expression was carefully blanked. "And you're *in* it."

I nodded gravely. "So is my sword."

Now she was startled. "Sword?"

I hefted it illustratively.

"That's a *stick*, Tiger."

I clicked my tongue against the roof of my mouth. "And here you've been telling me for years I have no imagination." I pointed with said stick. "Go get yourself one. I put a few over there, by that pile of rocks."

Both brows shot up toward her hairline. "You want to spar?"

"I do."

"I thought—" But she broke it off sharply. Then had the grace to blush.

Delilah blushing is not anything approaching ordinary. I was delighted, even though the reason for it was not particularly complimentary. "What, you thought I was lying to you, or giving in to wishful thinking? Maybe fooling myself altogether about developing new skills and moves?"

She did not look away—Del avoids no truths, even the hard ones—but neither did the blush recede.

I shook my head. "I thought you understood what all the weeks of physical training have been about."

"Recovery," she said. "Getting fit."

"I have recovered, and I am fit."

She did not demur; it was true. "But you did all that without a circle."

So I had. And then some. Though I had yet to sort out how I had managed it. A man entering his fourth decade cannot begin to compete with the man in his second. But even my knees of late had given up complaining.

Maybe it was the ocean air.

Or not.

It was the *'or not'* that made me nervous.

Clearing my throat, I declared, "I will dance my own dances, Del."

"But—" Again she silenced herself.

But. A very heavy word, that 'but,' freighted with all manner of innuendo and implication.

But.

But, she wanted to ask, how does a man properly grip a sword when he's missing the little fingers on both hands? *But*, how does he keep that grip if a blade strikes his? *But*, how can he hope to overcome an opponent in the circle? How can he win the dance? How can he, who carries a price on his head, win back his life in the ritualized combat of the South, when he has been cast out of it by his own volition? When the loss of the fingers precludes all former skill?

But.

I saw the assumption in her eyes, the slight flicker of concern.

"I have every intention of dancing," I said quietly, "and none at all of dying." For as long as possible.

"*Can* you?" she asked, frank at last.

"Dance? Yes. Win? Well, we've never properly settled that question, have we? Some days you'll win, other days I will." I shrugged. How many of those days I had left was open to interpretation. "As for the others I'll dance with . . . well, we'll just have to wait and see."

"Tiger—"

In the distance, the stud neighed ringingly. I blessed him for his timing, though he wouldn't have much luck finding the mare he wanted. "Get the 'sword,' Del."

She held her ground. "If I win this dance, will you stop?"

"If you win this dance, I'll just have to practice harder."

"Then you still mean to go back to the South."

"I told you that. Yes." I studied her. "What, did you think I meant to live out my life here on this benighted island?" Which had, nonetheless, saved our lives in more ways than one.

"I don't know." Her tone was a mixture of frustration, annoyance, and helplessness. "I have no inkling as to what you will or will not do, Tiger. You're not predictable any more."

Any more. Which implied that once I had been.

I bared my teeth at her. "Well, good. Then I'm not boring." Once again I waved my stick. "The sooner we get to it, the sooner we'll know."

Her expression suggested she already knew. Or thought she did.

"Not predictable," I reminded her. "Your own words, too."

Del turned on her heel and stalked over to the tree limbs I'd groomed into smooth shafts. There was no point, no edge, no crosspiece, no grip, no proper pommel. They were not swords. They were sticks. But whichever one she chose would do.

"Hurry up," I said. "We're burning daylight, bascha."

The world, through glass, is magnified. Small made large. Unseen made visible. Dreams, bound by ungovernable temperaments and unpredictabilities, may do the same, altering one's vision. One's comprehension. The known made unknowable.

Grains of sand, slightly displaced. Gently jostled one against another. Gathered. Tumbled. Herded.

I blink. The world draws back. Large is made small; immense becomes insignificant. And I see what moves the sand.

Not water. Not wind.

Blood.

First, they rape her. Then slash open her throat. Twice, possibly thrice. The bones of her spine, left naked to the day in the ruin of her flesh, gleam whitely in the sun.

Blood flows. Gathers sand. Makes mud of malnourished dust. Is transformed by the sun into nothingness.

Even blood, in the desert, cannot withstand the ceaseless heat.

It will take longer for the body, for flesh and bone are not so easily consumed. But the desert will win. Its victories are boundless.

They might have left her alive, to die of thirst. It was their mercy to kill her swiftly. Their laughter was her dirge. Their jest was to leave a sword within reach, but she lacked the strength to use it against herself.

As the sun sucks her dry, withering flesh on bone, she turns her head upon the sand and looks at me out of eyes I recognize.

"Take up the sword," she says.

I jerk, gasping out of sleep into trembling wakefulness, tasting sand in my mouth. Salt. And blood.

"It's time," she says.

Her breath, her death, is mine.

"Find me," she says, "and take up the sword."

Del felt me spasm into actual wakefulness. She turned toward me and sleepily inquired, "What is it?"

I offered no answer. I couldn't.

"Tiger?" She propped herself up on an elbow. "What is it?"

I stared up at the dark skies. Something was in me, something demanding I answer. I felt very distant. I felt very small. "It's time." Echoing the dream.

"Time?"

The words left my mouth without conscious volition. "To go home." *To go home. To take up the sword.*

After a moment she asked, "Are you all right? You don't sound like yourself."

I didn't *feel* like myself.

She placed a hand upon my chest, feeling my heart beat. "Tiger?"

"I just—I know. It's time." No more than that. It seemed sufficient.

Find me.

"Are you sure?"

Take up the sword.

"I'm sure."

"All right." She lay down again. "Then we'll go."

I could feel her tension. She didn't think it was a good idea. But that didn't matter. What mattered is that it was time.

ONE

HAVING SAILED at last from the island, we now were bound for Haziz, the South's port city. We had departed it months before, heading for Skandi; but that voyage was finished. Now we embarked on an even more dangerous journey: returning to the South, where I carried a death sentence on my head.

Meanwhile, Del and I passed the time by sparring. She didn't win the matches. Neither did I. The point wasn't to win, but to retrain my body and mind. Tension was in me, tension to do better, do more, *be* better.

"You're holding back," I accused, accustomed now—again— to the creak of wood and rigging, the crack of canvas.

Del opened her mouth to refute that; holding back in the circle was a thing she never did. But she shut her mouth and contemplated me, though her expression suggested she was weighing herself every bit as much.

"Well?" I challenged, planting bare feet more firmly against wood planking.

"Maybe," she said at length.

"If you truly believe I'm incapable—"

"I didn't say that!"

—"then you should simply knock me out of the circle." We didn't really have a proper circle, because the captain had vociferously objected to me carving one into his deck, but our minds knew where the boundaries lay.

Del, who had set one end of the stick against the deck, now made it into a cane and leaned upon it idly with the free hand perched on her hip and elbow outthrust. "I don't think anyone could knock you out of the circle even if you were missing two *hands*."

Not a pretty picture. "Thanks." I grimaced. "I think."

Blue eyes opened wide. "That's a compliment!"

I supposed it was.

Now those eyes narrowed. "You *are* using a different grip."

"I said I would." I'd also said I'd have to. Circumstances demanded it.

She unbent and put out the arm. Her tone was brusque, commanding. "Close on my wrist."

I clamped one big hand around her wrist, feeling the knob of bone on the left side, the pronounced tendons on the underside. A strong woman, was Delilah.

Her pale brows knit. "There is a difference in the pressure."

"Of course there is." I was not altogether unhappy to be holding her wrist. "I have *three* fingers and a thumb, not four."

"Your grip will be weaker, here." She touched the outside edge of my palm. Nothing was wrong with that part of my hand. There simply wasn't a little finger extending from it any more. "If the sword grip turns in your hand, or is forced back at an angle toward the side of your hand . . ."

"I'll lose leverage. Control. Yes, I know that."

She was frowning now. She let her own stick fall to the deck. She studied my hand in earnest, taking it into both of hers. She had seen it before, of course; seen them both, and the knurled pinkish scar tissue covering the nub of severed bone. Del was not squeamish; she had patched me up numerous times, as well as herself. She regretted the loss of those fingers—hoolies, so did I!—but she did not quail from their lack. This time, in a methodical and matter-of-fact examination that did not lend itself to innuendo or implication, she studied every inch of my hand. She felt flesh, tendon, the narrow bones beneath both. I have big hands, wide hands, and the heels of them are callused hard with horn.

"What?" I asked finally, when she continued to frown.

"The scars," she said. "They're gone."

I have four deep grooves carved in my cheek, and a crater in the flesh over the ribs of my left side. I raised dubious brows.

"On your *hands*," Del clarified. "All the nicks are gone. And this knuckle here—" She tapped it.—"used to be knobbier than the others. It's not anymore."

I suppose I might have made some vulgar comment about Del's intimate knowledge of my body, but didn't. There was more at stake just now than verbal foreplay.

I had all manner of nicks and seams and divots in my body. We both did. Mine were from a childhood of slavery, an enforced visit to the mines of a Southron tanzeer by the name of Aladar, and the natural progression of lengthy—and dangerous—sword-dancer training and equally dangerous dances for real. The latter had marred Del in certain characteristic ways, too; she bore her own significant scar on her abdomen as a reminder of a dance years ago in the North, when we both nearly died, as well as various other blade-born blemishes.

I had spent weeks getting used to the stubs of the two missing fingers, though there were times I could have sworn I retained a full complement. Beyond that, I had paid no attention to either hand other than working very hard to strengthen them, as well as my wrists and forearms. It was the interior that mattered, not the exterior. The muscles, the strength, that controlled the hands and thus the grip. Not the exterior scars.

But Del was right. The knuckle, once permanently enlarged, looked of a size with the others again. And the nicks and blemishes I'd earned in forty years were gone. Even the discolored pits from working Aladar's mine had disappeared.

Wholly focused on retraining myself, I had not even noticed. I pulled the hand away, scowling blackly.

"It's not a *bad* thing," Del observed, though a trifle warily.

"Skandi," I muttered. "Meteiera." I looked harder at my hands.

"Did they work some magic on you?"

I transferred the scowl from hand to woman. "No, they didn't work any magic on me. They cut my fingers off!" Not to mention shaving and tattooing my skull and piercing my ears and eyebrows with silver rings. Most of the rings were gone now, thanks to Del's careful removal, though at her behest I had retained two in each earlobe. Don't ask me why. Del said she liked them.

"You do look younger." Her tone was carefully measured.

Ironic, to look younger when one's lifespan has been shortened.

"Of course, maybe it's the hair," Del suggested. "You look very different with it so short."

"Longer than it was." I rubbed a hand over my head; and so it was, all of possibly two inches now, temporarily lying close against my skull, though I expected the annoying wave to start showing up any day. Del had said the blue tattoos were invisible, save for a slight rim along the hairline. But that would be hidden, too, once my hair grew out all the way.

"I don't mean you look like a *boy*," she clarified. "You look like you. Just—less used."

Hoolies, *that* sounded good. "Define for me 'less used.' "

"By the sun." She shrugged. "By life."

"That wouldn't be wishful thinking, would it?"

Del blinked. "What?"

"There are fifteen-plus years between us, after all. Maybe if I didn't look so much older—"

"Oh, Tiger, don't be ridiculous! I've told you I don't care about that."

I dropped into a squat. The knees didn't pop. I bounced up again. Still no complaints.

Del frowned. "What was that about?"

"Feeling younger." I grinned crookedly. "Or maybe it's just *my* wishful thinking."

Del bent and picked up her stick. "Then let's go again."

"What, you want to try and wear down the old man? Make him yield on the basis of sheer exhaustion?"

"You never yield to exhaustion," she pointed out, "in anything you do."

"I yielded to your point of view about women having worth in other areas besides bed."

"Because I was *right*."

As usual, with us, the banter covered more intense emotions. I didn't really blame Del for being concerned. Here we were on our way back to the South, where I had been born and lost; where I had been raised a slave; where I had eventually found my calling as a sword-dancer, hired to fight battles for other men as a means of settling disputes—but also where I had eventually voluntarily cut myself off from all the rites, rituals, and honor of the Alimat-trained sword-dancer's closely prescribed system.

I had done it in a way some might describe as cowardly, but at the time it was the right choice. The only choice. I'd made it without thinking twice about it, because I didn't have to; I knew very well what the cost would be. I was an outcast now, a blade without a name. I had declared *elaii-ali-ma*, rejecting my status as a seventh-level sword-dancer, which meant I was fair game to any honor-bound sword-dancer who wanted to challenge me.

Of course, that challenge wouldn't necessarily come in a circle, where victory is not achieved by killing your opponent—well, usually; there are always exceptions—but by simply winning. By being better.

For years I had been better than everyone else in the South, though a few held out for Abbu Bensir (including Abbu Bensir), but I couldn't claim that any longer. I wasn't a sword-dancer. I was just a man a lot of other men wanted to kill.

And Del figured it would be a whole lot easier to kill me now than before.

She was probably right, too.

So here I was aboard a ship bound for the South, going home, accompanied by a stubborn stud-horse and an equally stubborn woman, sailing toward what more romantic types, privy to my dream, might describe as my destiny. Me, I just knew it was time, dream or no dream. We'd gone off chasing some cockamamie idea of me being Skandic, a child of an island two week's sail from the South, but that was done now. I *was*, by all appearances—literally as well as figuratively—Skandic, a child of that island, but things hadn't worked out. Sure, it was the stuff of fantasy to discover I was the long-lost grandson of the island's wealthiest, most powerful matriarch, but this fantasy didn't have a happy ending. It had cost me two fingers, for starters. And nearly erased altogether the man known as the Sandtiger without even killing him.

Meteiera. The Stone Forest. Where Skandic men with a surfeit of magics so vast that much was mostly undiscovered, cloistered themselves upon tall stone spires ostensibly to serve the gods but also, they claimed, to protect their loved ones by turning away from them. Because the magic that made them powerful also made them mad.

Now, anyone who knows me will say I don't—or didn't— think much of magic. In fact, I don't—didn't—really believe in it. But I'll admit *some*thing strange was going on in Meteiera, because I had cause to know. I can't swear the priest-mages worked magic on me, as Del suggested, but once there I wasn't precisely me anymore. And I witnessed too many strange things.

Hoolies, I *did* strange things.

I shied away from that like a spooked horse. But the knowledge, the awareness, crept back. Despite all the outward physical changes, there were plenty of interior ones as well. A comprehension of power, something like the first faint pang of hunger, or the initial itch of desire. In fact, it was *very* like desire—because that power wanted desperately to be wielded.

I shivered. If Del had asked what the problem was, I'd have told her it was a bit chill in the morning, and after all I was wearing only a leather dhoti for ease of movement as I went through the repetitive rituals that honed the body and mind. But it wasn't the chill of morning that kindled the response. It was the awareness again of the battle I faced. Or, more accurately, battles.

And none of them had anything to do with sword-dancing, or even sword fighting. Only with refusing to become what I'd been told, on Meteiera, I must become: a mage.

Actually, they'd said I was to become a *priest*-mage, but I'm even less inclined to put faith in, well, *faith*, than in the existence of magic.

And, of course, it was becoming harder to deny the existence of magic since I had managed to work some. And even harder to deny my own willingness to work it; I had *tried* to work it. Purposely. I had a vague recollection that those first days after escaping the Stone Forest were filled with desperation, and a desperate man undertakes many strange things to achieve certain goals. My goal had been vital: to get back to Skandi and find Del, and to settle things permanently with the metri, my grandmother.

I got back to Skandi by boat, which is certainly not a remarkable thing when attempting to reach an island. Except the boat hadn't existed before I made it exist, conjured of seawrack and something more I'd learned on Meteiera.

Discipline.

Magic is merely the tool. Discipline is the power.

Now I stood at the rail staring across the ocean, knowing that everything I'd ever been in my life was turned inside out. Upside down. Every which way you can think of.

Take up the sword.

I lived with and for the sword. I didn't understand why I needed to be told. No; commanded.

"You're still you," Del said, with such explicit firmness that I realized she was worried that *I* was worried, not knowing my thoughts had gone elsewhere.

I smiled out at the seaspray.

"You are." She came up beside me. She had washed her hair in the small amount of fresh water the captain allowed for such ablutions, and now the breeze dried it. The mix of salt, spray, and sun had bleached her blonder. Strands were lifted away from her face, streaming back across her shoulders.

I have been less in my life, dependent on circumstances. But now, indisputably, I was more.

I was, I had been told, messiah. Now mage. I had believed neither, claiming—and knowing—I was merely a man. It was enough. It was all I had wanted to be, in the years of slavery when I was chula, not boy. Slave, not human.

I glanced at Del, still smiling. "Keep saying that, bascha."

"You *are*."

"No," I said, "I'm not. And you know it as well as I do."

Her face went blank.

"Nice try," I told her, "but I read you too well, now."

Del look straight at me, shirking nothing. "And I, now, can read nothing at all of you."

There. It was said. Admitted aloud, one to the other.

"Still me," I said, "but different."

Del was never coquettish or coy. Nor was she now. She put her hand on my arm. "Then come below," she said simply, "and show me *how* different."

Ah, yes. That was still the same.

Grinning, I went.

When we finally disembarked in Haziz, I did not kiss the ground. That would have entailed my kneeling down in the midst of a typically busy day on the choked docks, risking being flattened by a dray-cart, wagon, or someone hauling bales and none too happy to find a large, kneeling man in his way, and coming into somewhat intimate contact with the liquid, lumpy, squishy, and aromatic effluvia of a complement of species and varieties of animals so vast I did not care to count.

Suffice it to say I was relieved to once more plant both sandaled feet upon the Southron ground, even though that ground felt more like ship than earth. The adjustment from flirtatious deck to solidity always took me a day or two.

Just as it would take me time to sort out the commingled aromas I found so disconcertingly evident after months away. Whew!

"They don't need to challenge you," Del observed from beside me with delicate distaste. "They could just leave you here and let the *stench* kill you."

With haughty asperity, I said, "You are speaking about my homeland."

"And now that we are back here among people who would as soon kill you as give you greeting," she continued, "what is our next move?"

It was considerably warmer here than on Skandi, though it lacked the searing heat of high summer. I glanced briefly at the sun, sliding downward from its zenith. "The essentials," I replied. "A drink. Food. A place to stay the night. A horse for you." The stud would be off-loaded and taken to a livery I trusted, where he could get his earth-legs back. I'd paid well for the service, though the sailhand likely wouldn't think it enough once the stud tried to kick his head off. Another reason to let the first temper tantrum involve someone other than me. "Swords—"

"Good," Del said firmly.

"And tomorrow we'll head out for Julah."

"Julah? Why? That's where Sabra nearly had the killing of us both." Unspoken was the knowledge that not far from Julah, at the palace inherited from her father, Sabra had forced me to declare myself an outcast from my trade. To reject the honor codes of an Alimat-trained seventh-level sword-dancer.

"Because," I explained. "I'd like to have a brief discussion with my old friend Fouad."

" 'Discussion,' " she echoed, and I knew it was a question.

"With words, not blades."

"Fouad's the one who betrayed you to Sabra and nearly got you killed."

"Which calls for at least a few friendly words, don't you think?"

Del had attempted to fall in beside me as I wended my way through narrow, dust-floured streets clogged with vendors hawking cheap wares to new arrivals and washing hung out to dry from the upper storeys of close-built, mudbrick dwellings stacked one upon the other in slumping disarray, boasting sun-faded, once-brilliant awnings; but as she didn't know Haziz at all, it was difficult for her to stay there when I followed a route unfamiliar to her. She settled for being one step behind my left shoulder, trying to anticipate my direction. "Words? That's all?"

"It's a starting point." I scooped up a melon from the top of a piled display. The melon-seller's aggrieved shout followed us. I grinned, hearing familiar Southron oaths—from a mouth other than my own—for the first time in months.

Del picked her way over a prodigious pile of danjac manure, lightly seasoned with urine. "Are you going to pay for that?"

Around the first juicy, delicious mouthful I shaped, "Welcome-home present." And tried not to dribble down the front of my Skandic silks. Still noticeably crimson, unfortunately.

"And I've been thinking . . ."

Hoolies, I'd been *dreaming*.

And I regretted bringing it up.

"Yes?" she prompted.

"Maybe . . ."

"Yes?"

The words came into my mouth, surprising me as well as her. "Maybe we'll go get my true sword."

"True sword?"

I twisted adroitly as a gang of shrieking children ran by, raising a dun-tinted wake of acrid dust. "You know. Out there. In the desert. Under a pile of rocks."

Del stopped dead. "*That* sword? You mean to go get *that* sword?"

I turned, paused, and gravely offered her the remains of the melon, creamy green in the dying sun. I could not think of a way to explain about the dream. "It seems—appropriate."

She was not interested in the melon. " 'Appropriate'?" Del shook her head. "Only you would want to go dig up a sword buried under tons of rock, when there are undoubtedly plenty of them here in this city. *Unburied*."

Again the answer was in my mouth. "But I didn't make those swords."

Which conjured between us the memories of the North, and Staal-Ysta, and the dance that had nearly killed us. Not to mention a small matter of Del breaking, in my name, for my life, the sword that *she* had made while singing songs of vengeance. Boreal was dead, in the way of broken *jivatmas* and their ended songs. Samiel was not.

And something in me wanted him. Needed him.

Del said nothing. Nothing at all. But she didn't have to. In her stunned silence was a multitude of words.

I tossed the melon toward a wall. It splatted, dappled outer skin breaking, then slid down to crown a malodorous trash heap tumbling halfway into the street. "We'll stay the night, buy some serviceable swords and harness, then go to Julah, to Fouad's." I said quietly. "A small matter of a debt between friends."

And the much larger matter of survival.

TWO

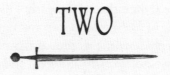

Del WAS a little leery about the two of us striding around Haziz, instantly recognizable to any sword-dancers who'd seen us before. I tried explaining that Haziz wasn't all that popular with sword-dancers, who generally kept themselves to the interior, and that I didn't precisely look the way I used to, thanks to my sojurn at Meteiera, but Del observed that even with short hair, earrings, the tracery of tattoos at my hairline, and no sandtiger necklet, I was still a good head taller than most Southron men, decidedly bigger and heavier, still had the clawmarks in my face—and who else traveled with a Northern sword-singer? A *female* Northern sword-singer?

Whereupon I pointed out we could split up while in Haziz.

Del, tying on her high-laced sandals as she perched on the edge of the bed—we'd spent the night in a somewhat squalid dockside inn, albeit in the largest room—lifted dubious brows. "And who then would protect you?"

"Protect me against what?"

"Sword-dancers."

"I already told you there's not likely to be any here."

"*We're* here."

"Well, yes, but—"

"And you already admitted you needed my protection."

I was astounded. "When was *that*?"

"On the island." Now she slipped on the other sandal. "Don't you remember? You were talking about starting a new school at Alimat. I was talking about Abbu."

Come to think if it, I did vaguely recall some casual comment. "Oh. That."

"Yes. That." She laced on the sandal, tied it off, stood. "Well?"

"That was pillow talk, bascha."

"We didn't have any pillows. We had sand."

"I'm fitter than I've been in months. Leaner. Quicker. You've sparred with me. You know."

Del cocked her head assessingly, pointedly not observing that I also lacked two fingers. "Yes."

"So, you don't need to protect me."

"Are you prepared to meet Abbu Bensir?"

"Here? Now?"

"What if he *is* here? Now?"

I gifted her with my finest, fiercest sandtiger's glare. "So, you want me to hide up here in this pisshole while you go hunting a swordsmith in a town you don't know?"

She was not impressed by the glare. "You don't know it much better. And I can ask directions."

"A lone woman? In the South? Looking for a swordsmith?"

Del opened her mouth, then closed it.

"Yes," I said. "We're in the *South* again." Which was very different from the North, where women had more freedom, and very much different from Skandi, where women ran things altogether.

"I could," she said, but there wasn't much challenge in it. Del was stubborn, but she understood reality. Even when it wasn't fair. (Once upon a time she ignored reality, but time—and, dare I admit it, my influence—had changed her.)

"Tell you what, bascha. I'll compromise."

With excess drama, "*You?*"

I ignored that. "We'll send a boy out to the best swordsmith in Haziz and have him come here."

Del considered. "Fair enough."

"And after that," I said, wincing, "I'll have to pay a visit to the stud."

"Ah, yes," she agreed, nodding. "Maybe he'll save the sword-dancers some trouble and kill you himself."

"Well, since you're so all-fired ready to protect me, why don't you ride him first?"

Del scowled. Grinning, I exited the room to scare up a likely boy to run the message summoning a swordsmith.

The swordsmith's two servants delivered several bulky wrapped bundles to our room as well as a selection of harnesses, swordbelts, and sheaths. Then they bowed themselves out to permit their employer to conduct business. That employer was an older man in black robes and turban, gray of hair and beard but hardly frail because of it. Anyone who spends years pounding metal to fold it multitudinous times trains his body into fitness. A different kind from mine, perhaps, because of different needs, but age had not weakened him. Nor his assessment of customers.

After formal pleasantries that included small cups of astringent tea, he had me stand before him, then looked at me and saw everything Del had described earlier, cataloging details. All of them mattered in such things as selecting a weapon. Most tall men had long legs but short to medium torsos; shorter men gained what height they had in a long torso. I, on the other hand, was balanced. My height came from neither, but from both. I had discovered that in Skandi mine was the normal build. Here in the South, it was not. Southroners were shorter, more slender but wiry, very quick, and markedly agile.

Fortunately, I had been gifted with speed despite my size, and superior strength. Both had served me well.

Now the old man examined me to see what kind of sword would serve me well.

After a moment he smiled. He lacked two teeth. Without a word he turned, knelt, and set aside four of the bundles. He pulled out a fifth bundle I hadn't noticed, much narrower than the others and more tightly wrapped, and began to undo knots.

Del, seated on the bed, exchanged a glance with me, eyebrows raised. I shrugged, as baffled.

The swordsmith glanced up, saw it as he began to unwrap the bundle. A spark of amusement leaped in dark eyes. In a Southron dialect I hadn't heard in well over a year, he said, "It is a waste of time to display my best to undiscerning customers. Then, I begin with the lesser weapons."

"And I'm a discerning one?"

Tufted brows jerked upward into the shadow of the turban. "With a body so carved and cut by blades? Yet still breathing?" He grinned again. "Oh, yes." He opened wrappings reverently, folding back the fabric with great care. Steel glinted like ivory ice in meager, sallow sunlight slanting through narrow windows chopped into mudbrick. He rose and gestured. "Do me the favor of showing me your hands."

Mutely, I put them out. Saw the abrupt widening of his eyes, the startled glance into my face. That he wanted to speak of such things as missing fingers was obvious; that to do so would offend a discerning customer was equally obvious and went against his training as tradesman as well as artisan. After a moment he took my hands into his and began to inspect them, measuring breadth of palm, length of fingers, feeling calluses. He took great care not to so much as brush the stubs.

Then, quietly, he bent, took up a sword, set it into my hands, bowed. And stepped away even as Del moved back on the narrow bed, giving me room to move, to lend life to the sword as I tested its quality.

It took me no longer to judge the blade than it took the swordsmith to judge me. He had selected the one he believed was most appropriate. And indeed it was, in every important way. It was more than adequate—for a temporary weapon.

But then, that was all I required, until I found Samiel.

The swordsmith's expression was a curious blend of surprise and reconsideration. Though he had correctly surmised I knew how to handle a blade—or had, at one time—it was clear he had been dubious because of the missing fingers. The stumps were still pinkish; anyone familiar with wounds, particularly amputation, would recognize that the loss of the fingers was relatively recent. He paid me tribute by displaying his best to me, but he clearly expected less of me in the handling of the weapon.

Unfortunately, testing a blade and going against another sword-dancer were two very different things.

"It will do," I said, after complimenting him on his art. "What is your price? I will need a sheath and harness as well."

He named an outrageous amount. I praised his skill, the product, but politely refused and offered less. He praised my obvious expertise, my experience, but politely declined my counter. So went the bargaining until both of us were satisfied.

His eyes glinted briefly. He knelt again and began to rewrap the bundle of his best.

"Wait." When he glanced up, I indicated Del.

At first he did not understand.

"A sword," I explained, "for the lady."

It was fortunate he spoke a dialect Del did not, or she very likely would have tested one of the blades on him. As it was she knew by his tone, his expression, by the stiffness in his body, what he said. She was a woman. Women did not use swords.

"This one does." I said. And then, grateful Del didn't understand, "Indulge me."

That, he would accept: that a man might be foolish enough, or lust-bound enough, to woo a woman by seemingly giving into her fantasies, however ludicrous they might be. It lessened me in his eyes, but so long as it resulted in the desired end, I didn't care. For this insult to his person, his skill, his Southron sensibilities, he would vastly overcharge, and I would vastly overpay, but Del would have her blade.

She rose from the bed and stood before him in creamy pale leather tunic, legs and arms bare, a plaited rope of fair hair fallen forward over one breast. He shut his eyes a moment, muttered a prayer, and asked to see her hands. As he touched them, his own shook.

Del shot me a look over his bent head. "Since you're the jhihadi," she said pointedly, "why don't you start changing the Southron male's perception of Southron women as inferior beings?"

I grinned. "I suspect some things are impossible even for the jhihadi."

"Changing sand to grass is very dramatic," Del observed, "especially for a desert climate, but changing women to humans in Southron eyes—*male* Southron eyes—would be far more proof of this jhihadi's omnipotence."

This jhihadi knew better than to travel that road. He smiled blandly and did not reply.

"Coward," she muttered.

Finished with his assessment, the swordsmith dropped Del's hands with alacrity and turned away from her. With skilled economy he selected a sword, rose with it, then gazed upon it with obvious regret. His beautiful handiwork, intended for a man, would belong to a worthless woman merely playing at men's games.

We needed the sword. Carefully avoiding Del's eyes, I told the swordsmith, in his dialect, "When she's done playing with it in a week or so, I'll sell it back to you. At a reduced price, of course, because of its taint."

That seemed satisfactory. He placed the sword in Del's hands, then moved back to the farthest corner of the room, pressing himself into it. Knowing what she would do to test the weight, balance, response, I moved only so far as I had to. The swordsmith stared at me out of astonished eyes.

I grinned. "Indulge me."

Del danced. It was a brief but beautiful ritual, the dance against an invisible opponent, intended only to allow one to establish a rapport with one's weapon, to let the hands come to an understanding of the fit of the hilt, how the pommel affected balance, how the blade cut the air. It lasted moments only, but enough time for him to realize what he was witnessing.

Impossibility.

Del stopped moving. Flipped the braid behind her shoulder. Nodded.

The swordsmith drew in a rasping breath. He named a price.

Knowing there was no room for bargaining under the circumstances, I accepted. Paid. Saw him to the door.

Del's voice rose behind us. In clear Southron, albeit not his dialect, she said, "I will not dishonor your art."

His eyes flickered. Then his face closed up. With his back to us both, he said fiercely, "Tell no one that sword is mine."

I shut the door behind him, then turned to look at Del. She had sheathed the sword and buckled on the harness, testing the fit. It would require adjustment, but wasn't bad. "Happy now?"

She smiled languorously. "With a sword in my hand again, I can indulge even pigs like him."

"Then indulge *me*, won't you? Let's visit the stud together." I grabbed up my own new harness, slid the sword home. "I may need you to pick up the pieces."

The stud was, predictably, full of piss and vinegar. I sighed as the horse-boy led him out of the livery, recognizing the look in the one rolling eye I could see. The pinning of ears, the hard swish of tail, a peculiar stiff readiness in body indicated the stud had an opinion and was prepared to express it.

I didn't really blame him. He'd been cooped up on a ship, nearly drowned in a shipwreck, deserted on an island, refound, then stuck aboard a ship again. Someone had to pay.

I sighed. "Not here in the street," I told the boy. "Someplace where no innocent bystanders might be injured."

He bobbed his black-haired head and led the way through a narrow alley between the livery and another building to a modest stableyard. The earth had been beaten into a fine dust, and the muckers had already shoveled and swept the yard. At least when I came off, I wouldn't land in manure.

Del, following, raised her voice over the thunking of the stud's hooves. "Shall I send boys out to invite wagering?"

The tone was innocent. The intent was not. Del and I had indeed managed to make some money here and there with wagers on who would win the battle—but that was when the stud was well ridden, and I was more likely to stick. Del knew as well as I that this battle would be worse than usual.

"The only wager here is how soon I come off," I said glumly as the boy slipped the reins over the stud's dark-brown neck. Ordinarily his mane was clipped close to his neck, but time on the island had allowed it to grow out. Now it stood straight up in a black hedge the length of my palm. I ran a hand through my own hedge. "I have a sneaking suspicion this is going to be painful."

In deference to the Southron sun if not Southron proprieties, Del had donned a striped gauze burnous before exiting the inn. Now she arranged herself against a whitewashed adobe wall, arms crossed, one leg crooked up so the toe of the sandal was hooked into a rough spot. The thin, hand-smeared slick coating was crumbling away to display the rough, hand-formed block of grass-and-mud brick beneath.

She smiled sunnily. "It won't be painful if you stay on."

Despite my desire to discuss things with the stud in private, an audience was already beginning to straggle in. Horse-boys, muckers, even a couple of bowlegged, whip-thin men I suspected were horse-breakers. All watched with rapt attention, murmuring to one another in anticipation. It felt rather like a sword-dance, except no circle was in sight. Merely an open-air square, surrounded on three sides by stable blocks and on the fourth by the solid wall of an adjoining building. With a horse as my opponent.

"Don't embarrass me," Del said. "I still need to buy myself a mount, remember?"

"I'll sell you this one cheap."

Her smile was mild. "You're burning daylight, Tiger."

Muttering curses, I stripped out of harness and sword, left them sitting on a bench near Del, and strode across to the stud.

Groundwork was called for, a chance to settle him to some degree before I even mounted by circling him around me at the end of a long rein, by handling head and mouth, by singing his praises in a soothing tone of voice. Actually, it's the tone of voice that counts; I often called him every vulgar name I could think of, but he was never offended because I did it sweetly.

However, I'd had the stud long enough to know groundwork was ineffective. It never seemed to change his mind when he was in the mood for dramatics. Certainly not on the island, when I'd mounted him after months away. *That* had been a battle.

And now another loomed.

There isn't much to a Southron saddle to begin with, and this one was borrowed from the livery since all of my tack had been lost when the ship sank under me on the way to Skandi. Supremely simple, it was merely an abbreviated platform of leather with the swelling humps of pommel and cantle front and back atop a couple of blankets, a cinch around the horse's barrel to hold the saddle on, stirrup leathers no wider than a man's belt, and roundish stirrups carved out of wood.

Almost simultaneously I took the woven cotton reins from the boy, grabbed handfuls of overgrown mane, and swung up into the saddle with a burst of nervous agility that put me right where I needed to be, even without benefit of stirrups. I'd done that purposely. It was a shortcut into the saddle and gave me an extra instant to set myself before the stud realized I'd beaten him to the punch.

I wore soft Skandic boots instead of sandals, the latter not being particularly helpful atop a recalcitrant horse, and the crimson silks bestowed weeks before on the island. Waiting back at the room was more appropriate Southron garb, but I'd opted to try the stud in clothing I could afford to have ruined. In the whitewashed stable yard, beneath the Southron sun, I must have glowed like a blood-slicked lantern as I eased boots into the stirrups.

Then the stud blew up, and I didn't have time for imagery.

Unless he falls over backward—on purpose or not—riding a rearing horse is not particularly difficult. It's a matter of reflexes and balance. Which is not to say a rearing horse can't do damage even if you survive the dramatics; if you're caught unaware, there is the very real possibility that the horse's head or neck will collide with your face. Trust me, the nose and teeth lose when this happens. And I'm not talking about the horse's.

A bucking horse is tougher to ride, because unless the horse gets into a predictable rhythm, which then becomes a matter of timing to ride out, a jolting, jouncing, twisting and repetitive rear elevation can not only hurl you over the horse's head and eventually into the ground, but can also shorten your spine by a good three inches. And turn your neck into a noodle.

Then, of course, there are the horses that can contort themselves into a posture known as "breaking in two," where they suddenly become hinged in the middle of their spines, drop head and butt so that the body forms an inverted V, and proceed to levitate across the ground in abrupt, stiff-legged, impressively vertical bounds.

Naturally, *my* horse was supremely talented. He could rear, buck, and break in two practically simultaneously.

The stud is not a particularly tall horse. Southron mounts aren't, for the most part. But he was all tight-knit, compact, rock-hard muscle, which is usually tougher to ride than a big, rawboned animal, and, being a stallion, he packed on extra heft. He was broad in the butt, round in the barrel, wide in the chest, and had the typically heavy stallion neck, crest, and jaw. It made it much more difficult for me to get any leverage with his mouth and head.

Which he delighted in demonstrating.

After I dragged myself out of the dirt for the fourth time, I noted a subtle change in the stud's posture. The tail no longer swished hard enough to lash eyeballs out of a skull. Ears no longer pinned back swiveled freely in all directions. He swung his head to peer at me quizzically through dangling forelock, examined me (maybe looking for blood?), then shook very hard from head to toe as if to say he was done with his morning warmup, and nosed again at the dirt in idle unconcern.

I slapped dust out of silks. Pulled the tunic into such order as was possible when seams are torn. Made certain the drawstring of my baggy Skandic trousers was still knotted. Managed to stand up straight and stride across to the stud. He stood quietly enough. I mounted, settled myself in the saddle, walked him out enough to know he was done with the battle.

Applause, whistles, and cheering rang out. Coin changed hands as wagers were paid off. But I knew better than to count it a victory, no matter what the crowd believed. The stud had merely gotten bored.

I dismounted and walked back over to Del with said stud in tow, supressing a limp. Her expression was sublimely noncommital.

In a pinched voice, I said, "Remember how just the other day I said I felt younger?"

Del raised brows.

"Add about two hundred years to the total."

One of the horse-boys came up, offering to strip down the stud and walk him. It was a warm day and all the excitement and exertion had resulted in sweat and lather. He needed cooling. I needed cooling. I wanted water, ale, and a bath. In that particular order.

Oh, and a new spine.

But of course under the eyes of the audience, many of whom had wandered in from the street when they heard the commotion, I stood straight and tall, saluted them, and strolled casually toward the alleyway leading to the street, pausing only to ask Del if she were coming, since she showed no signs of it.

"And stop laughing," I admonished.

"I'm not laughing. I'm smiling."

"You're laughing *inside*."

"My insides are mine," she observed, "to do with as I please."

"Are you coming?"

"I'll stay here and buy a horse, I think. And tack for both mounts. I'll meet you back at the inn."

I opened my mouth to oppose Del's foray into shopping without my presence, then thought better of it. She was a woman, and it was the South, but Del had proved many times over that only the rare man got the better of her.

That rare man being me, of course.

I gathered up harness and sword and took myself off to the inn. And ale. And a hot bath.

THREE

*F*LESH *has turned to leather be-*
neath the merciless sun. Eye sockets are scoured clean. Teeth shine in
an ivory rictus. Wind, sand, and time have stripped away the clothing.
She wears bone, now, little more, scrubbed to match the Punja's crys-
talline pallor. Modesty lies in rills of sand blown in drifts across her
torso—

I woke up with a start as Del came into the room, creaking the
door. Completely disoriented from the dream fragment, I stared at
her blankly, slowly piecing back awareness, the recognition that I
was still in the half-cask I'd ordered brought up and filled with
hot water. That the water had cooled. That there was a real possibility I might never move again.

Del's expression was quizzical as she shut the door. Her arms
were full of bundles. "I can think of more comfortable places to
sleep—and positions to sleep *in*."

With care I pulled myself upright, spine scraping against
rough wood. In an hour or so I might manage to stand. Scowling,
I asked if she'd spent every last coin we claimed.

Del was piling bundles on the bed. "Supplies," she replied
crisply. "I assume we're leaving tomorrow, yes?"

I rearranged stiff legs with effort and hauled myself dripping
out of the cask, swearing under my breath. "Yes."

Del tossed me the length of thin fabric doubling as a towel, examined my expression and movements, then frowned. "Your hands are hurting."

"Yes." I wrapped the cloth around my waist.

"Tiger—"

"Leave it, Del. I just banged them around on the stud, that's all." I bent, carefully grasped the jar of ale I'd set on the floor beside the cask, and upended the remaining contents into my mouth.

She clearly wanted to say more, but did not. Instead she turned back to the bed and began sorting through bundles. "Food," she announced, "suitable for travel. New botas; we can fill them in the morning. Medicaments. Blankets for bedding. A griddle. Flint and steel." There was more, but she left off anouncing everything.

"What about a mount for you, and tack?"

"Arranged. We can collect the stud and my horse first thing tomorrow morning."

"*Do* we have any money left?"

"Not much," she admitted. "Refitting is costly."

I could not get the memory of the dream fragment out of my mind. I turned away from Del and dropped the towel, rooting around in my belongings for fresh dhoti and burnous. I was done with Skandic clothing. I was in the South again. Home.

Where the dead woman was.

Del held out a small leathern flask. "Liniment," she said. "One of the horse-breakers gave it to me. He said it would help."

I tied the thongs on my dhoti. "I think the stud got the better end of the deal. I'm not sure he needs any help."

"He didn't mean it for the stud."

Ah. Trust a horse-breaker to know. And Delilah.

Sighing, I surrendered pride and annoyance and limped to the bed. "Be gentle, bascha. The old man is sore."

"It will be worse tomorrow."

I closed my eyes as she began to work aromatic liquid into my shoulders. "Thank you for that helpful reminder."

"There's a bota of aqivi in the supplies. For the road."

My eyes flew open. "You packed aqivi?"

"Only for medicinal purposes, of course."

I smiled and let my eyes drift shut again. Del herself was the best medicine a man could know.

She lifts an arm. Beckons. Demands my attention. When I give it, understanding, acceding to that demand, I see that the fragile bones of her hands have begun to fall away. A thumb and three fingers remain. The fourth, the smallest, is missing.

The jaw opens then. A feathering of sand pours between dentition. Shadowed sockets beseech me.

"Come home," she says.

"I am home," I say. "I have come home."

But it is not, apparently, what the woman wants. The hand ceases its gesture. The bones drop away, collapsing into fragments. Are scattered on the sand.

"Take up the sword," her voice says, before the wind subborns it as well.

I opened my eyes. Square-cut window invited moonlight. Illumination formed a tangible bar of light slicing diagonally across the bed. Del's hair glowed with the sheen of pearls. Her breathing was even, uninterrupted; though neither of us slept deeply in strange places, we had grown accustomed to one another's movements and departures.

Were the dreams my heritage from Meteiera? Would I spend my life viewing the remains of a dead woman in my sleep? Was I doomed to hear her voice issuing nightly from a broken mouth?

Or was there something I was to do, some task to undertake that I didn't yet understand?

I was too restless, too disturbed to sleep. Carefully I peeled back the threadbare blanket, warding tender stumps from rough cloth, and slipped from the bed, trying not to permit the ropes to creak. Trying not to groan about the stiffness of my body. The liniment had helped, but time and movement were the only true cures.

I halted three steps away from the bed, brought up short by a sense of—*something*. Something in the room. Something in the darkness. Something in the moonlight.

Something in me?

I lifted my face. Closed my eyes. Saliva ran into my mouth. Flesh prickled on my bones. Thumbs and six fingers splayed.

Something was *here*. Begging for recognition.

It sang in my body. The mantra of the mages.

Discipline.

Nihkolara, blue-headed mage of Meteiera—and apparent relative—had told me denying the magic was impossible. That to do so was to invite the madness, to commit self-murder.

I had no inclination to do either.

They had tried to steal my name, the priest-mages, and my knowledge of self, there atop the stony spires. Very nearly had succeeded. But something in me, something more insistent than burgeoning power, despite its insidious seduction, had given me the strength to throw off the infection. At least, enough that I retained my name, rediscovered knowledge of self.

I am Sandtiger.

I am sword-dancer.

More than enough, for me. I needed nothing more.

Even if I had it.

Sweat filmed my body. Soreness remained, bruises had bloomed. But such petty things as discomfort are bearable when weighed against the greater needs of the world.

Or the dictates of magic.

I took up the new sword. In the midst of the moonlight, with eloquent precision, I began yet again to dance, to hone the flesh that sheathed the bones. And the mind that controlled them.

So that I could control *it*.

I was, as expected, still stiff in the morning, though the midnight dance had helped. Del and I dressed respectively in tunic and dhoti, donned sandals, gauze burnouses, and buckled on harnesses over the clothing. Once we'd merely split the left shoulder seams to allow sword hilts freedom, but that was when challenges were to dance, not to die. Now we didn't have that luxury. We packed up the balance of our belongings and headed out to the livery to collect and tack out our mounts, grabbing something to eat from a vendor along the way.

The stud, when led out into the stableyard square in the kindling sun of early morning, gifted me with a sublimely serene expression suggesting he was nothing but a big, sleepy pussycat. Though one of the horse-boys offered, I saddled him myself to give my body the chance to get used to movement. I took my time examining the fit of new tack, including bridle, bit, long cotton reins knotted at each end, and of course the saddle. Satisfied, I loaded my share of the supplies, checked the weight distribution, tossed a colorful woven blanket over the new saddle, and turned to see what progress Del was making.

"What is *that?*" I blurted.

She glanced up from assessing stirrup length. "I think he's reminiscent of you after a particularly drunken cantina fight." She paused. "A little pale, with two black eyes."

A little pale? He was *white.* And she didn't mean his actual eyes were black, because they weren't, but the two circles painted around them. The actual eyes were blue, and looked even lighter peering out from black patches.

"Why in hoolies did you pick *him?*"

"Beggars," she declared succinctly, "cannot be choosers."

Well, no. But . . . "A white, blue-eyed horse in the desert?" Actually, he was a *pink*-and-white, blue-eyed horse, because he lacked pigmentation. His nostrils and lips were a fine, pale pink.

"That is why I've put grease around his eyes," she explained. "It will cut down on the sun's glare reflecting off his face. And I slathered alla paste on his nose and lips."

"Del, this is a *horse*, not a woman painting her face."

"Yes," she agreed equably, continuing to tack out the gelding.

"Do you know what you're doing?"

"Yes."

"Are you *sure?* We've got the Punja to get through."

"I had a white dog when I was a child," Del remarked casually after a moment. "He had blue eyes and no pigmentation. My father wanted to put him down, but I insisted he be mine. I was told that with the sun reflecting off the snow, he might in time go blind. So I mixed up grease with charcoal, and painted around his eyes. He lived to be an old, old dog. And he never went blind."

"Is that why you bought this horse? Because he reminds you of your dog?"

"I bought him because he was the only gelding." She glanced up. "Would you want to risk another stallion anywhere near yours?"

"There are mares."

"I tried that before. Your horse, as I recall, spent most of his time trying to breed her. Sometimes when I was on her."

I recalled that, too. "There are other liveries in town, I suspect. With other geldings."

"But not with one we can afford. I did look." Del reached up and tied something onto the left side of the gelding's headstall, then ran it beneath his forelock to the other side.

My mouth dropped open. "*Tassels?*"

"Fringe," she corrected.

"You're putting fringe on a *horse?*"

"It will help shade his eyes."

First she painted black patches around his eyes, now she hung fringe across his brow. Gold fringe, no less.

I shook my head in disbelief. "Where in hoolies did you find that?"

"I bought it from a wine-girl in one of the cantinas. I don't know what it once was. I was afraid to ask."

"You went into a cantina by yourself?"

"Yes."

"Kind of risky, bascha. Dangerous, even."

"Tiger, I was in a cantina by myself when I met you."

"Well, I *said* it could be dangerous."

Del slipped a foot into the left stirrup and swung up, settling herself into the blanketed saddle with ease. "Now, do you want to spend all morning arguing about horses, or shall we actually ride them?"

It was ridiculous. We were bound for the Punja and all its merciless miseries, including unceasing sun. Del herself certainly knew the risks; she had once been so sunburned I was afraid she'd never recover. A blue-eyed, white horse lacking pigmentation was a burden we couldn't afford.

But Del was right: neither could we afford something better. I suspected we had only a few coins left from Del's shopping expedition. If we didn't take the gelding, we asked the stud to carry two across the searing Punja, or we'd have to take turns riding and walking, which was slower going yet. Besides, if the gelding dropped dead on us from sunstroke, we could always eat him.

On that cheerful note, I mounted the uncommonly cooperative stud, winced at the creaking of my body, and began the careful process of relaxing complaining muscles fiber by fiber. Eventually my body remembered how it was supposed to sit a horse, and some of the soreness bled away. The stumps of my missing fingers were still a trifle tender, but once the stud hit his pace and settled, it wouldn't take more than index and middle fingers to grasp the soft cotton reins.

Del, mounted atop her white folly, leaned down to hand the horse-boy a few copper coins. Likely our last. I sighed, turned the stud, and aimed him out of the stableyard into the narrow alley between livery and adjoining building. He sucked himself up into stiff condescension as the gelding came up beside him, snorting pointed disdain. Then he caught a glimpse of one sad blue eye peering at him out of a circle of black greasepaint coupled with dangling gold fringe and shied sideways toward the nearest wall.

I planted a heel into his ribs, driving him off the wall before my foot could collide with adobe brick. "Let's not."

The stud took my hint and kept off the wall. Now he turned sideways, head bent back around so he could keep both worried eyes on Del's gelding. Ears stabbed toward the white horse like daggers. The accompanying snort was loud enough to drown out the sound of hooves.

Del began to laugh.

"What?" I asked irritably, trying to point the stud back into a straight line as we exchanged alley for street.

"I think he's afraid of him!"

"A lot of horses are afraid of the stud—"

"No! I mean the stud's afraid of *my* horse!"

"Now, bascha, do you really think—" But I broke off because the stud, now freed of the confines of the narrow alley, took three lunging steps sideways into the center of the street and stopped dead, stiff-legged, snorting wetly and loudly through widened nostrils. Fortunately it was early enough that the street was not yet crowded, and no one was in his way.

Del was still laughing.

"Maybe you should have gotten a mare after all," I muttered. "Look, bascha, just go ahead. I'll bring up the rear."

Grinning, she took my advice. The stud eased after a moment, ears flicking forward as Del departed. "What, you like the view from behind better?" I asked him. "Fine. Can we go now?"

And indeed we might have gone beyond the first two strides, except someone stopped dead in front of us. On foot. It was either ride over the top of him, or halt yet again.

I reined in sharply, swearing, and looked down upon the interruption. A young man in an russet-gold burnous, a Southroner, with smooth dark skin, longish dark hair, strong but striking features, and the kind of liquid, thick-lashed, honey-brown eyes that can melt a woman's heart. It might have been happenstance that he stepped in front of the stud, impeding my way, except that one hand was on a rein, holding the stud in place—and the other held a sheathed sword.

"You are the Sandtiger," he declared, raising his voice. Plainly he wanted an audience.

I might have denied his opening salvo in the interests of saving time, except I'd nearly lost myself in Meteiera and would never hide from my name again. I merely stared down at him.

Expressive eyes challenged me. "Will you dance? Will you step into the circle?"

I opened my mouth to explain I couldn't dance, not the way

he so clearly wanted, with a circle drawn in sand and all the
honor codes. Instead I said, "Not today," and jammed heels into
the stud's ribs.

Startled, he jumped forward. The young man, equally startled,
lost his grip on the rein. With agile alacrity he leaped aside so as
not to be ridden over, and I heard his fading curses as I struck a
crisp long-trot to the end of the street.

Del waited there atop her quiet gelding. The stud took one
look at him, considered spooking again, but was convinced otherwise when I cracked the long reins across his broad rump. There
was no further dissent as Del fell in beside us.

"So," she said calmly, "the secret of your return is out."

"Yes and no."

She frowned. "Why do you say that?"

"He isn't a sword-dancer. Just a kid trying to make a reputation."

"How do you know?"

"He invited me to dance. A sword-dancer won't. They all
know what *elaii-ali-ma* means: that there is no dance, no circle,
merely a fight to the death. There's a huge difference."

"And every sword-dancer in the South will know this?"

"Everyone sworn to the honor codes, yes."

"But he recognized you."

"That," I said, "is likely more a result of the swordsmith
spreading gossip."

"You think *he* recognized you?"

"Probably not. As I said, Haziz isn't a place many sword-dancers go, unless specifically hired. But as you pointed out before, we
don't exactly fit in with the rest of the crowd. All it would take is
a description, and anyone who'd seen or heard about us would
know."

"So. It begins."

"It begins." I glanced sideways at the long equine face with its
black-painted eye circles, the wine girl's dangling golden
fringe—I wondered briefly if Del had told her what she intended

to do with it—and mournful blue eyes. "That horse is a disgrace to his kind."

Del put up her brows. "Just because your horse is afraid of him is no cause to insult him."

"He looks ridiculous!"

"No more than yours did when he stood rooted to the ground, trembling like a leaf."

Probably not. Scowling, I said, "Let's go, bascha. It's a long ride to Julah—"

"—and we're burning daylight."

Well. We were.

Del and I stopped burning daylight when the sun went down. Then it lost itself in its own conflagration, a panoply of color so vivid as to nearly blind you. Desert orange, blazing red, yellow, vermillion, raisin purple, lavender, the faint burnished shadow of blue fading to silver-gilt. Out here twilight dies gently, shading slowly into darkness.

We were beyond the last oasis between Haziz and Julah, so there was no place in particular we wanted to bed down. We ended up settling for a series of conjoined hummocks carpeted in a fibrous, red-throated groundcover bearing tiny white blossoms, and the threadbare shelter of a thin grove of low, scrubby trees boasting a bouquet of woody limbs bearing dusty green leaves. Within weeks the leaves would dry out, curl up, and drop off, when summer seared them to death, but for now there was yet enough moisture in the mornings for the leaves to remain turgid. Mixed in with the groundcover were taller-growing desert grasses with frizzy, curled topknots.

"This'll do," I said, reining in even as Del dismounted.

Since the stud was not always trustworthy when picketed close to other horses, I led him to a tree eight paces away and had a brief discussion about staying put as I hobbled him. Del and I busied ourselves with untacking and grooming both mounts, swapping out bridles and bits for halters, pouring water into the squashable, flat-bottomed oiled canvas bags doubling as buckets, and offering them grain as a complement to the grasses. It wasn't particularly good grazing, but it would do; and the next night we'd be in Julah where they'd eat well.

Our dinner consisted of dried cumfa meat, purple-skinned tubers, and flat, tough-crusted journey-bread. Del drank water, I had a few mouthfuls of aqivi from the goatskin bota. Sated, we sprawled loose-limbed on our bedrolls and digested, blinking sleepily up into the deeping sky as the first stars kindled to life.

"That," Del observed after a moment, "was one huge sigh."

I hadn't noticed.

"Of contentment," she added.

I considered it. Maybe so. For all there were risks attendant to returning South, it was home. I'd been North with Del once, learning what real forests were, and true mountains, and even snow; had sailed to Skandi and met my grandmother on a wind-bathed, temperate island in the midst of brilliant azure seas, but it was *here* I was most at ease. Out in the desert beneath the open skies with nothing on the horizon but more horizon. Where a man owed nothing to no one, unless he wished to owe it.

Unless he was a slave.

Del lay very close. She set her head and one shoulder against mine, hooking ankle over ankle. And I recalled that I was man, not child; free, not slave. That'd I'd been neither child nor chula for years.

I remembered once telling Del, as we prepared to take ship out of Haziz, that there was nothing left for me in the South. In some ways, that was truth. In others, falsehood. There were things about the South I didn't care for, things I might not be cognizant of had Del not come along, but there were other things that meant more than I expected. Maybe it was merely a matter of being familiar with such things, of finding ease in dealing with what I knew rather than challenging the unexpected; or maybe it was that I'd met and overcome the challenges I'd faced and did not wish to relegate them to insignificance.

Then again, maybe it was merely relief that I was alive to return home, after nearly dying in a foreign land.

I grinned abruptly. "You know, there *is* one thing I really miss about Skandi."

Del sounded drowsy. "Hmmmm?"

"The metri's tiled bathing pool. And what we did in it."

"We can do that without the metri's bathing pool. In fact, I think we have."

"Not like we did there."

"Is that *all* you think about?"

I yawned. "No. Just most of the time."

After a moment she said reflectively, "It would be nice to have a bathing pool like that."

"Umm-hmm."

"Maybe you can build one at Alimat."

"I think I have to rebuild Alimat itself before building a bathing pool."

"In the meantime . . ." But her voice trailed off.

"In the meantime?"

"You'll have to make do with this." Whereupon she squirted the contents of a bota all over me.

The resultant activity was not even remotely similar to what we'd experienced mostly submerged in the metri's big, warm bathing pool. But it sufficed.

Oh, indeed.

FOUR

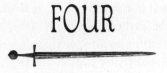

THE BALANCE of the journey to Julah was uneventful, save for the occasional uncharacteristic display of uncertainty by the stud when the white gelding looked at him. Del's mount was a quiet, stolid kind of horse, content to plod along endlessly with his head bobbing hypnotically on the end of a lowered neck—though Del claimed he didn't plod at all, but was the smoothest horse she'd ever ridden. I wasn't certain I knew what that was anymore, since the stud had forgotten every gait except a sucked-up walk that put me in mind of a man with the runs, trying to hold it in until he found a latrine. When this gait resulted in him falling behind Del's gelding, which happened frequently, he then broke into a jog to catch up and reassert his superiority. The gelding was unimpressed. So was I.

Julah was the typical desert town of flat-roofed, squared-off adobe buildings, deep-cut windows, tattered canvas awnings, and narrow, dusty streets. But there was water here in plenty, so Julah thrived. Opting to cool off before taking the risk of meeting other sword-dancers, we stopped at a well on the outskirts of town, dismounting to winch up buckets. We filled the horse troughs, permitted our mounts to drink, then quenched our own thirst and refilled botas. It was early enough in the season that the heat wasn't unbearable; but then, we hadn't reached the Punja yet. There was only one season in the Punja: *hot.*

Del dampened the hem of her burnous and wiped dust from her face. "Tonight *I* get the bath." Then, "How many sword-dancers are likely to be here?"

I backhanded water from my chin, realizing I needed to shave before we hit the Punja. "Oh, a few."

"Then we shouldn't stay longer than is necessary."

"We'll head out first thing tomorrow. In the meantime, except for a visit to Fouad's cantina, we'll keep our heads down."

"Walking into Fouad's, where at any time there may be half a dozen sword-dancers drinking his spirits, strikes me as keeping our heads *up*."

"Maybe. But we knew we'd face this coming back here."

Del said nothing. She had not argued when I said I wanted to return home—we had established that Skandi, for all my parents had come from the island, did not qualify—but she had quietly pointed out that to do so was sheer folly for a man sentenced to death by the very honor codes he'd repudiated. But the mere fact that she *hadn't* argued struck me as significant; I suspected Del was recalling that she was exiled from her own homeland and understood how much I needed to go back to mine. Unlike Del, I wasn't truly exiled. I wasn't under pain of death if I went back South. Oh, men would try to kill me, but that had nothing to do with exile. Just with broken oaths.

At my behest, we waited until sundown before entering Fouad's cantina. We had in the meantime secured lodging in an only slightly disreputable inn with a tiny stable out behind in an alley and had eaten at a street vendor's stall. The odors and flavors of spiced, if tough, mutton, sizzling peppers, and pungent goat cheese had immediately snatched me back to the days before we left for Skandi. I'm not sure Del appreciated that so much, having a more delicate palate—or so she claimed—but it felt like home to me. Then I led Del to Fouad's cantina, which was only fitfully lighted by smoking tallow candles on each small knife- and sword-hacked wooden table. I selected one back in the farthest corner from the door, a windowless nook veiled with smoke from a dying torch stuck in an iron wall sconce, dripping tallow. As we found stools to perch our rumps upon, I leaned forward and blew out our candle. Dimness descended.

"Oh, good," Del commented, brushing bread crumbs off the table. "Makes it so easy to see whom I'm to stick my sword into."

"We're not going to stick swords into anyone, bascha."

"Not even Fouad?" Del really seemed focused on the fact that my friend had betrayed us.

"Not immediately," I told her. "Maybe for the after-dinner entertainment."

Fouad, proprietor of my favorite cantina, was a small, neat, quick man of ready smile and welcome. Though he had wine-girls aplenty—Silk was working our corner, though clearly she hadn't yet recognized me—he enjoyed greeting newcomers personally. He approached the table calling out a robust greeting in Southron and offering us the best his cantina had to offer.

In bad light, wreathed in smoke, shorn of most of my hair, with double silver rings hanging in my ears and a tracery of blue tattooing along my hairline, I was no doubt a stranger to him at first glance, as I'd hoped. But Del, as always, was Del, and no man alive, having seen her even once, forgot what or who she was.

Or whom she traveled with.

Fouad stopped dead in his rush to greet new custom. He stared. He very nearly gaped.

He had, helpfully, placed himself within my reach. I rose, kicking back my stool, and leaned close, slapping one big hand down upon his shoulder in a friendly fashion. "Fouad!" I shut the hand, gripping him so firmly a wince of pain replaced his shocked expression. "Join us, won't you? It's been a long time." I shoved him toward the empty stool and pushed him down upon it. "There's much to catch up on, don't you think?"

He was trembling. Very unlike Fouad. But then, so was betrayal.

I yanked over another stool and sat down upon it. "So, what's the news? Any word out of Sabra?"

Fouad flicked a white-rimmed glance at Del, then looked back to me again. The robustness had spilled from his voice. "They say she's likely dead."

I raised a brow. " 'They say'? They're not sure?"

"She disappeared." His thin tone was a complex admixture of emotions. "Some say a sandstorm got her, or a beast, or the Vashni. But Abbu Bensir said differently."

I grinned. "Abbu would. He's always one to tell a good tale. So, what *did* Abbu say about Sabra?"

"That you killed her."

"He did not." That from Del, who was never one to let a good story get in the way of the facts. "Sabra died of her own folly."

In truth, Sabra had died because she laid hands on a *jivatma* which was, at the time, utterly perverted by magic, full of a sorcerer wanting very badly to get out. Which he had managed. Unfortunately, the vessel he chose for freedom—Sabra—was far too weak to contain him. But I suppose "folly" fairly well summed it up.

"And just when was good old Abbu here last?" I asked idly.

Fouad had stopped trembling. Color returned to his face. We had always been friends, and I supposed he was recalling that. But wariness remained. And guilt. "Weeks ago," he said. "He's north of here now, I hear."

Well. At least I wouldn't have to grapple with Abbu Bensir immediately. "Aqivi?"

"Water for me," Del said.

It gave him something to do. Rather than calling Silk over, Fouad sprang up.

"This time," I said quietly, "leave out the drug."

His face spasmed. "I will drink first of each, if you like."

I was prepared to wave it away, knowing my point was made, but Del was less forgiving. "Do so," she said, in a tone that lowered the temperature of the room markedly. "And you will remain at this table. Let it be brought."

After a moment, Fouad bowed to her with one hand pressed over his heart and quietly bade Silk, lingering nearby and trying to catch my attention now that she *had* recognized me—Silk had always been one of my favorites and, she said, I one of hers—to bring water, aqivi, bread and cheese. Then he sank down on the stool. He looked older than he had when we first entered the cantina.

I waited.

He drew in a deep, sharp breath, then let it out in a rush of helpless sound. "She would have killed me had I not done her bidding."

"Of course she would have," I agreed.

"I begged her not to make me do it."

"Of course you did."

"I *prayed*—"

"Enough," Del snapped. She glanced at me. "Do you intend to kill him, or shall I?"

Bloodthirsty Northern bascha. I smiled, and let Fouad start sweating again. When the water and aqivi arrived—and Silk was shooed away—he poured cups of each and tasted both. Del rather pointedly turned her cup so her mouth would not touch the rim where his had touched. Me, I just picked up the aqivi and knocked back a slug.

Long practice kept me from choking. Long abstinence—from aqivi, anyway—burned a line of fire from throat, through gullet, into belly. But being the infamous Sandtiger, I did not indicate this. I merely took another big slug.

Del's brows pulled together briefly, but she blanked her face almost at once.

"So." I grinned companionably at Fouad. "At Sabra's behest, in fear for your life, you drugged our wine. I, innocent as a woolly little lamb, wandered off looking for someone and walked into a trap you helped set. Del, meanwhile—*also* drugged—was handed over to Umir the Ruthless to become a part of his collection." Umir the Ruthless had tastes that did not incline to women but to unusual objects. He was ruthless not because he was particularly murderous personally, but because he'd do anything to get what he wanted. Even if he hired others to murder for him. "Del apparently feels what you did is worthy of execution. But I'm a more generous soul. What do you suggest I do about this?"

Fouad's tone was a carefully weighed mixture of resignation, suggestion, and hope. "Forget it?"

I nearly choked on a mouthful of aqivi. Far less amused, Del stared him down.

Fouad, suddenly smaller on his stool, sighed deeply. "No, I suppose not."

"We could have been killed," Del said.

"No!" Fouad exclaimed. "Assurances were made . . ." As if realizing how ludicrously lame that sounded, he trailed off into silence. "Well," he said finally, "they were. I'm only a lowly cantina keeper, not a sword-dancer to parse between what is threat and what is honesty."

"You've parsed enough in the past," I reminded him. Fouad had always been an excellent source of information and interpretation.

He debated whether to acknowledge flattery or avoid it altogether. He shrank further inside his yellow robe.

"So," I said, "you really didn't think they'd kill us—"

"And they didn't!" Fouad, having discovered a salient point, sat upright on the stool again. "Are you not here? Are you not sitting before me, eating my bread and cheese, drinking my liquor?"

"Water," Del clarified, displaying her cup. "But yes, I will give you all of that: we are indeed alive and sitting before you. Eating and drinking. Whether you intended it or no."

"I didn't want you dead! Either of you!" He looked from Del to me, and back again. "Why would I? I have nothing to gain from your deaths. I wanted merely to prevent mine."

"What did she pay you?" I asked.

"Nothing!"

Del was clearly skeptical. "Nothing?"

"She permitted me to keep my life," Fouad explained. "I am somewhat attached to my life and considered it payment enough, under the circumstances. Though undoubtedly others might not agree." He eyed me, clearly expecting a reaction. Then a frown pinched his brows together. "You look—different."

"A full life will do that to you," I replied gravely. "Especially if you're sold off to a murderous female tanzeer intent on punishing you for killing her father, despite the fact that said father deserved to be slowly roasted to death over a nice bed of coals." As Aladar had been the one to throw me into his mines and nearly cost me my sanity, I felt justified in my stance.

Color deepened in Fouad's face. He stared hard at the surface of the table. "I am not proud of it."

"Oh, that does change matters," Del said with delicate irony.

"You would do the same!" he cried; and then abruptly recalled to whom he spoke. Two sword-dancers, who defended the lives of others—and their own—without recourse to such cowardly acts as drugging customers' wine. His breath came fast. "What do you want, then? To kill me?" He paused. "Really?"

I smiled sweetly. "Two-thirds of this place."

Del cut me a sharp glance, not being privy to my plan. Fouad missed it, being entirely taken up with the magnitude of my revenge.

I lifted a forefinger before he could sputter out a protest. "You might have told Sabra no."

"She'd have had me killed!"

"So could we," I reminded him. "Though at least we'd do you the courtesy of killing you ourselves, instead of hiring a total stranger to do the job." My gesture encompassed the cantina. "Two-thirds, Fouad. One-third for you, one-third for me, one-third for Del."

Del concentrated on drinking more water so as not to give away her bemusement. Such are the dynamics of negotiation. Even if you aren't truly negotiating but merely informing.

Fouad did not believe. His tone was incredulous. "You want to be a cantina keeper? Here? But—but you're a sword-dancer!"

"I'd have been a dead man, had Sabra succeeded," I said bluntly. "But I am very much alive, and prepared to leave you that way . . . should we reach an equitable agreement." I cut him off before he could speak again. "And no, I am not proposing that I play host, or tell you what kind of curtains to put in your windows, or that Del be a wine-girl." I could imagine what she'd say to that image later. "I was thinking we'd be silent partners."

"I do all the work, you take two-thirds of the profits," Fouad said glumly.

"I'm glad you grasp the pertinent details."

"For how long?" he asked.

"How long?"

"For how long do I have to put up with you?"

"What, are you already planning to hire Abbu or some such soul to knock me off?"

Fouad was stunned. "I would *never* do such a thing!" Whereupon he recalled that while he hadn't done precisely that, he had indeed contributed to the trap that could very well have have ended in my death.

"Two-thirds," Del said crisply. "Payable four times a year."

I nodded with grave dignity. Fouad screwed up his face.

"And *I* may just have an idea for those curtains," she added.

I suspect a knife in the gut might have proven less painful to him. But he eventually agreed, with much moroseness of expression.

"Good," I said. "As for how long, it's a lifetime arrangement. If I die, Del gets my one-third. If she dies, I get her one-third."

I'd given Fouad an opening. "And if you both die? You are sword-dancers, after all. Sword-dancers die."

I drank down the rest of my aqivi, then scratched idly at the claw marks in my face. "I plan to live forever."

Fouad looked. He saw. His lips parted. "Your finger," he said hoarsely.

I displayed both hands. "Fin*gers*," I enunciated. "As I said, I've lived a full life."

He was stunned. "Sabra did that?"

"This? No." I didn't elaborate, which left him nonplussed.

"But—can you dance?"

I felt Del's look, but I did not return it. "Try me."

Fouad was perversely fascinated by the missing fingers. I saw him turn it over in his head, applying his knowledge of my past,

my reputation, to the present sitting before him and all the impli-
cations. He more closely noted the shorn hair, doubled earrings—
and whatever else you might see if you looked upon me now.

"I heard—" He paused and cleared his throat. "I heard a
rumor that you'd survived Sabra. That you'd declared . . ."

"*Elaii-ali-ma,*" I supplied, when he faltered. "You've been selling drink and women to sword-dancers for years. You know very
well what *elaii-ali-ma* means."

He did. "Forsworn."

"And subject to any punishment a sword-dancer—one who's
still true to his oaths, mind you—cares to give me." I shrugged.
"So you might get to keep my one-third of the profits, if it comes
to that. One of these days."

"They'll kill you, Tiger."

"Maybe," I agreed. "Maybe not."

His gaze was on my mutilated hands, which I did not trouble
to hide. "This is worse," Fouad said hollowly. "Worse than anything Sabra might have done."

"Possibly. But that does not absolve you of your responsibility." He had the grace to wince. "She intended me to die, Fouad.
This way, fingers or no fingers, I have some say in the matter."

Fouad was not convinced. "They'll kill you."

I gave him my friendliest grin. "Or die trying."

"Why?" Del demanded later in the inn's tiny room high under
the eaves. An equally tiny window—a lopsided square chopped
into thick mudbrick—tinted the room a sallow sepia as the sun
went down, glinting off the brass buckles of our belongings.

I knew better than to ask to what she referred. "Financial
security." I stripped out of my burnous.

Stretched out on the rope-and-wood bed atop its thin pallet
and even thinner blanket, she watched as I, dhoti-clad, began to
methodically undertake the forms I found beneficial to my
strength, flexibility, and endurance. For most of my life I'd depended on a natural wellspring of sheer physical strength, power,

and speed, with no need to work at keeping any of them. They simply *were*. Now I needed more.

"You just didn't want to kill him."

She sounded so disgusted a brief gust of laughter was expelled as I bent from one side to the other. "Fouad's a friend."

"A friend who betrayed you."

"At Sabra's insistence." I felt the joints of my spine stretch and pop. "She was a little hard to turn down when she got a bug up her butt. Hoolies, even *I* was going to do what she wanted." Die in the circle, facing Abbu Bensir.

"But you had a choice."

I clasped hands behind my head and pushed it forward against resistance. "Sure I did. I forswore all my oaths as a seventh-level sword-dancer. I don't think cantina keepers have any oaths. Though I suppose there could be some secret society dedicated to all the arcane secrets of selling liquor and hiring wine-girls."

Del had been leaning on one elbow. Now she shoved herself upright. "Speaking of wine-girls, you made reference to *me*—"

I cut her off before we could take that route. "Certainly not."

"Certainly, yes," she said dryly. "You also mentioned something about Fouad selling wine-girls to sword-dancers."

"Well, I suppose 'rented' would be a more accurate term."

"And I assume you 'rented' your share?"

"Nah," I replied off-handedly. "None of them ever charged *me*."

After a moment of stunned silence, Del said something highly explicit in uplander.

I changed the subject hastily. "Do you really want to kill Fouad?"

"No. But I *do* want to know why you've encumbered us with a two-thirds ownership of a cantina." She paused, considering. "Unless you figure it entitles you to free aqivi."

"Well, it does. Might save me a little money." I shrugged prodigiously, repeatedly, loosening the muscles running from neck to shoulders. "It's not an encumbrance, bascha. All we have to do is drop in four times a year and pick up our share of the profits."

Fortunately Fouad had been prevailed upon to give us an advance, since, having arranged for horse boarding, human lodging, and some food, we now needed money to pay for it all.

"But why, Tiger? You've never indicated any interest in owning property before. A cantina?"

"I like cantinas."

"Well, yes; you spend enough time in them . . . but why *own* one?"

"I told you. Financial security." I stopped loosening up and faced her. "I doubt I'll be taking on any jobs as a sword-dancer any time soon. I'm kind of proscribed from that."

Del was perplexed. "You told me you wanted to rebuild your shodo's place. Alimat. And take on students."

"I do. But that presupposes there will be students to teach and that they'll have money to pay me. We need to buy things, bascha. Fouad's cantina will at least cover expenses." I gave her a quizzical look. "Isn't that the responsible thing to do?"

"Of course it's the responsible thing to do," she agreed. "It's just very unlike you to *be* responsible."

I scowled. "Short of killing him, and he wouldn't be around to suffer or feel remorse if I did that, it's also about the direst punishment I could think of for Fouad. He's a pinch-coin."

"Is there anyone else you want to punish? Are we likely to wind up owning a weaver's shop, a vegetable plot, or a flower cart?"

"I doubt it. None of those people has ever drugged my wine and set me up to be taken by a spoiled, bloodthirsty, murderous little bitch bent on seeing me killed in the circle." I rolled my neck, feeling tension loosen. "What color of curtains were you thinking, bascha?"

Del made a sound of derision. "As if any cantina would boast curtains in the windows. Likely some drunkard would set them on fire the first fight he got into. And we, now partners with your faithful friend Fouad, would have to bear two-thirds of the cost of damages."

I hadn't thought about that.

"I knew it," Del said in deep disgust. "Men. All they ever think about are the profits. Not about all the work that goes into such things."

Well, no. "That's why we have Fouad," I said brightly. "He'll take care of all that."

Del scowled. "I still say it was foolish to go to Fouad's. Word will be out by morning, just like in Haziz."

"It won't be Fouad who spreads it."

"Of *course* it will be Fouad—"

"No."

"Why, because you're his partner now?"

"Because we really were friends, bascha. And because he feels guilty."

"As well he should!"

"You don't know *you* wouldn't have done what he did, faced with Sabra."

After a moment, Del declared, "I find that observation incredibly offensive."

I grinned at her, continuing to work out the tension in my body; going to Fouad's had kept me on edge, regardless of what I admitted. "You didn't face Sabra." Not in the same way, at any rate. By the time Del and Sabra were in close proximity, Sabra was unconscious and tied to a saddle.

"I'd have killed her," Del said shortly.

A sudden and very intriguing image rose before my eyes: Del and Sabra. One small and dark, one tall and fair. Two dangerous, deadly women. Except Del was far more honest when she killed: she did it herself.

"Word will get out," I said, "but it won't be Fouad."

"Such a trustworthy soul," Del said dryly.

"Let me see your wrist."

Obligingly, Del extended an arm. I shut my hand upon the wrist and squeezed. Tightly. *Very* tightly.

After a moment, she asked, "Are you purposely attempting to break my wrist?" She wiggled fingers. "Let go, Tiger."

Smiling, I let go.

Del sighed. "Point taken."

"I should hope so."

"But it will still be different," she cautioned. "More difficult."

"I agree, bascha."

And it was very likely, I knew, I'd discover *how* different to-morrow. Because word was bound to get out.

The Sandtiger is back.

Yes. He was.

FIVE

Del and I were only just crawling out of bed in the morning when a scratching sounded at the door. I might have said vermin, except it was too repetitive. I dragged on dhoti and unsheathed my sword even as Del hastily swirled a blanket around her nudity.

The scratching came again, coupled with a woman's soft voice asking if the sword-dancer and the Northern woman were in there. No names. Interesting.

A glance across my shoulder confirmed a well wrapped Del was prepared with sword in hand. She nodded. I unlocked the door and opened it, blade at the ready. It wasn't impossible someone might use a woman as a beard. Such things as courtesy and honorable discourse were no longer required.

The woman in the narrow corridor winced away from the glint of sharp steel. She displayed the palms of her hands in a warding gesture, displaying innocent intent. I blinked. It was Silk, the wine-girl from Fouad's cantina, swathed in robes and a head covering when ordinarily she wore very little.

"I'm alone," she blurted. "I swear it."

Her nerves were strung tight as wire. I opened my mouth to ask what she was doing here when I saw her gaze go beyond me to Del. She registered that Del was nude under the thin blanket, with white-blond hair in tumbled disarray, and something flared briefly in Silk's dark eyes, something akin, I thought, to recognition and acknowledgment of another woman's beauty. Her mouth hooked briefly. Not jealousy, though. Oddly enough, regret. Resignation. Silk was attractive, in a cheap sort of way, but infinitely Southron; Del, in all her splendid Northern glory, was simply incomparable. She wasn't to every Southroner's taste—too tall, too fair-skinned, too blonde for some of them, and most definitely too independent—but no one, looking at her, could be blind to what she was.

Ah, yes. That's my bascha.

"Fouad sent me," Silk said nervously. I gestured her in, but she shook her head. "I must go back. He wanted me to tell you someone recognized you, and word is already out of your presence here. He fears you may be challenged before you can leave."

I nodded, unsurprised, already thinking ahead to how it might occur.

"Thank you for this," Del said.

Silk resettled her headcovering, pulling it forward to shield part of her face. "I didn't do it for you."

After a moment of stillness, Del smiled faintly. "No. But we both want him to survive."

Silk cut me a glance out of wide, grieving eyes. I was startled to see tears there. I opened my mouth to speak, but she turned sharply and walked away, a small dark woman in pale, voluminous fabric.

"Door," Del said crisply.

I shut and latched it even as she shed the blanket and grabbed smallclothes and tunic. Without further conversation we donned burnouses and sandals, packed and gathered up belongings, reestablished the fit of our harnesses and that swords were properly seated in their sheaths.

The horses were stabled just out back in the tiny livery. So long as no one knew we were here at this particular inn, it was possible we might get them tacked out, our gear loaded, and our butts in the saddles before we were discovered.

But maybe not.

Del's eyes met mine. Her face was expressionless. She was once again the Northern sword-singer, a woman warrior capable not only of meeting a man on equal footing but of defeating him.

Shodo-trained sword-dancers wouldn't want to fight or harm her. It was me they were after; they'd let her go. But Del would take that convention and turn it upside down.

One of us might die today. Or neither. Or both. And we each of us knew it.

She opened the door and walked out.

Del and I made an honest effort to take every back alley in the tangled skein that made up the poorer sections of Julah. For a moment I thought we might actually get out of town without me being challenged, but I should have known better. Whoever the sword-dancer was who'd recognized me, he was smart enough to know he couldn't be everywhere; he'd need to make a financial investment in order to track me down. He'd hired gods know how many boys to stake out the streets and intersections, and eventually the alleys merged with them. It didn't take long for word to be carried that the Sandtiger and his Northern bascha were crossing the Street of Weavers and heading for the Street of Potters, which in turn gave into the Street of Tinsmiths.

And it was there, in front of one of the more prosperous shops catering to the tin trade, that the sword-dancer found us.

Mounted, he'd halted his dun-colored horse in the middle of the street. Del and I had the option of turning around and going back the way we'd come, but it was one thing to attempt to avoid your enemy, and another to turn tail and run once you actually came face to face with him.

Fueled by the overexcited boys and the promise of a sword-dance, rumor had quickly spread. The Street of Tinsmiths was not the main drag through town, but the entire merchants' quarter was always thronged with people, and today was market day. The buzz of recognition and comment began as Del and I reined in, and rose in anticipation, much like startled bees, as we sat at ease atop our horses, saying nothing, letting my opponent take the lead.

"Sandtiger." He raised his voice, though our mounts stood approximately fifteen paces apart. "Do you remember me?"

The street fell silent. I was aware of staring faces, expectant eyes. The sun glinted off samples of tinware hanging on display on both sides of the narrow thoroughfare. I smelled forges, coals, the acrid tang of worked metal.

I looked at him. Southron through and through, and all sword-dancer, torso buckled into harness and the hilt of his sword riding above his left shoulder. Yes, I remembered him. Khashi. He was ten or twelve years younger than I. He'd been taken on at Alimat about the time I left to make my own way. I'd witnessed enough of his training before I departed to know he was talented and had heard rumors over the years that he was good, but we'd never crossed paths on business, and I hadn't seen him since then.

"You know why," he said.

I didn't reply. The faintest of breezes ruffled our burnouses, the robes and headcloths of spectators, and set dangling tinware clanking against one another. A child's plaintive voice rose, and was hushed.

Khashi's thin lips curled. Disdain was manifest. "What's more, I heard you played the coward in Haziz and refused to accept a challenge."

I shook my head. "He wasn't a sword-dancer. Just a stupid kid looking for glory."

Brown eyes narrowed. "And what do you say of me?"

"Nothing." I shrugged. "That's all you're worth."

We weren't close enough for me to see the color burning in his face, but I could tell I'd gotten to him. His body stiffened, hands tightening on the reins. His horse shifted nervously and joggled his head, trying to ease the pressure on his mouth. Metal bit shanks and rings clinked.

"And what are you worth?" he asked sharply. "You declared *elaii-ali-ma*."

"Oh, I am lower than the lowest of the low," I replied. "I am

foulness incarnate. I am dishonor embodied. You'll soil your blade
with my blood."

He grinned, showing white teeth against a dark face. "But
blood washes off. Righteousness does not." Abruptly he raised his
voice, addressing the crowd. "Hear me!" he shouted. "This man
is the Sandtiger, who once was a seventh-level sword-dancer
sworn to uphold the honor codes and sacred traditions of Alimat.
But he repudiated them, his shodo, and all of his brethren. It is
our right to punish him for this, and today I willingly accept the
honor of this task. I call on every man here to witness the death
of an oath-breaker!"

I sighed, looping one rein over the stud's neck as I extended
the other to Del. "You talk too much, Khashi."

Stung, but still focused on the task, he hooked his right leg
over his horse's neck, kicked his left foot clear of stirrup, and
jumped down, throwing reins toward one of the boys. There were
clusters of them lining the shop walls, and merchants and customers spilled out of doorways. The street was a canyon of staring
faces. "Then we shall stop talking," he said, "and fight."

Unlike the stupid kid in Haziz, Khashi knew the difference
between dance and fight. He stripped off burnous, sandals, and
harness, wearing only the customary soft suede dhoti underneath,
and set them aside. He did not pause to draw a circle, or to invite
me to draw it, because there would be none. Lithely graceful, he
strode forward, sword in hand.

I heard the simultaneous intake of breath from the impromptu
audience as I stepped off the stud. I did not strip out of harness,
burnous, or sandals. I simply unsheathed without excess dramatics
and walked to meet my challenger in the middle of the street, six
paces away.

He smiled, assessing his opponent. The infamous Sandtiger,
but also an older, aging man who was too foolish to rid himself
of such things as would impede his movements. I had given the
advantage to the younger challenger.

Which is why he laughed incredulously as I halted within his
reach.

I did nothing more than wait. After a moment's hesitation—perhaps unconsciously expecting the traditional command to dance that wouldn't come—Khashi flicked up his sword and obliged with the first move.

I obliged by countering the blow, and another, and a third, and a fourth, turning his blade away. I offered no offense, only defense. I conserved strength, while Khashi spent his.

Though we did not stand within a circle and thus were not required to remain within a fixed area, lest we lose by stepping outside the boundary, we'd both spent too many years honoring the codes and rituals. There was no dramatic leaping and running and rolling. It was a swordfighter's version of toe-to-toe battle, lacking elegance, ritual, the precision of expertise despite our training. We simply stood our ground, aware of the mental circle despite the lack of a physical one, and fought.

It was, as always, noisy. Steel slammed into steel, scraped, tore away, screamed, shrieked, chimed. Breath ran harshly through rigid throats and issued hissing from our mouths. Grunts and gasps of effort overrode the murmuring of the spectators, the low verbal thrum of excitement.

I countered yet another blow, threw the blade back at him with main strength. I felt a twinge in my right hand, and another in my left wrist. The hilt shifted slightly in my hands.

All of the things Del and I had discussed had indeed become factors: The loss of a finger on each hand did affect my grip, and that, in turn, affected wrists, forearms, elbows, clear up into the shoulders and back. I had worked ceaselessly since leaving Skandi to compensate for the loss of those fingers by retraining my body, but only a real fight would prove if I'd succeeded. Now that I was in one, I realized my body wanted to revert to postures, grips, and responses I'd learned more than twenty years before. The new mind had not yet taught the old body to surrender.

I could not afford a lengthy battle, because I could not win it. I needed to make it short.

I raised the blade high overhead, gripped in my right hand, wrist cocked so the point tipped down toward my left shoulder.

Khashi saw the opening I gave him, the opportunity to win. He did not believe it. But he lunged, unable to pass up the target I'd made of my torso. The audience drew in a single startled breath.

I brought the sword down diagonally in a hard, slashing cross-body blow, rolling the edge with a twist of my wrist even as I adjusted my elbow. The inelegant but powerful maneuver swept Khashi's blade down and aside. Another flick of the wrist, the punch through flesh and muscle, and I slid steel into his belly. A quick scooping twist carved the intestines out of abdominal cavity, and then I pulled the blade free of flesh and viscera.

Khashi dropped his sword. His hands went to his belly. His mouth hung open. Then his knees folded out from under him. He knelt there in the street clutching ropy guts, weaving in shock as his gaping mouth emitted a keening wail of shock and terror.

I did him the honor of kicking his blade away, though he had no strength to pick it up, and turned my back on him. I intended to go directly to the stud. But three paces away stood the stupid kid from Haziz. His sword was unsheathed, gripped in one hand.

Blood ran from mine. I watched his startled eyes as they followed the motion along the steel, red, wet runnels sliding from hilt to tip, dripping onto hardpacked dirt.

He looked at me then. Saw me, saw something in my face, my eyes. His own face was pale. But he swallowed hard and managed to speak. "There was no honor in that."

I'd expected a second challenge, not accusation. After a moment I found my own voice. "This wasn't about honor."

His brown eyes were stunned in a tanned face formed of planes and angles gone suddenly sharp as blades. "But you need not kill a man to win. Not in the circle."

"This isn't about the circle," I said. "Not about rites, rituals, honor codes, or oaths sworn to such. It's just about dying."

"But—you're a sword-dancer."

I shook my head. "Not anymore. Now I'm only a target."

"You're the Sandtiger!"

"That, yes," I agreed. "But I swore *elaii-ali-ma*."

Color was creeping back into his face. The honey-brown eyes were steady, if no less shocked. "I don't know what that is."

A jerk of my head indicated Khashi's sprawled body, limp as soiled laundry. "Ask him."

I walked past him then, because I knew he wouldn't challenge me. Not now. Likely not ever again.

But others would.

Before mounting I wiped my blade clean of blood on my burnous, sheathed it, and took the rein back from Del. Then swung up into the saddle. "Let's go."

The mask of her face remained, giving away nothing to any who looked. But her eyes were all compassion.

I heard the chanting of my name as we headed out of Julah.

Not far out of the city, after a brief but silent ride, I abruptly turned off the road. I rode to the top of a low rise crowned with cactus and twisted trees, dismounted, let the reins go, and managed to make it several paces down the other side, sliding in shale and slate, before I bent and gave up everything in my belly in one giant heaving spasm.

I remained bent over, coughing and spitting when the residual retching stopped, and heard the chink of hoof on stone. It might be the stud. But in case it was Del, I thrust out a splayed hand that told her to stay away.

I didn't need an audience. I'd had one already, in Julah.

Finally I straightened, scraping at my mouth with the sleeve of my burnous. When I turned to hike back up to the stud, I found Del holding his reins. Silent no longer.

"Are you cut?" she asked.

"No."

"Are you sure?"

"Yes."

"Have you *looked*?"

Sighing, I inspected my arms, then ran my hands down the front of burnous and harness, checking for complaints of the flesh, though I was fairly certain Khashi had not broken my guard. I was spattered with blood, but none of it appeared to be mine. And nothing hurt beyond the edges of my palms where the fingers were missing.

"I'm fine." I climbed to the stud, took the reins from her, then pulled one of the botas free and filled my mouth with water. I rinsed, spat, scrubbed again at my mouth, then released a noisy breath from the environs of my toes. "Butchery," I muttered hoarsely, throat burned by bile.

"It was necessary."

"I've killed men, beheaded men, cut men into collops before. Borjuni. Bandits. Thieves. It never bothered me; it was survival, no more. But this—" I shook my head.

"It was necessary," she repeated. "How better to warn other sword-dancers you will not be easy prey?"

That was precisely why I had done it, knowing the tale would be told. Embellished into legend. But the aftermath was far more difficult to deal with than I had anticipated.

"Tiger," Del said quietly, "you spent many years learning all the rituals of the sword-dance. The requirements of the circle. It was your escape, your freedom, but also a way of life woven of rules, rites, codes. The formal sword-dance is not about killing but about the honor of the dance and victory. What you did today was the antithesis of everything you learned, all that you embraced, when you swore the oaths of a sword-dancer before your shodo at Alimat."

"I've been in death-dances before." They were rare, as most sword-dances were a relatively peaceful way of settling disputes for our employers, but they did occur.

"Still formalized," she observed. "It's an elegant way to die. An honorable way to die."

Killing Khashi had been neither. But necessary, yes.

"On another day, you and he would have danced a proper dance. One of you would have won. And then likely afterwards you'd have gone to a cantina together and gotten gloriously drunk. It *is* different, Tiger, what was done today."

"You can't know, bascha—"

"I can. I do. I killed Bron."

It took me a moment. Then I remembered. Del had killed a friend, a training partner, who otherwise would have kept her from returning to the Northern island known as Staal-Ysta, where her daughter lived.

But still.

I squirted more water into my mouth, spat again, then drank. Stared hard across the landscape, remembering the stink of severed bowels, the expression on his face as his life ran out, the weight of the blade as I opened his abdomen.

Butchery.

"Would you feel better if you had died?"

For the first time since the fight I looked directly at her. Felt the tug of a wry smile at my mouth. Trust Delilah to put it in perspective.

"You don't have to like it," she said. "If you did, if you began to, I would not share your bed. But this, too, is survival, and in its rawest, most primitive form. There *will* be others. Kill them quickly, Tiger, and ruthlessly. Show them no mercy. Because they will surely show none to you."

What she didn't say, what she didn't need to say, was that some of those others would be better than Khashi.

SIX

D<small>EL</small> was initially resistent to
going after my *jivatma*. She truly saw no sense in it, since very
likely the sword was buried under tons of rock, and we had new
blades. I still hadn't told her about the dreams of the woman commanding me to take up the sword, because I couldn't find words
that didn't make me sound like a sandsick fool. Instead, I relied
on Del's own respect for the Northern blades and on the loss of
Boreal. As I had by declaring *elaii-ali-ma*, she had made the only
choice possible in breaking the sword, but that didn't mean she
was immune to regret. Eventually she gave in.

There was not a road where we wanted to go, because no one
else, apparently, had ever wanted to go there. Del and I made our
own way, recalling the direction from our visit to Shaka Obre's
domain nearly a year before. We left behind the flat but relatively
lush desert of Julah and traded it for foothills, the precursors of
the mountain where we had encountered strong magic, where
Chosa Dei, living in my sword, had vacated it first to fill—and
kill—Sabra, then to encounter his brother. They hadn't been living beings, Chosa Dei and Shaka Obre, merely power incarnate,
but that was enough. What was left of them battled fiercely
within the hollowed rock formation that shaped, inside a huge
chimney of stone, a circle. And Del and Chosa Dei, using my
sword, my body, had danced.

Here there was rock in place of soil, intermixed with hardpan and seasonings of sand. Drifts of stone were like the bones of the earth peeping through the flesh, but there were tumbled piles of it as well as that beneath the dirt. Brownish, porous smokerock, the variegations of slate, sharply faceted shale, the milky glow of quartz, the glitter of mica coupled with glinting splashes of false gold. The Punja, with its crystalline sands, was yet miles away. This was a land of rock swelling like boils into looming stone formations crowning ragged foothills, merging slowly into mountains. Not the high, huge ranges of Del's North, shaped of wind and snow and ice, but the whimsy of Southron nature in sudden bubbles of burst rock, scattered remnants of wholeness and order, abrupt, towering upthrustings of striated stone shoved loose from the desert floor.

Movement against the uneven horizon of foothills and rock formations caught my eye. I looked, saw, and reined in sharply. Del, not watching me as she and her gelding picked their way through, nearly allowed her gelding to walk into the back of the stud. There was a moment of tension in the body beneath me, but he, too, knew what lay before us was far more threatening than what was behind.

"What—" Del began; but then she, like me, held her silence, and waited.

I had half expected it. We were in the land of the Vashni. No one knew where the borders were, or even if there *were* borders, but there was always the awareness of risk when one traveled here.

Four warriors. Vashni are not large, nor are their horses. But size wasn't what mattered. It was the willingness to kill, and the way in which they did it.

Four warriors, kilted in leather, wearing wreaths of fingerbone pectorals against oiled chests. Black hair was also oiled, worn in single, fur-wrapped plaits. Bone-handled knives and swords decorated their persons.

Del's voice was a breath of sound. "Could these be the same four who met us when we had Sabra?"

I answered as quietly. "I don't know. Maybe. No one sees the

Vashni often enough to recognize individuals." At least, no one
lived long enough to recognize individuals.

The warriors eased their small, dark horses into motion. They
rode down from the rocky hilltop and approached, marking our
faces, harnesses, swords. I felt the first tickle of sweat springing up
on my skin.

Is it possible to fight a Vashni? Of course. I imagine it has
happened. But no one, *no one* has ever survived the battle. They
are killed, then boiled. When the bones are free of flesh, the
Vashni make jewelry and weapons of it. The flesh is fed to dogs.

The only reason I know this is the Vashni don't kill children.
It is their 'mercy' to take children into their villages, to feed them,
have them watch what becomes of their parents, then deliver
them to a road where they will be found by others.

If they are found. Some of them have been.

Del and I had been in a Vashni village once, when searching
for her brother. They had treated us with honor; Jamail was considered a holy man, and she was his sister. Jamail, castrated, mute,
had not wanted to leave the people who gave him a twisted sort
of kindness after years of slavery elsewhere. Later—known by
then as the Oracle—he had been killed, but it hadn't been Vashni
doing. They revered his memory.

"Del," I said quietly, "come up beside me so they can see you
better."

She didn't question it; possibly she also realized safety might
lie in her resemblence to the Oracle, her brother. She moved the
gelding out from behind the stud, guided him next to me, and
reined in. Again, we waited.

That triggered a response in the Vashni. One of them stayed
back, but three others rode down. One stationed himself in front
of me, approximately three paces away; the other two took up
positions on either side of us.

The fourth rode down then. When he was close enough, I saw
his eyes were lighter than the others, the shape of his face somewhat different. I'd never heard of Vashni breeding with other
tribes, but anything was possible. They had taken a Northerner

into their midst. Del's brother, by the time we found him, had become one of them.

The warrior pulled up near Del. This close, we could smell them. Apparently rancid oil was considered perfume in Vashni circles.

The warrior's eyes were a dark gray. He looked hard at Del, then at me. Something moved in those eyes. He raised a hand to his face and touched one cheek, mimicking my scars.

I took it as invitation. "Sandtiger," I said.

Now he looked at Del. Now the hand rose to his hair, then indicated his eyes.

Blue-eyed, fair-haired Del said, "The Oracle's sister."

The Vashni closed in. We followed—or were made to understand it was wise to follow—the man with gray eyes.

It was a camp, not a village. A tiny clearing surrounded by boulders, a grove of twisted, many-limbed trees, a fire ring set in the middle with blankets thrown down around it. The stink of blood and entrails as well as the piles of hides told us the Vashni were a hunting party, as did the skinned carcasses hanging from the trees. Likely the village was a day's ride. Perhaps it was even the one where Jamail had been held.

Once in camp, Del and I were motioned off our horses. We dismounted, and one of the warriors led the stud and gelding away to tie them to a tree lacking the ornamentation of meat. The stud was not happy, but he didn't protest. Del's black-painted, fringe-bedecked gelding went placidly and stood where he was tied, lowering his head to forage in thatches of webby green grass spreading beneath the tree. The Vashni mounts were turned loose once their bridles were slipped; apparently even they knew better than to test a warrior's mood.

Gravely the gray-eyed man unsheathed knife and sword and set them down upon a woven blanket. The other warriors followed suit. Then it was our turn.

Unarming before anyone was not something I enjoyed. Doing it before Vashni set a knot into my guts. But a single misstep could get us killed. And they seemed to be peaceable enough—for the moment.

Del and I added our weapons to the pile. The gray-eyed man, whom I took to be the leader, sat down, motioning us to be seated on the blanket across from him, on the other side of the fire ring. We did so. It was a comfortable spot out of the sun's glare, shaded by trees. If we'd been with anyone besides Vashni, it might have been a nice little respite.

Then, surprisingly, the grey-eyed man placed a hand on his chest and identified himself: "Oziri." Botas were brought out and passed around. We were, they made it clear, to drink first, even before Oziri.

Peaceable indeed. Courteous, even. I unstoppered the bota, smelled the pungent bite of liquor, took a surreptitious deep breath, then squirted a goodly amount into my mouth. Even as I swallowed liquid fire, clamping my mouth shut so as not to gasp aloud, I passed the bota to Del. Without hesitation she drank down a generous swallow. Then tears welled up in her eyes, and she went into a spasm of coughing.

It might have been insult. Instead, the Vashni found it amusing. Grins broke out. Heads nodded. One warrior brought out a leather bag, dug inside, then tossed out sizeable chunks of meat to his companions. I was thrown a chunk big enough for two; Del, they clearly judged, was still too incapacitated to catch her own.

"If you die," I told her, "they'll likely take your body back to the village and boil the flesh off your bones."

Her voice was thin and choked. "I'm not dying."

"Here." I divided and passed her some meat. "Maybe this will help."

She cleared her throat repeatedly, then accepted the meat even as she thrust the bota back at me. "What is it?"

"Don't ask. Just eat." I sucked down more liquor. It was unlike anything I'd had before. Already my brain tingled.

Knowing Vashni eyes were on her, Del lifted the meat to her mouth and found a promising edge. She bit into it, froze a moment, then began to gnaw at it. Eventually she pulled the bite free and began to chew. Her expression, despite her attempt to mask it, spoke of a flavor not particularly pleasing to her palate.

Now that Del was eating, it was my turn. No more excuses. I bit into my portion, tore off a chunk, tasted the sharp, gamy flavor, and began the lengthy process of chewing it into something that might be swallowed. The warriors, I noted, had no problems. But then, they likely had been given tough and mostly raw meat from the day their teeth came in.

Del's words were distorted around the bite she was clearly reluctant to swallow. "Wha' i' it?"

I grinned as I risked it—one big swallow to get it all down at once—and tossed the bota back. "Like I said, don't ask. Just eat. Wash it down with that."

Oziri said, "Sandtiger."

I looked at him. "Yes?"

Something very like a smile quirked the corner of his mouth. He pointed to the meat. "Sandtiger. For the Sandtiger."

Oh. *Oh*.

Hoolies—I was eating my namesake!

Del stopped chewing. She stared at the hunk of meat in her hand, plainly trying to decide if she would be forgiven for spitting out what was in her mouth, or possibly killed for it. As I expected, she took the safer road. She swallowed with effort, then squirted more liquor into her mouth. This time she didn't cough, but a hand flew to her mouth. Droplets fell from her chin.

Sandtiger meat. No wonder it was so tough. They weren't exactly known as a food source. Usually we were theirs.

I bit off another chunk and began to chew before it could chew back. It was impossible to relax, but the Vashni, eating and drinking companionably, gave every indication we were guests, not quarry bound for the cookpot.

Of course, it could just be the last meal prior to the cookpot.

I didn't say that to Del. Just watched her struggle to chew and choke down the meat, leavening it with liquor. Eventually I took the bota back and did the same.

"Sandtiger," Oziri said.

I waited politely, wondering if he were addressing me or identifying my meal.

"The Oracle's sister took you into Beit al'Shahar and freed you of Chosa Dei."

Either that had become legend in his tribe, or this man had been one of the warriors who'd told Del where to find Shaka Obre, after she'd hit me over the head with a rock. Or perhaps he was one of the warriors who'd taken Jamail to the chimney formation where he somehow managed to learn how to speak again despite lacking a tongue.

"Yes," I confirmed.

"You are free now?"

"Yes."

He ran a forefinger along his hairline. "Chosa Dei did that?"

He meant the rim of tattoos at the top of my forehead, not yet hidden by hair. "No. This was done in Skandi. An island far away."

He didn't care about Skandi. "Did Chosa steal your mind?"

I smiled. "He tried. But no. I'm truly free of him." If I weren't, they'd likely boil me. "Thanks to the Oracle's sister."

He nodded once, glancing at Del. "We honor you, Oracle's sister."

Del was startled. But she retained enough courtesy to give him thanks for that, for his meat, for his liquor.

Oziri smiled. "You will be drunk."

Her face was rosy. "I think," she said, "I am."

He nodded once. "Good."

"Good?" she asked faintly.

"Good, yes." He glanced it me. "You, it will take longer."

"Oh, I don't know—I'm already feeling it."

"Drink more. There are tales to be told."

So I drank more, while the Vashni told us tales of the Oracle's prophecies of a man who would change the sand to grass, thus changing the future of the desert. I kept my face free of reaction, but I couldn't help wondering if that kind of future was anathema to them. Yet the warriors seemed merely to accept what their Oracle had prophesied, as if it hadn't occured to them to question what might come. Blind faith, sitting before me.

"Jhihadi," Oziri said, and the others murmured something.

I flicked a sharp glance at him.

"The Oracle said he will change the sand to grass."

I chewed thoughtfully at a final bite of meat, recalling the suggestions I had made to a young man called Mehmet about digging new wells and using cisterns linked to channels to bring the water to areas without. The suggestion had seemed quite logical to me, infinitely practical. So obvious, in fact, I found it amazing no one else had ever thought of it.

And for that suggestion, Mehmet had named me jhihadi.

A man could own a dwelling and a plot of land and call himself a king. A man could have an idea that suited a prophecy, and call himself a messiah.

And there were times when that kind of label could be valuable.

I swallowed the meat, then leaned forward, dug a shallow depression in the dirt, drew a line leading out of it, then poured liquor into the depression. After a moment, it flowed into the finger-wide channel. I reached out, plucked a sprig of grass, and set it at the end of the channel as the liquor arrived.

"Sand," I said, "is grass."

The Vashni stared at my little demonstration. Dark faces paled. Four pairs of eyes fastened themselves on my face, staring in astonishment. Clearly they were shaken.

"But don't mind me," I told them, shrugging. "I'm pretty drunk."

And indeed I was. This morning I had eaten nothing, killed a man, lost the dinner I'd had the night before, and swallowed most of the contents of an unfamiliar liquor under a warm afternoon sun.

"He *is* the jhihadi," Del declared emphatically. "My brother said so. Was he not your Oracle?" Now it was her turn to be stared at. She blinked, put a hand to her head, then said the words I never, ever expected to hear from her: "Oh, Tiger, I am so dreadfully drunk."

"Sometimes," I said, "this is a good thing." I put my arm around her shoulders, guided her close so she could slump against me without falling over, and smiled fatuously at the Vashni. "And now, if you don't mind, I think the Oracle's sister—and very probably the jhihadi—are going to pass out."

SEVEN

I WOKE UP to the sound of retching. Del, I realized, was no longer beside me. And she'd never been drunk before.

Ah.

I cracked an eye and realized the sun was up, filtering down through the trees. This is not a particularly strange discovery to make unless you've gone to sleep—or passed out—in the late afternoon, and it appears to be the *morning* sun.

I opened the other eye, squinted up at arching limbs with their feathery, waving leaves, then girded my loins for battle and managed to lever myself up on an elbow. The world wobbled. So did I. I caught sight of Del several paces away, clutching a tree and looking for all the world as if she'd fall down without it.

Poor bascha.

Belatedly, I became aware of a sense of absence. A sharp glance around the camp showed me no Vashni, no Vashni horses, no skins or carcasses. Only the stud and gelding, still tied to trees but unsaddled, and our belongings piled neatly nearby. Including knives and swords.

As I moved to get up, something shifted against my chest, getting caught on the harness. I looked down, saw a handful of ivory ornaments danging against the burnous. Some kind of necklet had been put around my neck as I slept. Closer inspection showed a string of human fingerbones carefully wired together.

Ugh.

But I elected not to take the necklet off in case Vashni were watching from cover. You never know when the repudiation of a gift might get you cooked. And then *your* fingerbones would adorn someone's neck.

There is no cure for the day after a good drunk—or a bad one, depending on your point of view—but there is something that helps. I groped around, found the bota, sloshed it to test for contents, unstoppered it and drank. The bite was just as bad, the smell just as pungent. But adding new liquor to old would improve morning-after miseries.

I raised my voice. "You going to live?"

Del didn't answer except to be sick again.

I sat up all the way, shut my eyes a moment, kept my own belly down with a massive application of determination, and swallowed more liquor.

Eventually Del made her way back to the blanket, clutching a water bota. I noticed she also had been gifted with a fingerbone necklet but decided against mentioning it just yet. She was very pale—more than usual, that is—and circles had appeared beneath her eyes.

She sat down, leaned her head into her hands, and mumbled, "You must be enjoying this."

"What, seeing you get sick? Trust me, bascha, it's one of the least attractive sights in the world."

"No. That I *am* sick. After all the times I reprimanded you for getting drunk." She sighed heavily into the heels of her hands. "I don't see how you do it. I don't see *why* you do it!"

"Well, usually that isn't the point. I mean, not to get so drunk I feel that bad the next day. Unfortunately, sometimes it is the price you pay."

"I don't want to pay it."

"You didn't have much choice. It was the polite thing to do when being hosted by murdering savages."

"*You're* not sick."

"I did that yesterday, remember?" I gently slapped the bota against one arm. "Here. I know you don't want to, but I promise it'll help."

"I have water."

"It's not water."

She lifted her head and looked at me. "You can't mean more of that horrible spirit!"

"I can. I do. Just a few sips, bascha. Then lie down and go back to sleep."

"Tiger—"

"I've already had my medicine. Your turn."

She looked and sounded desperate. "I don't want any!"

"Well, I could pour it down your gullet *for* you . . ."

She knew I'd do it, too. Del gritted her teeth, took the bota, winced from the smell, then tipped the skin up to drink. Her hands shook, but she squeezed a couple of swallows into her mouth.

I thought at first she might be sick again, but she managed to keep it down. "Another swallow," I prompted.

She managed that, then thrust the bota back at me. After a moment she lay down on her side with her back to me, one hand over her face. The sun through leaves spread a lattice of dappled shadow across her body.

Smiling, I sorted out her tangled braid. "Sleep. We're in no rush."

What she replied was unintelligible. Probably just as well.

I knew better than to attempt to go back to sleep myself. Once awake after a session of too much liquor, I stayed that way for a while. I'd sleep again later. Besides, other business called me. I got up, suppressing groans, stood there a moment until the world steadied, then made my way into the brush to find a likely bush. After offering a rather prodigous libation to the gods of alcohol, I set about assessing our situation.

First I checked the horses and found them content, lipping up what remained of the grain that apparently the Vashni had given them. Our oiled canvas buckets were on the ground within reach, and each contained enough water that I knew the horses weren't thirsty. Our weapons remained on the blanket where we'd put them, though the Vashni swords and knives were gone. Our saddle-pouches were stacked next to them, and there was an extra leather bag. I loosed the thong drawstring enough to discover the contents were more meat, nearly lost my belly then, and dropped the bag instantly. Later. Maybe.

So. They had guested us in their camp, fed us, given us drink, untacked, fed, and watered our horses, left our weapons and belongings, and gifted us with meat and bone necklets. All in all, I couldn't think of a more polite visit with anyone.

Hmmm. Being the jhihadi has its advantages.

I dug through our pouches and pulled out some dried cumfa. While it's hardly a delicacy, it was somewhat more appetizing this morning than barely cooked sandtiger meat left for gods know how long in a leather bag, plus it was preserved in salt. Salt in the desert is a must. I grabbed up a water bota and went back to the blanket, settling down to a meager breakfast. Del slept on.

Lucky bascha.

When next I awoke, Del was no longer retching. Or sleeping. In fact, she was up doing what I'd already done: checking the horses, our belongings. She was moving with much less grace than usual but had rebraided her hair and changed into a cleaner burnous, since she had, as I had, used her sleeve to clean her face, and looked altogether more prepossessing than she had earlier. Though there was no question she didn't feel *good*.

"It lives," I commented.

Del peered balefully at me, shielding her eyes from the sun with a raised hand. "Barely. I had more of the spirits. What do call it?—the bark of the dog?"

I grinned. "The *hair* of the dog. Told you it works."

"Marginally." She hooked a finger under the fingerbone necklet dangling against her harness and displayed it. "What's this?"

"My guess is it's some kind of guest-gift. You're the Oracle's sister, and I'm the jhihadi. Maybe they're some kind of safe passage tokens through Vashni territory. Not a bad thing to have."

It was an understatement to mention Del was not happy. "We didn't even wake up when they put them on us. They might as easily have cut our throats."

"They could have done that while we were awake. Anyway, I think we'd better wear them for a while, just in case."

She didn't like the idea, but nodded. Then she pointed at the Vashni sack. "Can we at least get rid of that? I think we should bury it."

I grinned. "Not too fond of sandtiger, are we?"

"It doesn't taste particularly good going in either direction."

Fortunately I'd only experienced the one direction. I grabbed a bota and sucked down more water, then made the effort to climb to my feet. It was easier this time. "Better take it with us, till we're out of Vashni territory. You never know what might insult them."

"Then *you* carry it."

I glanced up at the sun. "Midday," I muttered. "We ought to get moving. Maybe we can make the chimney before nightfall."

"Or not," Del said, "considering how we feel. You said yourself there is no rush."

"That was earlier, when I took pity on you."

"And I'm not deserving of any now?"

"You're standing, aren't you? If you can stand, you can ride."

Del said glumly, "I suppose that means I must stay on my horse."

"Well, I could always throw you belly-down over the saddle and tie you on. Of course, all the blood would rush to your head, and I'm not sure that would make you feel any better. I certainly recall how I felt when you did it to *me*."

She flicked me an arch glance. "That was the Vashni who did it to you. And it was either that or let them kill you. To kill Chosa Dei."

"Well, they *were* much friendlier this time around," I agreed. Then I scratched my head and sighed, staring at the horses. "I suppose they won't saddle themselves. Guess we'd better get to work."

And work it was, with a pounding head. Took longer than usual, too, though eventually we did have both horses saddled, repacked, and ready to go. The Vashni had left us two blankets as well, which I found downright neighborly of them.

I led the stud into the center of the clearing, sorry to leave the shade. With great deliberation I stuck a foot into the left stirrup, carefully pulled myself up, and swung my right leg over. Amazingly, everything stayed attached.

"Well, bascha, I guess—" But I didn't finish, because Del arrived with the gelding in tow, thrust his reins at me urgently, and disappeared with haste behind a clump of trees.

This time I didn't tease her. I dug out some of the red silk left over from my Skandic clothing, unhooked a water bota, and handed both down to her without comment when she reappeared. Del rinsed her mouth, spat, then washed her face. She looked terrible.

I made the sacrifice. "Maybe we should stay here another night."

"No." Del took the gelding's reins back from me, flipped them over his neck, and mounted. She was clearly shaky, but determined. "I know how badly you want to get your hands on your *jivatma*. If it were mine . . ." She shook her head. "We'll go on."

The poor, pitiful bascha had reverted to cold-faced Northern sword-singer. I knew better than to attempt to jolly her out of it.

Besides, she needed to concentrate on keeping her belly where it belonged.

I realized within a couple of hours that we were not going to make the chimney before nightfall. Though I was feeling much better as the day wore on, and Del seem resigned to a generalized discomfort—at least she wasn't sick anymore—a faster pace might upset the balance. Not only that, but footing was tougher as we wound our way closer to the dramatic rock formations in the distance, beyond the foothills. Skull-sized boulders sprouted like shrubbery, abetted by drifts of bedrock peeping above the soil. The horses had to pay more attention to where they set their hooves, and we had to pay more attention to the occasional misstep, prepared to bring equine heads up to reestablish balance before they went down onto their knees.

Then a sandy area caught my eye. Like water spilled from a pitcher, it wound its way through rocks, then spread into a wider patch.

"Over here," I called to Del, riding behind me. "Footing's better."

And indeed it was. The sandy area went down a rocky hillock and opened into something very like a shallow streambed, except there was no water. There had been once, before desert took it over. But now it was dry, with an underlayment of hard and uneven stone intermixed with sandy pockets and water-smoothed, hollowed-out boulders. Amazingly, there was a scattering of vegetation here, edging the streambed. Tough, reedy-looking shrubbery of a pallid green hue.

"Look ahead—there." Del pointed. "Are those wagon ruts?"

"Out here?" But even as I asked it, I saw what she meant. A few paces up there indeed appeared to be wheel ruts running across the streambed, visible only when they hit sand pockets. I moved the stud into a faster pace, then pulled up when I reached the ruts. "Hunh," I commented. "*Someone's* been out here in a wagon."

Del reined in beside me. "It makes no sense. There is nothing out here for settlers or caravans."

I shook my head. "Not enough tracks for a caravan. One wagon, I'd guess. Two mules. Maybe someone got lost." I marked how the ruts entered the streambed on one side and exited the other. "Let's follow the tracks," I suggested, reining left. "Maybe whoever we find will invite us to supper."

"If they haven't already been someone else's supper."

"I'm not sure we're still in Vashni territory," I said. "Which reminds me . . ." I untied the increasingly odiferous bag of sandtiger meat from the saddle and let it drop into the edge of the

streambed as the stud climbed out. The gelding followed, white
head swinging on the end of his long neck. Gold fringe dangled
lopsidedly. "You know, you could always hang your Vashni necklet across your horse's face. He's already wearing axle grease and
wine-girl fringe . . . human fingerbones might give him a little
added class."

Del, not surprisingly, did not deign to reply.

We followed the tracks as they wound their way through the rocks
and sand. After a while they turned in toward the mountains on
our left, gaining in elevation. We wound our way up, and then
almost abruptly the crude ruts gave out onto a flat area to our
right, opposite the massive boulders skirting the bottom of the
mountain on the left. The flat formed a plateau, the chopped
off crown of a shallow bluff overlooking where we'd come from,
including the streambed. A few straggly trees, low shrubbery, and
modest grassy patches skirted the edge near the continuation of
the ruts. I pulled up there to give the stud a blow and take a look
around. Del's gelding picked its way slowly up to join us. Del was,
I noticed, drinking water again.

"You all right, bascha?"

She nodded as she restoppered the bota. "Much better than
this morning. Just thirsty."

"Liquor does that." I glanced around. "You know, this
wouldn't be a bad place to stop for the night—" I broke off, whistling in surprise. "Hoolies—would you look at that?" I pointed.
"Up there against the boulders, there. Looks like a shelter to me.
And the remains of a cookfire in front of it."

"Where—? Oh, *that?*" Del rode past me, heading toward the
huge tumbled boulders lining the merging of mountain with flat
area. "It is a shelter, Tiger—it's a little lean-to. The wagon ruts
go right past it, but they're deeper by the shelter, as if they
stopped here."

I followed. Del was right. Someone had used one of the larger
boulder formations for the back wall and had built a rough lean-
to out of branches and canvas. The fire ring hadn't been used for a

while, but clearly this was a regular camping place. No one would sacrifice canvas in the desert unless he intended to return.

"Halloo the camp!" I called. "We're coming in!"

Del reined in next to the fire ring. "No one's here."

"You never know." I dismounted and drew my sword. Del had done the same. But there was no place to hide in the lean-to; it boasted only two sides, the boulder for a back wall, and a branch-and-canvas roof. It was large enough for possibly three people, if they were very close friends. "Good enough for tonight," I said. "Let's get the horses settled, and then we can think about food."

Del recoiled. Her expression clearly announced she wanted nothing to do with food. Possibly forever.

I disagreed. "You need to eat something. You've only had water all day."

"Yes, and in fact . . ." She turned abruptly and headed toward the hillside strewn with tumbled boulders, sheathing her sword.

"Are you sick again?" I asked.

"No. But I have had a *lot* of water."

"Ah." Grinning, I strode back to the horses. I decided to be a nice, kind, thoughtful man and untack her gelding. "Hold on, old son," I told the stud. "You're next."

I untied saddlepouches and piled them beside the lean-to, tossed Del's bedding inside. The gelding gazed at me out of mournful blue eyes, peering through dangling bits of fringe.

"You look ridiculous," I told him, undoing his girth. "No offense, but you do." I lifted saddle and blankets off his damp back, set both by the lean-to. "Amazing what we let women get away with, isn't it?" His response was to thrust his head against my chest and rub. Hard. "Ah, hoolies, horse—" In disgust, I stared down at the front of my burnous. "Now I've got black gunk all over me!" Of course, the gelding also had greasepaint smeared all over his face, like an overly painted wine-girl first thing in the morning. Quite a pair, we made.

I heard the rattle of fallen pebbles high in the rocks and glanced up to see Del picking her way down from one of the piles of boulders. You'd think that since we'd been sharing a bed for several years modesty would no longer matter, but Del was fastidious. She always went off to find privacy, and I'd been ordered to do the same. I just never went as far. Men have a certain advantage when it comes to relieving the bladder.

Her arms were spread for balance as she worked her way down. She was concentrating on her path, rope of hair swinging in front of one shoulder. It's difficult to look particularly graceful when clambering down over piled rocks and boulders. Even for my Northern bascha.

I drew in a deep breath, preparing to bellow complaints about her horse. But I lost the impulse the instant I saw movement behind her.

Vashni? No—

Movement flowed down the mountainside, disappeared behind rocks.

I dropped the reins. "Del!"

Then it sprang up onto a boulder, and I saw it clearly.

"*Del*—" I was running for the rocks, yanking sword out of sheath. Her face was turned toward me.

I'd never make it, never make it—

"*—behind you—*"

Atop the rock she spun, grasping for her sword hilt, and went down hard beneath the leaping sandtiger.

EIGHT

WHEN in the midst of deadly danger, time slows. Fragments. It is me, the moment, the circumstances.

As it was now.

I saw Del, down. The glint of sun off her bared blade, lying against stone. The spill of white-blond braid. The sandtiger's compact, bunched body, blending into the rocky background as it squatted over her.

I bellowed at the cat as I ran. Anything to distract him, to draw his attention from his prey. Del was unmoving: probably unconscious, possibly dead.

"Try *me!*" I shouted. "*Try me*, you thrice-cursed son of a Salset goat—"

The sandtiger growled, then yowled as it saw me. I threatened his prey. For a moment he continued to hunch over Del, then came up into a crouch, flexing shoulders. Jaw dropped open. Green eyes glared.

Everything was slowed to half-time. I watched the bunching of haunches, the leap; judged momentum and direction; knew without doubt what was necessary. My nearly vertical blade, at the end of thrusting arms, met him in midair. Sank in through belly fur, hide, muscle, vessels and viscera, spitting him to the hilt. I felt the sudden weight, heard the scream, smelled the rank breath, the musk of a mature male. Without pausing I ducked head and dropped shoulder, swung, let his momentum carry him through his leap. Over my head, and down.

I was conscious of the horses screaming, but I paid them no attention. I was focused only on the sandtiger, now sprawled on the ground, jaws agape, tongue lolling. For all I knew he was dead already, but I jerked the blade free, then swung it up, over, down, like a club, and severed his head from his body.

Then I dropped the sword. I turned, took two running strides, climbed up into the boulders. "*Bascha . . .*"

She lay mostly face-down, one arm sprawled across a cluster of rocks. Her torso was in a shallow gulley between two boulders. Legs were twisted awry.

"Del—?"

There was blood, and torn burnous. I caught the tangled rope of hair and moved it aside, baring the back of her neck to check for wounds. She had not had time to face the cat fully. His leap had been flat, then tending down. Front paws had curled over her shoulders, grasping, while back paws raked out, reaching for purchase.

He had leaped at her back, intending to take his prey down from behind. But Del had moved, had begun to turn toward him as I yelled, had begun to unsheathe her sword, and he'd missed his target. Instead of encircling her neck with his jaws, snapping it, piercing the jugular, the big canine teeth had dug a puncture and furrow into her right forearm and the top of her left shoulder at the curve of her neck. The main impetus of the bite had fouled on harness and sheath.

I planted my feet as firmly as possible in the treacherous foot-ing, then bent, caught a limp arm, and pulled her up. I squatted, ducked, levered her over one shoulder, head hanging, braid dan-gling against my thigh, while her legs formed a counterweight before me. I rose carefully, balancing the slack-limbed drape of her body. Teeth clenched, I made my way slowly down the boul-ders, found level footing on the flat, sandy crown of the bluff, and carried her to the lean-to. I had tossed her rolled bedding there while unpacking the gelding; with care I slid her over and down, arranged her limbs, set her head against the bedroll. Then, locking my hands into the front of her burnous, I tore fabric apart along the seam, exposing her body in its sleeveless tunic.

Exposing arms and legs, and the sandtiger's handiwork.

"All right, bascha—give me a moment here . . ."

Almost without thinking I unbuckled the harness, worked the leather straps and buckles over her arms and out from under her body. Tossed it aside in a tangle of leather and brass. Yanked my knife free of its sheath, cut swathes of her burnous, and began wadding it between torn flesh and what remained of the tunic's high neck. Claws had cut through it, into the flesh beneath, baring the twin ridges of collar bones. One claw had nicked the underside of her jawbone at the angle beneath her left ear, trickling blood across her throat.

More fabric was sacrificed for her right forearm as I bound it tightly. Then I worked my left arm under her back, lifted her, tipped her forward against me. Her head lolled into my shoulder.

"Hold on, bascha—I'm taking a look at your back."

The sandtiger had attempted to set hind claws into her lower back and the tops of her buttocks, but all he'd managed to do as she turned was pierce the leather of her tunic. Very little blood showed through. So, the worst of the damage appeared to be the bite wounds at the top of her shoulder and in her right forearm, plus the deep claw lacerations reaching from the first upswelling of both breasts nearly to her throat.

Of course, that was the *visible* damage. Inside, beneath the flesh and muscle, sandtiger poison coursed through her blood.

With Del slumped against me, I untied the thongs on her bedding, unrolled it with a snap and flip of my hand, eased her onto it. Now it was time. Time I knew.

I bent over her, then slowly lowered my head. Rested my ear against her chest, petitioning all the gods I'd cursed for all of my life that she not be dead.

The beating was slow but steady.

My breath left on a rush of relief. I did not sit up immediately.

I pressed dry lips against her brow and did more than petition. This time I prayed.

When it became clear the bite wound in the top of her shoulder did not intend to stop bleeding on its own despite my ministrations, I did the only thing I could. I built a quick, haphazard fire in the rock ring outside the shelter, arranged my knife so the blade would heat, and when steel glowed red, I wrapped a flap of leather around the handle and carried it back inside the lean-to. Del was as pale as I'd ever seen in a living woman, even to her lips. Apologizing in silence, I ground my teeth together and set the hot blade against the wound.

Blood sizzled like weeping fat over a fire. The smell of burning flesh was pungent. I felt my gorge rise and fought it back down; Del would hardly appreciate it if I threw up all over her. I was aware of a detached sort of surprise; I had cauterized various wounds in my own body more times than I could count. But never before had I done it to Del.

She stirred, twisting her head. Her mouth sprang open in a weak, breathless protest. I tossed the knife aside, caught both her hands, and hung on.

"I know, bascha. I know. I'm sorry. I'm sorry." Her eyelids flickered. "Del?"

But she was gone again, hands lying limply in my own. I set them down, noted blood had soaked through the bandage on her forearm, and turned on my knees to gather up more makeshift bandages.

The world around me wavered.

Not surprising. Reaction. I shook my head, wiped sweat out of my eyes, grabbed gauze and folded a section into a pad. After unwrapping blood-soaked bandages, I bound the pad to the seeping wound. What it needed was stitches, but I had nothing to use. The stud was gone; he'd departed in blind panic during the sand-tiger attack. It meant the loss of half our food and water and other supplies, including the medicaments Del had packed. I had nothing for treating her except the crude bandages I'd already fashioned out of burnouses, cautery, and a bota of Vashni liquor, which had been put into our pouches without either of us being aware of it.

I'd considered using cautery on the forearm bite wound, but decided against it in favor of pressure and tight binding. Del would scar regardless, but using hot steel on it would twist the flesh, binding it into stiffness. She needed the flexibility to handle a sword. Nor would she thank me if I did something that harmed her ability to wield one.

I sighed when finished, let my eyes close for a moment. The day was nearly done. The sun straggled down the sky, preparing to drop below the horizon. The long desert twilight would provide light for an hour or so, and then it would be night, with only the stars, the moon, and the dying fire for illumination. I needed to find more wood, but I didn't want to leave Del that long.

Still, two swords were lying out there, hers and mine. I'd taken no time to pick them up since pulling Del out of the rocks. For the moment she was lying quietly.

I stood up, crouching beneath the low roof, and ducked out the open front. Muscles protested as I straightened. Del's gelding nickered softly as he saw me. *He* at least had remained despite the sandtiger attack. When I had time to track down the stud, who probably wouldn't go far, I intended to have words with him.

I went hunting. Del's sword lay between two of the boulders. I picked it up, climbed back down to mine beside the dead cat. I set both blades aside, grabbed the hindlegs, and dragged the sandtiger farther away from the camp. Scavengers very likely would come for his carcass; I'd just as soon they did so from a greater distance.

Something occured to me.

Smiling grimly, I unsheathed my knife. With great delibera-tion I cut out each of the ten curving front claws. I tied them into the remains of my burnous, then gathered up the swords and went back to the lean-to.

Del lay as I had left her, very still upon her bedding. The sun, going down in a haze of red and gold, gilded her face and lent it the healthy color it lacked. I propped both blades against one crude wall, caught up a bota, and sat down to once again dribble water into her mouth, bit by bit so she wouldn't choke.

In the final vestiges of the dying day, seated next to Delilah, I cleaned my blade of sandtiger blood—hers had never made contact —propped it once again beside hers, then untied the sandtiger claws from the rags of my burnous. Employing knife, Vashni liquor, and grim deliberation, I began to clean them of blood and tendon. When I had time, I'd drill a hole in each one, string them on a thong, and set it around Del's neck.

I glanced down at her, noting the pallor of her face. "I made it," I said. "I survived. So will you. You're tougher than I am."

Later, she was restless. A hand to her forehead told me precisely what I expected: she was fevered. Quite apart from the wounds, the poison from envenomed claws was enough to make her deathly ill, even to kill her. As a boy I'd been clawed in the face and across one thigh and had been very sick from sandtiger poison for three days despite the fact much of the venom had been expelled before I was clawed. Years later a couple of shallow scratches laid me low for hours. But Del had sustained much deeper gouges than I.

Earlier, I had hacked down some of the branches used to build the shelter, tossing them onto the fire. Now I threw the last of those I'd cut on the coals, waited for the flare of kindling flame, then knelt by her side. In the reflected firelight her cheeks were flushed, blotched red and white from the poison. Her lips and eyelids were swollen.

I dampened a cloth with water, then pressed it gently against her face. Lastly I wetted a corner, laid it on her lips, and squeezed. Her mouth moved minutely, responding to the water; I slipped a hand beneath her head, lifted it, dribbled tepid water into her mouth. Her throat spasmed in a swallow; then she began to choke.

Swearing, I dropped the bota and pulled her upright, then bent her slightly forward over my right arm. I let her head hang loose, chin hooked over my wrist. With a spread left hand, I pressed sharply against her spine several times, compressing her lungs. In a moment the choking turned to coughing. When that faded, I eased her down again, smoothing sweat-damp strands of hair away from her face.

"I'm here," I told her. "I left you in Staal-Ysta, when I thought you would die—when I thought I had killed you . . . I'll never leave you again. I'm here, bascha."

The claw stripes above her breasts were oozing blood again. I dampened more cloth, cleaned the wounds, then pressed a folded pad against them, tucking it under the shredded ruins of her tunic.

The last of the roof branches I'd cut down no longer flamed. Light was fading. Outside the lean-to, the white gelding pawed at sand and soil. In a brief break from tending Del I'd watered him, given him grain, but he wanted grazing. Though he'd proven his willingness to stay put, I couldn't risk losing him as well as the stud. He was tied to the lean-to. If the gods were merciful, he wouldn't pull it down on top of us.

My own bedding, still on the stud, was gone. But the gelding's saddle, set next to the shelter, had borne a rolled-up Vashni blanket. I tugged it over, threw it across rocky soil, set my rump upon it. I ached in every muscle, and my eyes were burning with exhaustion. I rubbed them, swore at the gritty dryness that stung unremittingly, then slumped against the boulder forming the back wall of the lean-to.

Sharp pain forced a grunt of surprise out of me. I sat forward again, reaching over the top of my right shoulder. Stung? But the boulder had no cracks, no crevices to host anything, being nothing more than a giant, rounded bulwark at the bottom of the modest mountain.

I brought my fingers around, tipped them toward firelight, rubbed my thumb against sticky residue, then sniffed fingers.

Blood.

I felt again behind my right shoulder, sliding my hand beneath the tattered remains of my burnous. Found two curving gouges there the length of palm and fingers, bleeding sluggishly.

I shut my eyes. Oh, hoolies . . . when I'd slung the spitted sandtiger over my right shoulder—

In my rage and fear, I'd felt nothing at all.

I tore the burnous off my torso, grabbed up the Vashni bota, squirted liquor down my back, aiming for claw marks I couldn't see. A burning so painful it brought tears to my eyes told me I'd found the target. I hissed a complex, unflagging string of Desert invective, breathed noisily, nearly bit my bottom lip in two.

When I could speak again, I looked at Del, whom I had liberally drenched. "Sorry, bascha—" I croaked. "—I had no idea it would burn so much!"

The world revolved again. Now I knew why. Knees drawn up, I leaned my head into them as a stiff-fingered hand scrubbed distractedly at the back of my skull, scraping through short hair. Before, in ignorance, all my thoughts on Del, it had been a simple matter to ignore the signs. But now, knowing, feeling, they were manifest.

"Not now," I muttered. "Not *now*—"

Not yet.

We had only once been injured or sick at the same time. And then it had been on Staal-Ysta, forced into a dance that had nearly killed us both. Northerners had cared for her in one dwelling, while others cared for me. When I was healed enough to ride, knowing Del would surely die and that I could not bear to witness it, I left.

I wouldn't leave her again. I'd sworn it. But this time, now, there was no one to care for either of us.

I licked my lips. "All right," I told myself hoarsely, "you've been clawed before. Neither time killed you. You have some immunity."

Some. But enough? That I didn't know.

I traced the curve of my skull, growing less distinct as my hair lengthened. Beneath it there were elaborate designs tattooed into my skin, visible now only at the hairline above my forehead. They marked me a mage. IoSkandic. A madman of Meteiera.

I wiped sweat from my face with a trembling hand. Could magery overcome sandtiger poison? Could magery heal?

I knew it could kill.

Del made a sound, an almost inaudible release of breath coupled with the faintest of moans. I tried to move toward her, but my limbs were sluggish. Cursing my weakness, I made myself move. I nearly toppled over her, but a stiff arm jammed against the bedding kept me upright.

"Bascha?"

Nothing. Sweat ran from her flesh, giving off the stale metallic tang of sandtiger venom. I tasted the same in my own mouth.

Time was running out. Hastily, clumsily, I snagged the water bota, soaked the still-damp cloth, draped it across her forehead. Droplets rolled down into the hollows of closed eyes, filling the creases of her lids, then dribbled from the outer corners of her eyes, mimicking the tears Del never wept.

I tucked the bota under her right hand, being careful not to jar the bound forearm. I curled slack fingers loosely around the neck. I checked bandages for fresh blood. Found none. Felt a stab of relief like a knife in the belly.

"Hold on," I murmured. "Just hold on, bascha. You can make it through this."

The gelding whickered softly. I glanced out. There were, I realized, three fire rings in front of the lean-to, overlapping one another, merging, then springing apart again. I scowled, narrowing my eyes, trying to focus vision. Nothing helped.

I swore, then grabbed a corner of the Vashni blanket. Tugged it toward Del. Managed to pull it atop her, cover most of her body save head and sandaled feet.

"I know it's warm," I told her, "especially with a fever. But you need to sweat it out. Get rid of as much as you can." I stroked roughened knuckles against one fever-blotched cheek. "When I can, I'll go to Julah. Fouad can find us a healer. Then—"

I broke it off. *When. Then.* Who was I fooling?

If Del were conscious, she'd insist on the truth.

On Meteiera, near the Stone Forest where the new mage was

whelped atop a rocky spire, I had conjured magic. I had dreamed and made the substance of dream real. Set scars lifted by magery back into my flesh. Formed a seaworthy boat out of little more than stormwrack and wishing.

Now I wished Del to live.

I bore tattoos under my hair and lacked two fingers, souvenirs of Meteiera, where mages and madmen lived and died. I had been then, and could be now, what I needed to be.

Del's life was at stake.

"All right, bascha, I'll try." I drew in a deep breath, sealed my eyes closed. "If I'm a mage," I said hoarsely, "if I'm truly a mage, let me find the way . . ."

I had done it in Meteiera, knowing nothing of power beyond that it existed. Blue-headed Nihko had told me those of us— *us!*—with magery in our blood had to use it, had to find a way to bleed off the power, lest it destroy us. But I had escaped the Stone Forest before learning much beyond a few simple rituals and prayers and the discipline of the priests; I was but an infant to the ways of the mages of Meteiera.

Discipline.

It claimed its own power.

I gathered myself there beside Delilah, body and soul, flesh and spirit, and tried to find the part of me that had been born atop a stone spire in far-off ioSkandi. I knew nothing of the doing but that I had done it. Once, twice, thrice. Since then I had locked the awareness away, concentrating only on the physical, the retraining of a body lacking two fingers.

A shiver wracked me. Something slammed into my body, buffeting awareness like a wind snuffing out candleflame. Weakness swam in. I meant to move aside; I *tried* to move aside, to find and lean against the wall of stone regardless of claw gouges, needing the support. But my limbs got tangled. I could not tell what part of me were legs, which were arms, or if I even retained my head atop my shoulders.

Power eluded me. What strength was left diminished like sand running out of a glass.

Fear for Del surged up. "No—" I murmured, "—wait—" But all the strength poured out of my body. I slumped sideways, vision doubled; fought it, attempted to push myself upright; went suddenly down onto my back on hardpacked soil and sand. "—*wait*—"

An outflung arm landed against unsheathed blades propped against the sidewall. I felt one of them, in toppling, fall across my elbow. It was the flat, not the edge—but by then I didn't care.

I was dimly aware of a flicker of stunned outrage, and a voice in my head. *Not like this*—

In the circle, yes. If a man had to die. But not from the last wayward scratch of a dying sandtiger.

"Bascha—" I murmured.

But the world was gone.

NINE

*B*ONES. *Bones and sand. Bones and sand and sun. And heat.*

Parched lips. Burned flesh. Swollen tongue. Blood yet running, smearing her thighs. Except there are no thighs. No lips, no flesh, no tongue. All has been consumed.

From a distance, the bones are thread against sparkling silk. But closer, ever closer, pushed down from air to earth like a raptor stooping, thread takes on substance, sections itself into skull, into arms, and legs. Silk is sand. Crystalline Punja sand.

Scoured clean of flesh, ivory bone gleams. Delicate toes are scattered. Fingers are nonexistent. Ribs have collapsed into a tangled riddle. The skull lies on its side, teeth bared in a rictus, sockets empty of eyes.

I am pulled into them, lips brought to dentition, live teeth clicking on dead. Against my mouth bone moves. "Find me," *she says.*

I want nothing to do with her. With it. With what the bones had been.

"Find me," *she says.* "Take up the sword."

The hand captured my head. For a moment I feared it was sand, and sun, and death. But the hand cupped my head, lifted it, set bota against my lips. Living lips, not bone. Water trickled into my mouth.

It was enough to rouse me to something akin to panic. I lifted both arms, grasped with trembling hands, closed on leather water-skin. Squeezed.

"Not so much," he chided.

He. Not she. The dead woman was gone.

I drank. Swallow after swallow. Then he pulled it away.

"Not so much," he repeated.

I wanted all of it.

"Del," I croaked. Swollen lips split and bled. Swollen eyes wouldn't open. "Del . . ."

"She's alive." Damp cloth bathed my face. "I swear it."

"Poison," I said. "Sandtiger—"

"I know. I recognize the wounds. Here. A little more."

More water. I drank, wanting to drown. "Del?"

"Alive."

"Poison . . ."

"Yes."

Dread was a blade in the vitals. "She's dying . . ."

"Maybe," he said.

Del's bones in the sand?

"Don't let her die."

"It wants a healer," he said. "I need to go back to Julah."

Julah. "Fouad's," I told him. "Cantina."

"Later," he replied. "I'll stay awhile yet."

"I won't die," I said. "Not from a sandtiger."

I heard a breath of laughter. "I don't doubt it."

"Del?"

"Alive," he repeated.

"You swore."

"Yes. I'm not lying. She might die, but she's not dead yet."

It was something.

"Who are you?" I asked.

But before he could answer, the world winked out.

When next I roused, the weakness was less. I still lay on hardpan, itching from sand, but a light blanket was thrown over me and another, still rolled, pillowed my head. A bota lay at hand, as I had left one for Del. I shut fingers on it, brought to my mouth, drank and drank and drank.

"Del?"

No answer.

I opened my eyes. I had no idea what hour it was, or day. Merely that I was alive despite the best efforts of my body to die.

"Bascha?" My voice was hoarse.

No answer.

I collected strength. Hoarded it. Hitched myself up on an elbow. Saw the colorful Vashni blanket and the body beneath.

Shadow fell across me. I glanced up, staring blearily at the opening and the man squatting there. "You?" I croaked.

Stubble emphasized the hollows and angles of his face. He was dark as a Southroner, but with the faintest tint of copper to his tan. And those honey-brown eyes, liquid and melting, fringed in black lashes Del would claim too lush for a man, and infinitely unfair when women would kill for such.

"Me," he agreed.

I slumped back onto the ground, wanting to groan. Didn't, since we had company. "If you've come to challenge me—*again*—you picked a bad time."

"So I see. And no, I haven't. I've learned a little since you killed that sword-dancer in Julah."

When was that? I didn't remember. A day ago. A month. "Then what are you doing here?"

"I am," he said, with grave dignity entirely undermined by a glint of irony in his eyes, "looking after a man who has repudiated his honor. And the infamous Northern bascha who should be lacking in such, being merely a woman, but who appears to have it regardless. Or so some say." He crawled into the lean-to, sat down beside me. "I couldn't ask a dead man what *elaii-ali-ma* meant," he said, "but I asked another sword-dancer when he came into town."

"Oh, good." I managed my own irony despite the hoarse voice. "Then you know. You don't have to challenge me to a dance, because there can be no dance. But you can kill me if you want to." I paused. "If you can."

The faintest of smiles twitched one corner of his mouth. "Well, that would at the moment be a simple thing."

"And where's the honor in that?"

"So I asked myself." He placed a hand against my forehead. "The worst of the fever has passed, I think, but you're far from well."

I knew that without being told. "Who are you?"

"My mother named me Nayyib."

"This isn't the road from Julah. What are you doing here?"

"It's *a* road from Julah," he clarified, "now. And I came looking for you. Fortunate thing, yes?"

"I thought you said you weren't going to challenge me."

"I'm not. At least, not in that way."

That sounded suspicious. "In *what* way, then?"

"I wish to become a sword-dancer."

I grunted. "I figured that."

"I wish you to teach me."

"What, you just decided this?"

"I decided this in Julah, after you killed that sword-dancer."

"Khashi."

"After you killed Khashi."

"Why? Didn't you originally want to kill me?"

"No. I wanted to dance against you. I didn't know anything about this *elaii-ali-ma*. You were just—you. After I saw what happened to Khashi and learned what had happened to you, I decided to follow you."

I attempted to frown, which isn't easy when you're sick. "You followed us to Julah."

"Well, yes."

"And at that point you still wanted to challenge me."

"I did. At that point I thought I was good with a sword."

"You don't anymore?"

His mouth twitched. "Not good enough."

"So *now* you want to be taught by a man who has no honor?"

"A man who once was the greatest in all the South."

Once was. Once. What in hoolies was I now?

Well, sick. That's what.

"So you figure if you look after us while we're sick, you'll earn some lessons."

His tone was exquisitely bland. "I should think saving your lives might be worth one or two."

I shut my eyes. "You're a fool."

"Undoubtedly." He placed the bota under my hand again. "I've tended her, got more water down her, wet the cloth again. And I've watered your horse. Grained him. Tied him under a tree for what little shade there is, and the few blades of grass."

"Busy boy," I muttered.

He ignored that. "But he'll need more water later. So will she. Can you manage it?"

"I'll manage it." How, I didn't know. But I wouldn't admit it to a kid. Especially not this kid, who had a mouth on him.

He seemed to know it anyway. "I'll go to Fouad's and ask him for help. I'll bring a healer, food, and more water. There isn't much left. Ration it, if you want to live. I put wood by the fire."

He had indeed been a busy boy—and it just might save us. "Wait." I levered myself up on an elbow. "You say there's a road to Julah from here?"

"Such as it is. Paired ruts, nothing more."

"We didn't come that way."

"I crossed your tracks."

But Del and I had spent the night with the Vashni, and the kid—Nayyib—had only just reached us. "There's a shorter way. Follow our tracks back to the streambed, and go from there."

Black brows drew together. "Vashni territory. Or is that your way of getting me killed?"

"Oh, I'd do that myself. No—here." With a trembling hand—hoolies, I hate being weak!—I pulled the Vashni necklet over my head, fingerbones clacking. "Wear this. It's safe passage."

He stared at the necklet, then flicked a glance back at me. "You're sure?"

"Well, I suppose they might kill you for sheer hard-headedness, but it ought to get you safely through."

He took the necklet, eyed it in distaste, then hooked it over his head. My elbow gave out and I thumped back to the ground. Shut my eyes. "Do it for Del," I said wearily, "not for me."

Against my lids his shadow shifted. Retreated. "I will try," he told me, "to make certain she doesn't die."

When I opened my eyes, the sun was down. And he was gone.

Wind blows. Sand shifts. It creeps upon the bones, begins to swallow them. Legs. Arms. The collapsed cage of ribs. The jewels that are spine. All that is left is skull. And the sword.

"Find me," she says.

Could the bones belong to Del? Could she be dead?

I awoke with a start. "Auuggh," I croaked. "Stop with the dreams, already!"

Sweat drenched me. It stank of sandtiger venom. I rolled to my right side, started to use my elbow, thought better of it as the wounds in my back protested. After a moment I made the attempt to sit upright without the assistance of arms. Aching abdominal muscles warned me it wasn't such a good idea, but I managed to stay there. Eventually the world settled back into place.

The dream faded. Reality was bad enough.

I turned my head and spat, disliking the aftertaste of fever and poison. Dry-mouthed, nothing was expelled. I found the bota, rinsed my mouth, tried again. Much better. Then I drank sparingly, recalling the boy's warning regarding how much water was left.

I looked across at the blanketed form. Del did not appear to have roused. I set down the bota, took a deep breath, and made my body move.

Well, such as it could. In the end I flopped down on my belly, head near Del's pallet, and hitched myself up on a forearm.

"Bascha?" I peeled back the blanket with my free hand. Del's face remained slightly blotched, a network of red overlaying extreme pallor. Her swollen lips had cracked and bled. I rested a hand on her abdomen, waited in frozen silence, then felt the slight rising and falling. She breathed.

With effort, I pulled myself upright. Found her bota, shook it, heard the diminished sloshing. I had no idea when Nayyib had been here, when he'd left, or when he might return. For all I knew it was a week after he'd gone. I thought it more likely a matter of hours, though possibly it was the next day.

I hooked my left hand under Del's head and lifted it, placing the bota at her lips. I squeezed and dribbled water into her mouth. This time she swallowed without choking. I settled her head once more again the bedding.

The cloth across her forehead was dry. I wet it yet again, replaced it, cleared away the trickles that threatened her eyes and ears. "I'm here," I told her. "A little the worse for wear, but still here, bascha."

I did not know when Nayyib had changed her bandages. A torn burnous sat in a pile on her bedding, but I didn't recognize it. The boy's, apparently; and the fabric matched that now wrapping Del's forearm, so he had done that much. I peeled back the cloth to bare the bite wound. I bent, sniffed; did not yet smell infection or putrefaction.

So far.

I searched for and found the bota of Vashni liquor. Once again I poured it into the wound.

And for the first time in—hoolies, I didn't know how many days it was since the attack!—Del opened her eyes. They were hazy and unfocused.

"Bascha?"

But almost immediately they closed again.

"Del?"

Her lips moved, but no sound issued from her mouth. Instead of water, this time I dribbled liquor into her mouth.

Below the edge of the cloth, the faintest of frowns twitched her brows. Her left hand stirred, rose. Fingers touched her mouth. Then the hand flopped down to her neck.

I'd forgotten about the cracked lips when I'd given her the liquor.

I swore, stole the damp cloth from her forehead, and pressed it again her mouth. "Sorry, bascha. I didn't think."

I didn't think a lot.

She did not stir again. I took up Nayyib's burnous, made more bandages, wrapped her forearm again. Vashni liquor, I decided, ought to burn the poison out of anything.

I felt then at my own stripes on the back of my shoulder, cutting across the scapula. It was a bad angle, and even twisting my head until my neck complained did not bring the claw wounds into sight, but fingers told the story. The twin stripes were crusted, no longer bleeding. Leaving them alone was the best medicine.

Weariness intruded, as did dizziness. But there was the horse to tend. I drank a little of the liquor, breathed fire for a moment, then stoppered the bota and put it aside. I crawled to the opening of the lean-to, peered blearily out at the world, and wanted very badly to turn around and collapse into sleep—or unconscious-ness—once more.

A few paces away, tied to a scrubby tree, Del's horse stood with a black-smeared face. With the detached, exquisite clarity of fading fever, I wondered briefly what Nayyib had thought upon first sighting the paint and fringe.

The gelding saw me and nickered, ears flicked forward.

"Fine," I muttered, "I'm coming. It might take me a day, but I'll get there."

Nayyib had left a water bota and grain pouch by the lean-to. I grabbed both, gathered my legs under me, pressed both arms against the ground, and pushed.

In grabbing the shelter roof to steady myself, I nearly brought it down. I let go, took a step away, and almost fell flat on my face. I saved myself from doing so only because most of me would have landed in the fire ring, and that was not a particularly favored destination.

The gelding nickered again.

Sun stabbed into my eyes. A lurking headache flared into

existence. Everything, from bones and muscle to skin, ached un-remittingly. I drew in a breath, set my teeth, and began the horren-dously lengthy and perilous journey to the gelding, all of five paces away.

Upon reaching him I grabbed a hunk of mane to hold myself upright. "Hello," I said sociably, hoping he wouldn't move. "Nice weather we're having, isn't it?"

He blinked a white-lashed blue eye and nosed at the bota.

"Coming," I muttered, working at the stopper. Once free, I upended the waterskin and drained the contents into the canvas bucket. The gelding dipped his head and began to drink. I hung onto the curve of his withers, wondering if I could make it back to the lean-to. Possibly the gelding would have company tonight, right where he was.

Except Del was there. I'd make it back.

Done drinking, the gelding lifted his head. Clinging to him one-handed, I took the opportunity to relieve myself. The sharp tang of venom expelled with urine made the gelding shift uneasily.

"Not *now*," I suggested fervently, readjusting my dhoti. The gelding obliged. I thanked him with a pat, then opened the grain pouch and poured a handful into the empty water bucket. He needed good grazing, but there wasn't any. For now, this had to do.

I did not look forward to the journey back to the shelter. "One step an hour ought to get me there," I told the horse.

But he was no longer paying me any mind. He'd drawn himself up, head lifted, and pealed out a whinny of welcome. Steadying myself against his neck, I turned, expecting to see Nayyib. Re-lieved that I'd see Nayyib. He was bringing the healer.

And indeed, I saw Nayyib. Along with three other men on horseback. Nothing about them resembled healers. In fact, every-thing about them resembled sword-dancers.

Especially since I knew one of them.

He was highly amused. "Sandtiger." All his handsome white teeth were on display. "You look terrible."

I glared. It was all I could manage. "What do you want, Rafiq?"

"You."

Figured. I sighed, squinted at him, hung onto the gelding. "How about we skip the sword-fight and name you the winner," I suggested. "Right about now, as you can see, I'm not really up to a match. There'd be no challenge in it. As I recall, you like to tease an opponent for an hour or two before defeating him. Hoolies, I'd go down in the blink of an eye. No fun for you."

Rafiq was still grinning atop his palomino horse. "He said you were sick. Sandtiger, was it?" He laughed. "Appropriate."

I shot a glance at Nayyib. He sat his mount stiffly, not even looking at me. I wondered if they'd paid him to lead them back here. Or promised him a dance in a circle. Or lessons in being a sword-dancer.

"Sick," I agreed. "Probably even dying, and therefore not worth killing. So why don't you just ride on out of here and let me die in peace?"

Rafiq jumped off his horse, pulling something from the saddle. "Because," he said, approaching, "we have every intention of *not* letting you die. At least, not like this. If you're up and moving now, the poison's mostly out of your system."

"What's the plan?" I asked.

Rafiq had a loop of thin braided leather in his hands. "You're coming with us."

He intended to tie my hands. I debated avoiding it, even tensed to do so.

Rafiq saw it and laughed. "I can tie you standing here before me with some measure of dignity, or I can tie you with your rump planted in the dirt. Which do you prefer?"

I said nothing. He slipped the loop over my wrists and snugged it tight, preparing to knot it.

Then I moved.

TEN

WHEN I came to, my rump was not planted in the dirt. All of me was. Rafiq had one knee on my chest and was scowling into my face. I expected him to apply inventive curses to my aborted attempt to escape, but instead he asked, "What happened to your fingers?

I scowled back. "I got hungry."

Rafiq claimed a good share of Borderer blood and thus was larger than most men in the South. It wasn't an impossibility for him to jerk me to my feet, especially with me wobbly from venom residue and being knocked out. Especially with his two friends on either side of me, waiting to help. He lifted his knee, they grabbed my arms, and he yanked me up by dint of tied wrists. Which hurt. Which he knew.

His expression was odd. "What happened to your fingers?"

I blinked away dizziness, aware of how tightly the others gripped my arms. Surely they didn't believe I could offer much of a fight, after that brief travesty of a protest. "I was kidnapped by bald, blue-headed priest-mages, and they cut them off."

Rafiq accepted the truth no easier than falsehood. He studied my stumps with every evidence of fascination. "This isn't new."

Well, it wasn't that old, either, but I didn't say anything.

He thought about it. "At least I know you didn't lose them in the last couple of days."

I glared at him. "What does it matter?"

He looked at my face, searching for something. "You killed Khashi four days ago."

Actually, I'd lost count. Apparently I'd missed the night before and much of another day. Being poisoned will do that to you. "If you say so."

"You killed Khashi with two missing fingers."

"And easily," Nayyib put in.

Moral support. How nice.

Rafiq's eyes flickered. He looked again at the stumps, thoughts hidden. Then his face cleared. "Well, we'll let Umir decide. It's his business if he wants damaged goods."

"Umir?" I blurted. "Umir the Ruthless? What in hoolies does *he* want?"

"You."

"Me? Umir? What for? He never wanted me before." It was Del he'd wanted, and gotten, even if only briefly.

"He does now." Rafiq smiled. "You've apparently become a collector's item. A seventh-level sword-dancer who's declared *elaii-ali-ma*. It's never happened before. That makes you unique. And you know how Umir is about things—and people—he considers unique."

I shook my head, slow to grasp the essentials. They were simply too preposterous. "What does he want, to put me on display?"

Rafiq's brows arched. His hair was darker than mine, but not quite black. "You haven't heard about his contest?"

"Umir's holding a contest?"

The Borderer, who knew very well how fast news traveled among the sword-dancer grapevine, stared at me. "Where in hoolies have *you* been?"

Blandly I replied, "Trying to convince bald, blue-headed priest-mages I didn't want to join them."

"Ah. The same ones who cut off your fingers?"

"The very same."

Rafiq snickered, shaking his head. "You always did have a vivid imagination."

I gifted him with a level stare. "So did Khashi. He believed he could defeat me."

That banished the humor. Rafiq nodded at his friends. I realized abruptly that while I'd been briefly unconscious they had slipped leather nooses over my head, now circling my neck. I was cross-tied like a recalcitrant horse, one man on either side of me holding a long leather leash. And currently tightening it just to demonstrate how well the system worked.

When, having made their point, they loosened the nooses, I asked, "Leashing me like a dog these days, Rafiq?"

"A cat," he answered easily. "A big, dangerous cat. Umir gets what he pays for. Fingers or no fingers, I'm not underestimating you."

"Khashi did," Nayyib said.

Very helpful, he was. And it served to bring the image back, and the knowledge, that a man lacking two fingers might still kill an Alimat-trained fifth-level sword-dancer.

Maybe even Rafiq.

Rafiq looked at me again. Assessed me. "Then Khashi was a fool. You may have broken all your oaths, but that doesn't mean you've forgotten how to kill a man. You always were good at that, Tiger."

I suppose it could be taken as a compliment. But my mind was on other things. "I'm not going anywhere without Del."

The Borderer was blank a moment. "Del?—oh, you mean the Northern bascha I've heard so much about?" Rather abruptly, tension seeped into his body. He glanced around sharply. A subtle signal had his two sword-dancer friends tightening the nooses again. "Where is she?"

Ordinarily this would be the signal for Del to sing out, offering to show them where she was, to describe what she would do to them, and how she would do it. Ordinarily it would be amusing to witness Rafiq's anxiety.

But this time it wasn't, because she wouldn't be doing any of it, and now was no time for prevarication. "In the shelter," I told him. "I'm not leaving without her."

Nayyib, still mounted, flicked a glance at me, then away. "I wanted the healer for her," he told Rafiq, "not for him."

Rafiq looked at me. Then he told his sandtiger-tamers to keep an eye on their charge and strode over to the lean-to.

If going with them got Del to help, it was worth as many leashes as they wished to put on me. It wasn't the best of situations, but some improvement in this one was worth a great deal if it helped Del.

I watched Rafiq duck down inside the shelter. In a moment he came back and glanced at his men. "Put him on his horse. We're leaving."

They shut hands on my arms again, started to turn me. "Wait," I said sharply. "We've got to make arrangements for Del. A litter—"

"We're leaving her."

"You can't do that!"

"I can." He nodded at his men. "Do it."

The gelding had been saddled. They shoved me toward him. I planted my feet, not that it did me much good. My feet weren't cooperating, and neither were Rafiq's friends. Rafiq himself turned away to his own mount, gathering reins.

"*Wait,*" I said again. "If you want me to come peaceably—"

Rafiq cut me off. "I don't care if you come peaceably or not. The woman's too much trouble. She'll be dead by tomorrow." He swung up onto his palomino. "Get on your horse, Tiger. If you don't, you can walk all the way to Umir's place at whatever pace our horses set. Of course if you fall, we'll simply drag you."

Rafiq and I had never been friends. But cordial rivals, yes, in the brotherhood of the trade. Now, clearly, cordiality was banished, and rivalry had been transmuted to something far more deadly.

The two men made it clear I could mount Del's gelding under my own power, or they'd choke me out and sling me over the saddle. There was no way I could win this battle. It was foolish even to try. But this was Del we were discussing.

I was running out of options. Beyond Rafiq, Nayyib sat his

horse wearing a curiously blank expression. I shot him a hard stare but couldn't catch his eye. Then I turned, grabbed white mane and stuck a foot in the stirrup, pulled myself up. Kicking the gelding into unexpected motion in a bid to escape would not succeed; Rafiq's leather leashes would jerk me out of the saddle and likely strangle me before I landed.

But leaving Del behind . . . that I couldn't do. I'd made a promise. If I tempted death, so be it. I wouldn't leave her alone if it cost me my life.

Without a word Nayyib abruptly turned his horse toward the shelter and rode away from us. He dismounted, looped his rein loosely around one of the roof branches, glanced back at me over a shoulder. No longer did he avoid my gaze, but seemed to be courting it. His jaw was set like stone.

Rafiq glanced back. "Aren't you coming? I thought you wanted to see some real sword-dances."

Nayyib lifted that stubborn jaw. He continued to stare at me. "I'm staying with the woman."

I released a breath I hadn't realized I was holding. Maybe he *hadn't* betrayed us. Or maybe he'd had a change of heart. I wanted no part of leaving, but at least Del would have someone with her.

The two men were mounted, one on each side of the gelding. I felt the pressure of the slip-knots on either side of my neck. A change in pace by any of our mounts, be it a side-step, a spook, a stumble, and I'd be in a world of hurt. The reins were mine to hold, but they did me no good.

Rafiq laughed, calling to Nayyib. "Well, you can catch up to us tomorrow—after you bury her."

"I don't think so," I said lightly. "In fact, I'm pretty damn certain of it. It'll be you who gets buried, and if I don't do it, she will."

Rafiq looked at me. He was neither laughing nor smiling now. "You have no idea what you're going to face. You broke every oath we hold sacred, Tiger. What Alimat was founded on. What do you expect? We were all children there, who were taught to become men. There is a cost for such betrayal, and now you will pay it."

"In blood, I suppose."

His eyes were cold as ice. "One of us will have the honor of cutting you into small pieces. I would like it, Tiger—I would like it *very* much—if that honor were mine."

I opened my mouth to answer, but Rafiq's friends suggested I not respond by employing the simple expedient of tightening their leashes. I subsided.

Bascha, I said inwardly, *please don't die on me yet. I need you to rescue me.*

If she could, she would.

If she couldn't, I wasn't sure I cared if Rafiq—or anyone else— cut me to pieces.

As the horses moved out, as mine was chivvied along, I shut my eyes. Everything in me rebelled.

But then I glanced over my shoulder. Nayyib had turned. Was ducking into the shelter. She wouldn't be alone.

I will try, he had said, *to make certain she doesn't die.*

"Do better than try," I muttered.

When Rafiq asked me what I had said, I held my silence. After a moment he shook his head and kicked his horse into a trot. Mine, and theirs, went with him.

About the time I began to doze off in the saddle for the fifth or sixth time, Rafiq woke me with a comment and a question. "Your horse looks ridiculous. What made you do that to him?"

I sighed, shifted in the saddle, swore inwardly; it is not comfortable riding with your wrists tied in front of you and leashes around your neck. Especially when your body wants to slump forward over the horse's neck, and *your* neck has nooses around it. "Bald, blue-headed priest-mages."

He had dropped back to ride near me. Now he eyed me askance. "Sticking to that story, are we?"

Well, except for the gelding's adornments, it was the truth.

But I countered with a question of my own. "What exactly is this contest Umir's holding?"

"He wants to see who's the best sword-dancer."

"We already did that in Iskandar a couple of years ago." I recalled it very clearly. Del had killed the Northern borjuni Ajani there, satisfying her vow to avenge the death of her family.

"It didn't end quite the way anyone expected," Rafiq said.

That was an understatement. All hoolies had broken loose, and Del and I had left town as quickly as possible. "So Umir's decided to start putting on exhibitions? Isn't that a little odd for him?"

"He wants to find out so he can hire the best."

"The best for what?"

"Protecting his business interests. Full-time employment with one of the richest men in the South until retirement. Not bad work, if you can get it."

It was not unusual for a sword-dancer to hire on with one employer for a term of service, but it had always been situational. I'd never heard of a permanent employment. "And you want it."

"I want it, and I intend to get it."

"And these two friends of yours are just along for the ride?"

Rafiq laughed. "Oh, no. Ozmin and Mahmood will take their chances, too. But they know I'm better than they are."

"Sometimes," Ozmin said, from my left.

"Usually I just take pity on you and let you *think* you're better," said Mahmood from my right.

I ignored them and addressed my comments to Rafiq. "What does it have to do with me? I'm not a sword-dancer. I can't play with the big boys anymore."

"Oh, he's making an exception for you. Or maybe that should be *we* are. Not in the way you expect, maybe, but it ought to be worth it regardless."

"And what is that?"

"Dessert."

"*Dessert?*"

"Well, reward, really. You." He grinned. "You're not a stupid

man, Tiger, and you know the South very well—as was proven by
your disappearance. Everyone wants you. But it might take years
for any of us to track you down in order to kill you. This way,
you're right there at hand. An extra prize for the last sword-
dancer standing: the chance to kill the Sandtiger in a dance to
the death. Umir put out the word months ago, but you'd disappeared."

"You found me easily enough." Not that it made me happy.

Rafiq shrugged. "That was luck. I was at Fouad's waiting to
meet up with Ozmin and Mahmood when your young friend came
in asking about a healer. I had no idea where you were, or even
that you were back from wherever it was you disappeared to." He
grinned. "Probably you should have stayed there."

So, maybe Nayyib hadn't sold us out. Maybe he'd had no real
choice about leading them back to us.

Or maybe he had.

Maybe, maybe, maybe.

Frowning, I guided the gelding over a rocky patch, hoping he
wouldn't stumble and strangle me by accident. But he was a rather
comfortable ride, despite the circumstances. Del hadn't exagger-
ated. If I were on the stud, I'd have been choked ten times over
by now.

Which reminded me that he was still missing. And now likely
to stay that way; Nayyib wouldn't know to go looking for him,
and Del was too sick to suggest it.

To take my mind off that, I looked at Rafiq. "And Umir, I
suppose, will reward you for bringing me in."

"Handsomely. And this way if I don't win the contest, I still
benefit from it." He laughed as he saw my dubious expression.
"I'm not stupid, Tiger; there's always a chance something might
prevent me from winning. I could trip at the wrong time. Get a
blister on my thumb. Lose a finger." He glanced pointedly at my
hands. "All the other losers will just be losers. I'll walk away with
Umir's coin in my purse, and the honor of bringing in the Sandtiger to face punishment."

"*We* will walk away," Ozmin clarified.

Mahmood nodded. "We're splitting it, remember? Otherwise you could have taken him on by yourself. And we all know who'd have won that contest."

Maybe not, in my current condition. I contemplated leather knots glumly. I'd known returning to the South was a risk. Being challenged by Khashi in Julah was merely the first of many I expected to face. But that was one by one. Umir's scheme likely *would* get me killed. At Alimat we'd held many such contests to test our skills against one another, because competition brought out the best. It focused the mind, honed the talent. By the time the two finalists met, regardless of cuts, bruises, and slashes, they were prepared for anything.

Whoever came out of Umir's contest the winner would be very, very good, and very, very hungry for his—dessert.

"Doesn't sound like there's much in it for me," I said lightly.

Rafiq affected surprise. "But of course there is! You'll have the honor of dying in front of men you trained with, sparred with, danced with, even drank with. Men you respect, and who respect—respected—you. Who will never forget you and will speak your name to others. How better for a sword-dancer to die? It's our kind's immortality." Then his expression hardened. "Oh, but I was forgetting. You have no honor. You aren't a sword-dancer. You're just a man whom no one will remember, whose name is never spoken. A man who never lived, and thus can have no immortality." Rafiq added with elaborate scorn, "A man such as you might just as well have been born a slave."

The verbal blade went home, as he had intended. My origins weren't a secret. They'd been part of the legend: a Salset slave had, against all odds, risen to become a seventh-level, Alimat-trained sword-dancer, favored by the shodo. When you're a legend, origins don't matter except as seasoning for the story.

Now, of course, I wasn't a legend. And Rafiq wanted a reaction. Maybe he wanted me to choke myself trying to reach him. But I merely grinned at him. "So much for honor. I don't think there is much in killing a former chula."

His face darkened. After a moment he kicked his horse into a trot and went ahead again.

While I, meanwhile, blessed the bald, blue-headed priest-mages for forcing me to rededicate myself to one of the teachings of my shodo.

Discipline.

It was its own kind of magic.

ELEVEN

BY THE TIME we reached the place Rafiq identified as Umir's somewhere near sundown, I was tired, thirsty, hungry, sunburned, and more than a little sore from a long ride with my hands tied, not to mention the residual debilitating effects of sandtiger poison. Most of it had worked its way out of my system—and this was my third encounter, so my reaction was somewhat lessened—but I wasn't exactly feeling myself. Rafiq and his friends had given me water along the way, but they didn't claim a spare burnous among them, so all I had to wear was my dhoti. Not to mention I hadn't eaten for a couple of days thanks to the sandtiger attack, and now that the worst of the sickness had passed my belly was complaining.

Last time I'd looked, Umir had concentrated his holdings farther north. It was very unlike him to take himself so far south. But he was a tanzeer who enjoyed buying all manner of items he deemed worthy of his collections, and I guess domains qualified. For all I knew he'd added five or six since I'd sailed for Skandi.

The house was, I decided as we approached, fairly modest for a man of Umir's wealth and tastes, being little more than a series of interconnected, low-roofed rooms built of adobe, the pervasive mudbrick of the South, with timber roofs. Except Umir had had his adobe smoothed into silken slickness and painted pristine white with lime, so it glowed in the sun. Tall palm trees formed clustered lines of sentinels around the house, and masses of vegetation peeped over courtyard walls, indicating there was good access to water. Which I saw proved as we rode into the front courtyard: a three-tiered fountain spilled water into a large tile basin. This was wealth incarnate. Trust Umir to find water at the edges of the Punja.

Thirst reestablished itself. I wanted nothing more than to fall into the fountain, but good old Ozmin and Mahmood still had me closely leashed. Rafiq tracked down a servant, explained his business, and within a matter of moments we were politely invited to dismount in the cobbled, shaded courtyard. The horses were taken away by grooms. Damp cloths were presented to Rafiq and his two friends to wipe off the worst of the trail dust; I was ignored. Ozmin and Mahmood still shadowed me on either side, leashes coiled in their hands. In dhoti, dust, sunburn, and sweat, I was definitely at a disadvantage when it came to presentability.

We were permitted into the house and left to wait in a reception room of airy spaciousness, with tile floors and colorful tribal rugs. Priceless items were set in nooks and adorned walls. Low tiled tables displayed other items, including thin, colored glass bowls and bottles, which I found more than a little risky with numerous careless sword-dancers trooping through the house. But maybe that was part of the appeal for Umir.

After a suitably lengthy wait intended to intimidate lesser personages, Umir's steward appeared. Said steward then led us through the reception room out into what I thought was a courtyard off the back of the house. Except I discovered it was nothing like. The back of the house was constructed of plain walls bowing out from the main house like a bubble. Thick, curved walls approximately six feet high. No exposed bricks. No adornment. No windows. No vegetation. No fountains. No nothing, except elegantly curving walls that met precisely opposite where we were standing, and imported silk-smooth Punja sand raked into perfection.

A circle.

A very large circle, more expansive than a proper sword-dance required; I suspected the sword-dancers not fighting a given match would stand against the walls to watch. There was no danger in doing so; a man who stepped out of the circle drawn in the sand forfeited the match, and we all of us had learned to dance in close quarters. That was part of the beauty, the art, and the challenge.

Umir, I realized with a start of surprise, had had the house built with his sword-dancer contest in mind. If it were true he intended to hire the winner for life—or at least for the balance of his professional career—it was no surprise sword-dancers would come from all over the South. Likely at retirement Umir would settle some land and a dwelling on him; not a bad job at all. I'd even be interested myself, if I weren't scheduled to be the post-dance entertainment.

Waiting in the sun surrounded by white-painted walls wasn't my idea of fun, especially since I was tired enough my eyes kept trying to cross. I scrubbed with bound hands at the sweat and dust filming my face and considered plopping myself down in the sand, then eyed Ozmin and Mahmood and decided against it. But as Rafiq and his friends grew impatient enough to start complaining, the master of the house appeared.

Umir the Ruthless was a tall, slender, aristocratic man with high cheekbones, arched nose, and dark skin, all classic features of a Southroner save for his eyes, which were a pale gray. I'd always assumed Umir had some Borderer in him. As was habitual, he wore robes of the finest fabrics. The toes of soft, dyed-leather slippers peeked out from under the bullioned hems.

He spoke to Rafiq, but didn't look at him. His gaze was fastened on me. "Well done."

Rafiq had never claimed any subtlety. "When do we get paid? Now, or after he's dead?"

Umir was unruffled. "Oh, now, of course. I'll have my steward tend to it." He assessed me with a faint smile. "Well, Sandtiger . . . the last time we met, I wished to acquire your woman. Does it please you to know I now wish to acquire you?"

"Depends on what you want me for," I answered. "Now, if it was me you wanted to hire for lifetime employment, we could probably work something out. But if I'm meant to be dessert, probably not."

One brow lifted delicately. "Dessert?"

"I told him what you plan," Rafiq offered. "How he's to be the reward for the winner."

"Oh, but you should have left that to me," Umir murmured. "You have deprived me of amusement." Apparently he'd made some kind of signal, because two large men appeared from the house. Umir indicated them with a negligent gesture. "Rafiq, you and your friends are free to avail yourselves of my hospitality with the other sword-dancers, in the visitor's wing. This particular guest is now the responsibility of my house."

I just love the way a cultured man finds euphemisms for everything. Guest. Hah.

Ozmin and Mahmood were happy enough to hand over the leashes to Umir's large servants. The steward presented a coin pouch to Rafiq and led them back inside. Which left me outside with Umir, and my two keepers.

The tanzeer's expansive gesture encompassed his circle. "Do you like it?"

He waited expectantly. I hitched one shoulder in a half-shrug. "Rather attractive in a spare, unassuming sort of way."

"Oh, yes. Very minimalist. No distractions that way. Merely the pure, elegant art of the sword-dance."

He had not brought me out here to discuss the attractions of his architecture but to impress upon me this was to be where I died. I thought again of sitting down, or asking if I could go back out front and fall face-first into the fountain. Did neither, under Umir's examination.

The tanzeer's nostrils flared with distaste. "Why is it whenever I see you, you are in a state of utter filth and dishabille?"

I smiled winningly. "I lead an active life."

He made a dismissive gesture. "Well, for a short time, at least, you shall enjoy the best my poor house has to offer. Scented baths, oils, the finest of food and wine, comfortable lodgings; even women, if you like. I do not stint my guests."

At this point, wobbly as I was, it all sounded wonderful—except for the women. Well, even they sounded wonderful in the abstract. (Once upon a time the women wouldn't have been abstract at all, but Del had reformed me.)

"I'm not a guest," I said. "I'm dessert."

Umir smoothed the front of his figured silk overrobe with a slender hand weighted with rings. "I would be remiss if I offered my other guests dessert lacking in piquancy. By the time you step into the circle, you will be well fed, rested, and fit."

"Hasn't anyone told you?" I asked. "I can't step into a circle anymore. That's the whole point of *elaii-ali-ma*."

He waved that away. "Call it what you wish. A square, if you like. But you will fight for me, Sandtiger. As only you can."

I lifted brows. "What's in it for me? What possible motivation would I have for meeting the winner of your little contest?"

Umir's eyes and tone were level. "Until last year, you were a man of honor. An Alimat-trained, seventh-level sword-dancer of immense skill and repute. I saw what took place at Sabra's palace, how you stopped the dance against Abbu Bensir and declared *elaii-ali-ma*. It was for the woman, was it not? The Northern woman. Well, I understand her worth. Not for the same reason, perhaps, but that hardly matters. You made an outcast of yourself for her sake. It had nothing to do with disenchantment with the oaths you swore, the life you chose. You may deny it now, to me, but when you step into that circle—and it will be a circle—you will recall those oaths. They will once again rule your life. You will dance, Sandtiger—and yes, I do mean dance—because you will have no other choice. It is all you know. It is what you *are*. And you will die with whatever honor you may make of your last dance."

Umir was right. With my life at stake, I would not refuse to dance. But . . . "You know, I'm getting really, *really* tired of everyone assuming I'll lose."

The tanzeer stared at me with the faintest of puzzled frowns.

I spelled it out for him. "I might win, Umir. What happens then?"

He shook his head. "I have been given to understand that it is an impossibility you might win."

"Oh? Why? Did you ask Rafiq? Someone else? How can anyone be sure *what* will happen?" I took one step toward him, as much as I was willing to risk while on doubled leashes. "What if I win, Umir? What happens then?"

He was baffled. "But you have broken all your oaths. It was explained to me."

I laughed. "Yes, but broken oaths and loss of honor does not necessarily translate to loss of skill."

Clearly Umir had never considered I might win. Clearly none of the sword-dancers he'd consulted considered I might win. Which is just the way I liked it.

"So," I said, "does the deal apply to me? I win, and you offer me employment?"

His face was very stiff. "I find it highly unlikely you would win."

I lifted brows. "Why? Do you intend to drug me?"

Color stained his cheeks. "Of course not! I am not Sabra, who was interested only in punishing and killing you. I want a true dance. A true winner. There will be no trickery."

"Your winner won't dance with me," I said. "He'll fight me. He'll attempt to kill me. And I will do my very best to kill him. And *if* I do, I expect some reward for it. Something more than dessert."

There was only one thing worth having. And Umir knew it. "The freedom to leave my domain unchallenged."

I nodded. "That'll do."

His tone became aggressive. "But anyone may challenge you outside my domain."

"Of course. But that's not your concern. And I truly believe anyone who witnesses me killing the best of the best here in your homemade circle may think twice about challenging me anywhere."

His lips thinned. "You are overconfident."

" 'Over'? Don't think so. Confident, yes." I gifted him with a friendly smile. "I *am* the Sandtiger."

"You truly believe you can intimidate everyone?"

It wasn't false confidence or bluster. I'd done it before. Many times. It was one of my most effective weapons. I was bigger, quicker, stronger and more agile than anyone else I'd met in the South. I was simply better.

I smiled and said nothing.

"I wonder," Umir murmured, "what Abbu Bensir will say?"

Simply better—except possibly for Abbu Bensir. We hadn't settled that yet. I stopped smiling. "If Abbu's here," I said, scowling, "why have a contest at all? Offer him the job and put us in your circle."

Umir studied a ring, admiring its beauty in the sunlight. "But that would deprive me of the entry fees."

I had to laugh. No wonder Umir the Ruthless was one of the wealthiest men in the South. He charged sword-dancers to step into a circle against one another when they did it all the time for free, just to hone their skills.

A faint glint of amusement appeared in Umir's pale eyes. "I hope you do understand, Sandtiger, that my goal here is to find the best out of many. I'm not interested in death. Only in the unique. Your presence here, under the peculiar circumstances of *elaii-ali-ma*, offers uniqueness. All of the men who lose my contest will go out and find other employment, possibly even with tanzeers as wealthy as I. But I offer something no one else can."

I knew what that was, but he detailed it anyway.

Dusky color stained his dark skin, and pale eyes glowed. "The opportunity to kill the Sandtiger in front of other sword-dancers, thus plucking the greatest of thorns from their pride and adding unassailable luster to one man's reputation. His name will be spoken forever with reverence. Tales will be told. He will go to his death one day secure in the knowledge he avenged the tarnished honor of Alimat and killed one of the greatest sword-dancers the South has ever known."

"And just when do you plan to *serve* dessert?"

Umir smiled. "In ten days."

Ten days. In ten days Del could be dead. Ten days was too long. Ten *hours* was too long. Even though Nayyib was with her. "How about now?" I asked.

Umir nearly laughed aloud. "I think not."

"I'm serious. Give me a sword, and call for the dance right now."

"You are half-dead with exhaustion; do you think I can't see it? You can barely stand up." He shook his head. "I will not present a farce. Ten days, Sandtiger. After you have rested and recovered. *Then* you may prove to me if you're as good as you claim." He gestured to his servants. "Escort him to the bath chamber, then to his room. See that he is fed."

I dropped all pretenses, all facades. "Wait," I blurted sharply, as Umir began to turn away. "The Northern woman," I said, "the one you wanted so badly . . ."

He paused.

"She's ill," I told him. "Possibly dying. If you let me go to her—send any number of men with me you wish, tie me up, keep me on a leash, put *chains* on me if you like—I swear to return and take part in your contest."

Umir studied me consideringly. Then, with delicate disdain, he said, "I do not accept worthless oaths from men with no honor."

I was tired enough and dirty enough that a bath among the enemy—with the enemy's servants watching—did not unduly disturb me, especially since my wrists were finally untied and the nooses lifted from my neck. Nor did I fear drinking the watered wine servant-guards offered as I soaked in the huge hip-bath. I was too thirsty. And for all Umir had imprisoned me—and had done so before—he'd never actually tried to harm me. If he was offering the Sandtiger on a platter to his guests as a fillip to his contest, he would indeed want me fit enough to provide proper entertainment. His reputation depended on it. He was ruthless when it came to dealing for prized acquisitions—kidnapping Del was an example—but not a killer.

So, knowing I needed to be in the best physical condition possible if I wanted to survive—minor motivation—I took advantage of his hospitality and came out of the bath markedly cleaner and feeling more relaxed than I had in days. Upon being dried by female servants and anointed with scented oil, I was presented with a soft linen dhoti and a fresh house-robe of creamy raw silk and a russet-colored sash, but my leather dhoti and sandals were missing. Then the male servants escorted me barefoot down a cool, tiled corridor to a wooden door boasting a rather convoluted locking mechanism on the corridor-side latch. They gestured me in, and in I went. I knew better than to try Umir's servants. They were very large men, and I was on the verge of turning into a boneless puddle of flesh.

The room clearly had been built to house a prisoner. The edge of the door was beveled so it overlapped the jamb; there was no crack into which a knife or some other implement might be inserted in an attempt to lift the latch. Nor was there any bolt or latch-string in evidence. Just planks of thick wood adzed smooth, studded with countersunk iron nailheads impossible to pry out. The door could only be opened from the corridor, and even a concerted effort on my behalf to knock down the door with brute strength would result only in bruised flesh and, possibly, broken bones. No thanks.

Nor was there a window. Just four blank walls with a row of small holes knocked through mudbrick up near the roof in the exterior wall, well over my head, and an equally blank adobe ceiling. The floor was also adobe, lacking tiles or rugs. A large nightcrock—in this case, daycrock, too—sat unobtrusively in one corner. The only piece of furniture in the room was a very high, narrow bed. Next to the bed, on the floor, was set a large silver tray containing cubed goat cheese; mutton pie baked in flaky pastry; a sprig of fat, blood-colored grapes; a small round loaf of steaming bread accompanied by a bowl of olive oil; and a pewter cup, plus matching tankards of water and wine. Not to mention a

folded square of linen with which to blot my mouth upon comple-
tion of the meal. Umir believed in manners.

   Ten days. I wondered whether that included today or began
tomorrow. I wondered it all through the meal, the entire water
tankard, half of the wine, and as I fell backward onto the bed.
Umir had even provided a pillow and coverlet. Then I didn't wonder anything at all. I fell fast asleep.

   *In the echoes of the dream, I saw old bones. Heard a woman's
voice.*

   And took up a sword.

TWELVE

I WOKE UP not long after dawn to the sound of sword blades. For a moment I was disoriented, aware of unfamiliar smells, light, and the fabric beneath my body. Then I remembered.

Swearing, I crawled out of Umir's so-called guest bed and sat hunched on the edge, scrubbing at creased face. I'd been shaved the day before during my bath, so the stubble was short instead of its usual three or four days' worth of growth.

Swords clashed outside. In the pallor of the morning, I glanced up at the line of airholes cut through mudbrick near the ceiling. Apparently the exterior wall of my room faced Umir's circle off the back of the house. But obviously I was not to be allowed sight of the matches or of the individual who might be given the honor of killing me.

The door latch rattled. The door itself was thrown open. Had I intended to move, I wouldn't have had time to get off the bed. As it was, I just sat there, scowling at my unannounced visitor.

Umir. I stopped scowling and presented him with a blandly noncommittal expression of nonaggression.

Then the two large men who'd shadowed me yesterday came into the room, and even as I began to stand up they grabbed my arms and jerked me onto my feet. So much for Umir's hospitality.

"Already?" I asked.

The two men clamped grips on my wrists and extended my hands. Umir approached. His expression was outraged. "It *is* true!" he cried, staring at my hands. "I believed Rafiq was exaggerating."

Ah. The infamous missing fingers.

"I shall have to reduce his payment," he declared grimly.

My eyebrows leaped up. "Just how much are two fingers worth compared to an entire person?"

Umir glared at me. "I expected *all* of you to be delivered. Whole in body. Those were my orders."

I wanted to laugh; the whole topic was unbelievable. "Not that Rafiq and I are friends, Umir, but he didn't do it. This happened a few months ago."

"I heard nothing of it!"

"It didn't happen here." Hoolies, what did it matter?

He swung away, took two steps, swung back. His pale gray eyes were fierce. "Can you still dance?"

I suppressed a smile. "According to the rite of *elaii-ali-ma*, I am not allowed—"

He cut me off with a shout. "*Can you still dance?*"

"What, afraid your plan for me as reward will be ruined?"

Umir took one step toward me and swung. I ducked most of the blow, but the flat of his hand still caught me across the rim of my ear. The servants tightened their grips even more as I tried to lunge at Umir, holding me back.

"Try me," I said between my teeth. "Put a sword in these hands and try me—or why not ask *Khashi* if I can hold a sword?"

Umir's expression was blank. "Khashi?"

"A sword-dancer," I told him. "We had a little contretemps in Julah. Except he's dead now, so he's not here to tell you anything about who won and who lost."

Color began to steal back into his face. "He's dead?"

"Yes."

"You killed him?"

"Yes."

"Was he any good?"

I attempted a shrug made unsuccessful by the grips of the servants. "Apparently not, since I won. But I suspect that depends on your point of view."

Umir bent down and peered closely at my hands. I found the critical examination highly offensive, but there wasn't much I could do about it. So I just gritted my teeth and waited.

"Are they still painful?" he asked curiously, the way one might ask a guest if he wants more wine.

It took effort not to bellow at him, to retain some measure of decorum. "Explain why this matters to you."

Umir seemed surprised as he straightened. "Of course it matters. Your physical well being affects the quality of the entertainment I'll be offering."

I shook my head and began to say something, but Umir abruptly grabbed both my hands and squeezed.

This did not particularly endear my host to me.

After a moment he released them. Umir debated something internally. Then he nodded. "The plans are unchanged." And he turned and strode out of the room.

When I was locked in again, I loosed a lengthy volley of curses in every language I spoke, which was significant after my sojourn at Meteiera, and wished I had numerous breakable items I could hurl at the door and walls as I paced furiously, waiting for the pain to fade.

Of course such actions would merely trigger even more pain in my Umir-abused hands, so it was just as well I didn't have that recourse. And I wasn't about to use the slops jar to vent my frustration, because then I'd have to live with the rather messy results.

Eventually I ran out of curses. The pain diminished. I threw myself onto the bed, hands resting on my chest, and contemplated the blank ceiling overhead, thinking fiercely focused thoughts of such things as sword-dances and sword-dancers, broken oaths, missing fingers, idiots like Umir, absent baschas. And the discipline I'd learned atop the Stone Forest.

Outside, in Umir's circle, sword blades rang. I heard voices

raised in cheerful insults, vulgar suggestions, the occasional compliment.

I frowned. There was one voice that sounded familiar.

I heard it again. The frown dissipated. I recalled sparring
matches in one of Rusali's dusty alleys. With swords and without.

Inspiration. Motivation.

I swung out of bed, pulled it away from the wall, turned it on
edge, studied the legs. With care I sat on one, my own legs gathered under me. I bounced slightly, and felt the answering crack.
Smiling, I stood up, smashed a foot against the leg, and was
pleased to see it break off from the frame in one piece. I was left
with approximately three feet of wood. One end was slightly jagged, but that didn't matter. The other end, adzed smooth at the
bottom, afforded me a functional grip.

I set the bed upright again, swinging it around so the legless
corner was not obvious to the eye of a visitor, and pushed it once
again against the wall. Then I stripped out of house-robe to the
linen dhoti. Took up the broken bed leg. Closed my hands upon
it. Then, courting patience and self-control, I began the practice
forms I had first learned twenty-three years before at Alimat.

I had worked up a good sweat when I heard the latch rattle. Hastily I slung the leg under the bed and donned the house-robe again,
though I didn't have time to tie the sash. I thought it best not to
sit on the bed with only three legs, so I stood in front of it as if
I'd just risen. By the time the door opened, I wore a suitably expectant expression. Especially since I wondered if Umir was coming to inspect any other portions of my anatomy.

A woman entered with breakfast. Even as she set the tray on
the floor, they locked her in. Rather than seeming startled or dis-
mayed by her predicatment, she merely stepped aside from the
tray and made a graceful gesture inviting me to eat.

She was beautiful in the way of the loveliest of Southron
women, small in stature and delicately made, with huge dark eyes,
expressive face and hands, and dusky skin set off by blue-black
hair hanging loose to her waist. She wore luxurious silks of a

brilliant blue-green, and gilded sandals. That she was here for my
pleasure was obvious; she wore neither headress or veil, and did
not affect the extreme modesty of other Southron women. But
neither was she overt in any way. Umir's taste in all things ran to
elegance and understatement. Rumor claimed the tanzeer did not
like to bed women or men, but took his pleasure in acquiring and
owning those things he found intriguing and unique. Sometimes
this included people. This woman was definitely unique.

Once upon a time I would not have questioned her presence
in his house or her role. I would merely have enjoyed her. Traveling with Del had made me aware of certain Southron customs
that were not judged acceptable by other cultures. Traveling with
Del had also filled a place in my soul I hadn't known existed; I
certainly wasn't blind to other women, nor was I gelded or dead,
but appreciation now found outlets other than taking attractive
women to bed, be it in my mind or in reality.

Thus I gazed upon this lovely Southron woman and asked,
"What's a nice girl like you doing in a place like this?"

Startled out of her poised serenity, she blinked. The faintest
of blushes rose in her cheeks. She gestured again, more insistently,
to the tray containing breakfast.

"Later," I said. "Umir sent you?"

She nodded, lids lowering long enough to display long dark
lashes against her cheeks.

"Were instructions given?"

She moistened her lips with the tip of her tongue. Her voice
was low and perfectly modulated. "I am to do what you wish and
be what you wish."

"Is being here in Umir's house what *you* wish?"

The dark brows arched. "But of course. How not? It is better
by far than it might be."

That was likely true. But still I heard Del's voice in my head,
arguing the point. "Given a choice, would you leave?"

She was clearly baffled by my line of questioning. "My family
was well paid. They live in comfort now. But I live in even greater
comfort. Why would I wish to leave?"

"And when you are instructed to do what a man wishes, and be what that man wishes, don't you ever ask yourself if it's worth it?"

Unexpectedly, she laughed. "Do you?"

My turn to be baffled. "What?"

"When you hire a woman for the night, do you ever ask yourself if it's worth it?"

I hadn't hired a woman since meeting Del. But even before that, when I'd celebrated victories with women and liquor, or with women and no liquor, it had never once occured to me to ask myself if it was worth it. It was simply what I did. And there were always women who wanted me to do it.

She saw the answer in my face and smiled. "So, you see. We are not so very different."

But I was. Now. Yet there was no possible way to explain it to her. "Thank you for bringing breakfast," I said, "but I'll eat alone."

She was smiling, certain of me. "And afterwards?"

"Afterwards, I will also be alone."

That surprised her. "You don't wish my company?"

It was undoubtedly an insult, but I tried to soften it. "I choose my own companions."

A wave of color rose in her face. "Umir believed I would please you."

"What would please me, and Umir knows this, is to be given my freedom."

She studied me a moment longer, as if expecting me to change my mind. When I said nothing else, merely waited quietly, she finally accepted it for the truth. She turned at once to the door, rapped on it sharply, and slipped out without a backward glance when the guard opened it.

I listened to the latch being locked behind her. Then I walked to the nearest wall, turned, slid down with my back planted against it. Once upon a time . . .

But I regretted no part of my decision.

I sighed, thumped my head against the wall, shut my eyes. I

could hear Umir's sword-dancers. But all I could think about was
Del as I had last seen her, left to the ministrations of a stranger
while I was here, waiting to meet a man who would do his best to
kill me.

Nine days, or eight. I should have asked Umir.

*Bascha, where are you? Still in the lean-to, or did Nayyib get you
to Julah?*

This was not how I had envisioned it. For several years I'd
seen Del and me dying together, fighting any number of enemies.
I had never envisioned us as old people, but as we were now.
Certainly I had never considered Del might die of sandtiger
wounds or poison, and me sentenced to die in a circle I was no
longer allowed to enter.

Never in a thousand thousand years had I ever expected to
declare *elaii-ali-ma*. Despite my time as a chula among the Salset,
I considered myself truly born the day Alimat's shodo had accepted me for instruction. The day I had taken my name. The day
I had defeated Abbu Bensir in an impromptu practice match with
wooden swords.

That image, unexpectedly, was abruptly clear and immediate.
I had been seventeen, or as close as I could reckon my age. Abbu
was a good ten or more years older, the acknowledged sword-
dancer of sword-dancers. He wasn't taking lessons anymore; he
had made his living hiring out for years. But he had come back to
Alimat to visit the shodo. Where he had heard of a tall, gangly
kid who promised, with proper instruction, to be as good—or
better—one day.

I smiled crookedly. Abbu had intended to laugh at me, albeit
quietly, noting all of my bad habits for the benefit of others. And
when he had tossed the wooden sparring blade to me, he had
anticipated demonstrating to all the other wide-eyed students
how my height and gangliness would hurt me in a circle.

Instead, my greater reach and speed, despite my awkwardness,
had landed a blow to his throat. To this day he spoke in a husky
rasp.

I had eventually grown into my gangliness, adding flesh and

muscle. Strength had been trained, quickness refined. I was unlike Abbu or any other Southroner, and I could not apply all of the lessons to my particular body. Instead, the shodo had adapted to *me* by developing other forms. In a matter of a few years, more quickly than any prior student—including Abbu—I had attained the seventh level.

Then, and only then, had I departed Alimat to make my own way.

The way that brought me here so many years later.

I got up and stripped off the robe, tossed it on the bed, and knelt to retrieve the broken leg. Once again I opened myself to the power that wasn't magic but that might allow me to live. The rites and rituals of honing the body, controlling the reflexes, taught me by the shodo; and the discipline of honing the mind, controlling that power, trained into me by the blue-headed priest-mages of ioSkandi.

The woman was long-limbed and agile, winding her legs around mine in comfortable abandon. She wore no clothes and had teased me out of my own. The initial passion was spent; now we lay very close, almost as one. Smiling, I twined my fingers into the silk of her hair, wrapping each: thumb, forefinger, next finger, next, and eventually the little finger. I felt the binding, tested it, tugged, then let the hair side through. Fair hair, nearly white; and skin lightly gilded from the blaze of the sun. I ran hands across that skin, stroked it with fingers—

—and sat bolt upright on the pallet I'd pulled from the three-legged bed and put on the floor.

I could see nothing in the night but raised my hands regardless. I counted, tucking fingers down as I named them off in my head.

Right hand: Thumb. Four fingers.

Left: Thumb. Four fingers.

And again, and again. The woman was gone—Del was gone—but the fingers remained. I could feel them.

I stayed awake the rest of the night, arguing with myself.

When dawn finally crept slowly into the room, segmented by air-holes, I was able to see truth at last.

Thumb. *Three* fingers. And a stub.

I lay down again, making fists of my hands. With two thumbs and six fingers.

Thinking: No Del, either.

Dreams, I decided bitterly, conjured pain as well as pleasure.

THIRTEEN

On the morning of the tenth day, I awoke not long after dawn. As always, the room I inhabited was quiet, dim, isolated, cut off from the ordinary noises of Umir's rousing household. But this time my body was poised and alert, my mind calm and prepared. Even without counting the days, I knew.

I lay on my back on the pallet and extended arms into the air. Examined hands, front and back. I had not dreamed again of having all my fingers. What I saw now was what I expected to see: that which had been left to me atop the stone spire after Sahdri had amputated two fingers in an attempt to also amputate my identity, the awareness that I was sword-dancer before anything else. Because he knew very well I would not become what he believed I should be, and could be, unless my past was extinguished.

The weeks thereafter had been a true battle as I fought an enemy such as I'd never met, to retain my sense of *self*. I had very nearly lost. But eventually I had rediscovered what and who I was and had managed to tap into ioSkandi's power. There atop the spire I'd been mage, if never priest, but also sword-dancer. And that, I knew, was all that would serve me now.

Sword-dancer.

Sandtiger.

Both—or either—would be enough.

I pressed myself up from the pallet. Used the crock. Spent time stretching myself into flexibility, cracked my joints, put my body through forms I could do in my sleep until every portion of me was loose. Took up a position in front of the door in the center of the room, composed myself, closed my eyes, and let myself go as I had in Meteiera, soaring without wings over the fertile valley at the foot of massive spires.

Far below I saw a circle made of white stones set into the ground with expert precision. I soared lower, lower, and saw there a man, dhoti-clad; a man born of Skandi, with the height, breadth, power, and quickness characteristic of the Eleven Families who claimed themselves gods-descended. Both hands grasped a sword, a full complement of eight fingers and two thumbs wrapping hilt. It was a weapon, but also an extension of the man. Steel became flesh.

He was alone and oblivious to the world at large. He danced there, he and the sword-his-partner, transforming the initial fundamental forms into a series of linked, liquid movements shaped, despite his size, of grace mixed with strength, a tapestry of motion on the frame of his will and spirit. Sweat sheened his body, slicking sun-browned flesh into a copper-bronze human sculpture of ridged sinews, tendons, and delineated muscle: the hard, ungentle beauty of a mature male trained beyond all others, fit beyond expectation, in body and mind. And then the first routines gave way to those known only by the best, known only of the best, kindling from the coals of talent into the intangible flame of rare gift.

He was alone no longer. A woman came into the circle. She too carried a sword. She too was tall, long of limb and torso, powerful but inherently graceful, manifestly and splendidly female despite her size and strength. Blonde, pale, wearing only a leather tunic, she challenged him to a dance.

When it was done, neither had lost. Neither had won. They had merely proven how perfectly matched they were, how exacting their precision, and how neither could be defeated.

Smiling, sated on self-awareness, I wheeled away on the wind, soaring back toward the spire. I descended; and cool stone lay under my feet. Power thrummed in my bones, threaded itself through muscle, tingled in my scalp. I spread my arms and gazed open-eyed but blindly into the heavens, calling on all the skills of Alimat, the courage of a slave become a man, and the fierce determination of a Northern bascha.

"Fill me," I invited.

That moment faded. I inhabited another. When I opened my eyes, I found Umir standing in the open door, staring at me oddly.

Eventually he bestirred himself and spoke. "Dress yourself. My servants will prepare you, then escort you to the circle."

The tanzeer departed. His servants held a fresh leather dhoti, a flask of oil, new sandals, and an overrobe woven of gleaming bronze samite, the finest silk in the world. Once Del had worn one similar at Umir's request, albeit white; and the interior had been lined with priceless beads, glass, and feathers. Mine, fortunately, was unadorned silk.

Mute, detached, I stripped out of linen dhoti, pulled on the soft suede. The servants poured oil into their hands and began to work it into my flesh. Once I might have wondered if the oil was tampered with in some way, but I knew Umir would not do such a thing for this match. He wanted a true dance. He wanted no one to say the Sandtiger lost because Umir had cheated.

The servants shaved me, then attempted to help me put on the rest of the clothing. I refused both overrobe and sandals. Wearing only the dhoti, I was escorted out of the room in which I had been imprisoned for ten days, and taken out to Umir's white-walled circle.

My host had, as I had expected, assembled all of his guests along the curving, white-painted wall off the back of his house. Having been present at Iskandar, I could see Umir had not been successful in luring all sword-dancers to his contest. But the number was decent. They were most of them Southroners, but there was a fair proportion of foreigners. They were taller men, heavier; brown-haired, blond, even red-heads, and everything in between with eyes of every color. Skin was tanned, freckled, or burned a permanent red from exposure to the harsh Southron sun. Though Southroners all resemble one another because of similar coloring and builds, the only likeness among the foreigners was a hardness in their eyes and the swords at hips and shoulders. There is a marked difference between men who wear swords for protection or impression, and men who make a living with a blade. An ease exists among the latter, a casual confidence in carriage, in self-knowledge. A sword is more than a sword. It is a part of their souls.

Sabra, the first, if short-lived, female tanzeer, had made her exhibition garish and overly dramatic. Umir's tastes and intentions were different. He neither announced my arrival nor my name; he knew, and I knew, there was no need. The Sandtiger had been promised to the winner.

Some of these men had never seen me. Some likely hadn't been born when I first left Alimat. These men gazed at me with a quiet avidity, marking how the man matched legend and rumor.

Undoubtedly some found me larger than expected, others thought me smaller. If what Del had said of Meteiera's magic lifting a measure of harsh usage from me were true, then perhaps I looked younger than many anticipated. But there was no doubt in any of the eyes that I was who I was. It was why I could go nowhere truly disguised. Nothing can hide facial scars left by a sandtiger's claws.

Something inside me kindled abruptly into memory, and regret. Now Del would bear her share, though fortunately her face was spared.

If she had survived.

The sword-dancers, as expected, took the measure of me: noted stature, the way I moved, the length of legs and arms, the depth and spring of my ribs—and the massive scar left there by Del's *jivatma*—the architecture of bones and muscle, the fit of flesh over both. In the circle, everything counts. Particularly in a death-dance.

They also, every one of them, looked at my hands.

The pale sand was warm beneath bare feet, but Umir had selected a good time of day. Since it was Punja sand, the sun would

eventually heat the intermixed crystals beyond endurance. But it
was early summer and mid-morning, bright enough to see without
squinting, not so warm as to burn the callused soles of a sword-
dancer's feet.

I noted a few frowns, an occasional puzzled expression. After
a moment's detached reflection, I realized it was likely I resembled
nothing of what those who knew me by sight anticipated. Skandi
had changed me. But none of them knew about Skandi. I had
simply disappeared after Sabra's aborted sword-dance, after declaring *elaii-ali-ma*. All they knew was the here and now: an aging
man who somehow looked younger, wearing double rings of silver
in his ears, with hair cropped shorter than was his wont. The
build was the same, the features the same; but the man, somehow,
was not.

There were men I knew. I watched their eyes meet mine, then
slide away. Faces were stiff, set in expressions designed to acknowledge the seriousness of the situation while giving nothing
away of their thoughts. Some of them had been friends. Some of
them had been good friends. But such things meant nothing when
weighed against the shame of *elaii-ali-ma*. Here, I had no friends.
No honored opponents. Only enemies.

Umir gestured me to halt. I acquiesced, marking the slant of
shadows, how the sand had been raked. No clouds: Nothing
would alter the intensity of the sun, thus altering the dance. I was
aware of the servants just behind me. I smelled heat and sand and
oil, the faint tangy musk of assembled, active males.

Then I sent myself away . . . *lost myself once more in the wind of
ioSkandi, threading my way through the Stone Forest as I gazed down
upon the circle, the man, the woman.*

Memory endured.

I was sword-dancer.

Sandtiger.

Legend in the flesh.

I smiled, returning. I was ready.

Umir raised his voice. "Will anyone among you draw the
circle?"

No one moved. No one spoke. Everyone stared.

The tanzeer made a placatory gesture. "Yes; I do understand. There is the matter of *elaii-ali-ma*. I neither disparage it nor mean you dishonor, nor ask you to forget. What I wish is to present that which most closely resembles what this man, this outcast, threw away. He should know what he had, what he shared with you, and what he has lost. The best of you will remind him, so that he dies comprehending the worthlessness of his life." He paused. "Is there any among you who will draw the circle in which this man will die?"

I heard a murmuring among them as they discussed it. Umir was asking a lot. I had no business being in a circle of any kind, yet here I was. They could accept the tanzeer's suggestion or repudiate it even as I had repudiated the honor codes.

Then a man pushed out from behind the others, unsheathing his sword. A tall, wide-shouldered, fair-haired man, bred of Northern climes. I knew those eyes. Knew that face. Had heard the voice, intentionally raised beyond the wall of my room so I might hear and know he was present. Recognized the sword; I had met him before many times, to drink with, to spar against, to share his food. He, his wife, his two little girls—now three, if I remembered correctly. They had cared for me after injuries more than once.

Alric's eyes met mine, blue as Del's. I saw the faintest of flickers there, a tautening in his jaw. Though not born to Southron customs, he had learned them well. He lived among Southroners, danced among Southroners, was married to a Southroner. His habits were theirs. He understood them.

He walked nearly to where I stood, set his blade tip into the sand and began to pace out the circle, drawing the line.

Alric finished where he began. He turned to face me, studied me, seemed to look inside my soul. I wondered what he saw.

Abruptly he pivoted. With long strides the tall Northerner walked into the circle to the very center, bent, and set down his sword.

This time the murmuring became recognizable words of angry

protest. The other sword-dancers were not pleased that one of their own spit in their faces by presenting me with his sword. Alric had just done his reputation among them irreparable harm; but then, Alric had always gone his own way.

At least one man here would mourn my death.

His message was clear: I need not worry that the sword I would use had been tampered with.

And the other message: he had not won his dance. It would not be Alric I'd meet in the circle, who would, unlike the others, make no attempt to kill me.

He inclined his head briefly, acknowledging me, then left the circle. Alric found a place to stand against the wall. He was alone, apart, as he had made himself by declaring his loyalty.

Inwardly, I laughed. Already Umir's plan had gone slightly awry. Rafiq had brought him the sword I'd bought in Haziz, which one of the servants nearest the tanzeer held. But it would remain unused. Now I had another. One I could trust implicitly, one that suited me in weight and balance; Alric and I were very similar in build, and I had sparred with it before. It also was offered by a friend to a man who supposedly had none among those who lived in the circle.

Such intricacies of mind, such subtle subtexts, could do much for a man who meant to kill another, or to preserve his own life.

"Musa," Umir called.

After a moment bodies parted. A pathway was opened. A man came forward, walking toward the circle. I had half expected Abbu Bensir, but this man was not he. Much younger than Abbu, perhaps twenty-six or -eight; taller, though not as tall as I; heavier than Abbu, though not a big man; slightly lighter in skin, hair, and eyes. But he had the high-bridged nose and steep cheekbones present in so many of his countrymen. Not Borderer, I didn't think. But a mix of something that gave him greater size than most Southroners and, I decided, more power. He moved with the lithe, coiled grace of the snow cats I'd seen high in Northern mountains, up near Staal-Ysta.

He wore only a dhoti, as I did. No harness, no sandals. He carried his sword. His eyes were fixed on my own.

The others called out encouragement to him. He ignored them. There was a tight-wound intensity in Umir's new hired sword. His eyes did not leave mine. His expression was a predator's, fixed and unwavering. Not for him the camaraderie before a dance, the jokes and wagers exchanged. He had come to kill me. He wanted me to know it.

Musa, Umir had named him. I didn't know him. I'd never heard of him. But he was here among the others and had obviously defeated those others; I discounted nothing at all about him.

The tanzeer once again raised his voice. "As all of you have no doubt heard, the Sandtiger is no longer whole in body. But lest you believe him physically unable and thus offering no challenge, let me repeat what you may also have heard: this man killed one of you in Julah a matter of weeks ago. His name was Khashi."

There were quiet, abbreviated murmurs. Every man present knew already. Likely Rafiq had told them, bragging about how he had so easily captured the man who had so easily killed Khashi. Borrowing glory, Rafiq.

I looked at Musa. Musa looked back. He borrowed no glory. The man's carriage claimed the quiet confidence of the expert, requiring neither bragging nor flattery. The unsheathed sword dangled casually from his hand. His forearms and ribs were webbed with pale, thin, slit-like scars, unavoidable in the circle, but there were no scars of significance. Blades had gotten through his guard, had marked his flesh, but none of them had done true damage. Mere pricks and minor cuts. Either everyone he had faced had been no better than adequate, or he was truly good. Potentially great.

Based on the identities of many of the men I saw gathered in Umir's walled circle, the quality of much of the opposition, that he was good was a given.

"Umir," I said quietly, "forget the appetizer. This man wants his dessert."

The tanzeer glared at me. "Your places!"

For me, it was a matter of taking three strides to the edge of Alric's circle. I waited. Musa, opposite, crossed the circle, set his sword beside Alric's, then paced back to take up his position. There were perhaps four inches between our respective heights, and he was long-legged. The race would be of equals.

He also had hands boasting all four fingers.

I raised mine. Displayed them palm out. Let Musa and everyone else take a good look. "Surely," I said, "it will not take long to kill me. How can any man lacking two fingers hope to defeat the best of the best?"

It infuriated Umir, who clearly did not want his rebellious dessert ruining the moment. There was only one way to end it. "*Dance*," he said.

FOURTEEN

I DUG the balls of my feet into sand and thrust myself forward, crossing over Alric's line into the circle. Three strides and I reached the center, snatching up Alric's sword.

I let momentum carry me forward into a somersault that took me out of immediate danger as Musa reached for his own weapon. I spun as I came up at the edge of the circle, blade at the ready, and blocked the first slashing blow. The clash of steel rang through the inner circle encompassed by Umir's wall.

Block. Block. Block and block. Musa was fast with his sword, disengaging and returning immediately to try new angles the moment I halted his blade. As with Khashi, I let him take the offense, judging foot placement, balance, strength, agility, blade speed. He had learned well, no question.

I was already at the edge of the circle because I had put myself there. One step, and I would be outside. But I knew better than to expect that would stop the dance; I was meant to die, and I was no longer honored among my peers. Musa would follow and continue the fight with no risk to his reputation, because I was, well, me. Still, I wanted this to be a true dance at least in my own mind, so that if I died, or if I won, no one could accuse me of cheating.

Well, they could. But *I'd* know better.

Musa brought more weight to bear, trying to push me beyond the line Alric had drawn. I dug in one foot and stopped the motion with a braced leg, then trapped his blade, held it, let him have a taste of my own weight as I pushed against him. Back, back, and back.

We were now once more in the very center of the circle. I yanked my blade free as Musa cursed, and slashed beneath his. Tip kissed flesh. A thin line of blood sprang up against the skin above his left knee.

My turn for offense, his to defend. And he did so admirably, blocking my blows as I had blocked his. When we broke and backed away panting, considering other methods to find a way through respective guards, we circled like wary street cats on the stalk, waiting for the most opportune moment to attack.

The first series of engagements was completed; neither of us had won. In Julah, Khashi had been dead by now. In fights too many to count, I had won by now. I suspected it had been the same for Musa.

Usually, the first moments of any match are spent testing the opponent's skill. A sword-dance is, in most cases, a *dance*, an exhibition of ability and artistry in pursuit of victory. But there were certainly dances where defeating the opponent was all that mattered, not how it looked. Musa and I had both chosen the latter, hoping to surprise the other, and neither of us had succeeded. Now the dance would shift into the testing phase as we teased one another's skills and signature movements out into the daylight, hoping to create openings we might exploit.

I saw Musa's eyes flick down to my hands wrapped around Alric's leather-strapped grip. There was no hiding the missing fingers. He was likely somewhat surprised I had matched so well against him initially in view of the disability. I wasn't, but only because I had worked like hoolies to overcome the problem, and I knew what to expect of my grip. An opponent didn't.

Musa lunged. I met his blade with my own and realized at once what he meant to do. Instead of movements aimed at my body in hopes of breaking my guard, he now went for the sword itself. Whether he drew blood didn't matter; the point was to disarm me. And that he judged a simple enough matter. I wasn't so certain he was wrong.

There was no finesse, merely strength and tenacity. Musa banged at my blade again and again, smashing steel against steel. From above, from below; from either side. The angle he applied changed with every blow, so that I constantly had to alter my grip upon leather wrappings or risk having the weapon knocked out of my hands. Then Musa could kill me at his leisure. I was at a distinct disadvantage, since not only did I have to concentrate on hanging onto my sword, but I also had to remember to block any body blow he might attempt without warning.

Which in fact he *did* attempt, and indeed without warning; I managed to turn most of the impetus aside, but the point of his blade still nicked me along the ribs. It was no more noticeable a wound than the shallow slice I'd put in the flesh of his lower thigh. The most damage either of us had managed to inflict was to our wind; both of us were panting heavily, noisily sucking air to the bottom of our lungs.

Now I went at him. Musa blocked each blow, and with each block he threw in a slight twisting of his blade. It wasn't enough to place him in danger of losing contact with or control of the steel, which would give the advantage to me, but it did continue forcing me to shift my grip each time. At some point he expected my mutilated hands to betray me. It wouldn't require much; merely a subtle change in pressure on the hilt, a weakening of my grip, that he could exploit.

The rhythm of the dance had changed. We no longer held our places in the center of the circle or kept ourselves to one specific area a step or two away from that center point; now we used the entire circle. We smashed steel against steel; hammered at one another; locked up blades and quillons; spun, ducked, or leaped away, using the time apart to recover breath. Sweat ran down my face, tickled along my ribs and spine. Musa's dark hair dripped as he shook it back, sending droplets flying. Bare feet had scuffed the neatly raked sand into an ocean of foot-formed hummocks. I didn't doubt we'd blotted out in places the line Alric had drawn, but it didn't matter. Everyone knew where the boundary lay.

Musa's strategy was sound. The stumps of my fingers ached, and the edges of my palms felt abraded from the continuous movement of flesh against leather wrappings. So far the specialized strength training of my forearms had aided me, and what I'd learned from the fight against Khashi, but Musa was clever enough to find a way around such things. All it required was time.

I was aware the sun had moved in the sky. My body told me we had been at this longer than likely anyone had expected, including Musa and me. But Umir ought to be happy.

We stood at opposite edges of the circle, facing one another. Chests heaved, throats spasmed, breath ran ragged. A half-smile twitched briefly at his mouth. I saw it, met it with raised brows. In that moment we acknowledged one another as something more than mere opponents. We were also equals. He likely had never met one since attaining this level of skill, unless he'd faced Abbu. I didn't doubt Abbu could defeat him; though acknowledging that meant admitting the possibility that Abbu was better than I. We neither of us knew, having never finished a dance.

Then Musa came at me, running, and the moment was banished. My sword met his, screeching. Teeth bared, he jerked his sword back and swung it down and under, going for my legs. I dropped to one knee, trapped his sword, pushed it up, then shoved him back with the power of my parry.

Musa staggered backward, retaining his balance with effort. He had expected to have me with that maneuver. Now he was angry. Equality no longer mattered.

"Old man," he said, "I will outlast you!"

Possibly he could. But I merely got up from the sand, laughing, and gestured him to come ahead.

He did. And in that moment I was aware of the vision I'd experienced in my room before the dance: me free of the stone spire to soar over the valley, to look down upon the man who met the woman in the circle. The vision overlay reality as Musa came on. I saw him, and I saw myself as the man in the circle in the Stone Forest, facing Del. The man with four fingers in place of three.

The priest-mages had taught me discipline was the key.

And conviction.

That the choice, the power, was mine. To make, and to use.

Something in me broke loose, answering. It—no, *I*—was swept up and up, high overhead, looking down upon the circle as I had before. Looking down upon a man, down upon myself, as I had before, and my opponent. But this time, in this circle, the opponent was not Del.

Two men, one young, one older, met within three circles: one of smooth, white-painted adobe; the second a blade-thin etching in white sand; and the third, the circle drawn in their own minds.

The younger man charged. The older met him, his smile a grimace, a rictus of effort. Muscles knotted beneath the browned flesh of both bodies, tendons stood up in ridges from neck to shoulder. Sweat bathed them, running like rivers in the hollows of straining flesh. Hands gripped hilts: four fingers, two thumbs on each.

On each.

The older welcomed the younger, challenging every fiber of his strength, every whisper of finesse, every skill and pattern he had ever learned. Challenging his belief in himself. Challenging his certainty of the older man's defeat. And the older challenged as well his own inner fear that he was unable because he was no longer whole. In the valley, in the circle, in the shadow of stone spires, he had been whole.

And was again.

"Now," the older man roared.

Back, and back, and back. Blow after blow after blow, the older drove the younger across the circle, forced him to stagger back, and back and back; shoved him over the line; smashed him down into the sand as the onlookers moved out of the way. The younger lay on his back, red-faced and gasping, sword blade in one hand feathered with sand. The older placed a callused foot upon the flat of the blade and stepped down. Hard.

Vision faded. Detachment dissipated. I blinked. Shook sweat away from my eyes. Was, abruptly, myself again, here in Umir's circle.

I was aware of silence. No one even breathed.

The tip of my own blade lingered at Musa's throat, pinning him with promise. I took my left hand off the grip and looked at it. Counted three fingers.

Three, and one stub.

There had been four on the hilt. I was certain of it. Four fingers and one thumb on each hand.

How in hoolies?—never mind. Time for that later.

I bent then, breathing hard, reaching down as I shifted my left foot. I pulled Musa's sword up from the sand, then flung it away hard to clang against the opposite wall. I flicked a glance out of the corner of my eye and saw what I had expected: Alric stood just behind Umir.

"Alric," I said between inhalations, "take that sword Umir's servant is holding."

The big Northerner did so and quietly moved forward to place it across Umir's throat. "Anything else?"

"Yes. Escort Umir into the house and have him give you a book."

Alric blinked. "A book?"

I smiled as I watched the color spill out of Umir's face. "It's called the *Book of Udre-Natha*. Umir places great value on it. I'm going to hold it hostage." I glanced briefly down at Musa, still lying beneath my sword. His breath was audible, chest heaving. "In the meantime, Umir will also have our horses readied— packed with food, water, grain and, of course, the book—and waiting for us in the front courtyard." Now I slid a glance over the assembled sword-dancers, swallowed, and raised my voice. "It was promised to me if I won: no one would challenge me inside Umir's domain. Right, Umir?" No answer. "Umir, if you ever expect to get your book back—"

"Yes," he said sharply. "I did agree. I will honor that agreement."

"And I think no one here will argue over the results of this dance." I glanced down. A thin line of blood trickled across Musa's neck, mingling with sweat. "Will they?"

Musa said nothing. Neither did anyone else.

I drew in a breath. "I made a choice that day when I stepped out of Sabra's circle and declared *elaii-ali-ma*. We all of us make choices. Some are good, some bad, some are right, some wrong. And we all pay the price. I accept that I am dishonored, that I have no place among you. I made the choice. And I make another now: to let this man live."

I backed away, taking my sword with me. Musa remained sprawled in the sand a moment longer, then hitched himself up onto his elbows.

"Why?" he rasped.

I smiled. "Some day, when you meet yourself in the circle— and you will, because we all do—you'll know."

I turned away. Musa's sword lay against the opposite wall, well out of reach. Though I meant what I'd said, I wasn't entirely stupid; you don't leave a loser's weapon close at hand.

Of course, I had reckoned without the insanity of irrational pride.

I heard him move and knew, even as I spun. Musa was up on his feet again, charging at me. Time slowed as he came: I saw the ripple of a tic in his cheek, the strain of tension reforming his facial muscles.

Oh no. No.

He came on. Despite the fact that he lacked a sword, and I did not.

Stop now. Save yourself . . .

But he did not. He gathered himself. Took that fatal leap. Committed himself. So I committed as well. I ran him through with my blade.

There was no triumph. I felt hollow. Empty. "You had the world," I told him, meaning it.

Musa's world—and his legs—collapsed. He knelt in the sand, choking on blood. I withdrew the blade sheathed in his chest. Blood ran down steel and pearled in white sand.

I was aware of movement. I looked up, lifting the sword; saw men stirring. But no one spoke to protest. Musa had effectively killed himself, though I had been the man holding the blade.

Alric, escorting our friendly host, came out of the house again. "Everything's ready."

I nodded. I cast a glance at the waiting sword-dancers. I couldn't help but smile at the irony. "I expect I'll see some of you again," I said, "but not for a few days or so. Until then, why not avail yourself of Umir's hospitality? Since none of you won his offer of lifetime employment, you might as well enjoy it while you can."

I heard at my feet, from the kneeling man, an expulsion of breath. Musa seemed to fold in upon himself, upper body collapsing upon the lower. The sweat-drenched hair fell forward as his head lolled upon his neck.

A waste. A waste of pure talent, barely matched skill. Banished by pride even greater, and thus presented to death—like dessert on a plate.

The body fell.

I turned then and walked away. Alric let go of Umir. We swapped swords with practiced lateral tosses, then ducked into the shadowed coolness of Umir's house.

"Nicely done," Alric commented.

"I thought so."

"Do you think they'll wait until you're out of Umir's domain?"

I led him through the front door into the courtyard. "Not on your life." Well. Not on mine, at any rate.

"Where are we going?" he asked.

I headed for the gelding, waiting patiently with his reins in the hands of one of Umir's grooms. A harness was attached to the pommel; I shoved the sword home in the sheath. "I am going to Julah. Aren't you going back to Lena and the girls?"

"Eventually. Right now I thought I'd ride with a friend who's in trouble."

"Big of you, Alric." I grabbed reins and swung up.

He grinned as he mounted his own horse. "I thought so."

I sank heels into the gelding. Together, at a gallop, the Northerner and I departed Umir's courtyard.

FIFTEEN

Some DISTANCE from Umir's house Alric and I fell into the walk-trot-lope combination that transported us as far and as fast as possible without ruining the horses. I discovered the white gelding, for all he was a ridiculous mount for the desert, was indeed a comfortable ride in all his gaits. Too bad he needed black paint and fringe to make it practical. And just now he lacked both after his sojourn at Umir's; fortunately it was nearing sundown as we approached the big oasis a day's ride from Julah.

The oasis was a popular stopover for travelers, and thus five different routes met here. There were palm trees aplenty, plus water plants around the edges of the small artesian spring that had, over time and with human help, been widened into a pool. Desert folk honor such places by treating oases as sanctuary. Animals and humans are watered, then everyone retreats to their own patch of soil and sand to pass the night without fear of attack. Since it was early summer, more people were on the roads. The oasis was crowded.

Alric and I dismounted, led the horses to the pool, let them drink enough to cool their throats, then pulled them away and commenced the struggle of man against thirsty horse. Trouble was, they'd get sick if they drank too much too fast when they were hot. Alric and I walked them a bit as dusk approached, then led them to water again. We filled canvas horse buckets, gulped a few mouthfuls for ourselves, then made our wandering way, trailing tired horses, through the cluster of tiny campsites to find our own, settling finally for a single unclaimed palm tree on the outskirts. There we unsaddled, spent some time rubbing the horses down, then pegged them out—and carried botas back to the pool to tend our own thirst in earnest.

Kneeling at the water's edge, I sluiced my head and face, then squirted the contents of a bota down my bare torso, front and back. Once I'd refilled the waterskin, I released a gusty exhalation of relief.

Alric, squatting nearby, grinned. "He will live?"

"He will live." I used a forearm to wipe water from my brow. "But he's getting too old for this."

The Northerner grunted. "Didn't look like it to me earlier today."

I inspected the thin crusted slice along one of my ribs, dismissed it as unimportant. "Trust me, I am."

Alric stoppered his bota and rose. I splashed another handful of water through damp, spiky hair, then pressed myself up from the ground. At a more decorous pace we strolled through the oasis, exchanging nods of greeting with other travelers. I smelled sausage and spiced mutton and journey-loaf baking on a flat rock. Danjacs and oxen called to various brethren, while horses snorted disdainfully down haughty noses. I thought of the molahs of Skandi and the steep, zig-zagging trail up the caldera face.

"So," Alric said, "Just what *was* all of that about?"

"All of what?"

"All of everything."

Back at our lone palm, we grained the horses sparingly and began to unpack our gear, unrolling and spreading blankets on the warm sand. "*Elaii-ali-ma.*"

"Oh, I heard about that." It didn't mean the same thing to him since he was a Northerner born and trained, but he understood what it was for me. "I mean, where have you been, what's

happened to you, how'd you lose your fingers and get those tattoos, and why did you want Umir's book?"

"Oh, *that* everything." I sighed, shoved saddle pouches under
one end of the blanket, stretched out with my head pillowed on
wool and leather as I chewed idly at dried cumfa. I'd already told
him briefly about Del's predicament and how I hoped to catch up
to her in Julah, supposing Nayyib had taken her there. "We've led
rather interesting lives for the past several months."

Alric flopped down on his blanket, thrusting a thick, blond-
furred forearm beneath his head. "I always like an entertaining
story before I go to sleep."

So I told him. Not everything. Nothing about magic, save to
explain that Umir's book supposedly contained all manner of
powerful spells. And nothing at all about my limited life expec-
tancy, or my dreams of a dead woman and a sword. But I didn't
need to. Even abbreviated, it was story enough for Alric.

When I finished, he lay in silence for a time. Then he grunted.
"I see I'm missing a great deal, being a staid married man with
four children."

"Four! Last time you had three."

"Lena's expecting again."

"Hoolies, Alric, you and Lena are worse than sandconeys. Do
you plan to populate the entire South?"

"I like children."

"Good thing!"

"Lena likes children."

"Even better, since she has to bear them."

He cast me a speculative glance. "Don't you ever plan to have
any?"

I cast him a look in return that informed him he was sandsick.
"You and Lena can make up for my lack."

Alric laughed. "Fair enough. It gives us an excuse for more."

He *was* sandsick. "In the morning," I said abruptly, "you head
back home. There are five roads out of here; they can track us this
far from Umir's, but then they'll have to split up to sort out where
I've gone."

It caught him off-guard. "I'd thought to go on to Julah and help you with Del."

I shook my head. "I appreciate it, Alric, but you've got three children and a fourth on the way. You don't need any part of my trouble. Go home to Lena." I might not want my own kids, but I didn't want to be responsible for depriving others of their father. "I'll be fine."

After a moment he agreed. "You certainly handled Musa easily enough."

"Hardly 'easily.' I'll feel it in the morning. Hoolies, I feel it now!"

"Musa doesn't."

I swore with feeling. "*That* was sheer waste. Talent like his doesn't come along very often."

"From what I hear, not since you did."

I made a noncommittal noise. Once I might have complimented him on his insight, but Del had impressed upon me that one needn't brag to establish one's credentials.

Or something like that.

Chewing tough cumfa, Alric observed, "Musa made the choice. He might have let it be."

But Musa was—*had been*—young, supremely talented, confident, and he could not believe I had beaten him. Not a man who had dishonored himself.

After a moment, Alric asked, "Will you answer a question?"

I couldn't figure out why he felt he had to ask permission. "Sure."

"What will you do if Delilah is dead?"

Oh. Now I knew why.

"Tiger?"

"I haven't thought about it."

My tone did not dissuade him from further inquiry. "Not ever?"

"No."

"Why not?"

I hitched myself up on an elbow and scowled at him. "What

kind of a conversation *is* this? How about I ask you if you've ever thought about what you'd do if Lena died?"

"I have. I do. Every time she goes into labor."

I blinked. It's not the sort of thing men speak about very often, if at all. "Well, I suppose that's a risk you have to take if you're going to have kids." Which was a pretty lame comment, but I didn't know what else to say. I flopped back down on my blanket. Since he'd brought it up— "So, what *would* you do if Lena died?"

"I have three daughters to care for. That is what I'd do."

"As a sword-dancer?"

"Oh, no. I would have to find another life. Something with no travel involved, so I would be there for my girls." He spoke so matter-of-factly about giving up the life he had always wanted. Maybe that's what happened when you got married and had kids. Gave things up. No wonder I didn't want any.

"As you have no children," Alric said, "what will you do if Del is dead?"

I really didn't want to walk this particular conversational road. Especially when I had no idea where or how she was. "Go on," I replied briefly.

"Doing what? You can't accept dances anymore."

"I own one-third of a cantina."

Alric turned to stare at me incredulously. "You'd spend the rest of your days serving liquor and wine-girls?"

"No," I replied crossly. "I mean I'd collect my share of profits. They'd be enough to live on even if I can't dance. But it doesn't really matter, because I have plans."

"What plans?"

"Alimat fell years ago. The shodo died. There hasn't been one since then—at least, not of his ability." I raised my hands into the air, inspecting them. "Even if I hadn't declared *elaii-ali-ma*, I'm a little bit hampered as a sword-dancer. So I thought I'd take a whack at being a shodo."

"You? A teacher?"

I scowled at him, lowering my hands. "Why does everyone always sound so surprised?"

Alric examined my expression. "Because you are not in general known for your patience, Tiger. And those who have a particularly rare gift for something—in your case, sword-dancing—often make the worst teachers. They can't teach what comes to them naturally and unbidden."

"How do you know I can't?"

"Tell me how you defeated Musa."

"I just—beat him."

"See?"

"Come on, Alric! Do you want me to give you a blow-by-blow description? You were there."

"How do you know precisely where a man will be in the circle, Tiger? How do you know what move he will make before *he* knows?" He grinned as I stared at him in surprise. "Yes. I have seen it in you. As I saw it on Staal-Ysta, in one of the sword-singers there. I asked him once. He couldn't tell me. He said he simply knew. He saw it in his head."

"Time just—slows." It was the first time I had ever spoken of it to anyone. It sounded ridiculous. And impossible.

Alric sighed. "You can't teach that, Tiger."

It stung. "You don't know. I might be able to."

The big Northerner snorted. Then he rolled over, displaying a broad back. Such faith he had in me.

But maybe he was right. Maybe I couldn't teach anyone anything. I just didn't know what else I might do.

I stared into the deepening sky, watching the stars emerge out of daylight into darkness. Firelight flickered at ground level, illuminating soil and sand, the dark, angular faces of Southron travelers. The aroma of mutton and sausage drifted our way. I heard quiet murmurings in several dialects, laughter, a child crying, and a faint, yearning melody sung softly by a woman.

Bascha, I said, *please don't be dead.*

* * *

I awoke to the sound of a baby screaming. At first I tried to block it out by pulling a corner of the blanket over my head, but it didn't help. Eventually I gave up, squinted out at the early morning sun, then pushed myself upright. Musa may have landed only one minor blow, but the dance alone had resulted in sore muscles.

I got up slowly, swearing quietly under my breath. By the time I was standing, I realized Alric was already up. In fact, he'd taken the horses off for watering. I was in the midst of stretching and attempting to lengthen my spine when he came back. He looked altogether too alert for this early.

Which reminded me. "How was it you managed to lose your dance?"

He led the horses back to the pickets. "Musa."

"You danced with Musa?"

"I was his fifth opponent, or maybe it was sixth. I lasted fractionally longer than the fourth or fifth." He tied off the horses, apportioned more grain. "It was clear from the first time he danced that he would likely win."

"So, I take it everyone lost money when I defeated him."

He grinned. "I would assume so."

"Too bad." I glanced around for something behind which I might shield my morning donation, finally settled on the palm tree just beyond the horses. "Did you?" I called.

"What, lose money? Hoolies, I didn't bother wagering."

"At all?"

"No. It would have been disloyal."

"Ah hah! Even *you* would have bet against me."

Alric was rolling up his blanket as I came back around the horses. "I didn't know where you'd been or what you'd been up to since the last time I'd seen you. I did mention to the others I thought they were giving you short shrift, but once Rafiq spouted off about the missing fingers and your bout with the sandtiger, no one wanted to listen."

I started packing up my own belongings. "You could have put coin on me for old times' sake."

"Lena expressly forbade me to wager."

I nodded sagely. "And you, of course, do everything Lena tells you. Or, in this case, *don't* do everything Lena tells you *not* to do."

"We would not be having this conversation if Del were here."

"Sure we would. She'd just be giving us the benefit of her own opinion."

"You've been together how long?"

I thought about it. "Almost four years."

"Ah. Then you're still a work in progress. Lena has had more than ten years to remake me."

"Del knows better than to try to remake me."

Whereupon Alric collapsed in paroxysms of laughter, drowning out even the screaming baby.

Eventually I noted, "I meant that as a joke."

The Northerner got up again and finished packing, but it was punctuated by occasional chuckles. After a while I ignored him and hauled pouches and saddle to the gelding, who peered at me out of watery blue eyes.

"What happened to the stud?" Alric asked.

I slipped into my harness and buckled it, reseating the sword I'd bought in Haziz. It would be another day ending in sunburn, since I still lacked a burnous. Fortunately I'm tanned enough that the burn is only mild. "He ran off when the sandtiger attacked. If I'm lucky, he wandered back after Rafiq and his friends hauled me away to Umir's. Otherwise, he might still be out there wandering around." Or more likely dead. But I didn't want to think about that any more than about the possibility of Del being dead. "He's a tough old son. He's likely bedded down in a good Julah livery about now." And Del, I hoped, was bedded down on a healer's cot.

"Are you sure you don't want company?"

"Go home to your wife, Alric. Tell bedtime stories of me to your little girls."

He grinned, reached out an arm. We clasped briefly. "Bring Del to Rusali when you have a chance. Lena and the girls would like to see her."

The gelding was saddled and packed. I mounted, settled my

aching body. Whatever Meteiera may have done to me, it hadn't made life painless. "I will."

Alric's expression was serious. "Tiger—I mean it."

I nodded. "I know. I will."

His smile was of brief duration, as if something nagged at him. "May the sun shine on your head."

"And yours," I returned, then headed the gelding south, away from crying babies.

SIXTEEN

I WENT THROUGH the cantina doorway bellowing for Fouad. It was late afternoon, and only a couple of men had yet wandered in for drinks. By sundown the place would begin to fill up. As I strode across the hard-packed floor to the plank bar, shouting for their host, they watched in mild curiosity. In Julah, in cantinas, pretty much anything was commonplace.

Fouad appeared from the hindmost regions of the cantina smoothing the front of his yellow burnous, as I dumped saddle-pouches on the bar. His eyebrows ran up into graying hair. "You're back."

"Where's Del?"

He blinked. "Isn't she with you?"

"Isn't she with *you?*"

"No."

I felt a stab of disquiet. "That kid came here, he said."

"Who, Nayyib?" Fouad nodded. "He did. He wanted the name of a good healer. He planned to take the healer to where you and the bascha were." His dark eyes widened. "Didn't he do it?"

Oh, hoolies. "He showed up," I said, "but there was no healer with him. Only three buffoons hired by Umir the Ruthless." I tapped impatiently on the plank, understanding now that Rafiq and his friends had never allowed Nayyib to find the healer, just made him lead them to me. "I figured he'd bring her here after-wards."

Fouad shook his head. "I haven't seen the bascha since she left with you, and I haven't seen the kid since he left with the sword-dancers."

I was thinking furiously. "Maybe he took her to the healer you recommended. How do I find him?"

"No, Oshet stopped by earier today for ale. He said he has no new patients." He eyed me, clearly reluctant. "Forgive me, but if she was that badly injured, it's possible—"

I cut him off. "She's not dead." Then I swore feelingly, won-dering if Nayyib had brought her back to Julah but avoided Fou-ad's, since his last visit had ended badly. Or maybe Del was sick enough that he'd felt it best to remain at the lean-to and not risk moving her. But it made no sense that he wouldn't take her to the healer Fouad recommended. I had a hunt ahead of me.

"She might be elsewhere in town," he suggested, following my thought. "Maybe with another healer. Do you want me to ask around?"

"If Nayyib's avoiding you, you won't find him."

Fouad scoffed. "This is my town."

"He doesn't strike me as stupid."

"It's difficult to hide with a sick Northern woman."

Very true; unless she *was* dead, and he was on his own.

I dismissed the thought instantly, annoyed I'd succumbed to it. "Ask around," I said. "The sooner there's an answer the hap-pier I'll be. I'll spend the night at the inn just up the street. If I don't hear anything by morning, I'll head out."

"Stay here," Fouad offered.

"In a cantina?"

He laughed. "You used to stay here all the time."

"Not in an empty bed." I hadn't stayed in a cantina since hooking up with Del. Before then, such places had been frequent lodgings.

"*That* could be remedied," Fouad asserted. But his humor died away. "One of my girls left to marry, and there is an extra room.

It's small, but it claims a bed, a tiny table. You do own one-third of the place, now."

"Fine. Can you have one of your boys take my horse to the livery? I've got all my belongings off him."

Fouad looked dubious. "No one likes handling the stud."

"I don't have the stud. It's the white gelding tied outdoors." I sighed, running a hand impatiently through hair that was just beginning to regain some of its wave. "Food and drink would be welcome. And a burnous."

"I'll bring a meal out myself."

"No. To the room. I'm going to lay low."

Fouad gestured. "Back through the curtain, down the hallway, last door on the left."

As I picked up the saddlepouches I didn't remind him that I knew the layout from earlier days. I just nodded and went.

The room was indeed small. Smaller, in fact, than I remembered. But it did have the bed to recommend it, plus the tiny table next to it just inside the curtained doorway. I dumped the pouches next to the bed, then unsheathed the sword and leaned it against the bedframe. I shed the harness next. Sure enough, after two days with no burnous, I had paler stripes standing out against the copper-brown of my skin. I looked as though I were wearing the harness even when I wasn't. Leather had rubbed against the slice along my rib, but the annoyance was minimal when weighed against the rest of my body.

My smile was twisted. Nihkolara had said new scars would replace the old ones lifted from me by the mages. It looked as though I was on my way to starting a second collection.

The whisper of a step sounded beyond the privacy curtain. I caught up the sword and leveled it just as the fabric was pulled aside. Silk, Fouad's wine-girl, bearing a tray and carrying a burnous draped over one arm, stopped dead.

I gestured her in, smiling ruefully. "We're beginning to make this a habit."

This time she wasn't swathed in cloth or trying to hide her

face as she bore me a warning. She wore filmy gold-dyed gauze and a sash-belt of crimson tassels riding low on her hips that accentuated her Southron coloring and lush body. She accepted my invitation, set the tray on the table, then put the burnous on the bed. Fouad is a man who likes color; the gauze was a deep bluish-purple. Bright red in Skandi, now purple here. Whatever happened to subtlety?

Silk was gazing at me, black wings of hair hanging loosely beside her face.

"Thank you," I said feelingly, and set down the sword again. Fouad had, of course, included aqivi along with food. For just a moment, though, I thought longingly of Umir's excellent meals.

"You are alone?" Silk asked.

I nodded, realizing Fouad probably had said nothing of the circumstances. I sat down on the edge of the bed and dove into mutton stew in a bowl carved of hard brown bread.

"Will you be wanting company tonight?"

It stopped me cold. I looked at her over the spoonful of stew halfway through my mouth.

"Ah," she said, and the single word contained a multitude of emotions.

"Wait," I said as she turned to go. "Silk . . ." But I wasn't sure what I'd meant to say.

Her smile was sad. "It's the Northern bascha."

I nodded.

Her mouth twisted faintly. "All those years . . . we used to say you would never settle on one woman. But inwardly we all dreamed it might be one of us." She gestured with one square hand. "Oh, I know—it wouldn't be with a wine-girl. But even women like us have dreams, Tiger."

I felt vastly uncomfortable. "I don't know what to say."

"Then say nothing. Know only that you were—and always will be—special to me."

I groped for comforting words. I'd never been very good at them. "There will be someone for you, Silk. Didn't Fouad say one of the girls just left to get married?"

She nodded solemnly. "But she was much younger than I, and not so coarse."

The best answer was suddenly a simple matter of speaking the truth. "If you were coarse," I told her, "I would never have shared your bed."

After a moment, she said, "Thank you for that."

"I meant it."

She nodded and turned to go.

"Silk!" I stabbed the spoon back into stew and stood up. It took a single pace for me to reach the doorway, and the woman.

She wouldn't look at me. I cupped her jaw, lifted her face, brushed away the tears with my thumbs. Then I bent and kissed her gently.

No passion. No promise. She knew what it was. She knew what it meant. But still she twined arms around my neck and clung. My hands rested lightly on her hips. She smelled, as always, of wine and ale, and the faint undertang of the musky scent she wore.

Silk broke the kiss even as I did. She raised her hands to my face, fingers scraping against stubble. She traced out the sandtiger scars. "Be careful," she whispered, and the curtain billowed behind her as she left.

No message came with news of Del's whereabouts in Julah or that anyone had sighted Nayyib. Since I wasn't sitting out front watching the world go by with liquor at my elbow, for a long while I paced the tiny room, fighting back a growing feeling of impatience coupled with desperation. Finally my body explained that it was tired even if my mind was not. I sat down on the bed for a while, spine propped against the adobe wall with my legs stretched out, and tried to invent logical reasons for Del's absence.

It was entirely possible that she was still at the lean-to. Except that it had been twelve days or more since Rafiq and his friends had hauled me off to Umir's, and she ought to have recovered enough to be moved to Julah. Even if the stud hadn't returned, the kid had a horse. He could easily have fashioned a litter using the limbs and canvas from the lean-to and brought her to a healer.

They just kept going around and around in my head, all the possibilities. And the thoughts I didn't want to think. I finally scooted down to lie on the bed, staring blankly at the wood-and-mud ceiling. Alric's questions kept sifting to the forefront of my mind no matter how much I tried to ignore them. I cursed myself for it, cursed Alric, cursed Nayyib, cursed Rafiq, Umir, Musa, and the sandtiger who had attacked her.

What *would* I do if I were alone in the world again?

More than two years before when I had left Staal-Ysta, believing Del would die from the travesty I had made of her abdomen with my newly keyed *jivatma*, I had focused on the task of tracking down the hounds of hoolies and their master, to save the village of Ysaa-den. It had given me purpose. It had given me the chance to think about something other than Del, for fractions of moments.

There was, now, nothing else to think about.

I scrubbed at my stubbled face, stretching it out of shape. Then growled long and hard into my hands, needing to bleed off the tension. Finally I took the sword from beside the bed, set it on the bed between me and the wall, and closed my eyes. I did not expect to sleep. But my body had other ideas.

I dreamed of Del, which was much improvement over the skeleton in the desert and the sword I was supposed to "take up." I dreamed of Del in all her many guises, sparing no truths of her temperament. She could be cold and hard, faceted like Punja crystal, capable of killing at a moment's notice. She could be sharp-tongued and short-tempered, and there were times her words wounded. But she could also be a soft touch when it came to baby animals and human children, ruthlessly fierce in her tenderness; and, despite a poor beginning among borjuni, passionate in bed. She was woman enough to drive me mad on occasion, because women did that to men; but she also took my breath away with the power of her pride and strength of will.

Silk had said it *for* me as much as to me: I had never believed it likely I would settle on one woman. Unlike Alric, I wasn't made for a wife and children. I wanted no ties. Nearly two decades as a Salset chula had taught me never to be owned by anyone again; and what was a husband but a man owned by his wife?

Even Alric admitted Lena forbade him things. Who needs that?

And then Delilah arrived in my life, as driven as I to prove herself, if for different reasons, and having no more interest in putting down roots than I did. Except for an enforced stay on Skandi and then time spent on the island off Haziz to regain fitness, we had never stopped moving.

A sudden thought occurred: Now I was proposing to rebuild Alimat and take on students. Which would require me to stay put.

No wonder everyone thought I was sandsick!

I roused from sleep long enough to mutter something mostly incoherent about old men growing soft, then slid down again into the abyss.

Where the bones and the sword waited.

This time the skeleton wears flesh, and a face. It is Del, gazing at me out of empty sockets. A hand reaches, gestures. There, she seems to say, though her mouth does not move. There. Take up the sword.

It lies just out of her reach, as if flung down or lost in battle. It is more than a sword, I see, but jivatma, fashioned in the North of Northern rites. Yet it isn't Boreal. Isn't Del's sword.

It is mine. Samiel.

"There," she says, "take up the sword."

Sand drifts. Obscures the body. Carries flesh away. Bones remain. It isn't Del anymore but the other woman.

"Find me," she says. "Find—"

"—me," I finished, and realized I was awake.

The sword lay beside me, where I had placed it. Not Samiel, just the sword I'd bought in Haziz. It bore no runes, no Northern magic. Was nothing more than steel, with a leather-wrapped hilt.

In the darkness, I lifted the sword. Closed one hand around it. Felt again the pressure of four fingers.

Four, not three.

I closed my other hand around it, resting the pommel against my abdomen so that the blade bisected air. And again, four fingers.

After a moment I set the sword down beside me and inspected my hands. Felt two stumps where little fingers had lived.

Find me, she had said. *Take up the sword.*

Find who? What sword?

"What in hoolies do you want?" I said. "And what am I supposed to do about it? If you want me to do something, you've got to give me more to go on!"

Of course, then I felt utterly absurd for talking aloud to a dream. But I was getting more than a little tired of obscurity. I've always been a vivid dreamer, but this was new. And already old.

I considered the situation. I had fully intended to go to the fallen chimney formation to search for Samiel. Del and I were on our way there when the sandtiger had attacked. So if I was heading there anyhow, why would the dreams seem to be commanding me this way and that, like a recalcitrant child? And what did the dead woman have to do with any of it? There had been no one but Del and me in the chimney when Chosa Dei met Shaka Obre for the final time. We'd escaped. No one had been killed. What did my *jivatma* have to do with the skeleton?

I sat up, planting my feet on the floor. Out of sorts, I scrubbed at mussed hair. I was bone-tired still, since sleep had brought me no rest. Finally I lighted the candle on the table, then bent down to dig through saddlepouches. I found Umir's book and propped it on my lap as close to candlelight as possible.

It was a plain, leather-bound book. No inset gemstones, gold or silver scrollwork, no burned-in knotwork designs that might set it apart from other books. I knew it was expensive; *all* books are expensive and owned only by the wealthy. But it didn't look particularly special. The hinges and latch were made of tarnished copper, and time-darkened gut threaded the pages onto the spine. I wondered briefly if it was locked against me, but the latch opened easily enough. I turned back the cover and saw the first page: fine sheepskin vellum, scraped to a clean, level sheet. The first letter on the page was bigger than the rest, much more ornate, painted in remarkable colors. The print itself was plain black ink.

I squinted at it in poor light. Before Meteiera, I hadn't been able to read anything other than maps, since mostly those were made up of symbols denoting roads, mountains, water, rather than words. Words I'd never been able to sort out in my head, but I'd never really tried. Del could read, so I'd relied on her on the few occasions it mattered. Mostly, it didn't. Then in ioSkandi, atop the spires, something had happened. Something had changed me. Not only could I read, but I comprehended languages I'd never before learned. I'd always had a few to hand—you just learn phrases over time—but now I knew them all. Fluently.

I could read Umir's book.

Something deep in my belly fluttered. It wasn't quite fear, nor was it excitement, nor, happily, was it nausea. Then I realized it was the first blossoming of anticipation.

The *Book of Udre-Natha* was, supposedly, a grimoire containing spells, incantations, summonings, and other magical oddments. Umir had fancied himself a practitioner of the arcane arts, and indeed I'd seen him do a few tricks. But I had spent most of my life denying magic existed, so I'd paid little enough attention to such things. In time, I'd rather uneasily come to the conclusion that it did indeed exist, and some could even summon and manipulate it to almost any degree—as apparently I had managed to do once or twice. But I didn't like to think about it.

Certainly not in connection with me.

I carefully turned the pages, noting colorful first letters throughout, and diagrams, drawings, even maps. The handwriting changed frequently, which suggested more than one man had written it. Though I could read the words, they spoke of many things unknown to me. It was a comprehension of parts without understanding the whole.

Then, paging through, I came across a brief scribbled note

saying something about some kinds of inborn magic coming to life late, residing unknown in the body and mind. That a man might live most of his life ignorant of his power until something kindled it. Then, suddenly beset by magic like a blind man given sight, he could react in one of several different ways. All of them seemed to entail some kind of danger to himself or to others.

One line in particular caught my eye. *Magic must be used*, it said, *as a boil must be lanced, lest it poison mind and body.*

Very familiar words. Sahdri had said something similar, as had Nihko.

I wondered, then, if my unwillingness to use whatever power I supposedly had was causing the dreams. If I had locked my magic away somehow, was it now seeping out around the edges? Would it burst free unexpectedly one day, threatening me and others?

Sahdri had said Skandic mages went mad from the magic, and that was why they exiled themselves to ioSkandi. That the discipline and devotions learned there in Meteiera could control the worst of the power when coupled with judicious use of it. But it was a finite period of control, because eventually every priest-mage merged with the gods. Of course, their idea of merging was actually self-murder, since they leaped off the spires. So I guess they really did go mad.

I'd never thought of magic as a *disease* before, but the book sure made it sound that way.

I read another line. *Magic manifests itself in uncounted ways no one may predict, depending on the individual. But it is known that overuse of the power may kill the man, and denial of it after manifestation may also kill him.*

Oh, joy. Either way I could die.

Ten years, Nihko had told me I had left. Possibly twelve. Not exactly what I call fair compensation for having magic in your blood.

Sighing, I closed the book, fastened it, set it on the table. Blew the candle out. Went back to bed.

This time I didn't dream.

SEVENTEEN

FOUAD STARED at me. He wore brilliant orange this morning. "Are you sandsick?"

My face got a little warm. "No."

"What in the names of all the gods *for?*"

"The horse," I muttered.

In his eyes I saw all manner of thought. Likely none of them had to do with the sanity of one particular sword-dancer. "You want Silk's tassels for your horse."

I stared down fixedly at the saddlepouches on the bar, picking at leather thongs. "Yes."

Amusement was replacing the incredulous note in his voice. "Are you sure this is not for yourself?"

I glared at him. "No, it's not for me!"

He cocked his head thoughtfully, examining me. "I don't know—you might look good with women's tassels hanging from your—"

"*Never mind!*"

"—neck," he finished, grinning.

"He has blue eyes," I explained.

Fouad reverted to surprise. "A blue-eyed horse? In the desert?"

"I know! I know! Just get the tassels, Fouad. And if you've got any charcoal and axle grease, I'll take that, too. Mixed."

"Also for your horse?"

This time I leveled my most threatening sandtiger's glare at him, and he flung his hands into the air. "All right! All right. I'll get charcoal and axle grease. Mixed."

I watched him turn away. "What about Silk's tassels?"

"Oh, you can get those yourself!"

"But—" But. He was gone.

Swearing inventive oaths having to do with Fouad's nether parts and the decreasing amount of time he would retain them, I swung the pouches over one shoulder and went back through the curtain. I didn't know which room was Silk's, which was probably intentional on Fouad's part. So at each curtained doorway I had to stop, ease the fabric aside and peer in, hoping I wouldn't awaken anyone. After a late night of entertaining various dusty and lusty males just in from the desert, Fouad's wine-girls wouldn't exactly enjoy me waking them up this early.

Fortune followed me until I found the correct room. As I eased aside the curtain, looking for a string of crimson tassels, I discovered the owner of the tassels in the midst of a morning stretch. She stood in the middle of her little room, nude, arching her back with arms outstretched. A long, luxurious, languorous stretch. When a woman does that with her back, other parts of her body shift forward.

I realized, as my face got warm, that once upon a time I wouldn't have been embarrassed. But somehow that had altered when I hooked up with Del. I guess maybe you don't have to get married for a woman to start changing your perspective about naked women who are not the woman who's doing the changing.

Not a happy thought, I reflected glumly.

Silk's eyes sprang open. I yanked my head back and shut the curtain hastily, then cursed myself for behaving like a green boy who'd never been with a woman.

"Tiger?"

She *had* seen me. My face warmed again. "Yes?"

Silk now stood at the doorway, curtain pulled around her body. The long black hair was a tangle spilling over her shoulders. Brows lifted, she waited for me to explain myself.

I floundered my way ahead. "I know this sounds strange . . . but could I buy your tassels?"

Black brows arched higher. "My tassels?"

I pointed self-consciously. "Those tassels. The red ones."

She glanced back over a naked shoulder, marked tassels, then looked at me. "For *her?*"

"Her?" It took me a moment, but I got there. "No, not for Del! For my horse." Which I realized, as soon as I said it, didn't sound particularly complimentary. At least Del was a human. I floundered on as quickly as possible. "He's white. And blue-eyed. He needs shielding from the sun."

Silk eyed me a long moment, her expression curiously blank. Then she dropped the curtain and padded naked to the table where the tassels lay. When she turned around again, swinging the tassels on one finger, there was no attempt to cover herself. In fact, she was doing her best to display everything. I cleared my throat, averted my eyes, and busied myself digging through pouches for coins.

She appeared in front of me, offering the tassels. "No charge."

I looked up, wished I hadn't. "Why no charge?"

"Because I will have my payment over and over again," she explained sweetly, "each time I imagine you telling your Northern bascha that you got these tassels from me. And what I was wearing *when* you got them."

Hoolies. Women!

I muttered thanks through gritted teeth, grabbed the tassels out of her hand, and got myself back to the front room as quickly as possible. Fouad, straight-faced, handed me a small pot of grease mixed with charcoal.

In a purple burnous, carrying a pot of black greasepaint and dangling crimson tassels, I made my way from the cantina with what dignity I could muster.

The white gelding peered at me out of sorrowful—and watery— blue eyes. He was bridled, saddled, and packed. Nothing left to do save for two final touches.

"I'm sorry," I told him, "but I have to do this."

He blinked lids edged with long white lashes. I stuck two fingers into the pot Fouad had given me, made a face denoting disgust, then began to glop on the first black circle.

"I've seen dogs like this," I said. "White dogs with black patches. But they were *born* that way. They don't have humans painting the patches on."

The gelding dipped his head briefly and snorted.

"I don't blame you," I agreed. "I'd protest, too. You look like a buffoon." I moved to the second eye. "It's not your fault. I don't mean to offend you. But you must admit this is not exactly how a self-respecting horse is supposed to look."

He extended his nose and whuffled noisily.

I filled in the last bit of white hair, stoppered the little pot and stuck it in one of the pouches. I wiped off as much of the gunk from my fingers as I could on burlap grain sacking, then heaved a huge sigh and picked up the tassels. "It gets worse," I informed the gelding.

I had considered trading him in for a darker horse, but I decided against it for two reasons. First, he had truly smooth gaits and Del, wounded, might need them; second, he was Del's pick for a mount. I'd learned from experience not to discard any number of items she'd selected for whatever reason, even if I considered them worthless, because she always eventually found a use for them. (Or said she would.) Even if it meant packing them along for months at a time, taking up space. In her own way, Del was as much a collector of unique things as Umir, except she at least didn't collect humans.

Unless you count the men who lose all control of their brains at first sight of her. We'd probably have a goodly collection trailing along after us, annoying the hoolies out of me, if I didn't run them off.

So I kept the gelding. Who stood very still and obliging as I looped the string of tassels from ear to ear, tucking the ends under the browband of the headstall.

I stepped back and appraised him. Now he had two black

patches around blue eyes and an ear-to-ear loop of brilliant red tassels dangling down his face. I gazed at him a long moment perched somewhat painfully between outright laughter and stoic resignation, then with great sympathy patted his nose. "Don't worry—we're leaving town the back way."

It was still early as we rode out of Julah, and I was certain that by taking the shorter route through Vashi territory I could cut a fair amount of time off the journey. If all went well, I would see Del before sundown. So I looked for and finally found the almost nonexistent wagon ruts cutting off from the main road into town, reflected I'd better make speed now while the footing was decent, and asked the gelding to once again resume the walk-trot-lope routine. Tassels swung and bobbled.

Del and I had been in no hurry before. Now I was. By asking more of the gelding when the footing was decent and letting him drop into a ground-eating long-walk at other times, in good time I located the spot where Oziri and his three warriors had appeared. Here the footing was rocky, and I couldn't in good conscience ask the gelding to do more than walk at a slower pace. I'd watered him twice already, and myself, but still felt the warmth of the sun. Within a matter of weeks it would be high summer.

I bypassed the detour to the clearing where Del and I had gotten drunk on Vashni liquor, and found the dry streambed. I dropped down into it, following the left bank. Eventually I came across the leather bag I'd dropped off the stud in an effort to evade the rank stench of spoiling sandtiger meat. The bag had been chewed and clawed open. Someone—or several someones—had enjoyed a good meal.

I exited there, trading sand for stone drifts, broken rock, and hardpan. Riding in, we hadn't concerned ourselves with marking our route. Now I depended only on my recollection of those things I'd considered landmarks, such as a tree with a twisted limb or a spill of rocks forming a shape that caught my eye. During that ride I'd been studying wagon ruts, but the land rose steadily toward the massive rock formations thrusting upward in the dis-

tance, and so long as I headed in that general direction, I knew
I'd find the plateau.

I followed my inner sense of direction with a pervasive sense
of increasing urgency. As Umir's prisoner, I'd been helpless; and
I'd learned years before that when I could do nothing, it was best
for mind and body to wait until opportunity presented itself. Now
I was free, and the only thing keeping me from finding Del was
the time it took me to reach her. I wanted to shorten that as
much as was humanly possible.

As the route began to slope up toward the plateau, I asked the
gelding's forbearance and put him into a long-trot; farther on, as
the trail steepened to wind up to the tree-edged top, I gave him
his head and asked for a lope. Hindquarters rounded as he dug
into the incline, grunting with the effort.

I leaned toward his neck, shifting weight forward. "Not so
far," I murmured. "Just a little farther." But I wasn't certain if it
was the gelding I encouraged or myself.

As he topped out with one gigantic bunching leap over the
lip of the plateau, I reined in, kicked free of my right stirrup and
dropped off even as the gelding slowed. I released the reins and
ran toward the lean-to.

"Del? Del!"

Nothing.

"*Del!*"

In sand and loose pebbles, I skidded to a halt by the lean-to.
It was empty. No blankets, no supplies, no tack. Just the crude
shelter and sandy floor.

Foreboding replaced urgency. I lifted my voice to a shout that
rang in the rocks. "Hey, *Nayyib!* It's me—Tiger! Where are you?"

Nothing.

Then I heard a snort and turned, but it was only Del's gelding.
He'd begun wandering over to the nearest tree, seeking grass. He
found it in the shade and began to graze, tangled vegetation
caught in the corners of his bitted mouth.

No one answered my calls. All I heard was the clank of bit
shanks as the gelding ripped grass out of the ground and chewed

noisily, the high, piercing cry of a hawk in the cloudless sky, and the faint, distant chittering of ground vermin, scolding one another.

Sweat ran down my temples. I closed my eyes, feeling the initial clench of panic in my belly. After a moment I banished it. I needed focus now, not emotion. Emotion makes you miss things.

With deliberation, I set about doing what Del had originally hired me to do years before: track someone. Only this time it was Delilah I sought, not her brother.

My examination of the campsite established there was no blood in the shelter or anywhere in the vicinity of the bluff's flat crown. There was no grave that I could find, in sand, under trees, under rocks; and the fire ring hadn't been used in days. Hoof prints crisscrossed one another, and all were old, nearly gone; likely from Nayyib's horse and the mounts Rafiq and his friends rode, not to mention Del's gelding and the stud. Breezes had scuffed the prints, and the tracks of insects and animals, but where there was soil, the impressions remained. There were piles of horse manure in several places, which could mean one of two things: two or more horses had stayed here long enough to leave deposits; or one horse had been moved from tree to tree for the grazing. The manure wasn't fresh; beyond that I couldn't tell. In the dry heat of the desert, horse droppings degraded quickly. I even found the sandtiger's skeleton, bones picked clean and scattered by scavengers. The skull was missing.

Consolation: with no grave anywhere in the area, it was unlikely Del had died here. And it made no sense for Nayyib to pack the body anywhere. In the desert, the dead were buried pretty much where they fell. This didn't mean Del was alive—she could have died along the way—but at least she wasn't dead *here*.

The campsite felt very empty. I shivered, squatted, inspected another hoofprint, then picked up a rock and bounced it in my hand, looking around yet again to see if I had missed anything obvious. "Bascha," I murmured, "where are you?"

The gelding shook his head, rattling bit shanks, then recommenced grazing. I mentally kicked myself out of my reverie and

SWORD-SWORN   177

went to tend him. My next plan was to see if I could find tracks
leading away from the area, and though I wanted to do it as soon
as possible, dealing with the gelding came first. You don't dare
lose your mount to neglect in the desert. A man afoot is a dead
man.

Once the gelding was haltered, unsaddled, cooled, and watered, I began a careful inspection of the edges of the campsite. It
did not appear that Nayyib had constructed a litter for Del, because the shelter was whole and I found no signs of poles being
dragged through the dust. It was possible she had recovered
enough to ride, either in the saddle with him behind, or vice
versa; it was also possible the stud had returned at some point.
But the only prints I found coming and going were those Del and
I had made riding up the bluff, those made by Nayyib, Rafiq, and
the others, and the tracks leading away as Rafiq took me to Umir's

Which left one answer.

I stopped looking at soil and the edges of the plateau. I looked
instead at the tumbled carpet of porous smokerock, quartz, and
shale spreading out from the huge boulders like a river of stone. I
squatted, searching for the tiniest detail that might tell a story.
And there I found one: chips knocked off of rock, showing raw,
unweathered stone; the hollowed bedding where rocks had been
seated until hooves knocked them loose; the tiny trails left by
insects and others fleeing the heat of the sun when their cover
was stripped away.

It was impossible to judge how many horses, or if one was
being ridden double, because the stones and their crevices held
too many secrets. But *a* horse had certainly gone this way.

So I played the game. If I were Nayyib, left with an injured
woman, I'd want to get her to help as soon as possible. But going
back to Julah the way I'd come could be dangerous; who knew
how many sword-dancers were out looking for the Sandtiger? And
it was no secret he traveled with a Northern woman; they'd recognize her immediately, assume she knew where their quarry had
gone, and question her regardless of her health. So I—Nayyib—
would head for Julah another way, attempting to leave no tracks.

I would take to the rocks and, since I now had safe passage thanks to the fingerbone necklet, cut through Vashni territory. I'd already done it once on the way to Julah, going for the healer. It was tougher footing for the horse and thus tougher on Del, but safer in the long run.

I went back to the gelding, grained him, watered him. Then collected bedding and saddlepouches. "We're staying the night," I told him. "We'll lose the light soon enough. First thing tomorrow morning, we're going hunting."

I dumped pouches at the shelter, then knelt down to spread my blanket. "Fat's going into the fire," I muttered. "My fat's going into the fire."

Because if anyone had seen Nayyib and Del on their way to Julah, likely it was Vashni. And I didn't have safe passage.

EIGHTEEN

I SLEPT POORLY, and awoke tired and unrefreshed. Despite circumstances that might provoke them, I hadn't dreamed at all—at least, that I could remember. And I usually remembered something of my dreams, even if they lacked the dramatics of dead women lecturing me about swords. I got up with stinging eyes that felt full of grit after a day spent squinting hard at the ground, and even more itchy stubble clothing my jaw. I needed both shave and bath. But I didn't suppose the Vashni would care.

The gelding, of course, also did not take note of such things, but he did suggest from across the way that I should move him to fresh grass, give him water, and portion out more grain. I did all of those things, among others; then I shoved dried cumfa down my gullet, swallowed a few gulps of water, tacked out and loaded the gelding. But this time I put the halter on over the bridle (and tassels), tied loose reins to saddle thongs, and paid out the lead-rope to a distance that would keep the gelding off my feet while still being close enough to manage.

"You get the day off," I told him, slinging a bota over my shoulder. "I'm afoot, too."

I led him to the place I'd found hoof scars in the rocks, inspected it a moment in hopes of seeing some kind of route, but there was nothing indicating such. All I could do was head out and hope that eventually, upon trading stone river for sand and soil, I'd locate Nayyib's tracks. They'd likely be obvious in softer ground: either a man on foot leading a horse; a horse carrying double and thus leaving much deeper prints; or two sets of hoof-prints—if the stud had come back.

I sighed. "Let's go, Snowball."

The footing was worse than bad. If it wasn't me tripping over stationary rocks or having loosely seated ones roll out from under my feet, it was the gelding. Hooves were not made for balancing atop rounded rocks, be they firmly seated against one another or treacherously loose; and my sandaled feet were no more appropriate. This was a place for boots, but I'd left mine somewhere along the way. Possibly in Haziz, if I remembered right. Foolish decision, even if I had been trying to save room in saddlepouches. I could not even imagine Nayyib leading a mounted horse carrying an injured woman through here, but I didn't have to; from time to time I found additional signs of their passage. I wondered if the kid's horse would be lame by the time he got through; I wondered if the gelding would be lame by the time *we* got through.

Slowly, carefully, I picked my way, trying to find some kind of route between stones and boulders easier on the gelding. He was a game horse, coming along willingly without hesitation. At some point I noticed the rocks were decreasing in size. Footing remained a challenge, but the way was less demanding. Better yet, more sand and soil was in evidence, which not only made it easier to walk, but held prints better. I was still on Nayyib's trail.

"Almost," I murmured to the gelding. "Not much farther."

And indeed, neither of us was required to go much farther at all, because even as I turned back to encourage the gelding, I heard other horses approaching. I counted them by sound: four. They clopped down through rocks, rolling and knocking them one against the other.

Finally. I turned to face the Vashni, purposely not drawing my sword. I simply waited, easing my body into a poised awareness that wasn't obvious.

The gelding, spying other horses, pealed out an ear-splitting whinny of greeting. I winced; even the Vashni seemed somewhat startled by their mounts' answering noise. So much for the momentousness of the meeting.

In one sweeping glance I noted each man. Oziri was not among them. I didn't have the slightest grasp of Vashni politics, nor did I know if these four warriors were even of the same band, so I didn't attempt to invoke his name as safe passage. Besides, Oziri was not my goal.

What I wanted to do was immediately demand if they had seen Del and if she were alive. But haste is not the best strategy among strangers, especially dangerous ones. Instead, using the gift I'd gained in Meteiera, I told them in their own language, succinctly and without flourish, that I was the jhihadi, and the jhihadi was looking for the Oracle's sister.

No more, no less.

Vashni are not a demonstrative race on the whole, but I saw a faint ripple of response in their dark faces. They said nothing aloud, yet eloquent fingers, as they examined me from a distance, spoke a language I did not; apparently what I'd gained was limited to oral tongues. But possibly it didn't matter, because my gut was certain they knew very well who, and where, Del was.

I just needed them to *tell* me.

I waited for confirmation. The clenching of my belly tightened. It was all I could do to breathe. I applied every shred of discipline learned atop the spires to hold my silence with no indication of concern.

There was no confirmation. They simply rode down through the rocks, took up positions in front, on either side, and behind me, and gestured at the the gelding. They closed in once I had mounted, making it clear with no speech that I was to go with them.

Time turned backward. Years before, Del and I had ridden into a Vashni village. Now, as then, word had been given before we arrived, so that by the time I entered the cluster of hyorts built in the foothills, men, women, and children had turned out to witness my arrival. They formed up in parallel lines facing one another, acting as a human gate into their home. I wondered how many people had ridden the double lines to their deaths.

The lines ended in the center of the village, a common area surrounded by oilcloth hyorts. I was escorted there, still hemmed in by the four warriors, and made to wait. More conversation with hand gestures ensued, even as the double lines of villagers threaded themselves into a single circle of Vashni, a human wall between my little party and the hyorts.

Quietly, carefully, I drew in a breath, held it a moment, released it. My right hand felt naked, empty of sword. But this was not, I knew, the time to unsheathe. I sat in silence atop the gelding, ostensibly relaxed.

Then, from somewhere beyond the village, I heard the ringing call of a stallion.

My head snapped around. I knew that voice. That arrogance.

Inwardly a small knot untied. A flutter of relief blossomed briefly in my belly. I grinned like a fool.

The grin dropped away as a voice called out. At once the circle of Vashni parted, allowing a warrior to step through. He approached, flanked by two other men, both younger, both bigger, both bearing traditional Vashni swords across their backs, though he was unarmed save for a knife. Black hair was threaded with gray, and a childhood disease had left his face pocked. The seam of an old scar nicked the corner of his right eye, extending to his ear. He wore an intricate bone pectoral across his bare chest.

I know a chieftain when I see one. But I was the jhihadi. Preordained by the Oracle himself, whom Vashni had hosted for years. I did not so much as incline my head.

The chieftain halted. He eyed me briefly, then made a rapid gesture. The four warriors surrounding me absented themselves. It left me atop the gelding in the center of the human circle, facing the chieftain on foot with his two bodyguards.

Inspiration was abrupt. I eased myself out of the saddle, aware of the sudden tension in the Vashni. Without hesitation or affectation—and without offering any manner of physical threat—I moved out in front of the gelding, ran a hand down his muzzle, and knelt on one knee. I pressed two fingers into the packed soil and sand and drew a line. Shallow at one end, deeper at the other, with a slight depression made by the heel of my hand. Then I unhooked the bota from my shoulder, unstoppered it, poured water in the shallow end of the line, and watched it trickle its way to the other. I placed the blade of grass I'd pulled from the gelding's bit into the filling depression. Smiling, I looked up and met the chieftain's eyes.

After a lengthy consideration, he inclined his head very slightly. Then he turned and walked back through the ring of villagers.

For an odd suspended moment I thought I was going to be left to fend for myself in the middle of the village. But then a warrior appeared at my elbow as another took the gelding's reins and led him away. I was escorted through the silent villagers to a hyort. There the warrior pulled the doorflap aside and gestured me to enter.

I ducked in, aware the flap was dropped behind me. The light was permitted entry only through the smoke hole in the narrow, peaked top of the hyort, concentrated in the middle of the car-peted dirt floor, but it was enough. I saw the blanket-covered pal-let and the woman upon it. That she slept was obvious even though her back was to me; I knew the skyward jut of shoulder, the curve of elevated hip, the doubling up of one knee intimately. Del had always stolen more than her share of the bed.

Relief was so tangible it sent a spasm through my body. I took one step, stopped, and just looked at her, letting the tension of fear, the tautness of anxiety, bleed slowly out of my body. The knot that was my spine untied itself.

I sat down then, next to the bed, close enough to touch her. I did not. I simply sat there, watching her breathe. Smiling. Happy—and whole—merely to be in her presence.

I'm here, bascha.

* * *

Del slept a long time, but I didn't care. I stretched out on my back, contemplated the peaked roof where the smoke hole opened to sky, and waited in patient contentment until she turned over onto her back, releasing a breathy sigh. I rolled onto hip and elbow and leaned upon my hand. Her eyes were still closed, but her breathing had changed. I marked the pale lashes against fair skin, the threading of bluish veins in her eyelids. She wore a burnous that hid most of her body, so I didn't know if she was still bandaged or not. She was too thin; that I could tell from the bones in her face.

Del's eyes opened. She blinked up at the smoke hole. Then, frowning, she turned her head and looked right at me.

My smile broadened. "Hey."

She gazed at me a moment. "Where in the hoolies have you been?"

I grinned. "Not a very good effort at sounding angry, bascha. Want to try again?"

An answering if drowsy smile curved her lips. She reached out a hand. "You won the dance."

I met her hand with my own. "I won the dance."

"Was it Abbu?"

"No, he wasn't there. Somebody named Musa. I didn't know him." I arched both brows. "I take it Nayyib told you what Umir planned?"

"He said Rafiq and the others were quite taken with the idea of facing you in a circle in order to execute you."

"I think *everybody* was quite taken with the idea of facing me in a circle in order to execute me. Fortunately, they forgot I wouldn't be so enamoured of it, myself."

"Are you hurt?"

"Nope."

Her eyebrows indicated subtle doubt. "Nothing?"

"One little cut along a rib." I traced it against my burnous. "Honest, bascha. You can see for yourself the next time I'm naked." I wiggled eyebrows at her suggestively, then let go of her hand to stroke a lock of hair out of her face, letting fingertips linger on the curve of her brow. "What about you?"

"I," she began, "may now rival the Sandtiger himself for the dramatic quality of my scars."

I winced. "I'm sorry, bascha."

"Why? Did you attack me?"

"No, but—"

" 'No, but' nothing," she said firmly. "The last thing I remember is going down beneath the sandtiger. That I'm alive and un-eaten likely indicates you killed him before he could kill me."

"Yes, but—"

"No 'yes, but,' either," Del declared. "Understood?"

I knew when to *appear* to surrender even if I disagreed. "Fine. Now give me details."

She caught my hand in hers again. Neither of us was the cling-ing sort, but we did like physical contact. "I will do very well, Tiger. The wounds are almost healed, thanks to you, Nayyib, and the Vashni healer. The poison is out of my body. Mostly I'm a little tired still, and bone-sore, but that will pass." She grimaced. "Except the healer keeps sending me to bed. I'm tired of naps."

Having years before been badly wounded and poisoned myself by a sandtiger, I knew very well *why* the healer kept sending her to bed.

"But we can go in the morning," Del said.

It caught me off-guard. "Go where?"

"After Nayyib."

"Where is he? And why do we have to go after him?"

"He's looking for you."

"He *left* you here?"

"When it became obvious I was fine, and when I insisted, yes. He did."

"You're not 'fine.' "

"Fine enough. Anyway, two days ago I sent him to look for you."

It astonished me. "You sent him to Umir's?"

"Yes."

"Why?" An idea occured, preposterous as it was. "Did you expect him to *rescue* me?"

Del contemplated my aggrieved expression in silence a moment. "Actually, *I* expected to rescue you. But I needed Neesha to scout for me first."

"Neesha?"

"Nayyib. Neesha is his call-name."

"You sent Nayyib-Neesha to scout for you, so you could come rescue me?"

"That was the plan," she confirmed gravely.

I was only half teasing. "You didn't think I could handle it on my own? A sword-dance? When I've been dancing for almost twenty-five years—which is likely longer than the kid you sent has been alive?"

"You've been dancing longer than *I've* been alive."

Which was a devastatingly effective way to remind me just how old I was, and how old she wasn't.

"Hoolies," I muttered.

Del was laughing. She carried my hand to her mouth, kissed the back of it, then rested it beneath hers against her chest.

I noted again how thin her face was, and there were shadows beneath her eyes. "Did you really think I'd lose?"

"'Only an idiot believes he may never be defeated,'" Del quoted. "You said that, once."

"Yes, but I didn't expect *you* to believe it. You're supposed to believe I can do anything."

"And so you have."

Well, so far. Sort of.

"Anyway," Del continued, "I think we should go after Nayyib."

"Why? He should have reached Umir's by now, and he'll know what happened. I won. I left. I'm here."

Del gazed at me. "What if *he* needs rescuing?"

This whole conversation was bizarre. "Why would he need rescuing? He's not worth anything."

"That's unfair!"

"To Umir," I elucidated. "He's not worth collecting. He's just a kid."

"He's twenty-three."

"That's a kid."

"*I'm* twenty-three, Tiger."

It shut me up, as she fully intended.

Del smiled, pleased to have won. "As for not being worth anything to Umir, of course he is. Neesha can tell Umir and any other interested parties where I am. Because they know wherever I am, you will eventually be."

"He could simply *not* tell them."

"Under torture?"

I scowled. "Why doesn't he just tell them you're dead? You almost were."

"Well, perhaps he will. But that doesn't mean he won't be tortured before he says it."

"Then he should have stayed here."

"He went looking for you. Isn't that worth something?"

"I don't know," I growled. "Depends on if you think *I'm* worth something."

"*Some*times."

I closed my eyes, gritted my teeth, rubbed a hand over my face.

"He saved my life, Tiger."

"I thought *I* saved your life."

"You, and Neesha, and the Vashni healer."

I squinted at her. "This isn't another of your cockamamie female ideas, is it? I mean, he's human, a man, not a cat or dog. He's not a stray."

"You were."

"*I* was?"

"Yes. All those years ago when the shodo accepted you for training. He took in a stray human and gave him a home."

I drew myself up. "*And* I repaid him by becoming not only his best student but the South's greatest sword-dancer . . ." I thrust an illustrative finger in the air. ". . . which is, I might add, a title very recently reaffirmed."

Del's tone was elaborately innocent. "I thought you said Abbu wasn't there."

I glowered. "We're not talking about Abbu. We're talking about the kid. And now you're telling me you want me to ride back into Umir's domain, even though there will be men looking to kill me?"

"But you just reaffirmed you're the South's greatest sword-dancer. Will anyone challenge that?"

"Yes!" I cried. "Likely all of them!"

"Well," she said thoughtfully, "it shouldn't be so bad."

"No?"

"Not when *I'm* with you."

I looked for laughter in her eyes. But Del does blandly expressionless better than I do.

Of course, I knew she was overlooking one very salient detail that would give me the victory: she was still recovering from a sandtiger attack. Del could no more get up and ride out of the Vashni camp tomorrow than the kid—Nayyib, Neesha, whatever—could beat me in a circle. By the time she could, the point would be moot. Because the kid likely wouldn't even be at Umir's anymore.

"All right," I said.

The abrupt capitulation startled her. "All right?"

"Yes. We'll go tomorrow."

Del nodded. "Good."

Or he might still be at Umir's, under duress, because Umir might possibly believe he was worth something to Del and me. In fact, Umir might even expect to trade the kid to us for the book I'd liberated.

A book of magic.

"Gahhhh," I muttered. "You and your strays."

Del shifted over on her pallet. "Lie down." She tugged at one arm. "Lie down and tell me all about the sword-dance."

"I won."

"Details, Tiger."

I lay down beside her on the edge of the pallet. Hips touched. I rearranged my left arm so my shoulder cradled her head. "What do you want to know?"

"How it was you reaffirmed that you are the South's greatest sword-dancer."

So I told her. It was nice that at least two of us believed it.

NINETEEN

D EL AND I were dinner guests
of the Vashni chieftain. Apparently he'd decided I was indeed the
jhihadi and wanted to pay honor. We were escorted to his big
hyort, given platters full of chunks of various kinds of meat—
including sandtiger, I didn't doubt—wild onions and herbs for
seasoning, tubers, and bread baked from nut flour. Not to mention
plenty of the fiery Vashni liquor. I drank sparingly, still felt the
effects, and did my best not to make a fool of myself. Del was
permitted to drink water as a nod to her recovery, and I caught
her watching me out of the corner of her eye. Apparently she
expected me to fall face-first into the modest fire in the center of
the chieftain's hyort. I was tempted to remind her *I* hadn't gotten
sick from it the last time, but decided the jhihadi wouldn't do
such a thing before a Vashni chieftain.

Later, maybe.

Afterward we were allowed to wander away from the encampment without interference or company. Clearly we were not pris-
oners. Or else they simply knew we wouldn't get far without
mounts, and the horses were closely guarded. But since I wasn't
trying to escape, it didn't matter. I simply walked with Del a short
distance, and sat down upon a boulder even as she did the same.

I stretched braced legs out, crossing them at ankles. Studied
her face sidelong. "Tired, bascha?"

She hitched a shoulder inconclusively.

I gazed out at the deepening dusk. Vashni fires set a subdued glow over the village that would become more obvious as darkness fell. A faint breeze teased at Del's hair. I rubbed at my own, feeling added length. Maybe the tattoos along my hairline were finally hidden.

I glanced at her, noting the gauntness of her features. "You know we can't go anywhere tomorrow."

She sighed, kicking a stone away with a sandaled foot. "I know. Not together. But *you* could."

I didn't even have to think about it. "I just spent two hard days tracking you down. I'm not going anywhere without you."

Del looked at me, clearly wanting to say something. Debated it. But held her silence.

"A few more days," I told her. "We're safe here. It's probably the best place we could be, without worrying about who might come looking for us." I wanted to say she needed more time. Knew better than to do it.

Her mouth was set in a grim, unhappy line. "I have been here too long already."

I shrugged, maintaining an excessively casual tone of voice. "You'll stay here as long as you need to."

"But Nayyib . . ." She let it trail off. A frown set lines between her eyes. "I wish you would go."

I was beginning to get exasperated with all this focus on Nayyib. "We don't know that Umir has him. I mean, how can you be sure the kid actually went looking for me?"

"He said he would."

"We don't know anything about him, bascha."

Del looked at me again, comprehending the implication. "He isn't a liar."

"Maybe not, but it doesn't change anything. You can't go anywhere until you're completely recovered, and I'm not going anywhere until then."

Del's left hand touched her right forearm, raising the hem of her burnous sleeve. Gently she fingered the scars I knew were there.

I tried again. "If Umir has him, he'll hold onto him until we're found. He won't harm him. Not as long as he thinks the kid is worth something."

"And if he doesn't?"

"Well, that was the chance Nayyib took. It's the chance we all take, riding into a situation we don't fully understand. I've done it. You've done it. If he's done it, he'll learn from it."

"Or die."

"Maybe." I shrugged. "Like I said, that's always a chance."

Del nodded. Her head was bowed, expression pensive.

She is a woman who pays her debts, and obviously she felt she owed Nayyib one. I didn't dispute it; he'd cared for her until she could travel and then brought her to safety. I owed him, too, for that. But I wasn't about to immediately go chasing off after a kid I didn't really know now that I'd found Del again; nor was I thrilled by the idea of taking myself back to Umir's domain quite so fast. It was possible some of the sword-dancers who'd witnessed my victory over Musa would decline to track me further, but I was certain some would. Not only for the honor of killing me, but Umir undoubtedly would pay generously to get his book back.

A book that apparently knew all about me.

I slid off the boulder and stood up, reaching for her. "Let's go back to the hyort. You need to rest."

Her head snapped up. "I'm tired of resting!"

"Come on, Del." I closed a hand on her wrist, tugged gently. "A few more days, that's all."

She stood. "Will you spar with me tomorrow?"

"Tomorrow? Well, maybe the day after."

"Tomorrow."

"You're not ready for that."

"Neither were you. I did it anyway."

Nothing would be gained by arguing with her. I didn't say yes, didn't say no. Just pulled her to me, slid an arm around her shoulders, and guided her back toward the hyorts.

"Most men," Del said abruptly, "detest weakness, sickness in a woman. They ignore it, trying to convince themselves she's fine. Or tell the woman there is nothing wrong, so they don't need to trouble themselves with thinking about it. With the responsibility."

I glanced at her, wondering where the complaint came from.

"Most men want nothing at all to do with a sick woman. Some of them even leave. Forever."

I grunted. "As I said, I just spent two days looking for you. Even knowing you were sick. Hoolies, the last time I saw you there was a chance you might not even live. Did I leave then?"

Inwardly I winced. Well, yes, I had left; but that hadn't been my fault.

"You are not what you were," Del said after a moment. "Not as you were when we first met in that cantina."

I had a vivid memory of that cantina, and that meeting. "Well, no."

"You were a Southron pig."

"So you've told me. Many times."

"Tiger—" She stopped walking. Stared up into my face as I turned to her. "You are not what you were."

I had the feeling that wasn't what she meant to say. But nothing more crowded her lips, even as I waited. Finally I cradled her head in my hands, bent close, said, "Neither are you," and kissed her gently on the forehead.

For a moment she leaned into me, clearly exhausted. I considered scooping her up and carrying her to the hyort, but that would play havoc with Del's dignity. She already felt uncomfortable enough about being tired and sick, judging by her comments; I knew better than to abet that belief. I prodded her onward with a hand placed in the center of her spine, and walked with her to the hyort.

There a warrior waited, standing quietly before the doorflap. He looked at me. "Oziri will see you."

It was the first mention I'd heard of the man we'd met a couple of weeks before. I exchanged a baffled glance with Del, who seemed to know no more than I did, then saw her brief nod of acceptance. She ducked into the hyort and dropped the doorflap.

I accompanied the warrior to another hyort some distance away, the entrance lighted by stave torches. There I was left, with no word spoken to the hyort's inhabitant. I paused a moment, aware of the call of nightbirds, the flickering of campfires, the low-pitched murmuring of conversations throughout the village. It was incredibly peaceful here. I turned my face up to the stars. The night skies were ablaze.

A hand pulled the doorflap aside. "Come in," Oziri said. "You have hidden long enough."

The Vashni ignored my startled demand for an explanation. He gestured me to a place on a woven rug covered by skins, fur side up, and took his own seat across from me. A small fire burned between us, dying from flames to coals. Herbs had been strewn across it; pungency stung my eyes. I squinted at him through the thin wisp of smoke. At the best of times, Vashni stank of grease, but all I could smell now was burning herbs.

Seated, I looked at Oziri. No one had mentioned him, and I hadn't asked, but here he was, and here I was. He wasn't chieftain or bodyguard, but obviously he was something more than warrior. A quick glance around the interior of the hyort showed me herbs hanging upside down, dried gourds, painted sticks, small clay pots stoppered with wax, a parade of tiny pottery bowls arranged in front of Oziri's crossed legs. I began to get a sick feeling in the pit of my belly. Vashni were unrelated to the Salset, the desert no-mads I'd grown up among, but the accoutrements, despite differ-ences, were eerily similar.

I looked at Oziri suspiciously. "You're a shukar."

Oziri smiled.

I drew in a breath, hoping I was wrong. "Among the Salset, the shukar doesn't hunt."

"Among the Vashni, he does. We are not a lazy people. Priests work also."

I wanted to wave away the thread of smoke drifting toward me but knew it would be rude. And I'd been trained from birth to respect, even fear, shukars. It had been years since I'd seen the old man who'd made my life a living hoolies, but I couldn't suppress a familiar apprehension.

I reminded myself I was a grown man now, no longer a helpless chula. The old shukar was dead. I cleared my throat and tried again. "You said I was hidden. Hidden from what?"

"Stillness," Oziri said simply.

I waited. When nothing more was forthcoming, I asked him what he meant.

"You are never still," Oziri replied. "Even if your body is quiet, your thoughts are not. They are tangled and sticky, like a broken spider web. Until you learn to be still, you will not find the answer."

"Answer to what?"

"Your dreams."

Apprehension increased. "What do you know about my dreams?"

Oziri took a pinch of something from one of the bowls and tossed it onto the fire with an eloquent gesture. Flames blazed briefly, then died away. Yet another scent threatened my lungs. It was all I could do not to cough.

"You must learn to be still," he told me.

"I'm kind of a busy man," I said. "You know—me being the jhihadi. There's much to think about. It's hard to find time to be still."

Another gesture, another pinch of herbs drifted onto the coals. Smoke rose. The back of my throat felt numb. This time I couldn't suppress a cough. I wanted very much to open the doorflap, or retreat outdoors altogether, but I had a feeling that among the Vashni, rudeness might be a death sentence.

Oziri smiled, handed me a bota.

I unstoppered it, smelled the sharp tang of Vashni liquor. Just what I needed. But I drank it to wash away the taste of the herbs, nodded my thanks, handed it back. Oziri drank as well, then set it aside.

"What—" I cleared my throat, swallowed down the tingle of another cough. "What exactly are the herbs for?"

"Stillness."

"So I can understand my dreams." I couldn't help it; I scowled at him. "What *is* it with you priests? Why do all of you speak so thrice-cursed obscurely? Can't you ever just say anything straight out? Don't you get sick of all this melodramatic babbling?"

"Of course," Oziri said, nodding, "but people tend not to listen to plain words. Stories, they hear. They remember. The way a warrior learns—and remembers—a lesson by experiencing pain."

It was true I recalled sword-dancing lessons more clearly when coupled with a thump on the head or a thwack on the shin. I'd just never thought of it in terms of priests before. "So, how is you know about my dreams?"

"It is not a difficult guess." Oziri's expression was ironic. "Everyone dreams."

"But why do *my* dreams matter?"

His dark brows rose slightly. "You're the jhihadi."

I gazed at him. "You don't really believe it, do you?"

"I do."

"Because the Oracle said so?"

"Because the Oracle said so when he had no tongue."

"But—there must have been some kind of logical explanation for that."

"He had no tongue," Oziri said plainly. "He could make sounds but no words. I examined his empty mouth, the mutilation. Yet when we brought him down from Beit al'Shahar, he could speak as clearly as you or I. He told us about the jhihadi. He told us a man would change the sand to grass." His smile was faint. "Have you not shown us how?"

He meant the water-filled line in the dirt, with greenery stuck in the end of it. I'd done it twice before various Vashni. "It's just an idea," I explained lamely. "Anyone could have come up with it. You take water from where it is, and put it where's it not. Things grow." I shrugged. "Nothing magical about that. *You* could have come up with it."

"But I am just a humble priest," Oziri said with a glint of amusement in his eyes.

"And I'm just a sword-dancer," I told him. "At least, I was. There is some objection to me using the term, now."

"Among other things." Oziri took up another pinch of herb, tossed it onto the coals with a wave of supple fingers. "The jhihadi is a man of many parts. But he is not a god, and thus he is not omniscient. Therefore he must be taught."

Be taught what? I opened my mouth to tell him I didn't understand. Couldn't. Because no more was I seated across the fire from Oziri but had somehow come to be lying flat on my back, staring up at the smoke hole. The *closed* smoke hole. No wonder it was so thick inside the hyort.

Oziri's voice. "A man must learn to be still if he is to understand."

Understand what?

But I didn't ask it. Couldn't. My eyes closed abruptly. What little control of my body I retained drained away. I was conscious of the furs beneath me, the scent of herbs, the taste of liquor in my mouth.

It would be a simple matter for the Vashni to kill me. But he merely put something into one lax hand, closed the fingers over it, and bade me hold it.

Hard. Rough. Not heavy. Not large. It fit easily into the palm of my hand.

"Be still," Oziri said, "so you may hear it."

Hear what?

"Truth," the Vashni said.

I came back to myself with a jolt. For a minute I just lay there on the rug, staring up at the hyort's smoke hole, until I felt the hand insinuating itself behind my head and lifting it up. A bota was at my mouth.

"Drink," Del said. "Oziri said you would need to."

Del. *Del.* I wasn't in Oziri's hyort anymore. I sat bolt upright, saw the hyort we now shared revolve around me, cursed weakly, and slumped back down. I took a swallow because she insisted, discovered I was incredibly thirsty, and proceeded to suck most of the water out of the skin. Then I lay there on my back and hugged the flaccid bota against my chest, scowling up at the stars visible through the smoke hole as I tried to put my world back together.

"What happened?" Del asked.

I closed my eyes. Felt the residual burning from the herbs and smoke. "I have no idea."

"Don't you remember?"

"Only that Oziri kept dumping herbs onto the fire. I thought I was going to choke." I looked at her. "They brought me back here?"

Del nodded. "A while ago."

I worked myself up onto elbows, then upright. This time the hyort did not spin so rapidly. "Did Oziri say what they did?"

"He called it 'dream-walking,'" Del replied. "I'm not sure what it is, except that Oziri said you needed to learn it." She shrugged. "He asked me questions about what happened to you on Skandi."

"And you told him?"

"I didn't see why I shouldn't."

Well, Del didn't know the whole of it, either. Some things I couldn't bring myself to talk about, even with her. I squirted the last of the water into my mouth and tossed the bota aside. "I don't remember anything. Did he say I actually did whatever it is a dream-walker does?"

"No. Just that he expects to see you again tomorrow."

"What for?"

"I don't know, Tiger. I don't speak priest."

I glared at her. Del smiled back blandly. I closed my eyes again, tried to recall what had happened in Oziri's hyort. The back of my throat felt gritty. I cleared it, hacked, then began to cough in earnest. Del dug up another bota and gave it to me. After a few more swallows, the worst of the coughing faded.

"I don't see any sense in trying it again," I said hoarsely, "whatever *it* is."

"They are our hosts. It would be rude to refuse."

"And if he asked to cut off toes to match my fingers, would it be rude to refuse?"

Del, yawning, lay down on her pallet, dragging a thin blanket up over her shoulder. "It's hardly the same."

"The point is . . ."

After a moment, Del said, "Yes?"

Nothing came out of my mouth.

"Tiger?"

I toppled backward, landing on rugs. I felt the dribble of water across my chest, the weight of bota. Limbs spasmed.

Then Del was at my side. "Tiger?"

I couldn't speak. Hearing was fading.

Hands cupped the sides of my head. "*Tiger!*"

But I was gone.

TWENTY

ONCE AGAIN I came back to myself with someone pouring a drink down my throat, but this one was noxious. I choked, swallowed, choked some more. Then someone dragged me up into a sitting position, where I sputtered the dregs all over the front of my burnous. Fingers closed painfully on my jaw, holding my head still. I saw eyes peering into my own.

I wanted to ask who of the Vashni had four eyes in place of two, but then they merged, and I recognized the face. Oziri's. It was his hand clamped on my jaw, squeezing my flesh.

"Le'goo," I mumbled through the obstruction.

He let go. I worked my jaw, running my tongue around the inside of my mouth. No blood, though I felt teeth scores in flesh. "What was that for?"

Oziri ignored my question and asked one of his own. "What did you see?"

"See where?"

Del interrupted both of us. "Is he going to be all right?"

"What did you see?" Oziri repeated.

"*Is he going to be all right?*"

I answered both of them. "Hoolies, I don't know."

"Tiger—" Del began.

"Be silent!" Oziri commanded.

My tongue worked. So did my mouth. So, apparently, did everything. I frowned at him, because I could.

"Not you," he said more quietly. "Her."

Del's tone was the one you don't ignore, even if you don't know her. "I have a right to ask if he is well."

I put up a hand. "Stop. Wait. Both of you." I squinted a moment. "I feel all right. I think. What happened?"

Oziri's expression was solemn. "You dream-walked."

"I thought that was what you wanted me to do in your hyort."

"In my hyort, yes. This is not my hyort."

"I did it here? *Now?*"

"What did you see?" Oziri asked.

"I didn't see—oh. Wait. Maybe I did." I frowned, trying to dredge it up. "There's something, I think. A fragment. But—" I clamped my teeth together.

Oziri seemed to read my reluctance. His mouth hooked down in a brief, ironic smile. "This is why you must train yourself to be still. That way not only do you walk the dream, but you understand it. You recall it at need and allow it to guide you. Otherwise it's no different from what anyone dreams."

I glanced briefly at Del, who wore an expression of impatient self-restraint—she wasn't happy with Oziri—then looked at the Vashni. "I'm not sure I *want* it to be any different from what anyone dreams."

"Too late," he said dryly. "You are the jhihadi."

"Can I quit?" I asked hopefully.

He laughed. "But if you are no longer the jhihadi, then you are not a guest of my people. I would have to kill you."

"Ah. Well, then, never mind." I sighed. "So, I'm just supposed to remember what I dreamed?"

Oziri nodded. "No more, no less than any memory. Yes."

"And there's a message for me in it?"

"Not this one," he said. "This was merely the test, to see if you have the art. There is more, but I will explain that later." He gestured briefly. "Recall the walk."

To remember my dream did not seem a particularly dangerous challenge. I recalled portions of my dreams the day after on a regular basis, though the immediacy faded within a matter of hours, sometimes minutes. Some stray fragments remained with me for years and occasionally bubbled up into consciousness for no reason I could fathom, but I'd never purposely tried to recall them. It seemed a waste of time. But the explanation of dream-walking, which I didn't exactly fully understand, seemed to require *enforced* recollection.

Oziri spoke of stillness. Sahdri and his fellow priest-mages had spoken of discipline. One seemed very like the other.

I closed my eyes. Focused away from the hyort, going inside myself. I waited, felt the tumult of my thoughts and apprehensions—I hate anything that stinks of magic—and purposely suppressed them. In the circle, I could be still. I had learned to relax my body. Now I relaxed my mind, and found memory.

My eyes opened even as my left hand closed. I raised it. "I saw—death." I uncurled fingers. My palm was empty. "Here, in my hand. Death."

Oziri nodded. "What else?"

"A man. From Julah. He was searching for something." I frowned. Felt weight in my hand, though it remained empty. "You killed him."

"Not I."

"Vashni killed him."

"Yes."

"Because he trespassed."

"Yes."

"You kill everyone who trespasses."

No change in inflection. "Yes."

My hand snapped closed on air and flesh. "Bone." I could feel the details of it, the small oblong circle with slight protruberances. "Backbone."

"Yes," Oziri said.

I opened my hand. Stared into it. "He strayed off the road," I said. "He heard the scream of a coney being killed and thought

he might eat well, if he found it not long after it died. But he
found Vashni. A hunting party. The next scream was his own."
My hand was empty, but the memory was full. Fear. Pain. Ending.
I looked at Oziri. "You gave me a piece of his backbone."

Oziri smiled. "Yes."

Del's voice was harsh. "What have you done to him?"

"I? Nothing. This comes of himself. Here." The Vashni put
out a hand and tapped my chest. "The heart knows what he is."

"I'm glad something does," I said dryly. "Now, care to tell *me*
what's going on?"

"You remembered the dream-walk. I believed the walk itself
would happen in my hyort. We brought you back here when it
became obvious nothing would occur." Oziri shrugged. "I should
have expected it. You don't trust us."

I took a breath. Was frank. "Vashni are not known for their
courtesy toward strangers. Just ask the man whose backbone you
gave me."

Oziri was unoffended. "But he was neither the jhihadi nor the
Oracle's sister. He was a man, and a fool, and he paid the price
for it."

Del's voice verged delicately on accusation. "You kill everyone
who comes into what you perceive as Vashni territory."

"We do."

"But no one knows the borders of Vashni territory."

"They learn."

"Not if they're killed."

A smile twitched his mouth. "Others learn."

"You kill them even if they trespass by mistake?"

"Yes."

She considered that. Because I knew her mind, I saw the struggle to remain courteous, nonjudgmental. "It is a harsh penalty."

"It is a harsh land," Oziri replied. "We are a part of it. We
reflect it." His gesture encompassed her body. "You yourself were
attacked by a sandtiger. You know how harsh the land is."

I knew it, certainly, having grown up in the desert, but I
wasn't aware of another tribe quite so quick to kill as the Vashni.

Certainly other tribes killed people if they perceived a threat—I'd witnessed the Salset do it—but the Vashni did it even if no threat were offered.

And yet Del and I, Oracle's sister and jhihadi, were treated honorably. And Nayyib, apparently, because he served Del and wore the fingerbone necklet.

Oziri watched me think it through. Irony put light into his eyes. But he returned to the topic of dream-walking. "Here, in this hyort, you can be still. Because you trust the woman."

I glanced at Del, whose brows arched up.

"And the smoke was still in your body," Oziri explained.

"So, it's the herbs that do it?"

"The herbs assist," he answered with precision, "when one is new to the art. In time, you will be able to do it without such things. Just find the stillness, and it will come." He paused. "If you choose."

"This is a Vashni custom," I said. "I'm not Vashni."

"But you dream," he countered, "and your dreams trouble you. If you can walk them, you'll understand what it is you're to do."

Del and I asked it simultaneously. "*Do?*"

He smiled. "Listen," he said. "Find the stillness. Walk the dreams. They will tell you."

I glared. "You're being obscure again."

Oziri rose with his bota of noxious liquid. He glanced briefly at Del, then looked down at me. "They are *your* dreams," he said. "It's for you to find the meaning in obscurity."

I waited until the doorflap fell behind him. Then I flopped down on my back, grabbed the nearest waterskin, and dragged it over my face. I growled sheer frustration into leather.

After a moment Del lifted the bota to examine my expression. "Are you sure you don't want to leave tomorrow?"

I yanked the waterskin out of her hand and let it settle its gurgling weight over my face again. "Don't interfere." My words were muffled by leather. "I'm trying to smother myself."

"With a bota?"

"Why not?"

"I can think of better ways."

"Oh?"

She peeled the bota back, tipped it off my face. She studied me a moment. Then, as she leaned over my face, her mouth came down on mine.

When she was done, I reminded her that kiss or no kiss, I could still breathe.

She kissed me again. This time she also pinched my nose closed.

I ruined the moment—and the kiss—by laughing. Del removed her fingers, removed her mouth, and stared down into my face. Loose hair tickled my neck.

"Are you *truly* all right?" she asked.

I was still grinning. "I seem to be." I threaded fingers into silken hair. "It really was like a dream. Except it didn't feel like mine. It felt like—*his*. Or, rather, it felt like his life, and I was there. Watching." I frowned, stroking the ends of her hair across my mouth. "Except it was more vivid. I could smell, and taste, and feel, too. Usually I just see and hear in my dreams."

Del nodded. "Are you going to go to Oziri tomorrow?"

"*You* were the one who said it'd be rude to refuse."

"That was before you collapsed in a heap with your eyes rolled up in your head."

The image was perversely intriguing. "They did that?"

"They did."

I felt my eyelids. "Hmmm."

"Very dramatic," Del added. "I thought you might break out into prophecy at any moment."

"You did not," I said sternly. "Besides, that doesn't really happen. Only in stories."

Del shrugged. "Jamail apparently did it. That's why the Vashni called him the Oracle."

I gazed up at her. I didn't want to think about dream-walking or oracles or stillness anymore. I tugged her hair. "Come down here."

Del followed the pressure on her hair and stretched out next to me.

"Just how tired are you?" I asked.

She suppressed a smile. "Oh, very tired. Extremely tired. Excessively tired. Far too tired for what you have in mind."

I sighed very deeply. Extremely, excessively deeply. "And here I was hoping it might be *you* I dreamed about."

Her fingers were on my belt, working at the buckle. "If you walk anywhere," she said, "I'm going with you."

The belt fell away. I arched my back so she could pull it out from under me. It took but a moment to free myself of the damp burnous. Then I performed for her the identical service, stripping away folds of cloth.

I turned her under me, taking weight onto knees and elbows. "How tired was that again?"

Del's hand moved downward from my ribs. Closed. "You tell *me*."

True to my word—well, actually it was true to Del's expectations, because I didn't feel like opening a debate—I met her for a brief match the next morning. The last time we'd sparred was aboard ship on the way to Haziz, and it had been Del's task to challenge me enough to help me regain fitness and timing as I adapted to the lack of little fingers. This time it would be me leading her through the forms trying to improve *her* fitness.

She had, of course, not bothered to don her burnous. Her cream-color leather tunic showed the aftermath of her encounter with the sandtiger, but a Vashni woman had patched it and stitched up the rents as Del recovered. The new leather didn't match, being the pale yellow hue of foothills deer, but the tunic was whole again.

Del, however, wasn't. In exploring her body the night before I'd examined with fingers and mouth the scars she bore, but I'd seen none of them. I knew better than to react as she exited the hyort, sword in hand—I was already outside—but inwardly I quailed to see the damage. Her right forearm bore a knurled purplish lump of proud flesh around the puncture wound and a vivid ditch left by a canine tooth as she'd wrenched her arm free. At the point of her jaw a claw tip had nicked flesh clear to bone. There were other scars, I knew—those stretching from breast tops to collar bones; and the punctures and claw wounds, not to mention the cautery scar atop her left shoulder—but the tunic covered them.

I caught her eye, then tossed her the leather thong I'd bought with a smile from a Vashni woman repairing a hyort panel. Del caught it, suspended it in midair, noted the curving black claws. Between them, acting as spacers, were the lumpy red-gold beads formed of heartwood tree resin. She'd worn them strung as a necklet as I wore my claws; I'd stolen them earlier this morning, since the Vashni had taken the necklet off to treat her wounds.

"Welcome," I said, "to the elite group of people who've survived sandtiger attacks."

Del looked at me over the necklet. "How many are there in this elite group?"

"As far as I know, two."

She nodded, half-smiling, and hooked the necklet one-handed over her head. "Too long," she murmured. "I'll shorten it later." Then she lifted her sword and placed both hands around the grip. "Shall we dance?"

"Spar," I corrected.

Her jaw tightened. "Spar."

"Until I say to stop."

That did not please her. "You'll say to stop after one engagement."

"I will not. Three, maybe." I waved fingers at her in a come-here gesture. "We're too close to the fire ring. Let's go out into the common area."

"Here, then." Del tossed me her unsheathed blade, which I managed to catch without cutting off any vital parts—I scowled at her even as she smiled sunnily—and accompanied me out to the common as she worked at the knot in the leather thong.

By the time we reached the spot I'd selected, she'd shortened

the necklet and retied the knot. Then she flipped her braid behind her shoulder, gestured for the sword, and caught it deftly as
I tossed it. Well, that ability she hadn't lost.

More than two weeks before, I had been clawed and sick from
sandtiger poison, then unceremoniously hauled off to Umir's with
both hands tied at the wrists, and imprisoned in a small room out
of the sun and air. Such things should conspire to rob me of any
pretense to fitness and flexibility, but I'd spent my ten days of
imprisonment profitably in near-constant exercise accompanied
by good food and restful sleep. I had then met an excellent sword-
dancer in the circle, which had the effect of not only challenging
my body but my confidence. Aside from missing two fingers—
actually, *because* of missing two fingers—I was in the best condition I'd been in for years.

Del, on the other hand. . . . Inwardly I shook my head, even
as I pointed to the spot where I wanted her to stand. I took up my
own position, closed my hands on leather wrapping, nodded. She
came at me.

It is impossible to spar in silence. Steel brought against steel
has a characteristic sound; blade brought against blade is unmis-
takable. Before long we had gathered onlookers. I was too focused
on the match to listen to what they said, but many comments
were exchanged. I didn't doubt some of them had to do with a
man meeting a woman; Vashni women, who look every bit as
fierce as their men, do not avail themselves of the sword. No
women in the South did. Oracle's sister or no, once again Del was
opening eyes and minds to the concept that a woman too could
fight.

Probably everyone watching expected me to 'win.' But, as I've
said before, that's not what sparring is all about. Del and I worked
until the sweat ran down her flushed face, the breath was harsh in
her throat, and her forearms trembled. I let her make one more
foray against me, turned it back easily, then called a halt.

"Don't fall down," I told her cheerfully as she stood there
breathing hard, "or they'll think I'm punishing you unduly."

Del shot me a scowl.

"Not bad," I commented.

The scowl deepened.

"Go cool off," I ordered.

She wanted very badly to say something to me, but she hadn't the wind for it. Instead she turned, visibly collected herself, and stalked back through the ring of hyorts. Upon reaching ours, I did not doubt, she'd suck down water, then collapse. Or collapse, then suck down water. Once she could move again.

Actually, she'd gone longer than I had expected. It was sheer determination and stubbornness that carried her, but such things count, too, when it comes to survival.

After the physical exertion, the taste of Oziri's herbs was back in my throat. I hacked, leaned, spat. Heard onlookers discussing the origins of the scar carved into one set of ribs. I wanted badly to tell them Del had been the one to put it there so they'd understand she was indeed a legitimate sword-dancer, but I decided against it. Anything that demoted me from jhihadi could well end in my execution, if I believed Oziri's explanation that anyone else in Vashni territory was put to death. And I had no reason to disbelieve him. One had only to look at all the human bones hanging around the necks of men and women alike.

I turned to follow the departed Del, found a warrior standing in my path. "Oziri," he said merely.

Numerous refusals ran through my mind. All of them were discarded. Glumly, carrying a naked blade, I followed the warrior.

TWENTY-ONE

I DUCKED inside Oziri's hyort. "Do you mind if I check on Del?—oh, hoolies, not *this* again!" I waved herb smoke from my face. "I thought you said this wasn't necessary."

Oziri was once again seated on furs. The hyort, as before, was closed and stuffy. "It won't be necessary, eventually. It is now."

"You going to give me another bone?"

He tossed a pinch of herb on the coals with an eloquent gesture. "No. This time I want you to walk your own dream."

I squinted against the smoke. "You want me to dream while I'm awake?"

"Not to dream but to recall your dreams. In detail. That is the walk. A man with the art may summon them at any time, may return to them, so he may understand their message."

"And what happens if he doesn't wish to understand anything? If he just wants to go on about his life like everyone else, blessedly ignorant?"

"A man with the art can't ignore such things. There is no blessing in ignorance, only danger."

I eyed him warily. "Where are you going with this?"

Oziri sighed. "You have, I'm sure, been bitten by sandflies."

I blinked, wondering what that had to do with anything. "Anyone who lives in the desert has."

"And you recall the fierce itching that accompanies such bites."

Dryly I said, "Anyone who lives in the desert does."

"And if you were bitten but could not scratch?" Oziri smiled faintly. "It would be hoolies, as you call it."

An understatement. "So?"

"Consider dreams as sandflies, and walking them, understanding them, is the scratching of the itch. One or two sandfly bites, unscratched, are bearable, if annoying, but what of an infestation? Bite upon bite upon bite, until your flesh is swollen on the bones. Without relief. No scratch for the itch."

I grimaced, wanting to scratch simply because of the image he painted. "If you say so; I'm not going to argue with my host. But we haven't established that I have any art."

There was—almost—a scowl on Oziri's face. "Last night we established that indeed you have the art, when you reacted to the bone. Now you must learn to walk the dreams, to recall them at will, so you may understand them." He paused. "And scratch the itch."

"Uh-huh. And the sandflies are supposed to give me messages." I started to laugh, but then without warning something boiled up inside me, an abrupt and painful frustration so desperate, so powerful, it overwhelmed. I wanted to wheel around, tear the doorflap open, stride away from the hyort. I wanted to get Del, throw our belongings into pouches, saddle the horses and go. Just go. Forever. Away.

I wanted to run.

To *run*.

Oziri's eyes flickered. "I know."

Stunned, ashamed, angry, I guarded neither words nor tone. "You know nothing."

"I know," he repeated.

The anger separated itself from frustration. It was an alien kind of anger, shaped not of rage and therefore comprehensible but of a cold, quiet bitterness. "Do you have any idea," I began softly, with careful clarity, "how many people have told me I have

arts? Gifts? Powers? Have you any idea what it is to be told, again
and again, that if that art, or that power, is ignored, it could drive
me mad? Kill me on the spot? Shorten my lifespan?" I shook my
head, hand tightening on my sword as every muscle in my body
tensed. "I was nothing. I was a *slave*. How is it that strangers—
you, Sahdri, Nihko, others—can see something I can't feel? How
can you tell me I must do this thing, that thing, whatever thing
it may be, or the price will be too high to pay?"

He closed his eyes a moment.

"I'm just *a man*, Oziri! Nothing more. That's all I ever wanted
to be, when I was a slave. A man. And free. To go where I want,
be what I want. No arts. No gifts. No powers. No end-of-life-as-I-
know-it punishment if I don't—if I *can't*—measure up. Messiah?
—Hah. Mage?—I want nothing to do with magic, thank you.
And now dream-walker?" I shook my head vehemently. "No.
Never. I don't want it. And if that means you want to kill me
because I'm not what the Oracle prophesied, so be it. I'll meet
anyone in the circle you like. Because *that's* what I am. Just a man
with a little skill, a lot of training . . . and no need at all to
contend with arts and gifts and powers, be they Southron, Northern, Skandic, Vashni, or anything else." I shook my head again as
tension and anger, now vented, began to bleed away into weary
resignation. "This is *your* art, Oziri, this dream-walking. Not
mine."

After a moment he lowered his eyes and gazed into the coals.
His fingers twitched, as if he wished to take up herbs and toss
them into the fire. But he didn't. He simply sat there, expression
oddly vulnerable for a Vashni warrior, and after a moment his
mouth twisted as if he were in pain.

Then he met my eyes. "Will you trust me to lead you
through?"

The question astounded me. "I just *told* you—"

"Yes. And I understand; your truth is a hard one, even for a
priest. I have no intention of killing you; we accept what the Oracle prophesied—*wait*." He lifted a hand to belay my immediate
protest. "A man is welcome to his own beliefs, yes?"

It took effort to accede, but I dipped my head in a stiff nod.

"We have hosted the woman, the Oracle's sister; and the young man who brought her here. And now we have hosted you. I ask that the jhihadi repay us by allowing me to lead him through this dream-walk."

The ice of anger was gone; its bluntness remained. "But it doesn't mean anything. Not to me."

"Then you lose nothing but a portion of time, while I . . ." Oziri smiled ruefully. "Well, it means a great deal to me. I risk losing a portion of my reputation. The Vashni hold priests to be incapable of mistakes."

I couldn't help but mock. "Will they kill you for it and boil the flesh off your bones?"

"No."

I shrugged with deliberate exaggeration. "Then it's not so much of a risk after all, is it?"

"They will boil the flesh off my bones without giving me the mercy of death beforehand."

It banished all derision, all protests, precisely as he intended. It's hard to ridicule that kind of imagery when you know it isn't falsehood.

I still wanted to walk away. But his time cost more than mine. Finally I nodded. "Then let's get it done. What do you want me to do?"

"Be seated. Be at ease. Trust me to lead you through."

I grunted dubiously. "I can't promise either of the last two."

"Then achieve the first." Oziri paused. "And lay down your sword. It is hard for *me* to trust a man with a blade in his hand when he is the Sandtiger."

Once I would have been flattered. Now I just wanted to get it over with. I seated myself on the other side of the fire and set down the sword not far from my knee.

"Breathe," Oziri suggested. "I believe we have established you have *that* art."

I shot him a disgruntled look. He threw more herbs on the coals. I gritted my teeth and tried not to cough.

"Find your stillness."

That particular recommendation was really beginning to grate on me. I watched suspiciously as he cupped both hands and wafted smoke at me. Another pinch of herbs went on the fire. "All right," I muttered, and drew in a deep breath. "Now what?"

"What did you dream last night?"

Oddly enough, I couldn't remember. I'd slept very well after Del and I had made love, and no recollection tickled my memory. Maybe, after the dream-walking lesson, I was all dreamed out. "I'm not sure I did."

Oziri, saying nothing, took a generous amount of herbs from two bowls. He dumped them on the coals. A cloud of pungent smoke wreathed the air between us, then drifted unerringly into my face. It was nothing so much as a challenge to prove him wrong. To allow my childish obstinance to sentence him to death.

But I really couldn't remember that I'd dreamed. "Wait—" I began, then broke into a paroxysm of coughing, which succeeded in drawing even more smoke into my lungs. The world coalesced into a tiny pinpoint of existence, then burst into a vast array of fragmented awareness. I felt parts of my body, my mind breaking apart, spinning away. "*Wait*—"

Oziri laughed. "The gods are not gentle to unbelievers, especially those who repudiate their gifts."

I could barely see, could barely hang onto my senses. "You told me to trust you."

His eyes were like a dagger. His words opened my vitals. "I said I would see you safely through. I did not say it would be a painless journey."

I reached toward the sword. Then memory stirred. Stopped me.

Oziri was right: I *had* dreamed last night.

"I remember," I blurted, startled. "I—"

—*remember.*

And then forgot everything, including my name.

* * *

Del's face, when she dances—or even when she spars—wears one of two expressions: fierce determination or an oddly relaxed focus. The former comes from a true challenge, to prove herself and win; the latter from the knowledge that she *will* win, so the point is to refine her skill. Opponents and enemies have witnessed both. So have I.

But this time, for the first time, I saw fear.

We were yet again in the common area of the Vashni encampment, pretending a portion of it was a circle. After two more hard engagements Del stumbled back, regained her footing and balance, blocked my blow. Steel clashed. She was breathing hard. "Let's stop."

I repeated the series of maneuvers, pushing her harder. Waiting for her body to fail.

She blocked me again and again, frowning. "Stop."

I tried a new angle. Blades met, scraped, screeched.

Her teeth were bared in a brief rictus of sheer effort. The exhaustion was obvious, and oddly exhilarating. "—*stop*—"

Over the locked blades I looked into her widening eyes. I shook my head, on the verge of laughing joyously. "You can't win by quitting."

This time there was no determination. No relaxation. Not even fear. Just astonishment.

"Come on," I jeered. "We haven't even begun."

Something flickered in her eyes. Then her mouth went flat and hard.

Laughing, I expected her to renew the match. Instead, Del pushed forward briefly, released her sword entirely, threw both splayed hands into the air and took three strides backward as the blade fell. The expression now was anger.

It wasn't surrender. She didn't yield. It was—cessation. And it left me standing in the middle of a circle I'd drawn in the Vashni common, clutching my sword while hers lay at my feet.

I arched my brows. "Afraid, bascha?"

She was sucking air audibly. The single braid had loosened itself, strands straggling around her face. She was ice and sunlight, and much too tough to melt. "What," she panted, "is wrong with you?"

"You asked me to spar with you."

She managed one word. "*Spar*."

I shrugged. "You've always preferred a challenge to mere practice. Let's not waste our time."

Hands went to her hips and rested there as her breathing slowed. "That wasn't sparring. That was anger, Tiger."

I shook my head. "I'm not angry."

"Angry," she declared. "And bitter."

"You're imagining things." I bent, picked up her sword. "Let's go again."

Del shook her head with slow deliberation.

"Afraid, bascha?" I smiled, tossed the blade. "Catch."

She made no attempt to do so. She merely stepped back and let it fall into the sand. Sunlight flashed.

"That," I said severely, "is no way to treat a good blade."

Winter descended. "Nor is your behavior any way to treat me."

"Oh, come on, Del! This is how it is. You work your body, work your mind, challenge everything about yourself, until the weakness is gone. It isn't easy, no, but it's the best way. I've spent months doing it—can't you at least invest a few days?"

Del bent, retrieved her sword, turned on her heel and walked away.

"Hey. Hey!" In several long strides I reached her. Reached *for* her. "Don't turn your back on me—"

Del spun. I saw the blade flash even as my own came up. They met at neck level. My blade was against steel. Hers was against my throat.

She tilted her head slightly in an odd, slow, sideways movement almost like a cat preparing to leap. But there was no leap. She stood her ground. "Angry," she said very softly. "Bitter. And vicious."

I blurted a laugh of incredulity. "Vicious!"

"*And afraid.*"

Laughter stopped. "I'm not—"

"What did he do to you?"

"No one has—"

Her low voice nonetheless overrode my own. "What did he do to you?"

I smiled. "You really don't like to lose, do you?"

She made no reply. Just stared. Examined. Evaluated. I saw a series of expressions in her eyes and face, but none I could name. They came and went too quickly: the faintest of ripples in her flesh, a shifting in her eyes. Nearly nonexistent.

Delilah asked, "What did he say to you to make you so afraid?"

I denied her an answer. I took a step backward, breaking contact with her blade, and lowered my own. "Go," I told her. "We're done for the day. If you aren't willing to do what it takes, I don't want to bother."

A multitude of replies crowded her eyes. She made none of them.

I watched her walk away. The anger, the bitterness drained away. I felt oddly empty.

Empty. And afraid.

"Stop it," she said. "*Stop* it, Tiger!"

I said nothing. Did nothing. The voice was very distant. I could ignore it. Did.

"Tig—oh, hoolies," she muttered, and then a hand cracked me hard across the face.

She is a strong woman, and the blow was heartfelt. I came back to awareness abruptly, catching her wrist. Realized I sat in the hyort we shared. I blinked at her, shocked. "What was that for?"

"To bring you back."

"Bring me back from where?"

"From the dream."

"I was dreaming?"

"Not now," she said. "You were awake. But—away. As if you

returned to something you'd already experienced." She indicated her head. "Inside."

I felt disoriented. Detached. "I don't understand."

She knelt next to me. Desperation edged her tone. "You have to stop this. This dream-walking."

I frowned, baffled. "Why?"

Del pulled her wrist out of my hand. "Because it's changing you."

"Changing me! How?" I noticed then that it was nearing sundown. I couldn't remember where the day had gone. "I don't understand what you're saying."

"Five days ago you went to Oziri's tent after we sparred, and since then you've been—different."

I frowned. "I know you think I'm angry, but I'm not."

"I didn't say you were angry. I said you were *different*."

"And bitter, you said. Vicious, even. Just because you can't match me in the circle."

Lines creased her brow. "What are you talking about?"

"The match earlier today. You were losing. *You* got angry. You quit on me, Del. You threw down your sword and walked away."

Astonishment was manifest. "I have never walked away from a match in my life!"

"Earlier today," I insisted. How could she have forgotten?

Del recoiled. Pale brows knit together. I saw surprise and worry. "But we didn't . . ." She changed direction. "Was that your dream?"

"It wasn't a dream, bascha."

She shook her head slowly, as if trying to work out a multitude of thoughts. "There was no match earlier." Almost absently, she added, "Something's wrong. Something inside you."

I found it preposterous. "Del—"

She overrode me. "We haven't sparred since that first time, Tiger. Five days ago. That's the *only* time we've sparred. Five days ago. Two days after you got here."

I gritted my teeth, verging on frustration. "Earlier today," I repeated. "We had an argument in the circle, as we sparred. You quit on me."

Del sat back, putting distance between us. Astonishment had faded. Now she stared. Examined me. Evaluated. Comprehension crept into her eyes. "Tiger . . . we need to leave this place. We need to go."

"Oziri says—"

"I don't care what Oziri says!" She lowered her voice with a glance at the open doorflap. "We have to leave. Tomorrow, first thing."

"You're not ready to leave, bascha. You need to rest."

"*You* need to get away from here," she countered. "And I've rested enough. Trust me."

Oziri had said that. *Trust me.* "There are still things I have to do," I explained. "Things I need to learn. Oziri says—"

Del pronounced an expletive concerning Oziri that nearly made my ears roll up. With crisp efficiency she began to gather up her belongings. "We're going. Tomorrow."

"I'm not done learning what I need to know. I realize it's difficult for you to understand, but there are things about me that are—different. Things—"

"Yes! Different! *Wrong.* That's my whole point." Del stopped packing. She moved close, sat on her heels, reached up to trap my head in her hands. The heels cradled my temples. "Listen to me, Tiger. To *me*, not to the things Oziri has put in your head. Or to what you believe happened." Her eyes caught my own and held them. "You're right: I don't understand this dream-walking. But what I do know is that it's changing you. You spend most of each day inside your own head. You don't hear anything I say. You answer no questions. You don't even acknowledge I'm present. It's as though your body's here, but your mind is somewhere else. And what you've just told me, this conviction we sparred earlier today—you're confusing reality with what's in your mind. With the dreams. You have to stop."

"I have to learn how to control it, bascha."

Del leaned forward. Our foreheads met. Her skin was smooth,

cool. "Let it go," she murmured. "Let it go, Tiger. It's Vashni magic."

"It's just another tool—"

"Magic," she repeated, "and you know how you hate magic."

"If I don't learn to control it, it will control me."

She released my head, ran one supple, callused hand through my hair, almost as if I were a muddled child in need of soothing. "It's controlling you now, Tiger. Every time you go inside your-self."

"It's just stillness," I told her. "It's like ioSkandic discipline. What happened to me atop the spire, in the Stone Forest . . ." I shrugged. "Well, you know."

Del's hands fell away. "I don't know what happened to you atop the spire," she said. "You've never told me."

My brows lifted. "You were there with me."

"No."

"Del, you were. I saw you. I dreamed you, and you came." And put the *jivatma* scar back into my abdomen, after Sahdri had lifted it.

The color ran out of her face. "No, Tiger. I was never in Met-eiera. I never saw the Stone Forest. I stayed in Skandi until Prima Rhannet's ship sailed." Something flinched in her eyes. "We all thought you were dead."

"You were *there*, Del. I remember it clearly." So very clearly. I was naked. Alone. Bereft of everything I'd known of myself, whelped again atop the rock. Until she came. "You were there."

Del shook her head.

"You're forgetting things," I told her, beginning to worry. "What happened in Meteiera a few weeks ago, and the sparring match earlier today. Maybe if you talked with Oziri—"

"No." Her tone was certainty followed by puzzlement. "Tiger, we left Skandi months ago. Not weeks. And we sparred *five days ago*. Not since. Certainly not this morning."

I opened my mouth to refute the claim, but she sealed it closed with cool fingers.

"Listen to me." Her eyes searched mine. "Trust me."

I had trusted this woman with my life more times than I could count. I was troubled that she could be so terribly confused, but I nodded. I owed her that much.

"*I* need to go," she said. "*I* need to leave. Will you come with me?"

"Why do you need to leave? You're safe here. You're the Oracle's sister. They'd never harm you."

"I need to leave," she repeated. "I promised Neesha we'd meet him."

It took me a moment to remember the kid. Then I frowned. "You don't owe him anything."

Her voice hardened. "I owe him my life, Tiger. And so do you."

"Maybe so, but—"

"It's time for me to leave," she said. "Will you come with me?"

"Del—"

"Please, Tiger. I need you."

The desire to refuse, to insist she stay with me, was strong. I felt its tug, its power. Leaned into it a moment, tempted. I owed a debt to the Vashni for tending her, and Oziri had much to teach me. But I owed a greater debt to the kid for keeping her alive so she *could* be tended.

She'd said she needed me. That was very unlike Del. Something serious was wrong with her.

With her. Not with me.

I nodded. "All right, bascha. We'll go."

Del averted her head abruptly and returned to packing. But not before I saw profound relief and the sheen of tears in her eyes.

TWENTY-TWO

THE STUD, for some reason, didn't want me near him. I found it decidedly odd; he can be full of himself and recalcitrant, but not generally difficult to catch and bridle. When I finally did manage both, I noted the rolling eye and pinned ears. He quivered from tension, from something akin to fear, until Del came out to saddle the gelding. Then he quieted.

"He knows, too," she said.

I tossed blankets up on the stud's back. "Knows what?"

"That things are not right."

I had no time for oblique comments and obscure conversations. I had agreed to go, but I regretted it. "Things are what they are."

"For now," she murmured, and turned her full attention to the gelding.

Annoyed, I did the same with the stud. We finished preparations in stiff, icy silence.

It wasn't until Del and I had made our carefully courteous farewells to the chieftain and actually mounted our horses that Oziri appeared. I heard Del's hissed inhalation and murmured curse as she saw him walking toward us. I reined in the stud and waited. I could feel Del's tension. It was a tangible thing even across the distance between the two horses.

I had seen and heard him laugh. He was a man like any other, given perhaps to more dignity because of his rank but equally prone to expressing his opinion in dry commentary. But as he approached, I saw he wore no smile. His eyes, lighter than most Vashni's, were fastened on Del.

Yet when he arrived at my stirrup, the sternness vanished. "So, you have learned all there is to know about dream-walking. I am amazed; it takes most men tens of years to do so."

I tilted my head in Del's direction. "This is for her. There's an errand we must do. A matter of a debt."

Irony. "Ah. Of course. All debts must be paid."

The stud shifted restlessly, bobbing his head. He watched Oziri sidelong, pinning his ears, then flicking them at the sound of my voice.

"It's easier for me now," I told Oziri. "As you said, the herbs aren't necessary. It's just a matter of discipline and stillness." I shrugged off-handedly. "There's much left to learn—but it's a beginning."

"Beginnings," Oziri said, "may be dangerous."

I laughed. "More so than endings?"

The Vashni didn't smile. He reached to his neck, lifted a bone necklet over his head, and offered it. "This will guide you," he told me. "Wear it in honor."

On horseback I was too tall, even bending, for him to slip it over my head. So I took the necklet into my hands, noticed the meticulously patterned windings of the wire holding the necklet together, and put it over my head. Human bones rattled against sandtiger claws.

I opened my mouth to thank him but was distracted when Del's white gelding, painted and tasseled, sidestepped into me. The toe of her sandal collided with my shin bone. When I glanced at her, annoyed, she had the grace to apologize. But her eyes were not so abashed, and they were very watchful. Almost as if she'd done it purposely.

I shot her a quelling glance, then turned back to the warrior. "We'll be back this way."

Oziri smiled, looked at Del on the far side of me. "Yes." Then he dipped his head in eloquent salute. "May the sun shine on your head, Oracle's sister."

I glanced at Del, expecting her to reply. But something in her eyes said she would not return the courtesy. I was appalled. She was the one who'd been warning me about rudeness and the possible consequences.

Then something shifted in her posture. Tension departed. She inclined her head briefly, wished him the same.

As she rode away, I muttered an aside to Oziri. "*Women.*"

But the Vashni didn't smile. Didn't laugh. Didn't agree. After a moment I knew he wouldn't. Somewhat nonplussed, I turned the stud, saw Del ahead, waiting, and rode up to join her.

A strange thing: her eyes were anxious. But it faded as I reined the stud in and gestured her to go ahead down the narrow thread of a trail Vashni hunters used. She murmured a Northern prayer of thanksgiving I found utterly incongruous, and took the lead.

From the Vashni encampment it was a long day's ride to Julah, and Del wasn't up to it. She said nothing, simply straightened her shoulders from time to time and kept riding, but I could tell she was exhausted. When we came across an acceptable place to spend the night, I called a halt. We had water enough in botas for ourselves and the horses, and though there was no grazing, we also packed grain. Thin pickings for the gelding and the stud, but we'd make Julah easily the next day. I figured we'd stay overnight, then head out toward Umir's.

Del is not one for asking or expecting help, so I offered her none as we unsaddled and hobbled the horses. I kept an eye on her, though, and saw how stiffly she moved, how carefully she balanced the weight of saddle, blankets, and pouches, gear she'd ordinarily swing off her horse easily. The spot I'd selected was open ground save for a huddled fringe of scrubby brush, with more sand and soil than rocks; Del dug in against an upswell like a coney, flipping her saddle upside down to form a horseman's chair. Once she'd watered the gelding and made certain he was comfortable, she flopped down on her blanket and leaned against the saddle. Her eyes drifted closed.

She wore a burnous, as I did. Save for the nick at her jawline, none of her scars were visible. But she was still too thin, and weariness hollowed her face.

I walked over, dropped a bota down next to her, and announced, "I'm cooking."

Del's eyes opened. "Cooking?"

"Yep. Here." I tossed her a cloth-wrapped packet. "Jerked meat."

She grimaced, peering down at the packet that had landed in her lap. "What kind of meat?"

"Who knows? But it's not cumfa. That's enough for me." I dug more out of the pouches, slung a bota over beside my own saddle and bedding, found the flint and steel and placed it on my blanket. "Not much wood here. I'll go scout around."

"Tiger?"

I turned back, asking a question with raised eyebrows.

She studied me a moment, as if weighing me against some inner vision. Then she relaxed. "Thank you."

Now I frowned.

"For coming."

I shrugged. "Sure. I figure we can track down the kid, make sure he's all right, then head back to the Vashni."

Her hands froze on the packet of dried meat. Tension returned tenfold. "Go *back*? Why?"

For a moment I didn't know. I was completely blank. Then awareness returned, and the answer came without volition. "Because I don't know enough yet about the dream-walking. There's much left to learn." I gestured at the ground. "If you want to start digging a hollow for the fire, that would help. And find rocks for the ring."

Del said nothing. Just stared at me. Fear was in her eyes; stiffened her body.

"*What?*" I asked.

She opened her mouth the answer, then shut it. Shook her head.

After a moment, annoyed, I waved a dismissive hand in her direction and went off in search of decent wood.

Later, after we had a bed of good coals for warmth and eaten our fill of seasoned jerked meat, Del unsheathed her sword and began to hone and oil it. I knew I should do the same with my own, but I felt just lazy enough to stay put, relaxed against my upturned saddle. I blinked sleepily as I stared into the fire ring, transfixed by the red glow of chunky coals.

Del's face bore a pensive expression. "How many days has it been since the sandtiger attack?"

I thought about it. Realized I didn't know. "A week, I think. Maybe ten days. Why?"

Muscles leaped in her jaw. But she didn't reply. Her eyes assessed the blade as she ran the stone against it. Her expression was odd.

"Being sick can make you lose track of time." I hoped to set her at ease, if she was worried she lost a few days. I watched her hand move in an even, effortless rhythm: down the blade, running the stone against steel, then carrying it back to the hilt where the motion began again. I smelled oil, tasted the metallic tang in my mouth. The sleeve of her burnous fell back; I saw the knurled scar on her forearm. "You were lucky that healed so fast."

"I haven't lost track of time," she said quietly. "But I think you have." She glanced up, then set sword and whetstone aside. For a moment her hands were pressed against her thighs as if she sought self-control. "Could I see that?"

Her eyes now were on my chest. I glanced down at the Vashni necklet. Thin wire gleamed faintly in firelight. I pulled it from around my neck, tossed it across to her.

Del caught it, held it up, turned it in the glow of coals so she might examine details more closely. "The wirework is exquisite."

I watched her handle the necklet, noting how she tested the strength of the wire, examined how it all fit together. Her face was oddly tense. Then she slipped the necklet over her own head, arranged it against her burnous. "How does it look?"

"A little long for you. But it was made for a man."

Her fingers ran down the bones. Then she arched her back in a brief stretch, yawned, pushed to her feet. "I need to find a bush," she said, "and then I'm going to bed. Could you tend the horses?"

I nodded, leaning forward to add a couple of broken branches to the coals. Del disappeared. I got up and went to refill the horse buckets, check the picket pegs, exchange a few pleasantries with the stud, who had indicated no particular joy at having me back in charge of things; I made my own pre-bedtime donation, then settled down again beside the fire.

Del was gone longer than anticipated. When she came back, it was without the necklet.

I frowned. "What happened?"

She was arranging her bedding. "I found a bush."

"Not *that*. What happened to the necklet?"

One hand flew to her chest. She looked down, then back at me. "It must have broken."

She did not sound very concerned, which annoyed me; the necklet had been a gift. "It was *wire*, Del." I sighed, shutting my mouth on a complaint; she was clearly too tired to discuss it. "I'll go look."

"Oh Tiger, just wait until tomorrow. There's not enough light to see by."

I gathered bunched legs beneath me to push myself upright. "I'll just poke around anyway."

She uncoiled in a single sinuous motion and stepped beside the small fire, sword in hand. The tip kissed my throat, holding me in a kneeling position.

I was stunned. "*Del*—

Tersely she said, "You won't find it, Tiger. I buried it." Coal-glow painted her face into relief, underscoring the hard set of her jaw, the jut of sharp cheekbones. "I was hoping there would be no need for this. But it's time you came to understand that something is indeed very wrong with you. And has been since you took up with Oziri."

I was frozen in place, caught between rising and sitting. It was not an appropriate position for oblique movement, which I realized was deliberate. Del knew me. Knew how I moved. Knew how to effectively put a halt to any intentions I might devise.

She wore the mask I'd seen displayed to opponents. "Do you wish to try me, Tiger?"

I eased myself down. My own sword, still sheathed in its harness, was within reach, but I knew better than to dare it with her blade at my throat. "You didn't want to see the necklet," I accused. "You wanted to get rid of it."

Del said nothing.

"What is it you think is 'wrong' with me?"

She ignored the question. "Tell me again how many days it's been since the sandtiger attack."

I held myself very still. "Six or seven. Why?"

"How many days were you at Umir's?"

"Two or three. Why?"

"How many days did we stay with the Vashni?"

I wanted to laugh, but didn't. Not with the sword at my throat. "Del, this is—"

"*How many*, Tiger?"

My teeth clicked together.

The tip bit in. "Answer me."

"Five."

"And how many since we sparred? You know—the match you say I walked away from."

"Three or four, I think." I drew in a careful breath. "You really have lost track of time."

She bit down on a sharp blurt of disbelieving laughter. "*I have*—?" But she checked it visibly. I saw something in her face, something like pain. But the sword did not waver. The tip had seated itself in the hollow of my throat. The cut stung.

I attempted sympathy. "Bascha, put it away. You're exhausted and confused. You need more rest—"

She cut me off. "What I need is for you to come to your senses. To realize what he's done to you."

"What *who*'s done to me? What are you talking about?"

Her tone was bitter as winter ice. "The Vashni."

"Oziri? Hoolies, bascha, he was helping me learn how to—" I stopped. Couldn't breathe.

"How to what?" she asked, when I didn't finish.

Something built up in my chest. Something that twisted. Something that threatened to burst. I felt as if I were on the verge of a firestorm.

Oh, hoolies. Oh, gods, no . . .

Del's tone changed. No longer was there challenge. Now there was expectation. "How to what, Tiger?"

I couldn't speak. The heat, the pressure increased. Pain filled my chest.

Her tone was almost a whisper. "Say it."

I took the step into conflagration. Denial kindled, exploded, then crisped into ash. Was blown away. Comprehension, confession, slow and painful, began to come into its place.

I couldn't say it.

"He did this," she said. "The Vashni. He did something to you. Now do you understand why I wanted to leave?"

Years of being stubbornly, selectively blind and deaf to certain impulses and speculations had created habits I found comforting. Habits that I could live with. Denial afforded me freedom. But I had stopped denying it in Oziri's presence. Had accepted it.

"Say it, Tiger. What he was teaching you. Admit it."

A spasm ran through my body. The words, slow, halting, laden with need, seem to come from someone else. "How to work magic."

Oh, hoolies . . . Memories came back then, came pouring back, tumbling one over the other like stones in a flash flood. I took what I could of them and fitted them into a whole. Hours. Days. Weeks. All had been lost to the dream-walks, the learning of the art. Now I understood Del's concern. Del's fear. Her desperation.

The Vashni had indeed done something to me: stolen sense, taken time. Turned me from my course. Set me on a new one.

Nihko had begun the process. Sahdri had explained it. Oziri had advanced it.

Oh, but it was so much easier to *dis*believe, when faced with a terrible truth. A truth I could not accept, because the fear of it would overpower me. Incapacitation. I might as well be dead.

And I *would* be dead, according to the priest-mages of ioSkandi. To Umir's book.

Why would any man wish to be a mage, if the cost was so high?

Why would I?

I wished it because I'd wanted it. Needed it in the nights of my childhood, desperate to escape the Salset and the life of a chula: dreaming of a sandtiger, making it come to life; dreaming of Del atop the stone spire, who replaced a stolen scar and thus identity; dreaming of a boat to carry me to Skandi.

The intent had not been *magic*. Never. I had only ever, a very few times, wished to make a miracle to change what I could not bear.

Messiahs made miracles. Mages made magic.

Maybe one and the same.

I swore, then drew up my knees and leaned over them, elbows planted, clenching taut fingers in my short hair. I wanted to pull it out by the roots, as if that would erase the knowledge of what Oziri had done. Of what I had become.

Dreams could merely be dreams. But dreams could also be more. Now I walked them. Began to understand them. Summoned the magic within them, using the power Oziri sought, and found, and rekindled within my bones.

Nihko had told me. Sadri had told me. I had denied them both. But somehow, with Oziri, I had not. Maybe it was because enough time had passed since my "whelping" atop the spire. Maybe it was because I was in the South again, and my walls were down. Or maybe it was because Oziri forced the issue. Whatever the reason, he had made me understand what I was. What I could do. What I *had* done.

But not what I might yet do.

My walls were down now, shattered upon the sand. Del, who realized it, released a long breath of eloquent relief and set down her sword. Knelt beside me. Put one hand on my own where they viciously gripped my hair.

I closed my eyes. I closed them very tightly. I thought my teeth might crumble.

The hand closed, offering comfort. Her tone was meditative; as a Northerner, she had never feared or denied magic. Nor refused to employ it herself. "From when I met you, I knew. There were signs of it . . . but you denied it. Refused to believe, despite evidence. Even when I showed you Northern magic. Even when you *worked* it."

I said nothing.

"I learned my magic," she said. "It's part of being a sword-singer, part of Staal-Ysta. That's what *jivatmas* are. We sing the power into being, to wield the blade."

She had told me this before. I wanted her to stop. Wanted not to listen.

"*I* have no magic," she said. "Only the sword. Only the song." Her fingers traced the back of one hand. "But you . . . you need nothing but yourself."

I shook my head.

"It's a part of you, Tiger. Just like your sword skill. Don't deny it."

Eventually I untangled fingers and looked at her. "I have to."

"No."

"If I don't . . ." But I let it go. I shook my head again, releasing pent breath. "It's too late for that, isn't it?"

"I think so, yes."

I sighed heavily, scrubbed wearily at my face. My eyes felt gritty. The beginnings of a headache throbbed at the base of my neck. "Did you really bury the necklet?"

"I cut the wire into pieces with my knife, then buried each bone in a different place."

Relief was palpable. Then comprehension followed, and amusement. No wonder it had taken her so long to find the appropriate bush. I wasn't certain anything in the necklet had controlled me or was meant to control me, but self-awareness had returned only with distance from Oziri and separation from the necklet.

"Good." I could not meet her eyes, so I stared hard at the stars for a long time. I heard the coals settling, the faintest of breezes skimming the surface of the soil, the restless shiftings of the stud and Del's gelding. "Four weeks," I said. "Give or take a day."

Del was puzzled. "What?"

"Since the sandtiger attack." I was certain of it, as much as I could be. It felt—right.

Del smiled. "Yes."

"There's something I have to tell you. Something you must understand." I swallowed heavily, aware of pain in my throat, the fear she couldn't, or wouldn't, accept it. "Bascha—you really were there. Atop the spire in the Stone Forest. With me."

Her tone frayed. "Tiger—"

"In my dreams," I told her. "And that's what saved me. That's what kept me sane. So long as I could hold onto the memory of you, could conjure you in dreams, I knew I would survive. I lost myself for a while, even lost two fingers—but I came back from ioSkandi, came back from the spires." I took a deep breath. "I'll come back from this."

It was Del's turn for silence.

"I don't—I don't remember what Oziri did. What he told me, or taught me. Enough, obviously, to find and refine whatever was born in me, what bubbled up from time to time before going dormant again, until Meteiera. Apparently he brought it back into the open." I laughed sharply. "If I couldn't remember what *day* it was, how can I be expected to remember what he did? But what I don't understand is why."

Del pondered it. "Perhaps he realized what was in you, and wanted it for himself," she said. "I think as long as you denied what you were, he could use you. Perhaps he felt your magic might augment his, make him something more than he was. But if you knew what he wanted, you would have resisted."

"Would I?"

"Oh, yes. You let no man use you, Tiger. Not Nihko, not Sahdri, not Oziri."

"But they have. Each of them." Others as well, over the long years. "For a time."

"And you have walked away from them all."

Or been dragged away by a very determined woman. I sighed. "So, you think if I admit what I am, I'll be safe from manipulation?"

"Maybe."

I scowled. "That's not much of a guarantee."

Del's brows arched. "With the kind of lives we lead, that's the best I can offer."

True enough. I ran a hand through my hair, scrubbing at the chill that crept over my scalp. "Dangerous."

"What is?"

"A man with a sword who lacks proper training." I grimaced, said what I meant: "A man with *magic* who lacks proper training."

Sahdri had said it, atop the spires. Umir's book set it into print. Oziri had proved it.

"Unless he is strong enough to find his own way."

I grunted. "Maybe."

Del smiled. "I will offer a guarantee."

I laughed, then let it spill away. "I can't believe that all dreams are bad, bascha. Everyone dreams. You dream."

"But I am not a mage."

She had said it was born in me. So had Nihkolara, and Sahdri. Oziri. Even Umir's book. Dormancy until Skandi, from birth until age forty—except for a sensitivity to magic so strong it made me ill; until *io*Skandi, when Nihko took me against my will to Meteiera, to the Stone Forest; to others like him, like me. Where, atop a spire, a full-blown mage was born.

Denial bloomed again, faded. Was followed by the only logical question there could be.

What comes next?

TWENTY-THREE

I AWOKE with a start, staring up
into darkness lighted only by stars and the faintest sliver of moon.
Sweat bathed my body. I swore under my breath and rubbed an
unsympathetic hand over my face, mashing it out of shape.

"What is it?" Del's voice was shaded by only a trace of sleepi-
ness.

We lay side-by-side in our bedrolls with the dying fire at our
feet. Desert nights are cool; I yanked the blanket up to my shoulders. Muttering additional expletives, I shut my eyes and draped
an elbow over my face. "I was dreaming, curse it."

After a moment, with careful neutrality, she queried, "Yes?"

"I'd just as soon not, after my recent experiences." I removed
the arm and looked again at the stars, shoving both forearms
under my head. "How in hoolies am I supposed to go through life
without dreaming?"

"I don't think you *can* not dream," Del observed, shifting beneath her blanket. "You'll just have to get used to it."

I grunted sourly.

"Well—unless you can learn to control them. Make them
stop." She was silent a moment. "And perhaps you can. Being
you."

I chewed on that for a moment, then shied away from the

concept. That "being you" part carried an entirely new connotation, now.

"What was this dream about?"

I scowled up at darkness. "Actually, it was a piece of one I had before. At least, I'm assuming it was a dream. Before, that is. You swore up and down it didn't happen."

"*I did?*"

"The dance," I said. "The dance where you walked away."

"Ah." She was silent a moment. "No. It didn't happen. But—are you saying you dreamed about a dream?"

"I didn't think it was a dream at the time. In which case I'd be dreaming about something that *did* happen. But it didn't, so I guess I was dreaming about a dream."

Her tone was amused. "This is getting very complicated, Tiger."

"Then there's the dream about the dead woman . . ." Oh, argh. I hadn't meant to tell her.

Del's voice sharpened. "Dead woman?"

I tried to dismiss it as inconsequential. "Just—a skeleton. Out in the Punja."

"It's a skeleton, but you know it's a woman?"

"It's a woman's voice."

"This skeleton *speaks?*"

Now she'd really think I was sandsick. "It's not the kind of dreams I had with Oziri. This is just a dream. A dream dream. You know. The kind anyone has."

"*I* don't dream of skeletons who speak with a woman's voice."

I put a smile into my voice. "Of course not. *You* dream of *me.*"

"Oh, indeed," she murmured dryly. "What else would a woman dream about but a man? It is her only goal in life, to find a man to fill her thoughts during the day and her dreams during the night."

I rolled over to face her, hitching myself up on one elbow. "So. What kind of man *did* you think you'd end up with?" It wasn't the sort of thing I'd ever asked before. Nor had I ever heard a man, even dead drunk, mention curiosity about it. But that didn't mean we *weren't* curious.

"I didn't."

"Didn't? Not at all?" I paused. "Ever?"

"When I was a girl, yes."

"A Northerner."

"Of course. I lived in the North."

"And when you got a little older?"

"I stopped thinking about what kind of man I might end up with."

"Why?"

"Ajani," she said simply.

One word. One name. Explanation. And it came rushing back to me, the knowledge. A fifteen-year-old girl, witness to the massacre of her family. The sole survivor save for her brother, and subject to the brutality so many women suffered at the hands of borjuni. No, I didn't imagine Del had ever dreamed of a man again, except perhaps of the one she'd sworn to kill.

By the time she'd done it, we'd been partners for two years. Sword-mates. Bed-mates. I'd known the minute I laid eyes on her in the dusty, drag-tail cantina that I wanted her in my bed. I don't know when the idea occured to Del.

"What?" she asked.

I raised my eyebrows at her in a silent query.

Del frowned faintly. "You're staring at me."

"You're worth staring at." I reached out, hooked two fingers into the sandtiger necklet around her neck, pulled her toward me. "I think I know of a way to turn bad dreams into good ones."

"Ah," she said as our foreheads met gently. "But will you remember my name in the morning?"

I shifted closer, sinking a hand into the hair against the back of her head. "Who needs names? 'Woman' will do."

Stiffened fingers jabbed me warningly beneath the short ribs. "What was that again?"

"Delilah," I murmured against her mouth.

The mouth curved into a smile, then parted. The tongue flicked briefly against my own with the first word. "That will do."

So would a lot of things, with this woman.

In the morning I fought the muzzy residue of too many dreams crowded together inside my skull as I grained and watered the horses. The morning promised to bleed into a typical desert day: very bright, very warm, no moisture. Which is good for the bones, but bad for the skin. It wasn't high summer yet, nor were we in the Punja, but no part of the South lacks for heat. I could taste it on my tongue, an acrid trace of dry soil and sand; I could smell the tang of creosote and what was left of our fire, burned away to a thin scattering of coals amid the ash. Del, squatting beside it, raked the coals apart to expose all of them, then took care to blanket them in a layer of sandy soil so there was no threat of sparks that might kindle a conflagration.

I patted the stud as he nosed his morning grain, then turned back to Del. She looked tired; and it had nothing to do with our activities of the night before, which had been slow and undemanding, but satisfying nonetheless. She simply hadn't entirely recovered her strength following the sandtiger attack. "We'll make Julah in two or three hours, then spend the night before going on."

She glanced up, rising. "We'd make better time if we headed out this afternoon, after a good meal."

I hitched a shrug, turning back to gather up and pack canvas buckets away. "We'll see how we feel later today. No sense in wasting a decent bed, though, now that we own one." Or several.

"*Parts* of one," Del clarified. "Do you suppose Fouad will charge us rent on the other third?"

"Not if he wants to live."

She'd knelt and now was working on her bedroll. "Nayyib deserves better, after all he did for us."

"We'll go after him, Del. But we won't do him much good if we're both too tired to put up a decent fight. Besides, we don't even know if he *got* to Umir's place. Just because he said he'd go—"

"If he said it, he meant it." Del looped thongs around the bedding and knotted them. "I trust him."

It baffled me that she would. "We hardly know him, bascha."

"I spent nearly two weeks in his company." Her tone was clipped. "I would have died, had he not tended me. Hour after hour, day after day, at the shelter and then at the Vashni encampment. You can learn a great deal about a man in such circumstances."

"Look, I'm not saying he's a liar, just that—"

Del cut me off. "He went to look for you."

"I know that, but—"

"And likely he's risking his life for you, to walk into Umir's presence among all those sword-dancers. Look what happened with Rafiq."

"Which is precisely the point I tried to make once before: that he ran too high a risk going after me. Did he think to win Umir's little contest, then join forces with me?" I shook my head. "He's not good enough. They'd have eaten him alive in that circle."

"Which is why he came looking for you originally. To learn from you."

I placed blankets across the stud's back, then swung the saddle up. "No, originally he came looking for me to challenge me, until he saw me kill Khashi. *Then* he decided to ask me to teach him."

"We owe him, Tiger."

I wanted to growl aloud in exasperation. "We'll go, Del. I'm not saying we won't. I'm just saying we can afford a night in Julah."

"Neesha may not be able to afford—"

"*Del*." I turned toward her. "You need the rest. End of discussion."

She stood her ground, scowling at me ferociously. "Why is it you're so opposed to helping Nayyib?"

"I'm not opposed to helping Nayyib. I just think—"

"You try to argue me out of it every time I bring it up. Despite the fact he saved your life—"

"I wasn't in any danger of dying, bascha."

Her voice rose. "—as well as saving mine; and I *was* in danger of dying, Tiger! Not to mention he went for help in Julah and got himself abducted by Rafiq and his friends—"

"I don't think they actually abducted him—"

"—and risked being killed by Vashni—"

"I'm not sure the Vashni—"

"—and now may have been taken prisoner by Umir. How many times has he put himself out, or put himself in danger, to help us, yet you insist on denigrating those efforts and refuse to help him when *he* may need it?"

"I'm not denigrating those efforts, Del, and I'm not refusing to help him. I'm merely saying we should spend the night in Julah before we head off for Umir's. Where he may not even be."

"See? There it is, Tiger! Denigration. Is it because he's younger than you—*my* age, in fact—and handsome? Because I spent two weeks alone with him, mostly undressed, while you were elsewhere? Because we slept in the same tent? Because I came to know him, to trust him? Are you afraid I might be taken with him?"

I stared at her, mouth open. "You're saying I'm jealous!"

"Well? Are you?"

"No!"

"Are you *sure*, Tiger?"

"Yes!"

Clearly she was dubious. "You exhibited behavior somewhat similar to this in Skandi, when we met Herakleio. Young, strong, handsome, well-set-up Herakleio."

I glared. "I wasn't jealous of Herakleio, and I'm not jealous of Nayyib."

She glared back. "You have remarked many times on the years between us. No doubt some might even whisper I'm young enough to be your daughter."

I gritted teeth. "I don't care what anybody else thinks. Or

what they whisper, either." Though I'd heard it mentioned aloud a time or two.

Pale brows arched.

"I don't," I said crisply. "As for staying in Julah, it's one night. *One* night at Fouad's. That's all, bascha. Then we go."

"In one night a man could die."

"Hoolies, a man can die in one *moment*, Del! Between one breath and the next. But I find it very unlikely Umir will kill him—or that anyone else would—because there's still a price on my head, and by now they probably all know Nayyib has a better idea than they do where I might go. Plus Umir wants his book back. He won't kill Nayyib if he thinks he can trade him for the book."

Del held her bedroll in the crook of an elbow. "What book?"

In my zeal to change the subject, I'd forgotten she knew nothing about Umir's book of magic. I sighed, turning back to continue tacking out the stud. "I'll tell you on the trail."

Fouad seemed to have resigned himself to the fact that Del and I were now equal partners in his cantina. He was not in the least surprised to see us, nor that we expected to have private quarters. In fact, he led us rather dolefully down the hallway giving access to the rooms rented—along with the wine-girls—to men with coin. I fully expected Del to make some icy comment about women accepting the necessity of selling their bodies, but she held her tongue. Fouad took us to the very back of the building, then waved us inside a curtained door.

Plaster dust still lay on the floor. Raw wood and nail holes were obvious against the weathered walls. "I had a wall knocked down between two rooms," Fouad said, "and a wider bed put in." He glowered. "It's reduced the cantina by two rooms, you realize. And the income. Plus the cost of the changes will come out of your shares."

Two tiny rooms made into one slightly larger one by the deletion of a thin lath-and-plaster wall didn't leave us with much added space, but it was something. And the bed was noticeably wider. There were also two rickety tables, one battered, brass-hinged trunk, and a small, square window cut into one exterior adobe wall. I wondered inanely if Del would want to put up curtains.

"You can rent it out when we're not here," I told him, "and charge more for it because it's the best room in the house. Which reminds me—we'll need to sit down and have a good talk about how the place is run, so Del and I have an idea what to expect as partners." I caught her narrowed glance and added, "When we get back."

Perhaps he hadn't expected me to hit upon what was undoubtedly his plan. "You know where the kitchen is," Fouad said gloomily. "If you want food and drink, just ask."

I started undoing harness buckles. "I'm asking."

He sighed and nodded. "I thought so. I'll send one of the girls back with a tray."

Del stared after him as Fouad departed. I set harness, sword, and knife down on the trunk, then assigned myself the task of testing the feel of the mattress by sprawling across it, slack-limbed. I couldn't help the blooming of a lopsided smile. I was a Man of Property. I now owned one-third of a modestly successful cantina in a thriving town. But even better, I had a bed and a room to call my own for the very first time in forty years.

Well. *Our* own.

I smacked the bed lightly. "Room for two."

Del's gaze transferred itself from the curtained doorway to the bed. While I was pleased, she seemed stunned by events. Or maybe just too tired to take it all in.

"It doesn't bite," I said. "And *I* only do when invited."

Slender fingers worked at harness buckles. But she stopped before slipping out of it. "We should go after Nayyib."

I held onto my patience with effort. "Tomorrow, remember? First light. For now, we have the chance to rest under a real roof, in a real bed, and eat decent food for the first time in weeks." Well, cantina food didn't always live up to 'decent,' but it would be better by far than dried cumfa and flat, tough-crusted journey-bread. Especially when accompanied by something far more palatable than Vashni liquor.

Hmmm. Maybe the quality of food was something I should discuss with Fouad. After all, it was my reputation at stake now, too.

Del undid the buckles, set harness and weapons down atop mine, and sat on the edge of the bed. After a moment I wrapped a hand around the braid hanging down her back and tugged her down next to me. We lay cross-wise, feet planted on the packed-earth floor.

"Tomorrow," I said again.

Del's eyes drifted closed. She fell asleep almost at once, thereby proving my point about needing a good night's rest. I smiled, smoothing fallen strands of hair back from her face.

Then a thought occured. "I am *not* jealous," I muttered.

But I wasn't so certain I liked the idea of Del spending two weeks in a tent, mostly undressed—*mostly undressed!*—with a young, handsome, well-set-up buck like Nayyib while I was elsewhere. A young, handsome, well-set-up buck who, more to the point, was Del's age.

Now I scowled at the ceiling. What *did* she see in a man old enough to be her father?

Oh, hoolies. I got up, carefully shifted Del lengthwise on the bed, which occasioned a murmured but incoherent comment, and took myself and Umir's book into the common room. Such meanderings of the mind called for goodly amounts of aqivi.

TWENTY-FOUR

FOUAD EVINCED extreme startlement when I'd set up my study space at a table in the back corner of the common room, on a diagonal line from the doorway. I replaced the wobbly bench with the most comfortable one available, stuffed my spine into the confluence of walls, set out the book so the light from a window fell evenly upon its pages, and proceeded to sit there for hours, a cup and jug of aqivi at one elbow. I'd eaten earlier, but there was always room for aqivi.

After I'd insistently shooed away three curious wine-girls, intrigued by what I was doing, I'd been left alone. I was aware of whispered comments going on back behind the bar, discussing the new me in tones of disbelief, but dismissed them easily as I lost myself in the words.

Well, I suppose it *was* odd to see a man reading in a cantina, ignoring attractive women.

Fouad eventually arrived. His face was troubled.

I glanced up, marking my place with a finger. "What?"

"Is this a plan I should know about?"

"Is what a plan?"

He gestured. "You sitting here all afternoon."

"I've spent many an afternoon sitting here, Fouad. Not lately, maybe, but certainly often enough before."

He leaned closer. "People wish to *kill* you."

I figured it out. "You think I'm trying to lure sword-dancers to come in here after me."

"Aren't you?" Nervously he smoothed the front of his robes. "Damages can be expensive, Tiger. Broken stools and tables, shattered crockery . . ." He trailed off, figuring that was enough imagery to get his point across.

It was. "Fouad, I'm just reading. Nothing more. Del's sleeping, so I came out here."

His expression was a fascinating amalgam of disbelief and worry. "But you can't read."

"Who told you that?"

"*You* did. Some years ago."

Well, yes, I probably had. "I learned how." I didn't bother to explain *how* I learned how; some stories are better left untold.

"So, you're reading just to read?"

"Yes, Fouad. Reading just to read." That, and to learn what I could about magery, since it seemed to concern me in very personal ways now. "I'm not attempting to lure sword-dancers to come in here after me."

"And if they do come? You're sitting out here in front of the gods and everybody."

I dropped my right hand beneath the table, closed it around the sheathed sword, and raised it to a level where he could see the hilt. "Satisfied?"

Fouad's concern bled away, replaced by a relieved smile. "Yes."

"Good." I resettled the sword against the wall, hidden behind and beneath the table. "Now, if you don't mind, I'd like to continue my reading."

"Damages should concern you, Tiger," he pointed out. "It's not all profit, you know, operating a cantina."

"I'm sure you'll provide a thorough accounting of profits *and* expenses, Fouad. I trust you." I tapped the page with an impatient finger. "Do you mind?"

Shaking his head, Fouad wandered away muttering about losing his best corner to a man who wanted to *read* and who expected all his food and drink for free.

Well, sure. Why should I pay for what I own?

* * *

The next interruption was Del. "What are you doing?"

I scowled up at her, annoyed as her shadow slanted across the page I was reading. Since I was losing light as the sun went down, it mattered. With no little asperity, I replied, "I should think it's obvious."

Her face was creased from the mattress, flushed from recent awakening. She looked very young. "What are you drinking?" She bent forward as if considering helping herself to what was in my cup, then wrinkled her nose as she caught a whiff. "Never mind."

Del glanced around, looking for someone to take her order, then wandered over to the bar to place it herself when all of the girls disappeared into the back; it was their way of exhibiting jealousy. Apparently Fouad hadn't yet informed them Del was their boss as much as he was.

I followed her with my eyes, as did every other man in the cantina, though as yet there weren't many. Within the hour the common room ought to begin filling up. In the meantime, Del, oblivious to the stares, served as distraction and the object of lustful thoughts, even draped in a sleep-wrinkled burnous, with a sword hilt poking above her shoulder.

I heard raised voices from behind the curtain, including Fouad's. The three girls abruptly reappeared, each wearing an outraged expression that altered to sullen resentment as they saw Del at the bar. One of them, rubbing her rump, even deigned to inquire as to Del's wishes; the other two started working the tables, suggesting more drinks. None of them looked happy.

Hmmm. Maybe I ought to have a word with them. Couldn't have them displaying bad tempers to the customers. No doubt Fouad would appreciate me taking a hand in the running of the business.

Del came back with a cup and flask. "Water," she declared, eyeing my aqivi. "We musn't drink up all the profits."

I poured my cup full and availed myself of a portion of the profits. Del sighed and shook her head, hooking a stool to the table.

I closed Umir's book with a thump, latched the hook and

hasp, and set it down on the bench next to me so it wasn't in evidence to casual customers. "You're only half awake, bascha. Why don't you go back to bed?"

"Oh, no, I'm very awake. I doubt I'll be able to sleep again until well after dark." She drank her water, eyes guileless over the rim of the cup. "In fact, there's no need to stay the night here. We could get a start now."

"*I* haven't slept."

"But you've spent the balance of the day resting, Tiger, reading a book in a quiet corner. Unless you consider that exhausting labor."

"Well, it might be," I declared irritably. "It's written by several people in several different tongues. I have to translate all of them in my head before I can figure out what anybody's talking about, and even then I can't always sort through their meanings, since I've been a mage all of a couple of months. It's *mental* labor, bascha."

Her expression made an eloquent statement: she did not consider my explanation good enough.

"Come on, Del, we've been through this. We leave in the morning. *After* we've had a chance to sleep in a real bed."

"You could have slept in a real bed this afternoon."

"I was, in case you haven't noticed, being a considerate individual. I let you have the whole bed all to yourself."

"Considerate?" Del eyed my jug. "How much of that have you had?"

I brightened. "Enough that I wouldn't trust myself to stay ahorse."

"Hah," she retorted. "You wouldn't admit to being too drunk to sit a horse if you were lying face-down in a puddle of piss."

"I dunno," I slurred, blinking owlishly. "I might need you to help me to bed. You know, hold me up, take my sandals off, undress me . . ." I waggled suggestive eyebrows at her.

Del's face was perfectly bland, but I saw the faintest hint of a twitch at one corner of her mouth. "Dream on."

I stiffened on my bench. "That's cruel. I told you how I feel about dreams."

She was laughing at me unrepentantly even as she rose. "I will leave you to your reading, then."

"Wait—where are you going?" I started to reach for the book and my sword. "Back to bed?"

She paused. "Don't look so hopeful, Tiger. No, not to bed. I have it in mind to purchase some new clothing. Something— different."

"Why? What kind of clothing? *How* different?"

"Something suitable for serving liquor."

I stood up so fast I overset the bench. "You're not—you can't mean—tell me you don't . . ." I stopped, untangled my brain, started over from an entirely different direction, a more positive direction in view of Del's tendancy to disapprove of what she described as *my* tendancy toward possessiveness. With immense courtesy, I queried, "What is it you intend to do, pray tell?"

"Learn how to run a cantina."

Alarm reasserted itself. "By being a *wine-girl?*"

Del took note of the fact my raised voice, carrying, had stopped all other conversations throughout the common room, focusing abrupt attention on ours. With a glint in her eye she inquired, equally loudly, "What's wrong with being a wine-girl?"

I had committed a slight tactical error in the rules of war: I had taken the battle to the enemy's home. I could continue the fight valiantly if foolishly, or retire from the field with honor in- tact.

Not that Del ever allowed me any when she owned the ground.

"Why, nothing," I replied guilelessly. "I'm sure you'd make the very best wine-girl this cantina's ever seen."

Which, of course, did nothing at all to endear me to the wine- girls currently present, who already resented Del; yet another tac- tical error. Retreating with as much dignity as possible, I righted the bench and resumed my seat, whereupon I rescued the book, then promptly buried my face in a cup of aqivi.

Del said calmly, "A good proprietor understands all facets of a business."

I wanted very badly to ask if those facets included selling her favors, but I decided I'd said quite enough for the moment.

But later . . . well, later was a different issue altogether.

I gulped more aqivi as Del departed, thinking maybe it was best if I got drunk before she started serving liquor to men who were entirely too free with their hands.

Of course, Del was more likely to chop off a wandering hand than slap it playfully.

I reconsidered getting drunk, if only to bear sober witness to the justifiable murder of several men.

Then again, they were customers. It's tough to make any profits if you kill or maim the customers.

I went back to the aqivi.

Sometime later, as the girls took to setting out and lighting table candles, I gathered up book and sword and made my way back to the room that was now ours. It was kind of a nice feeling knowing we had a place to leave things as needed on a regular basis as well as to sleep. I'd bunked often enough at Fouad's in earlier days but almost never alone . . . well, come to think of it, I wouldn't be alone now, either, but back then I'd *ridden* alone, too.

I wondered as I slid aside the door curtain if this was a sign of getting soft or of advancing age, this appreciation of property. I'd never had a place of my own, nor needed one. With the Salset, as a chula, I slept on a ratty goatskin, but even that hadn't been mine; at Alimat, learning to sword-dance, I'd had a bedroll and a spot on the sand to throw it, but neither qualified as a home. A room in the cantina wasn't a home, either, but it was more than anything I'd claimed before.

I grinned wryly as I returned the book to a saddlepouch and slid them under the bed. For a while there, in Skandi, it had looked as though I might be heir to a vast trading empire, due to inherit wealth, vineyards, ships, and a chunk of property containing an immense and beautiful house. But that was when the metri had a use for a long-lost grandson; that use had changed, and so had her attitude. She had, in fact, eventually denied altogether I was her grandson, claiming her daughter had died before I was born. But Del made a surprising discovery on the way back home: I bore the keraka, the birthing mark that proved me a Stessa, one of the Eleven Families of Skandi. They claimed to be gods-descended, those families, but unless the gods they worshipped were petty and avaricious, I hadn't noted any resemblance or advantage.

Still, I couldn't help the hand that stole up to my head, fingers parting hair to feel behind my left ear. Had the priest-mages of ioSkandi not shaved my head, we'd never have known the truth. Del had once asked if I now considered the possibility of returning to Skandi and presenting my case to the ten other Families, but I wasn't interested. The metri had her heir in Herakleio, a cousin of sorts. He was Skandic-born, bred into island customs and convictions, one of *them*. I was Southron-born and -reared despite my Skandic ancestry; I belonged here.

Of course, only if I survived the current minor problems of sword-dancers out to kill me, and Umir the Ruthless.

My eyes were gritty from reading all day. For that matter, all of me was gritty; I hadn't bathed in days. It crossed my mind to ask Fouad to have the girls bring in a half-cask and fill it, but I decided not to push my luck. I was in their bad graces after my comment to Del. So I opted for the public bathhouse down the street a way. A hot bath, a filling meal, a drink or two, and a good night's sleep in a real bed. I felt my jaw: and a shave. Because come morning, we'd be back on the sand, sweating under burnouses, hunting one of Del's strays.

Of whom I was decidedly *not* jealous, thank you very much.

I donned harness, did up buckles, made sure the blade exited the sheath without catching, and took myself off to the bathhouse.

Del, who had explained that the scent of an unbathed, hot, active, liquor-imbibing male was not necessarily arousing in intimate moments, would undoubtedly appreciate it.

Me, I'd never noticed. But sometimes you just have to cater to a woman's wishes if you want her to yield to yours. It's the way of the world.

TWENTY-FIVE

JULAH'S public bathhouse was actually a bath*tent*. In a small courtyard set back from the street, not far from the main well, an enterprising soul years before had strung a cross-hatching of ropes from hooks pounded into the back walls of buildings, hung swathes of gauzy fabric over them to form tiny private "rooms," built three good-sized fires, and hired people to keep big cauldrons filled with heated water. Others filled smaller wooden buckets and hauled the water to the rough-hewn tubs in each "room." It wasn't much, but when you've been in the desert for weeks on end, it was sheer luxury. From time to time sun-baked ropes and fabric had to be replaced, but otherwise it was business as usual.

I paid the price for water and soap, which cost extra, gave the hirelings time to reheat the tepid water in a tub, waved away the attendant who offered to scrub my back, and pulled the draperies closed. There's not a lot of privacy in the bathtent, but since only men used it, it didn't really matter. I stripped down and draped the burnous over the nearest rope, bowing it slightly, then made a small pile out of sandals, dhoti, and harness next to the tub. I risked one foot in the water, hissed a bit, then worked the other one in. The introduction of netherparts required a bit more cour-age, but once I was down, rump planted against wood, water lap-ping around my navel, the contrast between cooling air and hot water faded. Sighing, I unsheathed the sword, balanced it across the width of the tub, and felt the knots in my muscles begin to loosen. Bliss.

I was about halfway through my bath when an overeager attendant pulled the curtain back, chattering to his customer, only to blush fiery red when he realized the tub already held a body. He apologized effusively and yanked the curtain closed, but not before the stranger had a good look at me hunched in the tub with one foot stuck up in the air as I scrubbed at toes.

Additional mortified apologies from the attendant were issued through the curtains. Smiling, I assured him that all was well and forgiven—even as I quietly climbed out of the tub, pulled on my dhoti (not easy over wet flesh), knotted sandal thongs together and hung them over a shoulder along with the harness. The sword was in my right hand. I bent over, sloshed my left through the water as if I was only just exiting, then waited.

Sure enough, within moments a sword blade sliced down through the back wall, severing the support rope. A body moved against falling fabric. I heard a blurt of shock, a curse—the former from an attendant, the latter from my attacker—and the clang of steel as I trapped the blade with my own and drove it down. Unweighting, twisting, I kicked out with one foot and made contact with the man's body, knocking him backward. He tripped, went down hard. Sheets of gauzy material collapsed upon him, fouling his sword. I bent, locked hands around the tub, upended it, spilling lukewarm water in my assailant's direction. Water on hardpack turns it slick; anything to slow him.

A series of quick slashes with my sword brought down every "room" in my immediate area, entangling customers and attendants alike in steam-dampened curtains and ropes. I heard angry shouting and cries of alarm. Barefoot, damp, half-naked, with harness and sandals flopping against my ribs, I light-footed into the alley, to the street, then raced toward Fouad's, hoping the sword-dancer had no idea where I might be staying.

At the cantina door I paused briefly, caught my breath, examined the customers even as I entered. The first thing I saw was

Del seated at a table with a man. She faced the doorway; his back was to me. Short of twisting all the way around on his stool, he wouldn't see me. Del's expression didn't change, but I did note the way she lifted a hand as if to smooth back hair, and saw the quick, subtle gesture with fingers: *go away*. Not polite, perhaps, but it got the message across: He wasn't an innocent customer making time with her but a threat, and she was making time with *him* to control his intentions. I tilted my head toward the back hallway, sending my own message, then soundlessly moved to our room.

By the time Del joined me, I had sandals and harness on and the saddlepouches packed. "We're leaving," I said. "Go back and keep him company so there's no suspicion, then meet me at the livery when you've got a chance to get away. I've got all of our things; I'll have the horses ready."

Del nodded and disappeared. I waited until I was fairly certain she owned his attention again, then made my way to the cantina's back door.

Fouad met me there. "Trouble?"

"The man with Del is a sword-dancer, likely on my trail."

"Ah. I wondered why she sat down with him." He offered me an armload of filled botas. "When Del disappears, I'll send Silk out to him with drugged wine. That'll delay him."

I opened the door. "He may have someone riding with him."

He shrugged. "We'll deal with him, too."

I grinned. "Kind of nice having another partner."

Fouad made a sour face and shut the door behind me.

It took Del a bit longer to arrive at the livery than I expected. Both the stud and the white gelding were tacked out and ready to go as we lingered in the stableyard; I tossed Del the reins to the gelding and swung up onto the stud. "What took you so long?"

"He was very curious about your habits."

She wore a fresh, pale burnous and had wound her hair up on top of her head in some kind of arcane knotwork fastened with a carved bone rod. Wisps straggled down her neck most fetchingly. "I doubt it was me he was asking about!"

Del mounted, gathering reins as she hooked her right foot in the stirrup. "Not initially, no. But we got around to you." She paused. "Where are we going?"

"North—" But I broke off as the stud sashayed sideways, snorting. I felt the tension in his body, the quivering of muscles. "What's *your* problem?"

"I think it's my gelding," Del said, amused.

"What—again?" But it was possible. Horses could be rather obtuse sometimes. I reaffirmed my control over the stud. "As I was saying, we're going north. We'll get out of town a ways, then find a place to stay the night." I shot her a glance over my shoulder. "Guess you got your wish."

"What wish?"

"To ride out after Nayyib tonight."

Del's smile was swift as she took out the hair rod, tucking it away in a saddlepouch. "Guess I did."

"And *I*, meanwhile—unlike a certain someone I could mention, who spent most of the day unconscious—did not get to sleep in a real bed."

She brought the gelding up next to the stud as we turned onto the main drag. "Take solace in the knowledge you are repaying a debt."

"Solace isn't as comfortable as a real bed."

Del nodded, tucking now-loose hair under the neckline of her burnous. "I did tell him you were a disagreeable soul. Cranky, even."

"Told who?"

"Ahmahd. The sword-dancer back at the cantina. A very courteous soul, he was—offered to buy me liquor, dinner, and a bed."

"So long as he was *in* the bed."

"Well, I suppose he had hopes, yes."

I shook my head, grinning; so . . . predictable. Just like me. "This way . . ." I turned the stud and led Del through one of the narrower alleys, twisting about like a tangled skein of yarn. When at last we left the last hedge of buildings behind, we were free of the town entirely, striking out northward beneath a star-pocked sky. "I suspect they won't think I'd head back *into* Umir's domain."

"I suspect Ahmahd won't, since I suggested otherwise." Del brought the gelding up next to me again. "I explained we hadn't seen one another for weeks. That you'd been hauled off to Umir's by Rafiq and his friends, and that was the last I'd seen of you. But before then you'd talked of going to Haziz to take ship back to Skandi. I was hanging around hoping you'd show up but was beginning to worry that you'd gone without me."

I grunted. "I doubt he believed you."

"There was no one left in the cantina who'd seen us together. Fouad had different girls working, and everyone else who'd seen us talking had left. Ahmahd will learn the truth, of course, at some point, but at least it will buy us a little time." A trace of dry amusement laced her tone. "Men tend to believe me, if I wish them to."

Present company included; nice of her not to mention that. "Here." I led her off the road. We rode some distance away, winding through scrubby trees and shrubbery, until I indicated a cluster of vegetation forming a leafy blockade against a rill of windblown sand and soil. It sloped into a slight hollow, good enough for a smidgen of shelter. "No one would believe anyone would camp out here, this close to Julah. This close to *real beds*." A glance southwards showed the flickering lights of the city, sparking against the dark horizon. "We should be safe. Come dawn, we can head for Umir's domain. And let's hope Nayyib's there, or this is all for nothing."

"He is." Del swung down off of her gelding even as I dismounted. "I asked Ahmahd."

Well, that was something. More than we had known. "Did he say if the kid was being held against his will?"

"That he didn't know. Just that Neesha arrived and had not yet departed when Ahmahd and his friend left."

"So it's likely the kid would have heard about any reward for me."

"It seems so."

"And how do we know Nayyib didn't tell Ahmahd about Fouad's cantina, hoping for a cut without involving himself personally?"

Del flicked me an icy glance.

"All right, fine." I was grinning as I dismounted. "We'll assume he didn't."

"He wouldn't. But if he had, don't you think Ahmahd and his friend would have arrived in Julah sooner?"

"Possibly," I conceded.

"Oh, and I did neglect to mention something Ahmahd said about you."

"About me? In between seducing you?"

"He did not seduce me. He *attempted* to seduce me."

"Ran out of time, did he?"

"He said," Del began, ignoring me, "that he had seen you dance there at Umir's and was quite impressed by your skills."

"At least he's being honest."

"He said you were better than he expected—especially for an old man."

I began untacking the stud. "He did not. *You're* saying that."

"Ahmahd said it." Del's expression was blandly serene. "Right before he asked me what a woman my age was doing with a man *your* age."

I scowled at the stud, undoing thongs and buckles, and changed the subject. "I don't suppose this friend of Ahmahd's felt in need of a bath."

"As a matter of fact, Ahmahd said he *did* go to the bathhouse. Why?"

"Because that's where I was when someone decided to interrupt my soak by taking off my head. Fortunately, I was ready. Last I saw of him, he was wrestling with curtains." I deposited the saddle on end, plus the tied-on saddlepouches, then peeled blankets off the stud's back. They were only slightly damp; we hadn't ridden long enough for the horses to work up a true sweat. "Did your friend Ahmahd happen to mention how many others might be tracking us?"

"Oh, *I'm* not being tracked," Del said, precise as always. "At least, not as prey. For information, yes. But it's you they want to kill."

"Comforting," I muttered, kneeling to hobble the stud.

"I'm assuming a goodly number are hoping to find you," Del added. "Though they won't kill you out of hand, Ahmahd said. Apparently Umir's far less concerned that you dishonored the circle and your vows than he is in recovering the book, despite what the sword-dancers want. The orders are explicit: you are not to be killed until the book is back in his hands, in case you've hidden it somewhere. Then they can do whatever they like with you."

"Comforting," I repeated. Although it was, a little; easier for me to defend myself if they didn't want to kill me. Not that all of them would accept Umir's terms. "Well, at least we know Ahmahd and his friend won't be following us immediately—Fouad was going to take care of that." The stud was hobbled, haltered, and watered; he'd already eaten at the livery. I took myself to my pile of gear and unrolled my bedding after grooming the soil beneath it, getting rid of rocks. Aggrievedly I said, "Here I am, being hunted by the gods know how many sword-dancers . . . and *you* want us to ride right into Umir's domain, maybe even into his very house, just to make sure the kid's all right."

Del knelt as she unrolled her own bedding. "Yes."

Nothing more. I shook my head, unstoppered a bota. "I sure hope this Nayyib is worth it."

"He is."

I watched her a moment, noting the slight stiffness in her movements, the pensive frown marring her face. She was defensive about the kid, as if there were more to him than she let on.

She glanced up, caught me staring at her. "What?"

I shook my head and began to unlace my sandals.

"Tiger—"

"I'm tired." And I was. "Let's get as good a night's sleep as we can, then head out at first light."

Her bedroll overlapped my own. Del took off her own sandals, her burnous, and set both beside her bedding along with harness and sword. She crawled beneath blankets. Bathed in the light of the moon, pale hair glowed. "Are you all right?"

I started to answer her flippantly, then reconsidered. Perched on one elbow, I leaned forward and kissed her lightly on the brow. "I'm fine, bascha."

With the abrupt change of mood I'd come to recognize over the years as purely female, she said, "If you truly don't wish to go to Umir's, we don't have to. Perhaps we could find another way."

I didn't wish to go to Umir's. But Del wanted it very badly, and I didn't really have a good enough reason to refuse. I did owe the kid. "We'll go, bascha. I said so." I pulled the blanket up to my chin. "Now, let's get some sleep."

After a moment of silence, "Tiger?"

"Hmm?"

"Did *every* sword-dancer at Umir's wish to kill you? Weren't some of them your friends?"

Beneath my blanket, I shrugged. "Friends. Rivals. Enemies. That was the way of Alimat. And there's the matter of *elaii-ali-ma* . . . I was as sworn to execute an outcast as they are; that was understood from the beginning. But no—not everyone wished to kill me. One man didn't." I smiled, remembering. "Alric. In fact, he helped me escape."

Her tone was sharp as she hitched herself up on an elbow. "Alric was there? And you didn't tell me?"

"We've been a little busy, bascha."

"But if he helped you, isn't he an outcast now?"

"Alric was never an *incast.* He's a Northerner. He didn't make any friends by helping me, and he probably lost some—or all—of those who were there, but he didn't break any Southron vows. And it's only Alimat where the codes were so binding." I shrugged. "It was the shodo's way of fashioning true men out of worthless meat."

"A very rigorous binding."

"Are the Northern vows made on Staal-Ysta any less binding?"

No, they were not. Del's silence made that clear.

She changed the subject. "Did Alric say how Lena and the girls are?"

"Fine. Lena's expecting again." I made an indeterminate sound of derision. "You know, you'd think three daughters would be enough!"

Del settled down again. "Some men insist on sons, and their poor wives keep having babies until they get one. Even if it kills them."

"*You've* met Lena. You know she loves children. She likely wants a dozen."

"Well, yes," Del conceded.

"And it's Alric who'll have to support them. See, bascha? There are always two sides. The woman has them, which, mind you, I *don't* suggest is easy or without risk, but the man pays for them. That, too, isn't easy or without risk."

"Maybe."

"Fools," I muttered, trying to get comfortable against hard ground, "both of them."

"If it's what they want, then they aren't truly foolish."

"It's one thing if you're a farmer, bascha. Or a tradesman. But a sword-dancer? If something happens to Alric—and he's not exactly in a safe line of work—Lena's stuck with raising the children on her own." I shrugged. "Though she'd probably marry again as soon as possible."

"You mean, once she found a man to provide for her and the girls?"

"Well . . . yes." I was wary of where the conversation might be heading; you never know, with Del. "I mean, it is what many women do."

"It is what *most* women do," she said curtly. "They have no other choice."

Not being up for the verbal sword-dance, I kept my mouth shut.

"Or they could do what I did, and give their child away."

After that comment, I wasn't going to sleep any time soon. I contemplated holding my silence in case that was what Del preferred, but I just couldn't let it go. "You mean Kalle."

"Of course I mean Kalle." Del sighed, staring up at the stars. "She has a good home. Better parents than I could ever be—or you."

The defense was automatic. "I might be a superb father, for all you know—I just don't particularly care to find out."

"You can't be a superb father if you have no children," Del declared. Then amended it almost immediately. "That is, if you *know* you have children and don't stay around to raise them. Otherwise you're not a father at all. Just the means for making them."

Did the same apply to a woman? I decided not to bring it up for fear it was a sore spot; pointed debate is one thing, but engaging in it to hurt someone is another thing altogether. I wondered how often Del's daughter crossed her mind. She never spoke about her. "You miss her, don't you?"

Del turned over, putting her back to me. "I don't even know her, Tiger."

"I mean, you miss what you might have had."

"I made my choice before Kalle was even born. There was nothing to miss."

And yet Del had once insisted on going North to see Kalle against my preferences, though I didn't know the girl existed then; she had been driven to see her daughter six years after her birth, as if it were some kind of geas. The journey had tested us both in many different ways, had taught us about strength of will, determination, the power of the binding between us; had nearly ended in both our deaths. Kalle was around eight now, I thought. Old enough to understand her mother had given her up in a quest to execute the men who'd robbed Del of a family. And Kalle as well.

"Maybe someday," I said, purposely not mentioning that Del,

by breaking *her* vows, was exiled from the North and thus from her daughter.

"What?"

"Maybe someday you'll see her again."

The tone was frigid. "And how would that come to be, do you think?"

"If Kalle came looking for you."

Del's single burst of throttled laughter was bitter. "Oh yes, they would let her come searching for a woman who has no honor, a woman exiled from her homeland. And why would Kalle wish to? She has a mother and father."

"But they aren't her blood."

She was silent a moment, then turned over to face me. Her eyes, black in the glow of the moon, were steady. "Do you believe that matters? Blood? To children whose true mother and father have disavowed them?"

"You didn't disavow Kalle."

"They will have told her I did."

I scratched at the stubble I hadn't gotten the chance to shave. "I think blood matters, yes. I think a child might wish to search for her mother. Hoolies, I went all the way to Skandi, didn't I?"

"And repudiated your family."

"The metri wanted nothing to do with the son of a disobedient daughter who dishonored her exalted Family by daring to sleep with a man well below her class."

"Your mother left Skandi to be with the man she loved, below her class or no. Do you really believe she'd have disavowed you if she was willing to go that far?"

"Doesn't matter," I dismissed. "I ended up a chula with the Salset anyway. And how in hoolies did we get onto *this* subject? We were talking about Kalle."

"You say it matters to children that they know their own blood."

"I believe that, yes."

"Does it matter to men or women that they know their own children?"

"You're the one who dragged me all the way into the ice and snow so you could see Kalle again, bascha! I would say yes to that as well, based on your example."

Del did not answer. When I realized she didn't mean to, I shut my eyes and, when I could slow my thoughts, gave myself over to sleep.

TWENTY-SIX

*B*REEZE *becomes wind. Wind be-
comes gust. Gust becomes storm: simoom. The sky is heavy with sand,
the sun eclipsed, occluded by curtains of it, pale as water, hard as ice.
At the edges of the Punja it scours the earth of vegetation; in the Deep
Desert, where the tribes take care to protect themselves, it stings but
does not strip; to strangers, wholly innocent but thus sweeter victims,
it is death. Clothing is torn away. Flesh abraded. Eventually flayed. In
the end, long past death, the ivory bones are polished white. And buried, only freed again by yet another fickle, angry simoom, digging up
the dead.*

*White bones in white sand. Fingerbones scattered, the vertebrae,
the toes. The skull remains, but lower jaw is lost. Teeth gleam, that
once were hidden by lips.*

*I walk there, find them: pearls of the desert. Out of boredom, I
begin to gather them, to arrange them against the flat sand. Not many
left. The skull, lacking half its jaw; upper arm, forearm; the ladder of
ribs. The knobby-ended thigh. I reassemble the pieces and stare at the
puzzle, wondering who and what it might have been, when it wore
flesh.*

*I sit back, studying the forgotten remnants of a living being. Then
pick up the curving, fragile short rib. Close my hand upon it.*

Over the skull, as I watch, flesh grows. Hollows are filled, angles

*coated, like moss on a rock. A face stares up at me, though it lacks a
lower jaw. Even without eyes, I know her.*

*"Time runs away," she says. "You must be faster, if you choose
to catch it."*

Her words are clear despite deformation. "And if I don't?" I ask.

"It is best to be the hunter, not the prey. The prey perishes."

"Unless it escapes."

"But you will not."

*Sobering pronouncement, especially from a woman dead a month,
a year, a decade. "If I'm to find you," I say, "how about a hint?"*

"The answer is in your bones."

I hold up the rib. "Yours are more accessible."

*The upper lip, lacking a lower, achieves only half a smile. "Your
bones know where to find mine."*

*I replace the rib in the collection on the sand. "And if I am to
sacrifice flesh in order to hear them? To become like you?" I hold up
mutilated hands. "Why would I wish to? I have already donated two
fingers."*

"Count mine," the woman says, who lacks even hands.

I smile wryly. "Point taken."

"The bones know. Listen. Then come and find me."

And the flesh retreats, and the woman says no more.

"The bones know," I echoed.

"What?" Del asked.

I blinked into chilly dawn. "What?"

"What did you mean? The bones know what?"

"What bones?"

She sat up, folding back blankets. "The bones you were talking about." Del picked a stray hair out of pale eyelashes. "I hope
you aren't referring to the fingerbone necklet Oziri gave you. Because if you are, it means I'm going to have to kill you."

I grunted, scrubbing at an itchy, sleep-creased face. The sun
was barely up, peering over the blade of the horizon.

"Find me," she had said once. Or twice. Maybe thrice. "And
take up the sword."

"The bones know," I declared, though mostly it was distorted by a tremendous yawn. "Mine, though, not those." Awareness coalesced. "Oh, hoolies, not that thrice-cursed dream again!"

Del crawled out of her bedroll, untangling twisted burnous from around her hips. "If we didn't have so much to do today, I'd tell you to go back to sleep. Maybe next time you woke up you'd make more sense."

I frowned. "What do we have to do today?"

Del laced up sandals. "Rescue Nayyib."

I watched her walk off, hunting privacy. I grumbled a protest, yawned widely again, contemplated going back to sleep. My bones ached.

My eyes flew open. "Bones." I sat up, threw back covers. All I wore was my dhoti, since I'd neglected to grab my burnous back at the bathhouse. That left me with an expanse of flesh tanned a deep coppery-brown, with the fine hairs bleached bronze-gold. I couldn't see any bones. Not naked ones. Just the lines and angles covered by muscle and flesh. I knocked on a kneecap, then inspected an elbow, since they were closer to the surface. "Is there anything any of you have to tell me? Like, how it is I'm supposed to find this woman?" Or whatever she was, buried in the sand.

For all they supposedly knew the answer, my bones remained stubbornly silent. Muttering, I pulled on my own sandals, crossgartered them up my calves, then got up and limped off to make my own morning donation even as Del returned from hers.

"Don't take long," she called. "I want to get started."

Not something a man wants to hear first thing in the morning when he's only barely awake. "It'll take as long as it takes," I muttered, scowling at the sunrise.

Del had everything packed and the horses loaded by the time I returned, reins in her hands; and no, I had not taken that long. She was clearly impatient to get going.

"Hold your horses," I said, wondering if she'd get the joke.

She didn't. "According to you, we could reach Umir's today if we leave early enough."

"And we will reach Umir's today, even if we leave after we eat."

"We can eat on the way." She had packed my things, leaving behind only my harness, sword, and knife. Ready to go.

I wasn't. I picked up the knife, went over to a spike-fronded plant, cut off a flat, wide, thorn-tipped leaf. "You weren't in this much of a hurry last night."

"Last night we couldn't do anything but sleep. This morning we can . . . Tiger, what are you doing?"

Methodically I trimmed the sharp tip from the leaf, then carefully slipped the knife blade into the plump edge and slit the leaf from top to bottom, peeling them apart. I now had two halves, turgid with pale green sap. I turned over one half of the leaf and began to smear the greasy sap over my shoulder. Once worked into skin, it was colorless.

"Tiger—"

"If you want to save time," I interrupted, "you might cut off some leaves and give me a hand."

"What *is* it, and why are you doing that?"

"Alla oil," I explained. "The same stuff you put on your gelding's pink skin, remember? It protects it from sunburn."

Del, who had only seen alla oil mixed with a paste in cork- or wax-stoppered pots, not in its pure form, was surprised. "Oh. But why are *you* putting it on?"

"Because I'm fresh out of burnouses, and the last time I made this trek to Umir's, I arrived with at least one layer of skin peeling off. I'd just as soon skip the experience this time." I dropped the depleted half of leaf, began to work with the other. "Gee, bascha, I can think of a lot of women who'd just love to spread oil all over me. Have you grown immune to my charms? I did bathe yesterday." I reconsidered. "Well, *half* of me got bathed. I'll let you do the clean half. And you might want to put some on your face, even with the hood."

Del shook herself out of her reverie and bent to cut off leaves. I watched her. Clearly the body was present, but the thoughts were not.

"*Have* you grown immune to my charms?"

With great concentration she slit the leaf open, frowning. "What?"

"You're not listening to a word I say, are you?"

She flicked a glance at me, then walked around behind me and slapped the leaf sap-down on my back. "I want to get going. We can talk on the way." Strong fingers began to rub oil into my skin.

She wanted to eat on the way, talk on the way. I suppose I was lucky she hadn't insisted I piss on the way. "Fine," I said tersely.

After that we worked in silence, which seemed to suit Del. Me, I just got grumpy. It's a sad thing when a dead woman's bones are more talkative than a living woman's mouth.

I insisted we stop briefly at the big oasis at which Alric and I had spent the night. Del clearly wanted to continue, but she'd learned that in the desert one never passes up the chance to refill botas and rest the horses.

She did, however, protest as I pulled up at the outskirts of the oasis, taking time to mark the other travelers present. "What are we waiting for?"

"Oh, I don't know—maybe checking to see if any sword-dancers are here," I remarked pointedly. "We ride straight in without looking and I could end up dead in very short order, and *then* where would your precious Neesha be?"

Del was annoyed, but she shut her mouth on further protest.

"There's a spring about halfway in. Follow the main path. Keep your eyes open. I'll take the perimeter, then come in from the other side. All right?"

She nodded, giving the gelding a touch of her heels. Sighing, I reined the stud aside and began to reconnointer as I rode the perimeter of the big oasis.

I did not see anyone lying in wait for me, but that didn't mean no one who might challenge me was absent. I aimed the stud down the center path leading toward the spring and remained mounted. Being ahorse gives a man an advantage, usually. Being atop the stud gives me a huge advantage always, as he doesn't take kindly to assailants rushing up at him, even if his rider is the target.

Of course, I didn't know any sword-dancers stupid enough to do such a thing. We—they—aren't assassins, though we will take on death-dances depending on circumstances; the goal is the ritual and the challenge, not out and out murder.

Then again, there were no guarantees all sword-dancers would adhere to that unspoken custom. Me killing Musa in a dance had proven to all witnesses that out and out murder might in fact be easier. Of course, supposedly Umir wanted me alive, but I suspected there'd be a few sword-dancers willing to forgo the reward simply for the pleasure of killing me.

I rode down the path, poised for attack. There was a scattering of wagons here and there, with unhitched dray animals resting quietly in such shade as palm trees offer; half-dressed children running around, heedless of the heat—why is it we notice it more when we're adults?—and burnous-clad men and women visiting in small groups, exchanging tales of their travels, describing plans for when they arrived at their destinations. Someone was playing a reed pipe; the thin, wailing melody cut the air. No fires, as there had been the evening Alric and I stayed, merely fire rings with quiet coals hoarded against the evening meal.

As I rode up, Del was at the spring watering the gelding. He had lost his brilliant red tassels at the Vashni encampment, where someone had presented Del with a browband of dangling leather thongs, ornamented with blue beads. He still looked rather silly, especially with the black paint around his eyes, but not as ridiculous as he had wearing Silk's crimson tassels.

She had watered herself as well as her horse and had braided her hair into a single thick plait. To tie it off she'd robbed the gelding of one thong; blue beads clacked quietly against each other when she moved her head. They matched her eyes.

"All right," I said in answer to her expression, "so we didn't run into any trouble. But we *might* have." I dropped off the stud

and let him nose his way in past the gelding, urging him aside
with an absent nipping motion of his mouth.

Del handed me a dripping gourd ladle. "I didn't say anything."

I drank, swallowing heavily, not caring when water splashed
down my bare torso to dampen my dhoti. I now wore a gritty layer
of fine dust sticking to the alla oil from head to toe. So much for
the half a bath in Julah.

"You didn't have to." I handed the gourd back. "I can read
your expression: Hurry up; let's go; stop wasting time. And *don't*
try to tell me none of those comments passed through your mind.
I know better."

Del did not attempt it, though clearly she was irritated. "You
said Umir's place wasn't far from here."

"We'll make it well before sundown."

"Then hand me your empty botas," she said, "and I can fill
them." Because, I knew, it would speed things up.

Shaking my head, I unhooked and handed her two flaccid
botas. The others I unloaded and dipped down via tie-ropes into
the water, soaking the rough sacking that formed an outer casing
for the leather. While wet it helped cool the water, but it wouldn't
stay that way for long beneath the sun. And since I doubted Umir
would be much interested in replenishing our supplies, and Nayyib might have none as we departed, we needed to conserve.

"You're filthy," Del commented, sounding somewhat concilia-
tory—if you want to call being told you're dirty a peace offering.
"You could wash off here, cool down a little."

"It'll strip off too much of the oil." I stood, botas dripping,
and began to tie them back onto the stud's saddle. "And I doubt
you'd allow me the time to go bargain for a burnous."

"If the oil is working . . ." Wisely, she let it trail off.

I took the refilled botas from her, tied them on. "Let's go,
basha. We're burning daylight."

I suspect she knew I was not pleased. But she didn't ask why
or suggest I shouldn't be; she simply mounted the gelding and
allowed me to take the lead as we rode out of the oasis.

*   *   *

Umir's place wasn't far, and we did arrive well before sundown. There were no gates, merely an arched opening in the white-painted walls, and I pulled up in front. "Whatever happens," I said, "you've got my back."

"What are you planning to do?"

"Ride up to his front door and ask for Nayyib." I set the stud into a walk.

"Tiger, be serious."

"I am being serious. Sometimes the only way to get what you want is to ride up to the front door and ask."

"Umir may set some sword-dancers on you!"

"Or not." I rode under the archway and into the paved court-yard with its tiled fountain. "Do you want the kid or not?"

Del kept her mouth shut. She held the gelding a few steps behind the stud, undoubtedly examining every visible nook and cranny in Umir's walled gardens. I suspected she had unsheathed and now held the sword across her saddlebow. That belief was confirmed when I caught a metallic flash of light thrown against the white-painted walls.

I halted the stud beside the fountain, marking how much room there was for him to pivot and take off if given the order. Del knew better than to crowd him, so there was no chance of a collision. I reached down to the pouch behind my right leg and undid the thong, flipping back the flap.

"Umir!" I shouted, as the stud rang a shod hoof off courtyard pavers. "Umir the Ruthless!"

As expected, it was a servant who came out to see what the ruckus was all about.

I greeted him politely. "Now, go fetch your master. Tell him we have business to transact, he and I."

The servant opened his mouth to refuse—I looked about as disreputable now as I did when Rafiq and friends had brought me in—then thought better of it. He departed.

After making us wait just long enough to notice, Umir put in an appearance. He wore a costly gold-striped robe, gem-weighted belt, soft kidskin house slippers. His expression was austere. "I do not conduct business out here in the heat and dust." His eyes assessed my condition, found it lacking. "I am a man of refinement."

Cheerfully, I told him what he could do with his refinement. "You have someone here, Umir. A young man, name of Nayyib. In fact, you're very likely guesting him in the same room I occupied. Have you replaced the bedframe, yet, or is it still missing a leg?"

"I have no guests at present," Umir retorted. "All of the sword-dancers have left to look for you."

"Well, too bad for you I decided to come here on my own. Makes them all look kind of bad, doesn't it? Especially after I outdanced Musa." I flicked a glance past him, toward the depths of the house. "We've come for Nayyib. Have someone saddle his horse while someone else escorts him out here."

"Why should I do any such thing, Sandtiger?"

"Because you want your book back."

His eyes sharpened. "You have it? With you?"

I reached into the pouch, closed my hand on the cover, and dragged it out.

The tanzeer took a hungry step forward. "*Give* it to me!"

I smiled. "Nayyib first."

Umir turned and snapped out an order to an invisible servant. Then he swung back. "Let me have it."

I rested the fat book atop the saddle pommel. "Not until the kid is brought out here and is mounted on his horse."

"You don't have any idea what that book is!" Umir said. "Don't be a fool—let me have it!"

"No wonder you don't conduct business out here," I observed. "The sun boils yours brains."

"The boy is being brought!"

"Fine. Once he's mounted and on his way, you'll get your book back."

A white indentation circling Umir's mouth appeared on his face. Pale eyes were icy with anger. "Do you expect this to lift the reward I've placed on you?"

"As I understand it, the reward was for my return—alive. Well, here I am. How about you pay up?"

"Pay *you* the reward?"

"Call it a delicious irony," I suggested. I traced with two fingers the scuffs in the leather binding. "The *Book of Udre-Natha*." I turned back the cover, began to riffle pages. "Interesting."

"Don't touch it!" Umir cried. "You'll soil the pages!"

I pinned down a page with a forefinger. "What do you suppose this says?"

"Don't read it!" He glared up at me. "Not that you could. I doubt you can read your own language."

"Just a big, dumb sword-dancer, am I?" I shrugged. "Ah, well. We can't all be born tanzeers."

"Chula," he spat.

I continued turning pages. "Hmmm . . . what do you suppose *this* means?"

Umir couldn't control himself. "Stop it! Stop it!" Hands reached out. "Give it to me!"

I looked beyond him as I saw movement in the doorway. Nayyib, escorted by Umir's servant, exited the house. His near-black hair was sticking up all over his head as if he'd been rousted from a nap. In fact, his eyes looked a little bleary, too. Had Umir drugged him?

I looked at the tanzeer. "Horse."

"Coming," he retorted.

And so it was, as another servant led the bay around from the stable block. Bridled and saddled, saddlepouches and botas tied on, ready to go.

I glanced at Nayyib. He was in a sad way, blinking woozily out at the sun-washed courtyard. Umir's little joke, to drug the boy. And neither Del nor I could chance giving him a hand, or we'd endanger the entire rescue. "You," I began, "have caused me no small amount of trouble. How about you get up on your horse and head out of here? *Now.*"

Nayyib nodded vaguely, scrubbing vigorously at his stubbled face. But didn't move.

I pointed. "That horse right there."

"Neesha," Del said, still waiting behind me. The tone was a complex combination of relief, concern, and command. And something I couldn't identify.

Umir glared at me. "The book."

"When the boy is mounted and heading out of here."

Nayyib finally bestirred himself to walk haphazardly to his horse and stick a foot in the stirrup. With great effort he pulled himself up. I heard the sound of a burnous seam ripping as he fell into the saddle. I wondered if I'd have any teeth left by the time we exited the courtyard. Already my jaw ached from clenching it.

"Go," Del told him, as Nayyib lifted reins.

The stud, taking a closer look at the bay, suddenly filled the courtyard with a ringing neigh. I winced.

Del's voice again: "Neesha. Go."

Neesha went.

"You too, bascha." I heard retreating hoofs clopping agains the pavers. Then I smiled down at Umir. "Your book."

I thought he might send a servant to take it from me. But Umir came himself, lower lip caught in white teeth as he reached up for it.

"I've locked it closed," I told him, "for safety." I handed over the book. "It may take you a few weeks or years, but eventually you'll figure out how to open it."

Eyes wide with alarm, Umir attempted to undo the latch holding the book closed. "No—no—"

"A little insurance," I remarked, "in case you felt like trying a spell on me when I wasn't looking."

He hugged the book to his chest, staring up at me. "But—how did you do this? It requires a spell to lock it!"

"Let's just say I picked up a few things while visiting an island paradise." I tossed him a jaunty wave as I backed the stud toward the opening in the wall. "Happy reading, Umir."

Outside the walls, I found Del and Nayyib waiting. I motioned them to ride on as I headed past them.

Del's face was white. "I can't believe you did that."

"What—give him the book? Why not? It worked, didn't it? Nayyib-Neesha is now our guest instead of Umir's." I glanced at the boy. "Are you drugged? Did Umir drug you?"

Owl-eyed, he shook his head.

Suspicion stirred. "Drunk?"

His tone was excessively grave. "I believe so, yes."

I swore deeply and decisively.

Del was still stuck on the book. "I thought you said it contains magic spells."

"It contains a number of things, including magic spells. It's a pretty amazing book, actually."

"And you gave it to *Umir?*"

"Well, I'd read it already." I grinned at her. "What did you think I was doing all day when you were asleep in bed?"

Del was stunned. "You read that whole book in an afternoon?"

"Just a little trick I picked up in Skandi." I took a hard look at Nayyib. "Are you sober enough to stay on your horse?"

"I believe so, yes."

"Do you know where the oasis is from here?"

"I believe so, yes."

"That's where we're going."

Nayyib nodded amiably. "All right." Then a hiccup emerged, attended by a modest belch.

I planted the flat of my palm against my brow. "Gods save me from a sandsick woman and a drunk boy!"

Del scowled at me. "I am not sandsick, and he's not a boy."

"But he's drunk."

Nayyib offered, "I believe so, yes."

"Oh, hoolies," I groaned. "Maybe I should take my sword to him. Or go on ahead and let him find his own way to the oasis. I only might have been killed in there getting him free, and it turns out he's drunk. Drunk!"

"Neesha," Del said gently, "I would be quiet now."

"All right." He gifted her with a luminous smile and a worshipful stare from those melting, honey-brown eyes. "You're so beautiful."

"Oh, hoolies," Del muttered.

TWENTY-SEVEN

W E MANAGED to get the boy
to the oasis. Or, rather, *Del* managed to get the boy to the oasis; I
was so disgusted by his condition I refused to have anything to do
with him. He managed to stay aboard his horse, which was all
that mattered to me, and upon finding a quiet little place at the
oasis that we might call our own for an hour or two, I dismounted
and led the stud off to the spring. I left Del to deal with the kid.

Which maybe wasn't the wisest thing in the world to do, in
view of his obvious infatuation, but I wasn't in any mood to put
up with either of them. And since I knew Del had no tolerance
for drunkenness, I doubted she was any more entranced with Nayyib than I was. The main thing was, he was free of Umir and my
debt was repaid. Del and I could now get on about our business.

I was heading back to the trio of palm trees when I met Del
leading her gelding and Nayyib's bay. "Did you get him settled all
safe in his own little bed?"

Del, pausing, shot me a hard glance. "You might have a little
sympathy for him."

"I just risked my life for a drunken kid! Why should I have
any sympathy for him?"

"Umir could have killed him."

"Umir wanted his book back too much for that."

"Which you *gave* him."

"In exchange for the boy. The one *you* were so all-fired determined to rescue. Well, he's rescued. He can stay here and sleep it
off, and you and I can get on with our lives."

She seemed startled. "I don't want to leave him here."

"Why not?"

"He's drunk."

"He can sleep it off."

"What if he gets sick?"

"*I* never died from it." I paused. "Neither did you, when you
got drunk on Vashni liquor."

Color flooded her face. "We are not discussing me."

"Maybe we should."

"Why? This has nothing to do with me!"

"He's not a stray kitten, bascha, or a puppy with a broken leg,
or even an orphan sandtiger cub—though you might not be so
thrilled with the idea of saving baby sandtigers, now, after our last
meeting with one. He's a grown man; he can take responsibility
for his own binges."

Del's eyes narrowed. "You *are* jealous."

I sighed with long-suffering patience. "I think not."

"If you weren't, you'd have nothing against helping him."

"Rescuing him isn't helping?"

"He spent days nursing us both after the sandtiger attack, and
weeks with me at the Vashni encampment."

"Yes, I'm aware of that."

"Yet you want to just ride off and leave him here to fend for
himself when the gods know *who* might try to rob him."

"Sometimes that's what happens when you get drunk. It's
called a learning experience."

"And I'm learning a little more about you just now, aren't I?"
She clucked to the horses and started to move them out. "Do
whatever you like, Tiger. I'm staying here with Neesha at least
until morning."

I watched her disappear between two wide horse butts as she
led them down the path. I found the image extremely appropriate,
in view of her behavior.

Aloud, I said, "I think this was the most ridiculous argument we've ever had." I patted the stud's face. "And we've had a few."

Being a very wise horse, he did not comment.

Nayyib was sound asleep when I got back to the little encampment. Del had unloaded gear and set out his bedroll; he lay sprawled upon it on his back with one bent arm flung across his eyes. I contemplated the rest of him, which was partially hidden beneath his burnous. But the legs were free of encumbrance, and one shoulder, and a forearm. Not a big man, not like me, but not small, either. His coloring was Southron, including the big brown eyes that he used to such advantage, curse him. A good-looking kid, no doubt, if still a tad soft around the edges; and certainly closer to Del in age than I was. Maybe that's why she wanted to mother him. She couldn't do it to me.

Not that she'd ever indicated she wanted to.

Scowling, I turned my attention to the stud, pulling off pouches, saddle, and blankets. I had thought to ride on after a rest, believing the oasis too obvious if Umir sent anyone after us or if there happened to be sword-dancers in the vicinity, but there was not much time before sundown. This place offered water, a little shade, safety in numbers.

Or maybe just more witnesses than usual.

I hobbled the stud, grained him, draped the halter-rope over one of the spiky bark segments sheathing the bole of the nearest palm tree. Someone else had built a modest fire ring not far from Nayyib's unconscious body, but we lacked kindling for it, and I didn't feel like going on a lengthy hunt for wood. Over the years pickings had become very slim near the oasis, so that most people on wagons carried wood with them if they wanted a fire, and a pot of embers they kept alive by feeding it twigs regularly. Del and I didn't pack that heavy; if there was no wood for a fire, or circumstances warranted it was safer to go without, we didn't bother.

I didn't bother now. I just set up my own little area with upside down saddle, drying blankets spread next to it, and bedding unrolled. I shed the harness and sword and set the blade within reach. Then I lay down in a posture very similar to the kid's, if without the accompaniment of liquor fumes, and let myself drift.

Del came back a little later. Eyes closed, I listened as she finished untacking her gelding and Nayyib's, hobbled them, told them to behave themselves, then crunched over to where the kid lay.

"He's alive," I remarked.

She didn't answer. She just arranged her own bedding—closer to him than to me—and settled down.

"We'll spend the night, all right? Make sure he's alive in the morning. Then we'll go."

There was no reply. Swearing under my breath, I rolled over onto one hip and pulled the corner of a blanket over my face. With one hand draped across the hilt of my sword, I went to sleep. If she was so concerned about the kid, Del could keep watch for any stray sword-dancers looking to get some of Umir's reward money.

I woke up to morning when I heard the sound of a body moving nearby. My hand locked around the sword hilt, lifted the blade even as I sat upright—and discovered Nayyib staggering off from our little camp with the frenzied focus of a man in dire need of relief. Since it was very likely his head, bladder, *and* belly were ready to burst, I hoped he found it in time.

Dropping the sword back onto my bedroll, I arched backward to stretch my spine and shoulders. Del, coming out of the cocoon of blankets between me and the kid's bedding, squinted at the early sunlight. Not far from our camp a danjac brayed and was answered by another, which began a whole chain of ear-shattering morning greetings from one end of the oasis to the other. No one could have slept through that.

Del finger-combed hair off her face as I crawled out of bed and stood. Across the oasis other bodies were doing the same, murmuring to one another as the day began.

I bent and picked up the sword. "I think the kid's got the right idea—" I yawned. "—though I don't believe I'm in quite the same distress. Be back in a bit."

Nodding, Del gathered up horse buckets and headed for the spring. Everyone carried water to their animals first thing in the morning, since to take livestock to the spring would form a milling mass of thirsty, impatient animals all insisting they deserved to drink first. Much safer to do it this way.

When I got back to the camp, I found Nayyib standing near his bedroll, staring at mine and Del's as if he had no idea who they belonged to. He heard me coming and turned sharply. Momentary alarm faded.

"Oh," he said.

"Yes, oh. It's us. Or did you forget what happened yesterday afternoon?"

"I think I have forgotten *all* of yesterday, not just the afternoon." He scooped up a bota, unstoppered it and took a long pull. The last mouthful he turned and spat out. "Yeilkth," he remarked—or something like it. He backhanded excess moisture from his jaw and looked at me. "What happened?"

"We rescued you."

"Oh." He nodded vaguely. "Good."

Near-black hair stood up in clumps all over his head. Stubble darkened the hollows beneath his cheeks, enhancing the steep, oblique angles of the bones above them. He had the look of a slightly disreputable but appealing young man coupled with boyish innocence down to perfection. But the honey-brown eyes, I saw with a stab of satisfaction, were bloodshot, and his color was slightly off.

"Bright day," I commented cheerfully.

Nayyib squinted.

"Feels like it'll be a warm one." I set down the sword, then gathered up my bedding and began to shake it out.

Nayyib very carefully sat down on his own and squirted more water into his mouth, then soaked his hair and let droplets run down his face.

I spread my blankets, began rolling them up. "You probably

won't feel much like riding today, huh?" He scrunched up his face thoughtfully as he slicked hair back into the merest shadow of obedience.

"Probably better if you stayed here, waited another day." I tied thongs around my bedroll. "No reason to get in a rush. Del and I'll make our goodbyes and head on out."

That got his attention. "Head out?"

"We've got business to attend to." I set the bedroll by my saddle, checked the condition of the saddle blankets. Dry. "Del and I." Just to make it clear who the "we" meant. "I imagine you've got things to do, too."

"Not really."

Figures. "Well, I imagine something will come up."

Del was back with the buckets. Nayyib immediately stood up, took a somewhat wobbly sideways step to regain his balance, then gallantly offered to assist her.

She took one look at his face and smiled. "No, but thank you. Tiger can help me. Why don't you sit back down—or *lie* down—and rest?"

Recognizing an order disguised as casual comment, I took one of the buckets from her. "He's a little worse for the wear this morning," I remarked cheerfully as she and I hiked over to the horses. "But he'll get over it by tomorrow, and then he can be on his way."

Del set the bucket down in front of her gelding. "Why don't we have him come with us?"

Startled, I nearly tripped over my bucket as I put it down in front of the stud. "What for?"

"He said he wanted to take lessons from you."

"Yes, but I never said I wanted to give them."

"But that's what you're going to do. Give lessons. Remember?" She patted the gelding's neck. "The plan is for you to resurrect Alimat and take on students. At least, that's what you told me. Has that changed?"

"No." Though I wasn't certain when it might come to be, since we were a bit busy trying to keep me alive.

"Then you've got your first student in Neesha." She grabbed the bucket, shoving the gelding's nose away, and lugged it over to Nayyib's horse.

"That sounds like a very tidy arrangement—from your point of view—but maybe I'm not ready to start lessons yet."

"Why not? Aren't we heading to what's left of Alimat? Couldn't he help us rebuild it?"

I glanced over my shoulder at Nayyib and saw him lying on his bedroll with an arm draped over his eyes once again. I lowered my voice. "What *is* it with you, Del? Why do you care so much about someone who's practically a stranger?"

Her face was set, though her tone was pitched as quiet as mine. "I told you, he helped me when I was ill. I would have died without his help."

"Does this mean we have to adopt him?"

She cut her eyes in Nayyib's direction, then stepped close to me. Since Del is six feet tall, you tend to notice when she gets that close. "Why don't you just say what's on your mind, Tiger? That you'd rather he didn't ride with us because you don't want a good-looking man my own age spending time with me."

I ground it out between my teeth. "That's not it."

"Then what *is* it?"

"I like it the way things are. You and me. *Just* you and me. It has nothing to do with the fact he's a good-looking kid with eyes that can likely get any woman to spread her legs for him with the first puppy-dog glance and who just happens to be your own age."

A wry male tone intruded. "Really?"

Del and I both turned as one. Nayyib stood three strides away, legs spread, arms folded against his chest. "I wasn't asleep—*or* unconscious—and I'm not deaf. I don't particularly care to eavesdrop, either, but when one hears his name mentioned, one tends to pay attention." His brows arched up as he met my gaze. "Do you think I really can get *any* woman to spread her legs for me?" He touched a finger to skin below one eye. "With these?"

I said, "Not the way they look today."

His rueful grin was swift, exposing white teeth; at least he could laugh at himself.

"Maybe by tonight," Del said thoughtfully.

Outraged, I glared at her.

"Really?" Nayyib repeated, sounding more than a little hopeful.

"Really," Del confirmed.

"This is ridiculous," I announced. "We're standing here talking about how this kid can get women to sleep with him when there are any number of people who want to kill me?"

Del seized the opening. "Which is *another* good reason for him to come along."

"Why, bascha? He's not a sword-dancer. I don't think he'd be much of a challenge." I glanced at Nayyib. "Hey, I'm telling it the way I see it."

He nodded. "Fair enough. But if you taught me, maybe I *could* be good enough to provide something of a challenge. I do have some skill, you see . . . though actually you never have, have you? Seen my sword skill." He shrugged. "So I believe you're making assumptions with no evidence to shore them up."

"Stay out of this," I suggested.

"Why? It's *about* me."

"Because you've already proven you're unreliable," I retorted.

"How has he proven that?" Del demanded.

"Hoolies, bascha, he got drunk while he was a prisoner!"

Del's disdain was manifest. "*That's* your evidence?"

"I got drunk," Nayyib said, "because Umir felt I might know some things about you that *he* wanted to know. Something to do with a book. But I didn't know anything about any book, nor do I know anything about you—except what everyone in the South knows, and Umir already knows all that, too."

"What does that have to do with you getting drunk?" I asked, failing to see any point.

"Because after it became evident that beating me wouldn't gain him his information, he tried another tactic. He had a supposedly sympathetic servant slip me a jug of—something. I don't know what it was, but it was certainly more powerful than anything *I've* tasted before. And while I lack your vast experience with liquor—you are old enough to be my father, after all, and thus you have the advantage of *significant* additional years—I have made the aquaintance of it in various forms." He shrugged. "It made me very, very drunk."

Del was furious. "Umir had you beaten?"

I was beginning to be intrigued in spite of myself. "Did you tell him anything?"

"No, because you arrived before he could ask me anything. But it would have gained him nothing anyway. I *don't* know anything more about you, or whatever this book is."

"The *Book of Udre-Natha*," I said, "is a grimoire. It contains all manner of Things Magical: spells, incantations, conjurations, recipes for summoning demons, notes made by men who studied it for years, and so on and so forth. Pretty much anything you want to know about magic is in that book."

The kid had the grace to look stunned. "And you *gave* it to him?"

"Gave it *back* to him," I clarified, "and yes, because it was the only way to get you free."

Nayyib looked somewhat diminished, losing the cocky stance as he stared at me in surprise. "You gave it to him for me?"

"I did."

But confidence reasserted itself. "Why didn't you just ride in there and take me? Without the book. I mean, you are *you*. Umir couldn't have stopped you."

"He might have."

"Stopped the Sandtiger?"

"I'm eminently stoppable," I told him. "Permanently, even. What, did you think I was immortal?"

His chin rose and assumed a stubborn tilt. "You've never yet been killed."

"Well, no, since I wouldn't be standing here involved in this ludicrous conversation if I had been. But 'not yet' doesn't mean 'never.' "

Del said, "Which is another reason Neesha should come with us. So 'not yet' doesn't become 'now.'"

I stared at her. "You really want him to come along."

"I've said that several times, I believe. Yes."

"Fine." I stalked past the kid. "Get your sword."

He turned. "What?"

"Get your sword." I bent and picked up my own. "Let's see just what kind of skill you have that I haven't seen. And then maybe my assumptions will be proven by evidence."

Nayyib was aghast. "*Now?*"

I smiled. "Why not?"

His mouth opened, then closed. Opened again. "Because . . . now is not a good time."

"You don't always get to choose your times, Nayyib-Neesha. Let that be your first lesson." I indicated his bedroll and pouches. "Your sword."

"I can't," he said faintly.

"I thought you wanted me to teach you."

His color was fading. "I do."

"Well then?"

"Because now . . . because now—" He swallowed heavily, looking pained. "—I'm going to be sick." He turned, staggered two steps, bent over—and promptly suited action to words.

"Gee," I marveled, "I've never had quite *that* effect on anyone before."

Del scowled. "Are you happy now?"

I grinned. "Yep." Particularly since it's hard for anyone, even a pretty kid like Nayyib, to look particularly attractive to a woman while he's bringing up the inside of his belly.

She picked up an empty bucket and slung it at me. "Go fill this up. The horses need more water."

I caught it, laughing, and took it and my sword with me to the spring, whistling all the way.

TWENTY-EIGHT

SOME WHILE LATER, Nayyib presented himself to me. He had washed, dusted himself off, neatened his hair. His eyes looked better, and his color was also improved. I had readied the stud and now occupied myself with splitting alla leaves and applying a new coating of oil, waiting for Del to finish tacking out and loading the gelding. It was taking a suspiciously long time, and when Nayyib stopped in front of me and drew himself up, I knew why.

I sighed and assumed a patient expression.

He didn't beat around the bush. "I would like to come with you."

I smoothed oil across the back of my neck. "We've had this conversation before."

"And you have never given me a definitive answer."

"*No* isn't definitive?"

"You haven't said 'no.' You have made objections. There's a difference."

Well, yes, there was. "You're absolutely certain you want me to teach you to be a sword-dancer."

"Yes."

"Why?"

Something in his eyes flickered briefly. It was neither doubt that he could answer nor fear that he'd answer wrong. Maybe it was merely a question he'd never expected of *me*.

The stud nosed my shoulder. I patted his muzzle, then eased his head away. "Well?"

"It's what I've wanted to be since I was very young."

I wiped alla oil across my abdomen between harness straps and began working it in. "Why?"

"My sister and I . . ." A quick smile curved his lips as he thought of her. "We made swords out of sticks. Drew circles in the sand. Eventually my mother made her spend more time in the house, so I had to dance alone. But my sister knew, and I knew, that someday it would come to this."

"What made you choose me?"

A muscle jumped in his jaw. "I didn't, at first. There was a sword-dancer in the village, on his way to Iskandar. For the dances there two years ago." His eyes flickered again. "Do you recall?"

Did I recall? Oh, yes. With infinite clarity. Del did too; it was where she'd killed Ajani.

I tossed used leaves aside, worked at splitting a new one. "So this sword-dancer rode through your village, and you asked him for lessons?"

"Yes."

"Did he give them to you?"

"Yes. He needed money, and I offered to pay him."

I nodded, bending to work oil into thighs. "And you decided by the time he left that you wanted to challenge me."

Once again color warmed the dusky tan of his face. "I didn't mean it as a challenge. I just wanted to step into the circle with you. I knew I would lose."

I grinned lopsidedly. "Not necessarily."

"Against you? Of course."

"Nayyib, the first time I stepped into a circle against a legendary sword-dancer, I won."

"But you're you."

I straightened up. "I wasn't me *then*," I said in exasperation. "I was just a gangly seventeen-year-old kid with hands and feet too big for his body, who was underestimated by a man who should have known better. Complacence in the circle is danger-ous—it nearly got him killed, and I had only a wooden sparring blade, not live steel." I shook my head, remembering Abbu's shock. I waved a depleted leaf at him. "And there, Neesha, is another lesson."

His mouth twitched in a half-smile. "Will you give me more? It would be my honor—and I have the money to pay *you*, too."

I laughed, tossing aside the leaf. I was aware of Del moving even more slowly as she prepared the gelding. Nayyib's horse was already tacked out and loaded, ground-tied some distance away. "Look . . ." I paused, thought about it briefly, gave it up. "I have every intention of reopening the school at Alimat, but not quite yet. There are a few things to settle first. If you truly want to learn—if you haven't lost interest or gotten distracted by some-thing else by then, like a woman—come find me then."

His jaw tightened. There was nothing puppy-doggish about his eyes now; he was angry, but he was suppressing it with unex-pected self-control. Some of the boyishness faded behind a harder veneer. Suddenly he wasn't a kid at all, but a man.

His voice was very quiet. "What would it take?"

"Time." And then I heard my shodo's words come out of my mouth. "There are seven levels. But there is no prescribed length of time required to reach any of those levels. It may take two years to reach the first level. You may leave after you reach it, if that is your choice—but to leave before you can walk means you'll be killed before you can even dream of running."

"And to achieve seven levels?"

I shrugged. "Few men last that long. They leave to make a living."

"You are a seventh-level sword-dancer."

"I was. I'm not anything now, other than outcast."

"*Elaii-ali-ma*," he said. "Rafiq told me, when I asked."

"Time and oaths," I told him. "It's a demanding service, the circle. Too many believe it's about glory. Rafiq does, and it's why he'll never survive. In truth, it's mostly about honor, and oaths, and service. The elegance of the dance, the beauty of live steel. Glory comes, if you win enough, *well* enough—but that's not the point. It only *seems* like it to young men who don't want to stay in the village, get married, and father babies on the first village girl they bed."

He had controlled the anger. His voice was steady. "And if I choose to achieve the seventh level, as you did?"

"Can you afford ten years?"

He blinked. "It took you ten years?"

I bent to apply oil to my calves and shins. "No, it took me seven. But I was the first to do it that fast."

Nayyib nodded once. "Seven levels. If it requires *twelve* years, then I will give you twelve."

Del led the gelding around in front of the stud. Waited, saying nothing.

"Don't swear any oaths just yet, Nayyib," I suggested. "Not until you know what they are. Because at Alimat, the oaths you swear are for life."

He didn't shy from it, was not afraid of me. "You broke yours."

"And every sword-dancer in the South is trying to kill me."

His glance slid to Del. Quietly, he said, "There are times when certain oaths must be broken, if to keep them breaks oaths you have made to others."

So. She'd told him. It seemed the Northern bascha had been doing quite a bit of talking to the Southron boy.

Who wasn't really a boy. Just considerably younger than I.

Like Del.

He was still gazing at her. She didn't avoid it. I saw a look pass between them, though I couldn't interpret it.

Something pinched deep in my gut. Jealousy? No, not really. But an awareness that things were changing; that they would continue to change.

And Del knew nothing about my limited time. *Her* life would change, too.

I looked back at Nayyib. He said he'd give me twelve years. In twelve years, or possibly ten, I would be dead.

Abruptly I tossed away the rest of the leaf. Turned and mounted the stud. I reined him in and looked down at Nayyib, waiting for my answer. "You can come with us as far as Julah. We'll spar there, and then I'll decide."

The stud has a very comfortable long-walk, once he consents to settle into the gait. Too often he has a burr under his blanket, or a bee up his butt—figuratively speaking, of course—and takes it out on me. But for now he was content to just walk on, head bobbing lazily at the end of his neck. I very nearly fell asleep, until Del's voice woke me up.

"Tiger!"

I let the stud go on, twisting in the saddle to look back. Del and Nayyib had stopped some distance away and were staring at me. "What?"

"Where are you going?" Del called.

"Julah!"

"Julah's *this* way."

I reined in. "No, it's not." I pointed. "This way. South."

"That's east," she declared.

Was she sandsick? "No, it's not. This is south. Julah's this way."

Del stabbed a finger in front of her horse. "There's the road."

"That's *a* road," I told her. "Five of them meet at the oasis. This is the road to Julah."

Nayyib shook his head and said something to Del I couldn't hear.

"What?" I asked, irritated.

"It's east," he answered.

"How would *you* know? You're not from around here."

"No, but I do know my directions."

"That's not a road at all, Tiger," Del called. "Take a look."

This was ridiculous, having this pointless discussion in the middle of the desert. I looked. Blinked. Saw that indeed the stud and I were striking out across the desert with no road, trail, or track in sight.

I scowled. It *felt* right, this direction. It felt south. Or else I really had fallen asleep, and the stud had chosen his own route.

I turned him around and headed back. Felt an abrupt sense of wrongness so powerful I reined in sharply. "No," I insisted, "it's this way."

Del pointed down the road. "South. Julah. I'm not from around here, either, but I know that much."

But it was wrong. *Wrong.* I knew it. Felt it in my bones.

And abruptly I swore, remembering the dream. My bones would know, she'd said.

Del's voice, "Tiger?"

I closed my eyes tightly. Tried to reorient myself. Tried to let my lifelong sense of direction tell me which way was the correct one. Yet when I opened them again, I still felt that they were wrong and I was right, despite the evidence of the road.

Or maybe we were both right. Julah lay south, but where I was *supposed* to go lay east.

"*Find me*," she had said. "*And take up the sword.*"

I looked at Del. "Which way is the chimney from here?"

"The chimney?"

"The rock formation we brought down when you broke your sword. When Chosa Dei fought Shaka Obre." Oziri had called it Beit al'Shahar.

Del pointed. "That way."

"West."

She nodded. So did Nayyib.

The stud and I were facing west. Del's gelding and Nayyib's bay faced south, toward Julah, with the oasis not terribly far behind them. East lay behind me, and that was the way I—or my bones—wanted to go.

Well, we don't always get what we want. I clucked to the stud and headed him toward the road. Once there, I stopped. Shuddered from head to toe.

Del's expression was concerned. "What is it?"

"I don't know. Something . . ." I shook my head, knowing how it sounded. "Something keeps telling me we need to go east. Or I do, at least."

"What's east?" she asked.

A dead woman, apparently. A scattering of bones: pearls of the desert.

"The Punja," I said.

A line appeared between her brows. "It makes no sense."

"And I agree with you wholeheartedly," I said. "All I know is, something in me wants to go east."

Nayyib, wisely keeping out of the conversation, looked past me and changed the subject. "Someone's coming."

I turned in the saddle, looking in the direction of the oasis. A cloud of dust accompanied the ride, obscuring the horizon. I noticed then that one arm was waving. A man's voice was raised over the hoofbeats of his horse.

"Wait!" he cried. "Wait!"

"Someone from the oasis?" Nayyib wondered.

"Wait!" He sounded frantic; had something happened at the oasis that required help?

"Guess we'll find out," I said. At least the distraction kept me from heading east.

The stud snorted, pawed, shifted sideways restlessly, not happy to be standing in one spot. I reined him in, had a brief discussion with him when he protested, and glanced up as the rider grew closer. I could make out his features, but I recognized none of them.

"Wait!" he called.

Then I saw the flash of steel.

I twisted, gesturing at Del and Nayyib with a sweeping left arm. "Move! Out of the way!"

As I swung back, yanking blade free of sheath, everything around me slowed. Swearing, I reined the stud back sharply, off the road, but by then it was too late. The rider neither reined in nor reined aside. With sword raised above his head, he crashed his dun horse into the stud.

Perception fragmented into shards of images, impressions. I

felt the impact rock the stud, knocking him sideways. Was aware of the dun's head smashing into my left elbow, of rolling eyes and hot breath. The stud staggered, nearly went down. A flash of steel blinded me even as I tried to yank the stud's head up into the air, trying to keep him on his feet, to pivot left so I would have a clean line for my own blade. But we were too cursed close, my assailant and I, with our horses jammed together.

I dropped the reins and, cursing, hammered a fist into the dun's nose, trying to get him off me, off the stud. I saw the flash of a blade, brought up my own. In the mass of tangled horseflesh it was impossible to parry properly, but I did block the worst of the blow's impetus. Then the stud was trying to fight the dun, mouth agape, neck snaking, head swinging sideways, teeth snapping.

The dun reared, screaming. My stirrups were gone anyway; I pushed off, diving sideways, and lost my sword on the way down. I landed hard, tasted sand and blood, saw stars; I tried to scramble up, to get out of the way, but my momentum was off, and I tripped over my sword and fell. Escape was now impossible in the midst of the equine battle; I couldn't tell which way was up or down, in or out. I just rolled myself up in a tight ball, arms hooked over my head, and prayed no hoof would land on any part of my anatomy.

Dimly I was aware of shouting. Del's voice. Nayyib's. And a stranger's. The screaming was terrible, the frenzied trumpeting of an enraged stallion. I focused on it, sorted out which direction it came from, and decided to take the chance. I lunched upward from the ground, ran two steps, fell again, rolled, came up into a crouch. In the midst of the battle I saw Nayyib dart in on foot and bend, sword bared. He sliced at something, and nearly got his head smashed for his trouble. But I saw the dun go down as Nayyib leaped back out of the way, and realized what he'd done.

The rider flung himself off as his mount, hamstrung and pressured by the stud, crashed to the ground. He rolled away, scrambling even as I had, and lunged upward—only to come face to face with Del. He had lost his sword in the melee, but grabbed for his knife. Del, who still claimed her blade, used it with fierce efficiency, driving it through his belly.

The stud reared, trumpeted again, came down with both front hooves striking. I heard the sickening crunch as he smashed the dun's skull. He spun then, took two leaps away, whirled back and stood trembling, front legs twitching, tail slashing. Ribbons of sweat rolled down his flanks.

And blood.

Nayyib was there immediately. Not everyone will approach a horse in the stud's condition; probably no one should. He could easily strike again, or bite. But Nayyib caught the cheekstrap of his bridle, quickly looped the rein around his nose, then through bit shanks, and pulled it taut. He was done so quickly the stud had no chance to react. Nayyib held him there, soothing him with his voice, using the looped rein as a makeshift stud-chain.

Del was with me. "Are you all right?"

I spat blood and sand, felt grit in my teeth. Wiped a hand across my mouth and managed only to smear things around. "Fine." I tried to get up. My left leg protested vociferously. I sat back down. "Well, maybe not so fine." I inspected the sore leg. The side of my knee was scraped and sore. But what—? Oh. Yes. I recalled the dun's shoulder slamming into the stud, with my leg trapped between.

Del knelt, putting one hand on the reddened, abraded area. "Is it broken?"

"I don't think so. But I'm betting it'll color up nicely by morning." I tried again, arrived on my feet. The leg was very sore but whole. I was lucky it hadn't been crushed. "I've got to see the stud."

"Nayyib has him. He'll be fine."

I limped over anyway, talking to the stud as I approached so I wouldn't startle him. "He's cut," I said sharply.

Nayyib, still holding the stud's head, nodded. "Sword blade. Just a slash, I think, but painful."

It was in the fleshy part of the stud's left haunch, about six inches long. It wasn't deep enough to sever muscle, but it had laid the flesh back. Blood bathed his left hind.

"Oh, son," I murmured, "the bastard got you."

"It'll need stitches." Nayyib stroked the stud's nose gently even as he worked the rein. "I have silk thread in my pouches, and a needle."

The stud, bothered by dripping blood and sweat, kicked out sideways with his left hind. I shook my head. "He's not about to put up with that right now."

Nayyib nodded. "We'll need to get him down, have someone sit on his head. And tie his legs—and probably his tail—so he can't kick or blind me."

I looked at him sharply. "You?"

"I've done it before." He smiled crookedly. "When I was no longer a child playing with sticks, I dreamed of being a sword-dancer in my head. What I did outside of it was work with stock; my father has a small horse farm near Iskandar."

"Then why aren't you there?" I asked. "Or do you have so many brothers he doesn't need you?"

"Oh, no, there is only me and my sister. But we had a disagreement, he and I."

"Don't tell me. You told him you wanted to be a sword-dancer."

Nayyib soothed the stud with his hands and voice. "He did not approve."

I sighed, winced as I put too much weight on my aching leg. "I think about all I'm good for is sitting on his head. But he'll go down if I give him the signal; I trained him to that for sand-storms."

Nayyib looked doubtful. "After a fight?"

I considered it. Possibly not. "Let me try," I said.

Nayyib nodded.

I went to the stud's head, looked him in the eye, told him I needed him to go down, then gave him the signal: a slap on the left shoulder. He wrung his tail and made no move.

"Oh, come now," I said. "You've done this before."

Another slap, plus a prodding thumb.

Nothing. Except for a very stubborn look in his eye.

"All right, we'll do it my way," Nayyib said. "Del can mind the rope snubbing up his one leg, while I stitch." He glanced over his shoulder at Del, who had caught her gelding and Nayyib's and waited out of the way. "Can you get into my saddlepouches? There is a leather pouch in there, dyed blue. It contains medicaments. And I need you to bring me every halter rope and my spare burnous."

She nodded and turned to his horse.

Nayyib eyed me sidelong. "I've stitched men, too."

I shook my head. "Bruised, not bloodied. I'll wrap my knee later for support." And maybe my elbow as well.

His tone was coldly angry. "I have never seen anyone purposely run a horse into another. To purposely risk a mount with such brutality, just to kill another man."

I wasn't sure if he was angrier about the risk to horseflesh or human. "If you live long enough, I guess you see everything."

And then Del was back, bringing ropes, burnous, and pouch, and we forgot about dead men, dead horses, and tended a live one.

TWENTY-NINE

By DEL'S tense silence, I knew she was worried. It's not often you attempt to drop a stallion to the ground when he has no interest in going there. But Nayyib was right: the only way we could get the slash stitched up was to put the stud out of commission temporarily. He wasn't a man; you couldn't explain to him what needed to be done and why and expect him to agree. Nor could you get him drunk, and none of us was strong enough to knock him unconscious. So while Del and I got him unsaddled, with blankets and pouches pulled off and deposited on the ground, Nayyib calmly rigged a lip-twitch and a rope harness, winding wide strips of his spare burnous around the hemp to pad it.

"Hobble his back legs." He handed me a pair of sheepskin-padded hobbles he'd conjured from his saddlepouches. "And bind up his tail."

Very dictatorial, Nayyib, when it came to horses. But I deferred, impressed by his confidence and quick thinking. Carefully I did as he asked, snugging the padded cuffs around both back legs. They were shorter than usual, also, meant to keep the legs closer together. A long leather thong controlled the tail, which was long enough—and strong enough—to blind a man if it slashed tough horsehair across his eyes.

"Hold him a moment," Nayyib told Del quietly, and as she

took the bridle the kid efficiently set about looping padded ropes around various parts of the stud's body. "All right," he said. "Tiger, come hold his head. Del, take this rope. When I say to, pull as hard as you can.

It sound risky to me. "What will *you* be doing?"

Nayyib's smile was brief. "I'll be on the other leg. If all works well, he'll go over onto that right shoulder. Once he does, sit on his head. *Hold* him there. Use the twitch to take his mind off everything else." He glanced at Del. "Keep that rope snubbed tight. I'll stitch as fast as I can. If I'm lucky, the rear hobbles will keep him from kicking my head off."

"Then what?" I asked.

"Once I'm done, I'll clear out. Del, you'll loosen your rope. Tiger, you get off his head. He'll come up lunging, but the hobbles will hold him in place. All right?"

"Yes," Del said. I nodded.

Nayyib drew in a deep breath, moved to the stud's left fore. "Pull, Del!"

She pulled. Nayyib grabbed the left leg and folded it up. The stud flung his head, which nearly decapitated me, then went down hard on the ground, rolling onto his right shoulder as the kid had hoped. I was aware of Del working swiftly to snub and hold taut her rope. Then I plopped myself down on the stud's head up behind his ears, where the neck began, and caught hold of the rope twitch in my left hand. He was breathing hard, muscles twitching, nostrils fluttering with explosive snorts that raised puffs of dust. The visible eye rolled, displaying reddened membranes.

"Hurry up!" I gritted, gripping the twitch and bridle.

My back was to the stud's body, so I couldn't view anything Nayyib did. If I glanced to my right, I could see Del leaning against the rope crossing over the stud's neck But mostly I watched his visible eye, balancing my weight evenly. With a knee on either side of him, one hand locked into the headstall of his bridle and the other tightening the rope twisted around his bottom lip, I realized my gehetties were in a rather perilous position. If he flung his head up, I'd likely be unmanned.

I swore again, spitting a faint sifting of dust from my mouth.

"How is your leg?" Del asked tightly.

"Ask me when we're done."

Stitching seemed to take forever. But eventually Nayyib warned us to be ready. "Del, loosen the rope just a little. When Tiger gets off his head, give the stud as much slack as you can. He'll come up hard and fast, but clumsy." He paused. "Tiger?"

"I'm ready."

"Del?"

"It's loose."

"All right, Tiger."

I let go of twitch and bridle and pushed up and away with planted legs, propelling myself forward. I rolled, crouched, stood, hopped briefly as my left leg complained. Saw Del feeding more rope, then jumping back. Nayyib was near the stud's head, freeing the twist of rope around his bottom lip. And indeed the stud came up hard and fast, lunging frenziedly. The padded rope slid from his neck and chest, pooled on the ground around his right leg. He wobbled a little, discovering his rear legs were still hobbled, then found his balance. He stuck his big head high in the air, eyeing me, then released a pent-up snort of severe annoyance that sprayed slime in all directions.

I wiped muck from my chest. "Thank you."

Nayyib held his bridle again, soothing him. Quietly he told me, "You can take those hobbles now."

Ah, and let *me* get my head kicked off. Smart kid. Smiling crookedly, I limped toward the stud's rear quarters, sliding my left hand over his spine and rump so he'd know I was there. I carefully avoided the wound, marked by a curving row of neat silk-thread stitches, then bent and quickly untied the padded hobbles and tail thong. And skipped back out of the way with alacrity as the stud took to slashing his tail in indignation.

"There now," Nayyib crooned, and led him forward. "See? Not so bad. An affront to your dignity, I do know, all this abuse, but you will survive it. You are the best of all horses, a stallion among stallions—even if you are a jug-headed ugly son of a goat."

"Hey," I protested.

"Not so bad, not so bad," Nayyib continued, leading the stud in a wide circle. "You'll have a fierce scar, you will, much like your rider. But you are *much* more handsome."

Del wandered over to my side. "He's like a horse-speaker."

I remembered the fair-haired kid we'd met years before at the kymri, a gathering of peoples in the North. "I don't think Nayyib can read their minds."

"He doesn't have to. He knows what they need. See? The stud's calming."

She was smiling. I watched her watching Nayyib.

Horses weren't the only thing the kid could handle.

Nayyib brought the stud up to me. "I would recommend we go on," he said. "The cut hasn't interfered with his muscles, so he can be ridden. But if we stay the night here, or even if we go back to the oasis, which isn't that far, he'll stiffen. Best to keep him moving."

Del glanced at me warily. "To Julah?"

I shrugged, taking the stud's reins. "Let's see what happens when I'm in the saddle again."

As Nayyib packed away his supplies again, I set about readying the stud. He was unusually subdued, as if he'd spent all of his temper and strength. Once he was saddled and loaded, I filled a canvas bucket with water from a bota and let him drink. He sucked it up greedily, lifted his dripping muzzle out of the bucket, then shoved it against my chest as if asking me to commiserate.

I smiled, scratching his jaw. "I'm sorry, old son. You didn't deserve that. It's me they want to kill, not you."

I packed away the bucket, turned to mount him, and discovered how much a half-crushed leg doesn't like being asked to bear all my weight. Swearing, I managed to make it up into the saddle, left knee throbbing. So much for the healing I'd encountered at Meteiera. I'd been told any new injuries would be mine to keep; seems like I was repeating old habits.

I turned the stud. "This way. To Julah, right?"

In concert, Del and Nayyib shook their heads.

"East?" I asked reluctantly.

"East," Del confirmed.

"What's east?" asked Nayyib.

I ran a hand over my face, trying to rein in anger and frustration. "Who in hoolies knows? Something that seems to think I need to be there." A dead woman who spoke to me in dreams. "Look, it doesn't feel *far*, whatever it is. If you two want to go on to Julah, go ahead. Maybe I'm supposed to do this alone anyway."

Del shook her head. "If you go east, I go east."

I looked at Nayyib.

He hitched one shoulder in a dismissive half-shrug. "You said I could ride with you to Julah. We're not there yet."

I sighed deeply. "Fine. Let's go east, shall we?"

East. Toward the sunrise—and whatever else might be lurking out there.

I became dimly aware of voices. Del and Nayyib were talking quietly, as if I weren't present. I felt rather as if I were waking up from a dream, except I hadn't been sleeping. I was working like a human lodestone, following the compulsion that pulled me east. For the moment that compulsion had slackened, and I glanced up at the sun. By its position, I knew we'd been riding about two hours.

Then I became aware of the surroundings. A vast ocean of cream-pale sand, sparkling with crystals afire from the sun. The Punja, the deadliest of the South's deserts.

I pulled up, stopping the stud. Del and Nayyib, reining in also, were staring at me warily. I frowned, scratched idly at facial scars, then reached to pull up a bota hanging from the saddle and slake increasing thirst.

"We need to water the horses," Del said.

I nodded as I unstoppered the bota. "Apparently I'm being allowed time to do just that. Or else whatever it is insisting I come has decided we're far enough." I knew how it sounded, but it was the only way I could think to describe it. I sucked down water, climbed down out of the saddle, easing onto my left leg, and unhooked another bota. This I emptied into the canvas bucket and let the stud drink.

"You said it wasn't far," Del remarked.

"I said it *felt* like it wasn't far. I can't say for sure." I shook my head, grimacing. "I sound sandsick. Hoolies, maybe I am."

"No." Del's voice was quiet. "You have instincts I have always trusted—and now more than instincts."

Ah yes, more. Magic. Magery. I'd used a little on Umir's book, spelling the lock, and then shied away from the idea like a spooked horse.

As the stud drank, I squinted across the expanse of sand, sheilding my eyes with the flat of one hand. The Punja had killed more people than would ever be counted, sucking the life from their bodies, scouring flesh from their bones. Whole villages had been swallowed by sand carried miles in dangerous simooms, burying all signs of life. Caravans, crossing from oasis to oasis, paying huge amounts of money to guides who knew the Punja, often disappeared despite their best efforts to anticipate the dangers. Sometimes you just can't anticipate everything.

I certainly hadn't, when Del had hired me to guide her across the Punja. I'd have never guessed a few years later we'd still be together as sword-mates, bed-mates, life-mates.

I smiled, recalling those first days. The ice-maiden from the North, summoning frigid, killing banshee storms with her magical sword. Boreal was long dead, broken and buried in the chimney formation in the mountains by Julah. Beit al'Shahar. My Northern *jivatma*, Samiel, was there as well, whole and unblemished, left behind as the chimney collapsed.

"*Find me*," the woman had said, "*and take up the sword.*"

If the sword she meant was Samiel, why were we out here in the Punja, at least two day's ride from Beit al'Shahar? I had intitally wanted to go get the *jivatma*, if possible; it was why we'd headed for the mountains in the first place, once out of Haziz. It hadn't felt like a compulsion then, merely a plan. Something I wanted to do.

Now, here, I *needed* to do it. Yet there was no *jivatma* anywhere nearby. That I knew. So maybe I was meant to find another sword, a different sword.

Unless only the woman was here for me to find. Or what was left of her.

Shaking my head, I packed the squashable bucket away, hung empty botas back on my saddle, made to remount. Then stopped. Stood there, clinging to the stud.

"What?" Del asked.

I flung up a hand, stopping her from saying more.

Silence, save for the familiar sounds of horses. They shifted position, pawed at sand, shook manes, rattled bit shanks, snorted, chewed at the metal in their mouths. I heard nothing else.

But I *felt* it.

Abruptly I stuck my foot in the stirrup and swung aboard, ignoring the complaints of my leg. "Turn back," I said urgently. "Simoom!"

I reined the stud around. Del and Nayyib mounted quickly and turned as well.

But that was where the storm came from. Behind us before; now ahead. The first faint haze was visible along the horizon, like a wisp of ruffled silk.

"The other way!" I shouted, sinking heels into the stud. Maybe my sense of direction was forever skewed, thanks to— whatever.

We ran, but the wind and sand ran faster. The storm spilled across the land like a vast, rolling wave, filling the sky from horizon to sun. The day grew dark.

"There's no shelter!" Nayyib's voice, pitched to cut through the first whining of the wind.

No. None. In such circumstances the best bet was to put the horses down and use *them* as shelter. I suspected Nayyib's horse was trained for it, if the kid had grown up on a horse farm in the South; but then Iskandar was up near the border, more soil than sand, and he might not know much about simooms. He probably knew even less about the Punja, though he had made it to Haziz. Probably paid a guide.

No guide could help us now. The leading edge of the storm was very close, collecting gouts of sand as it howled across the land. Del's gelding probably wasn't trained to lie down—I couldn't see anyone taking a blue-eyed white horse into the Punja—and the stud, after his experience earlier in the day, would likely refuse all inducements. We didn't have time to try Nayyib's trick of cross-tying and hobbling legs.

Knowledge flickered deep in my mind. Fear followed swiftly, churning in my belly.

Not me, I said. *Don't expect* me *to do this.*

But of course something did. Something inside. Something that had been teased back into awareness with the writings in Umir's book, full of spells, incantations, conjurations. Despite what I'd said, I hadn't quite read it all, but enough. More than enough.

I could build us shelter, the way I had conjured a boat on ioSkandi, to search for Del.

If I didn't do so, we'd likely all die.

Swearing, I reined the stud in. Del and Nayyib hadn't seen me and kept riding. But I had more to think about than when or if they'd realize where I was. I turned the stud loose and swung to face the storm.

It was magnificent and malevolent. Even the sun was shrouded, hazed by the towering storm. By the time I counted to ten on my hands—well, to eight—it would have us.

I went into my head, thinking. Wind was air. It was air that carried sand. Air was the impetus. If the air itself could be used, could be manipulated, I could make us shelter.

I wore no burnous, only dhoti, sandals, harness, and a sword across my back. It was not a *jivatma.* Was just a sword. But I was a *sword-dancer,* and in my hands a sword, any sword, could be made to conquer anything.

I unsheathed. Slitted my eyes against wind and sand. Shut the hilt in both hands as firmly as I could and raised the sword. Set the blade into the air over my head. Felt the wind buffet it, sand grains hissing against steel. I closed my eyes, bit into my lip. Even as I stood there, my flesh was abrading. Chest and legs stung.

I heard someone call. Del, then Nayyib. I shut them out.

Wished them away. Made myself alone. Just me—and the simoom.

I saw the spell in my head. Unraveled the words I'd read but days before, comprehending only half of them. I *knew* the words but not their meanings. I was but a first-level mage, as sworddancer skill was measured. Full of potential but raw, wild, dangerous.

Abbu Bensir learned that.

We stood no chance unless I surrendered denial and accepted truth. As I had to Del, saying the word. Naming myself.

Mage. Whelped upon a spire in the Stone Forest, weeks away from here.

I gripped the sword, felt two thumbs and four fingers. *Four.* Slowly brought the blade down, sundering the sky.

The fabric of the storm, the heavy curtain of sand, split apart. Poured around me, roaring. Sand whirled by, carried on wind. But wind was merely air, and I could command it.

Mage I might be, but I was also the Sandtiger, and *that* I valued more than magic. The greatest sword-dancer legendary Alimat had ever produced. No one, and nothing, could defeat me. Not even a simoom.

Paltry, petty storm. Insignificant.

I grinned into it, knowing no sand would touch my scarred, stubbled face, scour out fragile, gelid eyes. I had parted the simoom, cut through its gritty fabric, shattered gemstones made of crystal, and gave us room to live.

In a matter of moments, the storm, like torn silk, flapped itself into shreds. The curtain of sand fell to the earth. Crystals dulled, then flared anew into dusty sunlight. Haze dissipated. The air began to warm.

The sword was still in my hands, tip set against sand. Slowly, aware of trembling in my arms, I raised it, resheathed it, then turned to see if I was alone.

No. Three horses and two humans. A man and a woman. The latter two knelt on the sand, hands shielding their heads. But slowly the heads raised. The faces opened. Del, whose smile was as odd as it was faint, spat grit out of her mouth. Then she stood up.

"Nicely done," she observed. "That one will come in handy."

Nayyib still knelt, looking dazed as well as windblown. "That was magery?"

Del laughed. "That was Tiger."

I bent, ruffled my hair vigorously to free it of the worst of the sand. Nothing had gotten through once I'd applied myself to cutting open the storm to divert it around us, but we'd gotten a faceful before then. The horses, being horses, not foolish humans, had promptly turned their rumps to the wind. Now they shook violently, banging stirrups and botas against sandy sides. A cloud of fine dust rose from each of them.

I staggered, laughed, cut it off sharply, lest I lose the last shreds of self-control. "Ah, yes, the wonderul sensation of bones turned to water. And one hoolies of a headache." I shut my eyes, pressed the heels of my hands to either side of my head. "Why don't they warn you about this part of it? The book didn't say a word."

Del came to me, put one hand on my arm. "Are you all right?"

"No, but I'll likely survive it." I opened my eyes and looked at her. "Maybe you can put cool cloths on my brow and croon to me, the way Nayyib crooned to the stud. Lay me down, cradle my poor, aching head in your lap, stroke my tender temples, and tell me repeatedly I am a man among men."

Del brushed a rime of sand from my forehead. "I rather think not."

"A mage among mages?"

"No more that than the other."

"Why not?" I asked plaintively. "Didn't I just save your life?"

Del opened her mouth to answer, but Nayyib's voice intruded. "Come look at this!"

Del turned. I took my hands away from my temples. "What?"

He stood several paces away, staring at something. At several somethings, actually: odd, lumpy shapes uncovered by the storm. Simooms swallowed, but they also uncovered.

Del and I walked over. It was a scattered graveyard of wood

boards, scoured smooth like gray satin over years of burial and disinterrment. The Punja, goaded by storm, had tossed back one of its victims.

Nayyib knelt, fingering a section of wood. An edge showed, and inches of a flat surface. He locked fingers around it, pulled up with effort. The board broke free, showering sand. Nayyib sat down hastily, then held up the section of wood. "What is it from, do you think?"

I took it from him, studying it. "Looks like part of a wagon." I gestured to the other remnants poking above the sand, like tilted grave markers. "Likely the rest of it is still buried."

"Would it be whole?" Del asked. "If we dug it up?"

Aside from the fact that we couldn't do that, lacking shovels, I doubted it. "It's probably been here for years, bascha. The weight of the sand has broken it apart. We'd only find pieces."

Nayyib feigned deep disappointment. "No treasure?"

"Well, likely borjuni on a raid took everything of value and left the wagon—along with the people in it, I'd assume—or a simoom got them. Either way, there'd be nothing left worth digging for." I tossed the board aside. "For all we know, there could be a whole caravan buried under the sand."

Del had wandered to the far side of the wagon remnants. I saw her stop, roll something over with the toe of her sandal, then drop to her knees. She picked up something, examined it, blew a feathering of sand from it, then set it aside. Hastily she began brushing sand away with her hands, but carefully, as if whatever she'd found was fragile.

Curious, I went to see what had caught her attention. Nayyib was still playing with the exposed wood, digging up fragments and sections of boards, stacking them like cordwood.

I stopped next to Del. "What did you find?"

She set it into my hand. Said nothing.

It lay in my palm. Grains of sand remained caught against my flesh, flecks of mineral, a tracery of Punja crystal. The wind- and sand-polished fragment lay atop it, with a faint oily sheen of pearl. It had three worn protrustions, and a hole through the middle.

My hand clamped shut.

"Bone," Del said.

Human bone.

Find me, the woman had begged.

I looked down at Del's excavations. I didn't recognize the hoarse timbre of my voice. "What else is there?"

She bent close to the sand, blew it away from the suggestion of a shape. She picked it out of the sand, smoothed and blew it free of dust and crystal, then offered it to me.

Time-weathered, sand-polished bone. A slender piece perhaps five inches long. Curved.

In one hand: vertebra. In the other: rib.

I fell down to my knees. "She's here. She's *here*. We've found her."

Del asked, "Who?" Then she stilled. "You think—the woman you dreamed about? The skeleton?"

I displayed both palms. "Bone."

Del's eyes were full of wonder as she lightly touched the rib in my right hand. "This is what brought you here?"

"I think so."

Her eyes lifted to mine. "Who do you think she was? A mage?"

"I don't know," I said. I locked eyes with Del. "But I can find out."

"How can you—?" She broke it off. "Oh, Tiger. No."

"I did it back at the Vashni encampment."

Her face was pale. "It's dangerous. Remember what Oziri did to you?"

I closed my hands. The bones were warm. "This is the woman in my dreams. The one who told me to find her. Now I have, and I have to know who—and what—she was."

"Tiger," she begged, "don't do it. You worked magic only a matter of moments ago. You're weak—you said so yourself. You have a 'hoolies of a headache.'"

I sat down on the sand. Opened my hands. Gazed at the pearls of the desert. "I have to do this."

So I shut my eyes, and did it.

THIRTY

THE VOICE was the voice of a stranger, yet also mine. I heard it inside my head; heard it in my ears. In fits and starts, stumbling to find its way, it told the story the bone had guarded for years.

"*The caravan was small, short-handed, traveling too late in the season. Its master was not well respected, and those with enough experience or money hired others to get them across the deadly Punja. But those who lacked both, those unaccustomed to the South, to the desert, and certainly to the Punja, knew nothing more than that the man promised to take them where they wished to go: from Haziz through Julah and then across the Punja to where South met North and formed the borderlands, cooler than the desert, warmer than the mountains. The most temperate of all locales but dangerous because of its raiders, both Southron and Northern.*"

I sat on sand, cross-legged, left hand hanging limply in my lap, right hand holding bone. My eyes were open, but blind.

"*The caravan, being small, short-handed, traveling too late in the season, and led by a man who prized coin over lives, was caught by a storm. The simoom was but an immature version of its larger relatives, but it was enough. The beasts were made to lie down, and the people took shelter in their wagons, trying to save the canvas that formed their roofs. Eventually the simoom blew itself out, and it was discovered by the folk, as they dug themselves free, that no lives were lost.*

"The road, however, was."

I choked, coughed, drew in breath. I felt shivers course my body, but I could not stop. It needed to be told.

"The caravan master and his guide, trusting to their questionable instincts to find the right way, led the caravan on, and into disaster. A party of borjuni, taking advantage of the storm and its aftereffects, swept down upon the wagons. Men and children, being worth nothing, were killed outright. The women were taken to be sold as slaves or kept as camp whores. The horses, mules, and danjacs were rounded up. Everything of value easily carried was taken; everything requiring too much effort, or beasts to haul it, was left."

I was dimly aware of being wet with sweat, but cold. Shivers coursed my flesh. Someone's hand was on my knee, urging me to stop. But I could not.

"And also left was the foreign woman big with child, deemed too much trouble to take with them but worth some sport. That sport left her half-dead and in labor. The borjuni, finding it amusing, deserted her as she bled into the sand, deserting also the body of her husband, who had brought her out of Skandi to find a new life where a man and a woman, despite differences in birth, might settle and be content. Alone, beaten, raped, the woman who had been raised the privileged daughter of the Stessoi, one of Skandi's Eleven Families, found her dead husband, wept for him, then crawled under their wagon and, in a river of blood, bore him a son. She managed to take that son to her breast, to suckle him, to cover him with the scraps of her torn clothing. And died before she could name him aloud to the gods that had surely forsaken him.

"The child lived. He grew hungry, emitting wailing cries, and grew weak when the cries were not answered. But there was strength in him yet, and when the desert tribe that named itself Salset came across the caravan, he cried again. Was found. Was taken."

I swallowed, aware of pain in my throat, of exhaustion, of fever.

"The child, when judged old enough, was made a slave. His name was chula."

"Tiger . . . Tiger, stop now. Please. Please stop."

I stopped, because I could. Because the tale was told. The truth was known.

I opened eyes that had, at some point, closed. No longer did I sit on the sand, cross-legged. Now I lay on the sand with my head in a woman's lap. Her hands were on my forehead, fingers stroking.

"Tiger, come back. It's done. It's over. It happened a long time ago."

"Forty years," I rasped.

Del took the rib bone from my hand. "Enough. Enough."

"She didn't abandon me." A hollow, hoarse voice. "Neither did he."

"No one abandoned you," she said. "Never. They wanted you. You would have brought them great joy."

"The Salset told me I was abandoned."

"They would never say, even had they known, that you were the grandson of the Stessa metri, of one of the most powerful of Skandi's Eleven Families."

"I was a chula."

"But not anymore. Not for many years." Del's fingers stroked. "You should be happy, Tiger. I have crooned to you, soothed your tender temples. After I said I would not."

I grinned weakly. "You never could keep your hands off me."

She smiled. Laughed. Her eyes were the blue of Northern lakes, glistening with unshed tears, her hair pale as Punja sand.

I shivered. Realized the sun was down. Someone had thrown a blanket over me as I lay with my head in Del's lap. I turned my head, saw a fire. "Where'd *that* come from?" We were in the Punja, in a sea of sand; there were no trees.

"Neesha made a fire with the wood from the wagon."

It felt odd to think that the wagon might even be the one my mother and father had bought in Haziz. Now set on fire to warm the son neither had ever known.

Nayyib came close, squatted down next to me. His color seemed pale, though it was difficult to tell in shadows and fire-light. "What you saw—what you *said* you saw . . . your mother?"

"Mother. Father."

"Did the bone take you there?"

A smile twitched my lips, but I was too weary to hold it. "Memories, Neesha. The bones know what happened. I can conjure up the memories if I hold a bone. I can walk my dreams to find out what they mean."

I had said too much. Nayyib's gaze slid away, avoiding mine; talk of magic bothered him. Then his eyes returned. "Was she a mage, then? Your mother?"

"No. Well, not that I know of. There is magery in some of the Eleven Families of Skandi, and apparently in the Stessoi, if I'm any indication . . . but in males, not females." And it drove them mad. But that I wouldn't say. Not to him. Not to Del.

"Then it could have come through your father."

"No. He wasn't one of the Eleven Families. It had to have come through my mother." I remembered the metri, my grandmother, dismissing me out of hand when she was done with me, swearing her daughter had died before I was born. I swallowed heavily against the dryness in my throat. "Is there water?"

"Here." Del picked up the bota by her knee. "Don't drink too much at once."

I drank as much as I could, until she took it away. I sighed, closed my eyes. ". . . tired."

"Sleep," she said. "You went far away, and came back the long road."

I let go a trembling breath. Felt her take the bone from my slack hand. "I still have to find the sword."

"But not tonight."

Ah. Good.

I faded then, slipping bit by bit out of reality, out of consciousness, as Del, with gentle fingers, smoothed the lines from my forehead.

"Will he die?" Nayyib asked.

"Oh, no." Her voice seemed to smile. "Not for a long, long time."

Ten years. Twelve.

Then darkness took me.

I awoke sometime later, feeling limp as shredded rags, still covered by the blanket. I lay on bedding; wondered if Nayyib and Del had simply rolled me onto it. I had no memory of waking to put myself there. Not good for a sword-dancer. But obviously something in my mind believed I was safe in their care, not to stir at all when they moved me.

I stared up at the sky. Still night, still dark, wreathed in brilliant stars. The fire had died to embers. It was very quiet; even the horses slept.

Del was close beside me. I sensed her there even without looking, as if every part of my awareness was attuned to her presence. She slept as she often did, coiled on her left side with a fold of blanket pulled over her ear. Loosened hair fell across her face and strayed onto bedding.

I wanted to reach out and touch it, to feel the silk. But it felt good just to lie here unmoving, letting the night bathe me.

Oh bascha, I don't want to die in ten or twelve years. I don't want to lose you. I want to be with you, to see you grow old even as I do.

Nayyib slept on the other side of the fire. I knew he was attracted to Del; I wondered if he thought he might win her from me. If maybe he considered me too old for her, wondering what she saw in a forty-year-old man. He was her age: young, strong, athletic, undeniably attractive. He had a gentleness about him coupled with strength of mind, a quiet confidence that set him apart from other young men. Maybe it came from working with horses, from understanding their needs and fears, their moments of inexplicable recalcitrance. Or maybe it was just him.

What *would* Del do when I was gone? Find another?

Find Neesha?

I had no way of knowing what to expect when my time approached. Nihko and Sahdri had said nothing of that, merely that a Skandi-born mage went mad if he didn't learn to control his magic, and that the magic would eventually burn him out merely by its presence. If I refused to use it, I might die that much sooner.

Well, I had used it. With Oziri, learning to dream-walk; spelling Umir's book; dividing the sandstorm; reading the bones of the woman who was my mother.

Had used it even in childhood, conjuring the living sandtiger out of a carved one, in order to find freedom.

I wanted none of it.

It appeared to want me.

I sat up, suppressing a groan. Everything ached, even my skin. I didn't feel forty; I felt sixty. An age I would never reach.

Slowly I pushed myself to my feet, wavered a moment, steadied, then picked my way across the sand to the dozing horses. The stud roused as I touched him, whickering softly. I felt his warm breath against my hand. Then I turned, went a few steps away and attended to my business, aware of a clenching deep in my kidneys. Maybe mages died early because they used themselves up, aging their organs ahead of time.

I turned, took three steps, found Del waiting at the stud's head. Maybe she'd heard my joints grinding as I walked across the sand.

I saw the question in her eyes. Smiling faintly, I hooked an arm around her neck and stood next to her. "I'm fine."

I heard the pent breath expelled. For a moment we just stood there side by side, staring across the Punja glowing faintly in moon- and starlight.

She spoke very quietly. "I don't want to lose you."

I kept my voice as low, not wanting to wake Nayyib. "What? You mean Neesha hasn't won you from me with a glance of those eloquent eyes?"

"Neesha's eyes may indeed work wonders on other women, but not on me."

"Are you immune?"

"Oh, no. He is a beautiful young man."

"Beautiful?"

"As a man may be," she clarified. "Not like a woman. He isn't *pretty.* But the bones of his face are well suited to one another, and he moves very well. He understands his body."

I hadn't really asked for that much explanation. But I'd never thought about how women view men, other than appreciating that many of them seemed to view me with favor. "What do you look at in a man? Women, I mean. Not just you."

Del's breath of laughter was a quiet expulsion of air. "We don't all necessarily see or want the same thing. There are pretty men, and handsome men, and men who lack the features that most would name attractive but claim a sense of *presence* that makes looks unimportant. There is no describing that. It simply *is.* Tall, short, heavy, thin . . . it doesn't matter."

I thought of brutal Ajani, long dead. Handsome, huge, filled with undeniable presence. Yet he had used the power to rape and kill, to alter forever the life of the woman next to me. "But there are handsome men who have it."

"Yes. And those are the men that turn a woman's knees to water and her brain to mush."

"I, of course, exude it."

"There are also men who are *too* confident, too certain of themselves and their appeal, and who believe they may blind women to their faults."

"Thanks very much for that."

"But I, however, am not so easily blinded."

"I sort of figured that."

"Some men may begin that way but are trainable when in the hands of the right woman. Other men are hopeless."

I wasn't certain either of those attributes was something I aspired to.

"And age doesn't matter," Del said. "Not when a woman meets the right man."

"Even if she's young enough to be his daughter?"

"Lo, even then."

I had been curious a long time. Now I asked her. "When did you know you wanted to sleep with me?"

"Oh, within days. But you were such a pig-headed, insufferably *male* Southroner that I was appalled by my response."

"Thank you very much!"

"I argued with myself for weeks."

"As I recall, it was months before we finally did the deed." Months and months, in fact; it had been very hard on me.

"I intended it to be never. But one day I realized that ignorance could be changed, even in a Southroner. Besides, by then you knew I would never be the kind of women Southron men prefer: soft, quiet, deferential little mice who keep their houses and bear their children."

"We don't have a house to keep and you can't, well . . ." I realized belatedly that blurting out her inability to have children was not perhaps the most tactful thing. Del loved children. Enough to give her daughter to good people who could care for her when Del, consumed with vengeance, couldn't. "Sorry, bascha."

She shied away from it, not even acknowledging my apology. "I am not like most Southron women," she went on, "but more of them could be like me if they let themselves be free."

"Maybe they're happy the way they are."

"Or maybe they don't know any better because they are trained from birth to be blind to their own ambitions."

"Maybe their ambitions are to keep house and raise children. Lena seems to be happy."

"Lena *is* happy. But then, Alric is a Northerner; he expects her to be free to express herself. I have no objection to women keeping house and bearing children, Tiger, if that is what they truly wish in their hearts, and not because their men demand it of them. I only object when men won't allow the women who wish to be more to acheive it. To even imagine it."

I thought of Del, Northern born and raised, allowed to learn the sword even before she went to Staal-Ysta to become a swordsinger. I thought of my grandmother, the matriarch of a powerful family, conducting business with ruthless brilliance. I thought of my mother, who willingly left behind that wealth and power to

go with the man she loved to a distant land known for its harshness and died because of it.

I sighed. "Maybe I was trainable because I'm actually Skandic,
not a Southroner."

"Or maybe you have more flexibility of mind."

"Is that a good thing? If one's mind is *too* flexible, one never
has an opinion of one's own."

"Tiger, you would never let anyone change your opinion until
you were certain they were right."

"So, am I inflexibly flexible, or flexibly inflexible?"

She elbowed me in the ribs. "What you are is incorrigible."

"Is *that* a good thing?"

"Only when I'm in the mood."

I turned to her, wrapped her up in my arms. Lightly rested my
chin on her head. "I'm a little too tired, bascha."

"Not that kind of mood."

I smiled into the darkness. "I know."

"He is attractive, Tiger, and not without charm and that sense
of presence I mentioned before. But he is not you."

"Next best thing?"

"Well, I suppose if you got yourself killed in a sword-dance
tomorrow, I might consider it."

"So as long as I'm alive, you're satisfied?"

"Unless you decided to revert to the Tiger I met in that dusty
cantina four years ago. Then I'd have to kill you myself."

Considering she'd nearly done it once, I knew she was capable. "Then I'll be on my best behavior."

"Oh, no, be on your worst. Because then I can train *that* out
of you."

I sighed deeply, rubbing my cheek against her hair. Stubble
caught on it. "I want to live to be an old man, with you there
beside me."

"So you will, and so I will be."

The truth was, either of us could die tomorrow. But we knew
it. Accepted it. Were unafraid.

For ourselves, that is. I know we feared for one another.

THIRTY-ONE

AT DAWN, as the others lay sleeping, I carried the vertebra and rib bone out to where Del had found them. Nayyib had dug up all the visible pieces of wood; hollows and indentations were left to show where he had worked, but the first whisper of wind would cover those up, leaving no trace of the wagon. A few paces away Del had found the bones. I knelt, set the two fragments aside, used the edge of my right hand to ease away more fine sand. After some time I gave up the search; the rest of the bones could be anywhere, carried away in countless simooms over forty years. That any had been left for our discovery was miraculous.

I smiled wryly, remembering that supposedly I was the jhihadi. It was a ludicrous idea—and utterly untrue. I was just a man who seemed to fit pieces of the prophecy certain religious zealots had adopted, and I'd come up with a good idea in channeling water to the desert. But *anyone* could have come up with that idea. It just happened to be me.

I sat there on the sand, vertebra in one hand, rib in the other. It was very difficult to believe they were from my mother; that with flesh over them, and muscle, tendon, ligament, not to mention the vessels carrying blood, they had been part of a living woman.

A living woman who had somehow sent a message to me in my dreams.

But I wished I could have seen her as she had been, before the borjuni raid killed her. When she had been woman, not a scattering of bones across the sand, or a speaking skull telling me to find her, to take up the sword.

I leaned forward, dug a pocket in the sand, pressed the bones into it. Feathered sand over the top. The next storm would bury them more deeply, or strip away the covering so that the wind, in its exuberance, might carry them on a journey.

It crossed my mind that perhaps I should have them sent back to the metri on Skandi, so she might have a little something of her daughter to bury or burn, according to Skandic rites, and to mourn. But my grandmother didn't strike me as the type of woman who would do that. Or appreciate the thought.

Love for my father had brought my mother here. Best they remained together.

I pressed three sword-callused fingers over the slight upswell of sand, bid her goodbye, then left her.

Some time later we rode out of the Punja, onto the road—this time I had no problem heading south—and into Julah. I suggested we put up the horses at a different livery, which we did, then went to Fouad's by way of alleys and entered via the back door. It startled Fouad half to death as we snuck in, but when he saw who it was, he settled. His look at me was oddly assessing; I wondered what he saw. I was still tired from the magery I'd used first on the storm, then to read my mother's bones, and was looking forward to a night's sleep in a real bed. Especially since I'd missed it the *last* time we were here.

Then Fouad looked at Nayyib, narrowed his eyes as he sought to figure out who he was; his face cleared, and he nodded. He recalled the kid from when he'd come looking for a healer. Del shut and latched the door behind us.

"Food, no doubt, and drink," Fouad said. "Yes?"

"Yes to both," I agreed. "Del and the kid will eat in the front room; how about you send something back to me? I'd rather keep my head down, after what happened the last time.

Fouad's eyes flicked to Nayyib again, clearly questioning his presence. The kid had been taught his manners: He bowed slightly, smiling. "Neesha," he said. "I am privileged to be the Sandtiger's student."

Fouad's eyebrows ran up into his hair as he looked at me. "Student?"

I shrugged, deciding now was as good a time as any to announce my intentions. "I plan to restore Alimat and take up my shodo's role."

"Alimat! But it was destroyed years ago!" Fouad shook his head. "And I doubt the other sword-dancers will let you. Particularly Abbu Bensir."

"If they want to take it up with me, they're welcome to. That in itself would provide a valuable lesson for the students."

"Watching you die? I would say so!" He glanced at Del. "You're amenable?"

Del mimicked my shrug. "Why not? There will be two teachers: a Southron sword-dancer and a Northern sword-singer. What other school may claim that?"

"And one student already," Neesha added.

Fouad wagged his head back and forth thoughtfully. "Well, you will most certainly draw students—until someone kills you."

I scowled. "I appreciate the confidence. Now, how about that food and drink?"

"I'll eat with you," Del offered, turning toward the back hallway.

Neesha grinned wickedly. "While *I* eat out front and attempt to charm Fouad's wine-girls."

Fouad grunted. "I suspect you'll have any number of offers before the food's on the table. But come along; I'll introduce you as a friend of the new owners. That ought to be good enough for a discount." His tone went dry as dust. "That is, if they don't decide to offer themselves for free, as has been known to happen with certain regular customers I won't mention in present company."

Neesha, still grinning, threw a conspiratorial look over his shoulder at Del and me as if to make sure we understood what he was doing.

"Well, at least he's not *entirely* oblivious." I turned Del and propelled her toward the back bedroom. "I guess if he's got enough sense to know when we need some privacy, it won't be so bad having him ride with us."

Del, allowing herself to be propelled, merely laughed. "I don't think he's doing that so much for *our* privacy as he is for his own! Fouad's right: The girls will be fighting over him the moment he sits down. I rather think our new student will be most busy tonight."

I pulled back our door curtain. "I rather think *we* will be most busy tonight."

"And tomorrow?"

"Tomorrow we load the horses and head out again for the chimney at Beit al'Shahar. There's a sword I need to have a discussion with."

Del sat down on the bed and began to unlace her sandals. "If you can find it. The whole formation collapsed, Tiger. Your *jivatma* may be completely buried."

"Worth a look anyhow." I stripped off the harness, unsheathed the sword, set it point down against one of the bedside tables. "If I can't get to it, no one can; but my mother seemed fairly certain it could be found. I mean, who would have thought I could find her bones out there in the Punja? On the basis of dreams? It may be possible I can find Samiel, too."

"And if—" She corrected herself, "*when*—you do?"

"Dunno." I sat down, yawned, rolled my head against my shoulders, stretching tendons.

"He's still a *jivatma*, Tiger. You used Northern magic to make him—and now you have your own magic as well."

"A magical sword, wielded by a mage who is also the long-lost grandson of one of the Eleven gods-descended Families of Skandi—and who also happens to be the jhihadi." I flopped down against the bed. "Something for people to write sagas and sing songs about, don't you think?"

Del, barefoot now, undid the buckles of her harness. " 'The Sword-Dancer's Tale.' Well, perhaps."

"Maybe 'The Tale of Tiger.' "

" '*And Del.*' "

My eyes drifted closed. "As long as my name goes first."

"Not when it's sung or told in the North, it doesn't."

I smiled. "Depends on the audience, I guess. Hmm—what about '*The Tiger's Tale*'?"

"Or '*The Tiger's Tail*'?"

I stuck my tongue out at her.

"If you're asleep when the food and drink arrives, do you want me to wake you up?"

"I'm not going to sleep. I'm resting my eyes."

"Do you want me to wake you up from resting your eyes?"

"Sure," I mumbled, "a man's got to keep up his strength to satisfy his woman." And slid into the abyss before she could respond.

Del did indeed wake me up when the food and drink arrived. She slapped a cupped hand across my abdomen, making odd, hollowed, clapping sounds against my skin. Not entirely the most subtle way to awaken a sleeper.

"Up," she said. "Food's here."

I scrunched up against the wall at the head of the bed, inspecting the skin of my abdomen. Then I helped myself to the platter bearing bread-bowls of mutton stew, cheese, grapes, and a small jug of what turned out to be ale.

"Tiger, we need a door on this room."

I slugged down about half the ale, then licked the foam from my upper lip. "We have a door."

"That's a door*way*. I mean a door. I'd like some privacy, if we're to stay here now and again."

"There's a curtain."

"I would like a *wooden* door. With a latch."

I plucked grapes from their stems with my teeth and spoke around them. "Why so formal?"

"Because unless you don't mind everyone else knowing our business, with all manner of false conclusions drawn about the fair-haired Northern bascha—for example, how much does Fouad charge for me?—I think we need a door. A wooden door. With a latch."

"You have a point." I dropped the denuded grape stems back on the platter. "I'll have a word with Fouad. Anything else you'd like, while we're at it?"

"Well, *I'd* recommend he dismiss all the wine-girls who double as whores, but I'm quite sure he would not agree to that."

"I think that's a safe conclusion. We'd probably lose all kinds of business and thus all kinds of profit. We'd have to close down."

"The gods forfend," Del said dryly, reaching for the other jug; water, no doubt.

I paused before putting a chunk of cheese in my mouth. "You don't sound particularly enamored of being a partner in a thriving cantina. Just think of the benefits!"

"What benefits? Other than free drinks for you?"

"We'll be the first to hear all rumors and reports of whatever may be going on in the world. At least, our little corner of it."

"That's a benefit?"

"It is when you know anywhere from ten to twenty men are bent on executing you."

"And you'll run back here to hide any time one of them comes into the cantina?"

"Oh, no. We'll clear all the furniture out of the common room, cut a circle into the hardpack, then charge admission for the dance. Plus take a percentage of the side bets." I grinned wickedly. "Rather like *we* used to do, when we needed money."

Del used her knife to carve curling strips of cheese from the hunk Fouad had sent along. "Those were not actual dances."

"Which means we can charge even more money for a real one."

Her eyes were on the cheese, but her idle tone was nonetheless underscored by solemnity. "What will it take to make them stop?"

"Once I kill enough of them, the rest will find other things to do."

"I'm serious, Tiger."

"So am I. It's true. I killed Khashi quickly and brutally in front of many witnesses. Then I won a difficult sword-dance against a very, very good young man, in front of a whole slug of sword-dancers. Once I kill a few more, most of them will stop coming."

"And will it be like Fouad suggested, that they'll want to stop you from resurrecting Alimat?"

"Very likely." I took up horn spoon and bread-bowl of stew and began scooping the contents into my mouth. Seeing Del's concern, I paused between bites. "I have to see it settled, bascha. We can't go North, and I have no desire to return to Skandi, where I'd likely be hauled off to ioSkandi again and stuck back atop the spires in Meteiera. I also have no desire to go haring off to foreign lands. The South, despite all its problems, is my home. Coming back made me realize that. I won't run away again."

She nodded, clearly troubled. "I know."

I sighed, set down the bowl and spoon. "Del, something happened to me. I became aware of it when I was Umir's 'guest.' I don't know how it happened, and I can't even be sure it will happen again, but when I danced, when I took up my sword—I felt as if I had all four fingers on each hand."

Blue eyes widened.

"I know it sounds impossible. But it's true. I mean, I *know* the fingers are gone—hoolies, I saw Sahdri throw them off the spire!—but when I dance, it feels as if I still have them."

Del was staring at my hands. One thumb, three fingers on each.

"I don't know, maybe I'm just imagining them there. But when I danced against Musa, I could have sworn I had all my fingers again."

She met my eyes. "Is it possible that it's—"

"—wishful thinking? Sure. And it could be. But it might also be something in me now, something that's a part of the magic. I conjured a living sandtiger out of carved bone once. Who's to say I can't conjure two fingers when I need them?"

"Does it—does it feel the same?"

"Not exactly. And when I look at them, I see the stumps, not the fingers. But when I take up the sword, I feel whole again. That my *hands* are whole again." I hitched one shoulder in a half-shrug. "I'm not saying I can't be defeated or that no one could use it against me. My grip is different. I'm not the same as I was before. Anyone looking at my hands would see only three fingers. But if I can dance as though I have four on each hand—"

"But you don't." Gently insistent, afraid I'd become complacent in something that didn't truly exist.

I heaved a sigh, ran one hand through my hair, scrubbing against my tattooed scalp. "I've heard men who've lost a limb talk about ghost pain. That they feel as if the missing limb is still attached, still functional. Maybe that's all it is. I sense the ghosts of my fingers somehow, and it helps." I tapped. "Up here, in my head."

Del nodded. "And if the ghosts ever go away?"

I laughed a little. "Bascha, I'm forty years old. I don't have many more good years left to me as a sword-dancer; and I'm *not* a sword-dancer, according to the oaths of Alimat. But I think I can teach."

The smile broke free from the tension in her face. "I still can't believe it. The Sandtiger, opening a school . . . and *teaching*!"

"Oh? What about you? You seem willing enough to stick in one place and take on students. Is that what you envisioned for yourself when you left Staal-Ysta?"

"I envisioned killing Ajani. Beyond that—?" She shook her head. "Nothing. My song ended that day in Iskandar. The South is not my home, but I can't go to the North. And it doesn't matter. I chose to be with you. If you want to restore Alimat and reopen a school, then I will be a part of it."

I was only half-joking. "Until Neesha steals you away from me."

Nothing in Del's expression suggested there was anything that supported what I'd suggested, even in the back of her mind. "Well, then we have a few weeks, at least."

Relief. I grinned, handed her the other bread-bowl, stuck the second horn spoon into it so it stood up in the center. "Here. Just don't eat up all our profits."

THIRTY-TWO

DEL AND I were packed and eating our morning meal by the time Neesha came dragging out of one of the smaller rooms to knock at the doorframe, since, as Del had noted, we had no actual door.

My mouth was full, so Del, tying saddlepouches closed, waved him in; he sidled through the curtain split. "Is everyone decent?"

Del and I assessed him silently. His face was stubbled, his eyes faintly bloodshot, his hair an unruly tangle. I swallowed and said, "Aparently more decent than you."

His smile blossomed, lighting honey-brown eyes. "Oh, no. I am far better than decent. Or so Silk tells me."

I nearly choked on my next bite, swallowed hastily. "Silk? You ended up with Silk last night?"

"Silk was the *last* one I ended up with last night, yes."

I glowered at him. "And I suppose she didn't charge you."

Neesha's grin was a superior smirk. "As a matter of fact, she said she ought to pay *me*."

Del looked from me to him and back again. "Is this for my benefit, this ridiculous male posturing?"

Neesha started laughing even as I grinned. Hey, in front of a beautiful woman you like it to be known that you have alternatives.

"But you do look, um, used up," I noted.

He attempted to tame his hair. "Ridden hard and put away wet," he agreed in horse parlance; then he glanced at Del solemnly. "And that *isn't* posturing."

She made a sound of absolute scorn and waved a dismissive hand. "You men."

Indictment in two words. Neesha and I exchanged grins. "*Women*," we said simultaneously.

Del scowled, buckling on her harness. "Are we ready to go?"

"My things are packed and by the back door," Neesha told her.

My mouth full again, I gestured illustratively at waiting saddlepouches.

"Good," she said. "Why don't you two *men* go saddle the horses? I'll be along in a few moments."

I washed breakfast down with ale. "What's keeping you?"

"Something *men* wouldn't understand." She gestured again. "Run along, boys."

I already wore my harness and sword; I hooked my set of saddlepouches over my shoulder, tossed Del's to Neesha. "By all means, let's allow the *woman* to do *woman* things."

Del scowled at us both as we departed the room.

The kid and I went to the livery housing the horses and set about getting them ready to go. It was companionable as we worked, exchanging a sentence now and again, but mostly just tending the horses. Neesha did indeed have a way with them that I envied. I wondered if I should have him ride the stud . . . nah, better not. I really didn't want to get the kid hurt.

Nor, for that matter, did I want to witness the stud's defection.

He had finished tacking up his horse and worked on Del's white gelding, smearing black paint around his eyes and stringing the Vashni browband across his face. When done, he looked over at me. "When do you want to try this sparring match?"

I was inspecting the line of stitches in the stud's left haunch. "Oh, let's wait till we get to Alimat. I figure what you did for the stud bought you a lesson or two, no audition necessary." I patted the stud's rump well away from the stitched wound. "It looks good."

"My father taught me well."

I shook my head, leading the stud into daylight. "If you are the only son, you stand to inherit."

Neesha followed with his bay and Del's gelding. "Yes."

"Owning a horse farm is not a bad way to live."

"It's a good way to live."

"Then—"

He replied over the beginnings of my question, knowing what it would be. "Because it's not what I dreamed about. Not what I wanted to do since—" He broke off, glanced away from me. "Since I first understood what sword-dancing was. My father followed *his* father's footsteps, and his before his, but I want to follow . . . well, I wanted to go elsewhere. To make my own way." Now we stood in the alley not far from the cantina. "It may be a good life—I don't suggest it isn't—but it isn't the one I want. Not yet. Maybe someday when I'm your age and want to retire, I'll use my winnings to buy my *own* horse farm."

I nodded inwardly; I could admire a kid who wanted to make his own way in the world despite having advantages. If he had any true talent for the sword, I'd find out; if not, I'd send him back to the horses. Most didn't have that choice.

"Sword-dancing is a very hard life, Neesha. The work isn't steady, it's often painful, and now and again there's a very real chance you could be killed, even if it isn't a death-dance. Accidents happen. And outside of the circle, there are any number of jobs that could get you hurt or killed."

He nodded. "Abbu told me so."

I went very still. "Abbu Bensir?"

"He was the sword-dancer who came through my village."

"Hunh." That put a different light on things. "How many lessons did he give you?"

"Four." A self-deprecating grin kindled quickly. "Enough to have him humiliate me but not enough to dissuade me."

"You took lessons from Abbu, then decided to find *me*?"

"I decided to find you before then." His gaze on me was level. "I heard stories about you."

Ah, yes. The legendary Sandtiger. Abbu would certainly appreciate that. "Did you tell him that was your plan?"

"No. It was my business, not his."

I released a low whistle of appreciation. "Had Abbu known, he might have offered to teach you some tricks."

Neesha's smile was slight. "I knew that. But I didn't want to learn tricks. I wanted to learn the *art*. I think Abbu believed I would change my mind."

I saw Del approaching. "You'll do," I said, patting the stud's neck. "At least, for a while."

He grinned. "Ten years? Or maybe seven, to match the shodo?"

"Or maybe six, to better him?"

Neesha didn't hesitate. He simply shook his head. "Who could?"

I laughed. "Abbu would say otherwise."

"Possibly. But I didn't come all this way to be Abbu's student."

Del came up and took the gelding's rein from Neesha's hand. "So, we are bound at last—again—to the fallen chimney."

"Beit al'Shahar." I gave it the Vashni name. "Yes. And if I manage to accomplish my task, then we'll head for Alimat. It's a good five or six days' ride from here, depending on the mood of the Punja. In the meantime, we can start beating up on Neesha so he understands what schooling is *really* all about."

Del cast him a glance, expression questioning.

He nodded. "I am duly forewarned."

I mounted the stud. "Then let's ride."

Not far out of Julah we found and followed the faint trail of wheel ruts Del and I had come to recognize, noting familiar landmarks. Somewhere along it we'd camped out on the way back from the Vashni settlement, where Del had scattered the pieces of the necklet Oziri had given me. I was aware that I no longer had any inclination to return to the Vashni encampment or to learn more about dream-walking. I had used a form of it to read my mother's bones, but there was no desire in me to sort out what my dreams meant. I *knew* what those involving the dead woman meant; by finding her bones, I'd fulfilled half of her repeated commandment. Now all that was left was to take up my *jivatma* and forget all about magery.

If I could.

Not long before sundown we rode up the familiar twisting trail to the top of the tree-hedged plateau. The lean-to against the boulders still stood. I shook my head in bemusement, recalling how Del and I had spent days there sick from sandtiger venom, and how Neesha had helped us both.

Apparently so did he, and so did Del. I saw them exchange long, intent glances. It was more than mere memory, more than a friendly recollection worth reciting to others over food and drink, but something strangely intimate. And indecipherable. It left me with an odd feeling in my belly. There was nothing in Del's behavior suggesting she was attracted to Neesha, and she had even come right out and *said* there was no interest on her part. When drunk on Umir's liquor the kid had divulged his attraction to her, but that didn't surprise me. Most men fell under Del's unintended spell merely by being in her presence. I was used to that. But I had seen looks exchanged between them before, glances I couldn't translate. Not the silent communication of lovers, but something else. Something—more.

But what more is there? You are lovers, friends, acquaintances, strangers, or enemies. I could attach none of those descriptions to what I saw passing between Del and Nayyib.

Could she be lying? I didn't think so. She had explained once in Skandi that if she ever intended to leave, she'd tell me. That, I believed. It wasn't Del's way to hide behind lies and subterfuge. She had also demonstrated her affection for me in physical ways, ways that were no different than had been employed before. Could a woman hide her attraction to a new man while sleeping with the old?

Well, yes. But not Del. Not with her honesty. She had never learned to dissemble.

And when Neesha had quietly bragged about his conquests of Silk and other wine-girls, it hadn't been done in a way to kindle jealousy or to make a point, the way a man might if he wanted a woman who refused him.

Which left—what?

I didn't know. Before Del, I'd kept myself to wine-girls and other women who wanted nothing more than a night or two together. I'd never sworn myself to any kind of bond. Del and I were not oath-bound, not vowed to one another save by what lived in our spirits. But I knew that could change. That it had, for others.

Hoolies, it was too complex to think about right now, after most of a day spent on horseback.

I dismounted over by scraggly trees rimming the edge of the flat-topped bluff and set about unloading and tying out the stud. The grass grazed down earlier by our horses had recovered somewhat, which suggested no one had been here since I'd come looking for Del. She and the kid found separate places for their mounts and began to unload as well. When the stud had cooled, I'd water and grain him; for now he was content to nose and lip at grass. I humped my tack and pouches over to the lean-to and dropped them outside.

"Wood," I announced tersely. "I'll be back."

"I'll go, too, when I'm done here," Nayyib offered.

"Not necessary." I stalked off, aware both were staring at me in startled bafflement.

Well, fine, so I'm prone to occasional bouts of jealousy. I'm human.

Maybe *that* proved I wasn't the jhihadi. Did messiahs get jealous? For that matter, did messiahs sleep with women?

Feeling somewhat better, I began looking in earnest for appropriate deadfall.

I made two trips to gather firewood. Nayyib made one; he piled it next to the fire ring, then lingered to talk with Del. From some distance away, it seemed an odd conversation. The kid stood with his head lowered, shoulders poised stiffly. Not deferential exactly, but not precisely happy, either. Del stood very close to him, and *her* body language suggested she was doing most of the talking.

It was interesting to see them together from a distance. Nayyib was an inch taller than Del, and certainly broader and thicker of limb, but, though larger in general than most Southroners, he was not truly a significantly big man. Still, he was young yet; I didn't truly fill out until halfway through my twenties, though I had my height. Del is no delicate flower, but a tall, strong woman who moves unencumbered by the perceived requirements of femininity. They matched well together, Nayyib and Delilah.

His head came up sharply. Posture stiffened even more. He said something to Del, something definitive, because *her* posture abruptly tensed. Then he turned and walked away, looking for all the world like a house cat offended by the taint of splashed water.

Del watched him go—perhaps he was after more wood—then shook her head slightly. She knelt, began building a fire.

All in all, it did not put me in mind of a lovers' quarrel. Or a woman withstanding the blandishments of a man who wanted her. In fact, I couldn't put a name to it at all, save to say that he wasn't pleased by what she had told him, and she was no more pleased by his response.

But how much of that was wishful thinking?

I went over with my second supply of wood, piled it by the fire, and looked at her questioningly. "Something wrong?"

Del denied it crossly, then ducked into the lean-to to begin arranging her bedding.

Which left me even more confused than before. Wood delivered, I went off to check on the horses and to water and grain them. When Nayyib came back, he dumped his wood on the pile and came over to tend to his bay, though I had things under control.

The day was dying quickly, the way it does in the desert, but I could still see the stubbled planes of his face and the hollows of his eyes. He was unhappy about something. It struck me as odd, since Neesha seemed a mostly equable sort.

In view of my own sharp temper earlier, I didn't think it would help to inquire if he had a problem. So I lingered as I tended the stud and Del's gelding, and eventually he sighed, let the tension go, and spoke.

"Why is it we're going to this chimney place?"

"Beit al'Shahar. It's a rock formation."

"But what's there?"

"Something I left behind." I collected emptied canvas buckets and set them out of reach, so inquisitive equine teeth wouldn't chew them to bits. "Del and I were out this way about a year ago, give or take."

"She said something about a sword."

"*Jivatma*," I clarified. "A Northern sword. Blooding-blade. Named blade." I smiled when I saw his frown of incomprehension. "Northern ritual. Mostly, it's just a sword."

"You have a sword. Why go looking for this Northern one?"

"Something I need to do."

"Like find the bones in the Punja?"

"Something like that." I smoothed a hand down the stud's neck. "Kind of hard to explain. There are swords—and there are swords. If you own one long enough—if you form a partnership, odd as it may sound—it becomes more than just a weapon or a means of making a living."

"Singlestroke."

"Ah, the infamous blade of the Sandtiger!" I dropped the melodramatic tone. "A good sword. Kept me out of serious trouble many times."

"But you don't carry it any more."

So, he didn't know everything about the legend. "Singlestroke was broken a number of years ago."

His head came up. "So you want the Northern blade in its place?"

I remembered Samniel's begetting at Staal-Ysta, the days and nights I spent in Kem's smithy. "It too is a good sword. A special sword." I shrugged. "It's hard to explain."

"Much about you is hard to explain."

"I'm a complicated guy, Neesha." True dark had fallen; there was nothing more to be read in expressions, which couldn't be seen. Only in voices.

"Del told me some stories when we were with the Vashni."

Finished with the horses, we fell in together as we drifted back toward the fire. "It's been an interesting life."

"And a dangerous one."

"I warned you about that."

"Yes." He sounded pensive.

"Thinking the horse farm sounds a bit better?"

His head came up sharply. "No."

"Then what's bothering you?"

He did not answer immediately. When he did, his tone was stiff. "You have your secrets. I have mine."

By then we were at the fire. Del sat next to it, drinking from a bota and gnawing on dried cumfa. She did not look at Neesha. She looked at me as if her eyes were knives. Seems we were *all* being complicated tonight.

And it hurt.

Ignoring the thought, I squatted beside the fire. "First thing tomorrow morning I'd like to head out for the chimney. You two can wait here if you'd rather—it's not that far—or come along and wait for me there at the formation."

Del stopped chewing. "Why would we not come?"

I hooked my head in Neesha's general direction. "You and he appear to have some things to discuss."

Their eyes met. Locked. Del seemed to wait. Nayyib's jaw and raised brows suggested *she* had something to say.

"Fine." I pulled my pouches over, dug through until I found my share of burlap-wrapped cumfa. "The kid said it best, I guess—we all have our secrets. I don't know if each of you has a different one, or if you share the same one. What I *do* know is I'm left out of it. Which is probably for the best; I'm really not in the mood to deal with childish nonsense."

Del's brow creased, but she didn't reply. Nayyib sat down and pointedly turned his attention to the contents of *his* saddle-pouches.

My jaws worked to soften the preserved meat. It's almost impossible to talk with a mouth full of cumfa, so I didn't even try. We all just ground our jaws and thought thoughts none of us wished to share.

I've got to admit it: I've spent more companionable nights in the desert. But it didn't interfere when I decided to go to bed.

Del and Nayyib, not talking, were still sitting by the fire as I unrolled my bedding in the lean-to and crawled into it.

I sighed, turned over, tried to go to sleep. It took me a while, but I got there.

I awakened in the middle of the night, heart pounding against my chest. A residue of fear still sizzled through my body. A dream . . .

Not one like the others. Nothing like the others. This was a normal dream in all respects, except for its content.

I've always dreamed vividly. Maybe it was because of the magic in my bones, incipient dream-walking, bone-reading, or some such thing. Sometimes the dreams were fragments, sometimes connected scenes that told some kind of story. Often they entertained me; usually they confused me, in that I could see no cause for them.

I saw no cause for this one, either.

I lay wide awake beneath a blanket, staring up at the haphazard roof of the lean-to. Del and Nayyib were deeply asleep. I let my breathing still, my heartbeat slow, and considered what I'd dreamed.

Me, in the desert. Older, but not old. I wore dhoti and sandals, held a sword in my hand. All around me were people I knew: Del, Alric, Fouad, Abbu, also Nayyib, and my shodo; even people from the Salset, including Sula and the old shukar who had made my life a misery. My grandmother. A younger woman whose features were obscured, but whom I knew was my mother. And any number of other people I'd known in my life.

One by one they turned their backs on me and walked away. I was left alone in the desert with only my sword.

Remembering it helped. Tension eased. Fear abated. I banished the images, relaxed against my bedding, and let myself drift back into sleep.

THIRTY-THREE

In THE MORNING the air remained chilly, but it had nothing to do with the temperature. Del and Nayyib both seemed out of sorts. Feeling left out but not sorry for it, I went about my morning routine. Eventually I had the stud fed, watered, saddled, and packed, and I led him over to the lean-to. Del and the kid were still repacking bedrolls. I suspected there had been a verbal exchange held too quietly for me to hear; they seemed tense with one another, and they were behind on preparations.

"All right, children, how long are you going to carry on with this?"

My tone and implication annoyed Del, who'd heard it before. It always annoyed Del. She gathered up her belongings and stalked past me on her way to the white gelding. It left Nayyib with compressed mouth, set jaw, and sharp physical movements at odds with his normal economical grace.

So I came right out and asked it. "Does this have anything to do with Del?"

He didn't look at me. "Yes."

"And you?"

He stood up, hooking saddle pouches over one shoulder. Paused long enough to look me in the eyes. "Ask *her*." And marched himself across the flat to his horse.

Oh, hoolies. And other various imprecations.

* * *

We wound our way along the wagon ruts, going deeper into the low, boulder-clad mountains. I led, Del followed, and Nayyib brought up the rear. We were strung out, allowing the horses to pick the best footing, since the boulders began to impinge on the tracks. Some things looked familiar, some did not; but it was years since Del and I had been here, and we'd certainly been in a hurry to leave once the chimney collapsed. Other than a slight delay as I was declared a messiah by Mehmet, part of a Deep Desert nomadic tribe dedicated to worshiping the jhihadi, nothing had prevented us from leaving. Del had purposely broken her *jivatma* after drawing Chosa Dei out of my body, freeing him to fight it out with his brother sorcerer, Shaka Obre. We hadn't been certain how violent that fight would be since both had been refined to essences of power, not physical bodies, so we'd departed the area as soon as we could.

More memories came back. I recalled Umir's incredible feathered and beaded robe, which he'd put on Del when she was his prisoner. The whirlwind in the chimney had been been so powerful that it stripped all the ornamentation from the white samite fabric. We had picked feathers out of our hair for days.

I tried to stretch my senses, to get a feel for my own *jivatma*, buried in the ruins of the rock formation somewhere ahead. Nothing answered. There was no compulsion to continue as there had been to find my mother's bones; perhaps she trusted to me to complete the task without resorting to walking my dreams. I wasn't aware of anything except heat, the smell of stone and dust, the stillness of the air, the unceasing brilliance of the sun, and the sound of horses chipping rocks as the walked.

The wagon ruts were more difficult to follow as they passed over ribbons of stone extruding from the earth. Someone not intentionally looking for them might miss them altogether. But it struck me as odd that anyone would travel out here. There was no known road from Julah heading this way, the area skirted Vashni territory, and there was no known destination. Or if there were, it was a Vashni place; they had named the chimney decades before. In fact, I recalled being told they'd brought Del's brother to Beit al'Shahar, and when he'd returned he could speak again despite missing a tongue. Some kind of holy place, maybe. Except Vashni didn't use wagons, so the tracks didn't belong to them. We rode on a little farther, and then the trail made a wide sweeping turn to the left around an elbow of mountain flank. The stud abruptly pricked up his ears, head lifting. I reined in. He stood at attention, almost vibrating with focus. He nickered deep in his throat, then let it burst free as a high, piercing whinny.

In the distance, echoing oddly, a horse answered him.

Del, halted behind me, voiced it. "There is someone ahead."

"A horse, at least," I agreed. "Possibly two, or maybe a team of four; the wagon ruts got here somehow."

"Who would be out here?" Del asked. "There's nothing."

I shook my head. "It's a bit more than a day's ride from here to Julah on horseback; it would take longer with a wagon and team. Someone built that lean-to as a stop-over, a place to spend the night."

Nayyib brought his horse in closer. "So you're saying someone *did* settle out here."

"It's a guess," I said. "But we can find out." I brushed heels to the stud's sides and went on, more attentive now than I had been.

The trail took us down and around another tight turn, then leveled out. We were hemmed in by mountain walls. Then those walls fell away as if bowing us into a palace. And palace it was; I pulled up abruptly. Del fell in beside me, while Nayyib ended up on her far side.

"But—it wasn't like this . . ." Del said, astonished.

"Nothing like this," I agreed. Something had happened. Something that had riven the mountains apart, shaping out of existing stone and soil a long, narrow canyon. It wasn't terribly deep, nor was it huge. A compact slot cut between mountains and rock formations, opening up into a flat valley floor.

"Water," Nayyib said, pointing.

There hadn't been before. Now, bubbling up from a pile of tumbled boulders and fallen mountain, was a natural spring. It flowed outward into the canyon, finding its way through scattered rocks, then carved a fairly substantial streambed through the canyon floor.

I looked left, following the line of fallen hillside. And found the chimney.

Beit al'Shahar.

It had collapsed, breaking apart into sections. You could still see the suggestion of the columnar formation here and there, but it no longer existed as a true chimney. Del and I had not left it that way. Something more had happened.

Something powerful enough to open the way for an underground spring.

I tapped the stud back into motion and rode on. We passed the tumbled pile of slab-sided rock sections that gave birth to the stream, still following wagon ruts. Here we traded stony ground for soil, the first sparse scatterings of grass. Ahead, vegetation sprang up along the stream's meandering sides: reeds, shrubbery, thick mossy growths. Grass increased. The canyon widened. Thin, infant trees stood no higher than my knees.Oasis. Sheltered by canyon walls, with access to water, it was cooler here, shaded, with grazing and fertile soil.

"It was *nothing* like this," Del murmured.

Nayyib raised his voice. "Someone's farming here."

Indeed, someone was. The spring fed narrow, manmade ditches dug to water patches of fields and gardens, set apart from one another by low walls built of stones no doubt hacked out of the soil. We left behind wilderness and entered a private paradise.

"There," Nayyib said.

There, indeed. A scattering of flimsy pens held sheep and goats. A small pole corral contained a handful of horses. They had already smelled our mounts; now that we were in sight, all came trotting over to the fence rails to offer interested greetings. The stud stuck his head high in the air and commenced snorts of elaborate superiority, stiffened tail swishing viciously.

Behind me, Del's gelding pealed out a whinny.

"Look," she called. "They've built houses against the walls."

Low, squared, small houses built of adobe brick, surfaces hand-smoothed, with poles laid side-by-side and lashed together for roofs, chinked with mud to keep the rain and wind out. Unpainted, the dwellings were the color of the clay mud from which they were built: rich tan with an undertone of red. They blended into the canyon walls.

Faces appeared in wide-silled windows. Then the bodies took residence in the open doorways. Wagon ruts continued along the stream, fronting the dooryards of mudbrick homes standing cheek-by-jowl. Chickens had free run of the place, pecking in the dirt around the houses, pens, and corral.

"Sandtiger! *Sandtiger!*" A man emerged from one of the little houses. He came pelting down the ruts, brown burnous flapping, turban bouncing on his head.

"Mehmet!" Del exclaimed.

I grinned. "And his aketni."

"Sandtiger! May the sun shine on your head!" Mehmet arrived, dark eyes alight. At once he dropped to his knees, bowed his head, slapped the earth with the flat of his hand, then drew a smudged stripe across his Desert-dark forehead.

"Oh, stop that," I said. "You know how I hate it."

He sat back on his heels, enthusiasm undimmed. "Jhihadi," he breathed. And then he sprang up and began shouting in a dialect spilling so quickly from his mouth that I could only catch a third of what he said.

"Jhihadi?" Nayyib asked dubiously.

I arched supercilious brows. "Didn't you know? I've been declared a messiah. I'm even worshiped by—" I paused. "—however many people remain in Mehmet's aketni."

"Aketni?"

"His little tribe. An offshoot of his original tribe. Apparently not everyone wants to worship me."

"And the Vashni," Del put in. "Remember?"

Nayyib's expression was odd. "This is a joke."

I sighed. "No, actually, it's not. Though it certainly feels like one to me."

"You're a messiah?"

"I'm not a messiah. They just *think* I'm a messiah."

"My brother said you were," Del remarked.

Nayyib was totally lost. "Your brother said Tiger was a messiah?"

"It's complicated," I explained.

"A *messiah?*" he repeated.

I made a dismissive gesture. "Don't worry, it's not true."

"You're a legendary sword-dancer, the grandson of a wealthy Skandic matriarch, a mage—*and* a messiah?"

"A man of many parts," Del told him. "That's what the prophecy says."

I knew she was taking great joy in this, despite her bland expression. I shot her a quelling look. "Look, I have no control over what people say or think. Or that my grandmother is wealthy and powerful, or that I'm stuck with whatever this magic is inside me. What *I* know is that I'm a sword-dancer. That's good enough for me."

Neesha's expression was indescribable. Del took pity on him.

"We rescued them," she explained. "They'd been led into nowhere by unscrupulous guides, robbed, and left to die. Tiger and I found them, helped them."

Neesha's brows rode high on his forehead. "So they declared Tiger a messiah?"

"Not exactly." Del seemed to realize no explanation could sound reasonable. "But they worship the jhihadi, and they think Tiger fits."

"Why are they *here?*" Neesha asked.

"Because this is Beit al'Shahar," I answered crossly, knowing the whole thing sounded ludicrous, "and this is where I led them." I paused. "Supposedly."

Mehmet was waving his people out of their little homes. I saw the old women swathed in veils and robes, gray braids dangling from beneath head coverings, but also a few younger men and women and even a handful of children. Mehmet's aketni had increased in size since we'd last come across the tiny caravan.

Everyone gathered around, falling into a semicircle. All eyes were fastened on me, staring avidly. Mehmet stood in front of them, eyes alight with pride.

"We have done as you wished," he announced.

Since I didn't know what he was talking about, I prevaricated. "And you've done it well, Mehmet."

An outflung hand encompassed stream, ditches, grass, pens, corral, fields and gardens, and the small, square adobe houses huddled against the canyon walls. "We have turned the sand to grass!"

Ah, yes. The infamous prophecy.

And then I realized it was true.

Del, behind me, began to laugh.

Nayyib muttered, "I don't believe *any* of this."

Mehmet was exceedingly proud to know the jhihadi personally. After everyone had offered deep obeisances, he sent them all away to begin preparations for an evening feast. In the meantime, he offered us the hospitality of his own "unworthy house." He and his wife would sleep in the front room, while Del and I were gifted with the tiny bedroom.

He tripped a little over what to do with Nayyib, until the kid said he'd be perfectly happy sleeping outside near the water, if that was all right. He even added he was unworthy to be under the same roof as a messiah, which earned him a scowl from me and a snicker from Del.

"When did you get married?" I asked Mehmet. "And where did you find a wife?" The first time we'd met, Mehmet had been the only young male left in his aketni, which was comprised of old women and one old man, who'd later died. There was no one to marry in his own small tribe.

"I found my wife in Julah," he said proudly. "A caravan came through and stayed a few days. I went out to their encampment to welcome them, and I preached the prophecy of the jhihadi. A few of them decided to stay on and serve. Yasmah was one." His joy was infectious. "Now, come—these men will take your horses and make them comfortable."

I decided against protesting the preaching part for the moment. Certainly the sand *had* been changed to grass, at least right here; when we'd left it was desert, if not the sere harshness of the Punja and its immediate vicinity. But I rather had my own idea about what had caused the change.

Mehmet bowed us into his house, whereupon he presented us to his wife. She was a small, slight, black-eyed woman wrapped in robes and veils, quite shy, unwilling to meet my eyes at all. The gods only knew what Mehmet had been telling her about his jhihadi.

We were served food and drink at the low table surrounded by lumpy cushions rather than stools or benches, while Mehmet explained that they grew most of their own food, raised goats and sheep for wool, milk, and meat, chickens for eggs, and only infrequently went into Julah for additional supplies.

"And no one knows you're out here?" Del asked. "No one knows this canyon exists, or the water?"

Mehmet shook his head. "No one."

"Someday people will come," I warned. "We came. We found your ruts and followed them here."

Mehmet spread his hands. "Were you not already coming here?"

Well, yes. Come to think of it.

He nodded even though I'd said nothing. "No one has cause to come here, except for the jhihadi."

"I didn't come here as the jhihadi," I explained. "I have business in the chimney, and then we'll be on our way."

His eyes widened. "But—are you not staying?"

I felt bad about disappointing him. "No. We're headed for Alimat, across the Punja."

"But—but we did this for you." He spread his hands. "All of this. You told me, remember? Find water where none exists. We have made a home here."

"You and your people have done very well, Mehmet—but I didn't mean *I* wanted to live here. I'm sorry."

He leaped to his feet, gesturing sharply. "Come, then. All of you. Hurry."

The meal apparently was over, even if we weren't quite done eating it. Mehmet's little wife collected the dishes from the low table and took them swiftly away even as her husband ushered us out of doors.

Two young children were playing down by the stream; Mehmet called to them to find some of the men and have them bring our horses.

I looked up at the chimney formation, or what remained of it, on the other side of the canyon across the stream. No horse could make it up there through the tumbled rocks and scree. I'd have to go on foot.

The horses were brought. The stud had a wisp of lush grass hanging out of the corner of his mouth. Apparently they'd been enjoying a meal, too.

"Go on, go on," Mehmet insisted. "Get on your horses. Hurry!"

We did as we were told. Our host nodded. "Now, ride into the canyon. You see that elbow of hill up ahead? Go around that. The canyon curves to the right. Follow the stream. You will see."

"See what?" I asked.

"Go, go. Go and see."

"And do what?"

"Go and *see.*"

I gave it up. Until we went and saw whatever it was he wanted us to go and see, we'd make no progress toward actual communication.

"You're not coming?" Del asked Mehmet.

He shook his head vigorously. "It's for you. We kept it that way. Now, go and see."

"Let's go," I said to Del and Nayyib, and led the way.

As Mehmet instructed, we followed the stream around the designated elbow. Here the canyon narrowed until there was very

little good footing on either side of the stream, mostly the steep
sides of canyon walls. Huge sections of stone had broken off the
walls, falling to the floor where they blocked most of the way. The
stream, undaunted, had found a new way through. But I noticed
the fallen rocks were all sharply angled and faceted, not yet worn
smooth and round by water. Whatever brought them crashing
down was but a few years in the past.

The horses picked their way over dribbles of fallen stone.
There was no actual trail through here, and clearly none of Mehmet's people had ever attempted to bring in a wagon. The only
tracks I saw belonged to animals.

And then the walls reared back. A passageway lay open, and
the stream purled through. Beneath hooves, grass sprang up,
thick, lush grass. Rocks in the water were mossy, wearing stream-
ers of vegetation. Canyon walls became crumbled hillsides,
cloaked in a tangle of shrubbery and trees.

Old trees. Mature trees. Mehmet's little canyon was new. This
one was not.

The path we made took us out of shadow into sunlight. Out
of canyon into valley. Out of paradise into perfection.

We stopped, because we had to. We gazed upon it, marking
how the stream cut through the middle of meadow. Here was the
true heart of the canyon with high walls surrounding us except
for the throat we'd passed through.

Nayyib released a blissfully appreciative sigh. "Good grazing."

Del climbed down off her gelding and knelt on one knee,
digging into the soil. She brought up a handful, rolled it through
her fingers, then smelled it. "It should be," she agreed. "This is
fine, fertile soil." She shook her hand free of damp dirt, then led
the gelding by me, intent on something. After a moment Nayyib
and I followed.

Del paralleled the stream. All around her lay the meadow,
stretching from canyon wall to canyon wall. We were nearly to
the far end when she stopped and shielded her eyes against the
sun's glare as she looked up and up, studying the rim of the canyon and the blue sky beyond.

I saw her smile, and then she pointed. "Eagle."

Nayyib and I looked. Sure enough, an eagle spiraled lazily over the canyon.

Del's smile didn't fade, but grew. She stood in one spot and turned in a full circle, taking it all in. Her expression was rapturous. "It's almost like the North, this place. Not exactly, but very close."

I frowned. "In the borderlands, maybe."

"There are high valleys in the mountains very like this. You just never saw any of them." She began unbuckling her harness.

"What are you doing, bascha?"

"I'm going wading."

"*Wading?*"

"Maybe even swimming." She gestured up the way. "There's a pool, Tiger. See where the stream is partially dammed by rocks? On the other side there's a natural pool."

I hadn't paid any attention to it. But she was right. Nayyib rode up a little way, seeing for himself.

I recalled the big tiled bathing pool in the metri's house, heated by some means I didn't understand. Del had splashed around quite happily in it. I'd never learned how to swim and thus wasn't as enamored, though it did feel good, but the pool was shallow enough that I could stand in the middle with water up to my shoulders and not worry about going beneath the surface.

Mehmet had said this place was for us. That he'd kept it for us. His people had settled just inside the mouth of the new canyon. This one had remained untouched. This one, much older, had been untouched forever.

Del, who had tied up the reins so the gelding wouldn't trip over them, stripped out of harness, sandals, and burnous. She wore only the patched leather tunic a Vashni woman had repaired for her. Long-limbed, fair of skin, she strode to the water's edge as she unplaited her braid and shook it free. She was magnificence incarnate.

I realized it was the first time in months I'd seen her looking so relaxed. The tension had fled her face, leaving an incandescent joy. Every fiber of her body was reacting to this place.

I smiled, enjoying the sight. *Ah, bascha, if you only knew what I see when I look at you.*

Then I noticed Nayyib but a couple of paces upstream, staring at her. Del glanced at him and laughed. "Come in, Neesha. Lift the dust from your skin."

She had invited *him*. Not me.

Pleasure was extinguished. A chill washed through my body. It left me sick, angry, and afraid.

"I'm going back," I told her abruptly. "I'll leave the stud with Mehmet, hike up to the chimney and try to find the sword."

Del, picking her way carefully into the water, was startled. She halted, bare feet perched on round, slick stones. Sunlight gilded her skin. "*Now?*"

"I need to do it." And as she made as if to turn back, I waved her away. "No, no—you stay here. I'd rather do this alone." Which wasn't true, but I couldn't face taking her away from the canyon. I swung the stud. "I'll look for you when I'm done."

"And if you can't find it today?"

"I'll look again tomorrow morning." I turned my back on them both and headed out the way we'd come in.

THIRTY-FOUR

MEHMET, who knew nothing about *jivatmas* or that I'd left one behind, was perplexed when I said I wanted to climb up to the chimney. He reminded me that its collapse might have killed me. I reminded him that it hadn't and that I had business up there. Whereupon he, recalling I was the jhihadi, offered to guide me there.

I shot him a strange look. "Mehmet, I've *been* there."

"Things have changed," he explained. "After you and Del left, the earth trembled. Rocks fell. Mountains shook. This part of the canyon came into being. You don't know what's up there."

"Do you?"

He was forced to admit he didn't.

"Fine. You stay here. I'll be back before nightfall."

"But, Tiger—"

"I'm going. Look after my horse." I unsheathed my sword and offered it to him. "And look after this."

He was startled. "Why not take your sword?"

"Because I hope to find another one." I clapped him on the shoulder. "I'll be back in time for the feast. I promise."

Mehmet was unhappy, but he nodded. I left him carefully cradling my sword to his chest.

* * *

The climb up to the chimney was more demanding than I remembered or expected. But Mehmet had confirmed my suspicions: Something indeed had happened after Del and I left to collapse the remains of the chimney and crack open the earth to form the newer canyon Mehmet's aketi had made their home. Probably it had opened the entrance into the older canyon, which looked as though no humans had ever been there. I groped my way up, clutching rocks for handholds, trying not to stub my toes. Sandals are not approriate footgear for climbing, but they were all I had.

Originally the chimney had been the hollow core of a mountain. Del and I had found a tunnel and made our way into the heart of the mountain. There we'd discovered the ribbed, rounded chamber open to the sky far overhead. It was purportedly the home of what was left of Shaka Obre, the so-called *good* sorcerer; his brother, Chosa Dei, who had taken up residence in my *jivatma* and later in me, was considered the bad one.

I'd go along with that.

I found no trace of any tunnel or passageway. What remained of the chimney lay in pieces, broken up as if a capricious god with a giant ax had chopped it into sections. Parts of it were indistinguishable from the shattered mountain. But something drove me on.

"*Take up the sword,*" she had said. I would do my best. But it was possible I couldn't. That I might not even find it.

In which case, what?

Portions of mountain towered over my head. I picked my way carefully, gripping boulders as I pulled myself up. I remembered our flight from the collapsing chimney, knowing we might be crushed at any moment. I remembered how Del had shoved me out into the passageway when I wanted to turn back for the *jivatma*. She had no doubt saved my life.

Up and up. Eventually I found the bottom portion of the chimney surrounded by fallen segments of rock. Sections had broken off and collapsed all of a piece, like a stone cairn purposely kicked over. I prowled around, trying to sort out one part from another. If there was no actual chimney left, where might my *jivatma* be? How could I find it?

I stopped, looked around at the remains of the mountain. I wondered if Shaka Obre and Chosa Dei had brought about the additional change in topography.

Had they died? Had their essences faded away? Or had they merely taken their battle to another part of the world?

I went on, rounding a bulge of stone. And found the opening.

Here. *Right* here. The last section of tunnel. It was mostly blocked by fallen rock, and beyond the jagged mouth the interior was dark. I lingered on the cusp a moment—I hate closed-in places—then decided that jhihadis and mages had no reason to fear anything at all.

Or so one might think.

I took a breath, ducked my head, began to make my way in.

"Tiger!" It echoed oddly in all the rocks. "Sandtiger!"

Startled, I stood up and whacked my head on the tunnel roof. Cursing, I backed out. "Here!" Rubbing my head, I made my way around the nearest boulder. "I'm up here."

Nayyib was picking his way through rockfalls and boulders, head bowed as he watched his footing. He had taken off his burnous and now wore only a dhoti, as I did, and sandals. He was brown all over, darker than I, with no scars of significance and none at all from a blade.

If he was serious about becoming a sword-dancer, that would change.

When he reached me, there was no sign of shortness of breath. Very annoying. "What?" I asked testily.

His gaze went past me to the tunnel mouth. "Is that where the sword is?"

"Maybe. I can't be sure. Everything's changed. But this is a portion of the tunnel that existed, so it's possible I can get to the chimney floor."

He nodded vaguely, looking everywhere but at me. Something was on his mind.

Having seen how he stared at Del in the stream, I had a good idea what it was. "Why are you here, Nayyib?"

His eyes flicked to my face, then swiftly away. He turned and stared down the way we had come. "You can see part of the valley from here."

I waited. His posture was stiff even as he ran a hand over his head, smoothing springy hair.

And I knew. Even though I asked. "Neesha, why are you here?"

His back was to me. It nearly vibrated with tension. "Del sent me. She said I should come."

I closed my eyes a moment, then made myself cold and hard. "Not now."

"She said—"

"I don't care what she said." Because I knew. "I don't want to hear it." Because I *knew*. "I have business to attend to."

I bent and began to make my way into the tunnel section, leaving the kid behind. In the darkness I took care not to bash my head once again on some unseen protrusion. Hands followed the line of the walls, testing solidity. There was air aplenty but no light. I should have brought a torch.

I heard Nayyib's sandals crunching on grit. He was right behind me.

"Cool in here," he remarked.

I wasn't happy that he'd followed, but I felt a little better knowing someone, even he, was with me in a confined space. "There was ice in here originally. Not much, but a little." I peered ahead. "I think there's light up there."

So there was. The tunnel ended against two large boulders, but sunlight crept down through the cracks. It wasn't much, but it allowed me to see.

There was a slot to the left. The tunnel ended against the boulders straight ahead, but the narrow opening gave into something else. I pressed myself up against it and peered through. "I think that's it."

"The chimney?"

"What's left of it." I thought about it a moment, trying not to shiver in front of the kid; then reconciled myself with the memory that I'd been in here before and survived. I turned sideways and tried to edge my way through. Abdomen and spine scraped against rock. "There's a little light in there . . . it sure looks like it's a portion of the chimney. There's sand."

"Why does sand matter?"

"The floor of the chimney was sand. Just big enough for a circle." I grunted, sucking in my belly. Left a little more skin on the rock behind me.

"You're too big," Nayyib said. "Let me try."

I didn't want to let him do anything. "If I can just get through this one narrow spot—"

"Don't," he said sharply. "You'll get stuck."

He had a point. It was tough enough being in and under all this rock. The idea of being *stuck* here did not appeal.

"Let me try," he repeated.

I couldn't help the snap in my voice. "Why would you want to?"

For a fleeting moment there was pain in his eyes. Then it passed. "Because I'd like to."

No way could I get in there. It was Nayyib or no one. "All right." I slid back out, gritting my teeth. "It's tight, though. I'm not sure you'll have any more luck."

"I'm not as big as you." Nayyib poked his head through the slot, saw what appeared to be part of a chamber, sand floor and all, then sucked in his belly, straightened his shoulders, and started the slow, careful journey.

"Don't breathe," I suggested.

He released a brief hissing puff of air that served as laughter.

"If you find a sword in there, don't touch it."

His face was turned toward the chamber. All I could see was a body attempting to work its way through the slot. He seemed to be making progress.

And then he scraped through to the other side, disappearing

from my range of vision. I heard cursing, though I couldn't see anything. "You all right?"

His voice echoed weirdly. "I think I left fourteen layers of skin on that rock."

"Well, having less meat on your bones will make it easier to get back out." I couldn't contain the frisson of dread that scoured my flesh. I wanted to go back out into the sun. Hurry up, kid. "See anything?"

"Anything like a sword? No. But there's not much light in here."

"I left it lying on the sand. It wasn't under anything."

His voice sounded hollow, deformed by rock. "Well, it probably is now." A pause. "Maybe I should get down on my hands and knees and feel around for it."

"Don't touch it! If you find anything at all like a sword, don't touch it."

"Then how am I supposed to bring it out to you?"

"Strip out of your dhoti and use that."

I heard the ghost of laughter. "I don't much favor coming back through that slot naked, thank you. There are parts of my body I don't want to scrape off against stone!"

"Then push the sword through first. You can cover up your precious parts afterwards."

He was silent. I waited impatiently.

Finally I gave up holding my silence. "Anything?"

After a moment his voice came back. "Lots of cracks and crevices. I'm checking them all."

"It wasn't *in* a crack or crevice."

"Then," he agreed, sounding irritated. "It may be now."

Well, that was true. I subsided again into silence, wishing I could pace. Wishing I could leave.

Then I heard a choked-off expletive make its way through the slot.

"What? What happened?"

"Is your sword broken?"

"No. It's whole. Why? Did you find a broken sword?" Hoolies, he'd found Del's broken *jivatma*. "Don't touch it!"

"I didn't intend to!" he called back. "But when you're bare-foot and you stumble over it, it's hard not to."

"Why are you barefoot?"

"I took my sandals off."

"What for?"

"So I could feel the sand with my feet."

"You *stepped* on the sword?"

No answer.

"Nayyib?"

Nothing.

"Neesha?"

His voice sounded muffled. I couldn't understand.

"What are you doing?" I called.

Now he sounded cross. "Taking off my dhoti."

Was he bringing Del's *jivatma* out? Was that what Del had asked him to tell me, that he bring Boreal out if we found her?

"Neesha?"

"Here." His voice sounded closer, but pinched off. "Here, take the sword . . ." The hilt appeared through the slot.

Not Del's. Mine.

Samiel.

Mine.

I closed one hand around the hilt. Felt the familiar warmth, the welcome of Northern named-blade to wielder.

Mine. *Mine.*

Samiel.

Something deep in my soul surged up. I had forgotten what it felt like to hold a keyed *jivatma* bound to me. I couldn't restrain the fatuous smile that split my face.

Mine.

I heard grunts and mutters. Nayyib, dressed again, was working his way back through the slot. I saw a hand and arm reaching, a sandaled foot sliding through; heard the hiss of indrawn breath.

In a moment he was free, pressing a hand against his abdomen. "There went a few more layers."

"Let's get out of here." I turned, stepped back into the darkness of the tunnel.

"Wait," Nayyib said. "Tiger—wait."

I didn't want to wait. "I don't want to wait."

"Please."

"It's dark in here."

"That's why I want you to wait. It might be easier."

The pleasure in finding the sword spilled away. For a moment I had been able to forget. "*What* might be easier?"

"To tell you."

I said nothing. I couldn't. There was only pain and acknowledgment. An understanding that had everything to do with practicality and none whatsoever with the feelings of the heart.

Oh, bascha.

But I could be alone. I'd been alone all of my life, until she had come.

And now she wanted to go.

"Del said I shouldn't put it off any any longer. That if I didn't tell you, she would."

Suddenly I was grateful we were in darkness. I didn't want him to see my face; didn't want to see his.

More silence.

Then, "I don't know how to say it."

I wasn't about to be patient as he tried to find the right words to tell me what I didn't want to hear. "I'm done in here." I turned, took a step.

"Tiger, *wait*—"

I swung back, filled to bursting with dread and anger. "Spit it out!" I bellowed. "Get it over with! Tell me what you've come to say!"

"All right!" he bellowed back. "You're my father!"

THIRTY-FIVE

<sub/>

N_o.

No.

Of course not!

Of course not.

Not possible.

He had come to tell me something else entirely. Something to do with Del.

Hadn't he?

Not possible.

"It's true," he said, when I did not respond.

Because I couldn't. I could not make a sound. I wasn't even certain I was breathing. I had prepared myself to hear something entirely different. This was . . . this was wholly alien, like an unknown language that sounds familiar but you can't make out the words.

"It's true," he repeated.

I was numb all over. The hairs stirred on the back of my neck. It took everything I had to force halting words past a throat tight with shock. "You said your father has a horse farm."

"He does. That is, the man who raised me does. He married my mother when I was a boy. He *is* my father in all ways—except blood and bone. He raised me. *You* made me."

My chest constricted. I felt the banging of my heart against

ribcage. I didn't know how much of that had to do with his words
and how much with my hatred of small, enclosed places. Breath
rasped noisily through my throat.

"It's true," Nayyib said.

Couldn't be.

Wasn't.

Couldn't be.

My voice came out sounding very hoarse. "I don't have any
children."

"That you *know* of. Del said."

Del had said a great deal.

My bones felt oddly hollow. "Why should I believe you?"

He released a long, resigned breath, as if I had finally said
something he'd anticipated. "You were seventeen. Newly freed
from the Salset. You wanted to be a sword-dancer. You stopped at
a tiny village on the way to Alimat and spent the night with the
headman's daughter."

I went on the offensive. "Not to brag, but I've spent the night
with a lot of women over the years."

"She was, you told her, your first as a free man. And you intended to take a name—a *true* name—to mark that freedom."

"So? A lot of women know my name."

"You told her Sula had named you, when you lay sick from
the sandtiger poison."

Only Del knew that. And Sula, who was dead.

Seventeen then, barely. Forty now.

Twenty-three years.

Del was twenty-three. So was Nayyib. He'd said so; she had.
Not a kid, she'd said. Not a boy.

I had said I was old enough to be her father. And thus his.

"And you told Del this?"

"Del and I talked about many things when she was ill."

My voice sounded rusty. "There's one way to find out if this is
the truth."

Startlement edged his voice. "You still don't believe me?"

I wanted to ask, Why should I? "Go out into the light."

"But—"

"*Go out into the light.*"

Nayyib went out into the light. I followed him. Both of us blinked against the sun. Samiel, forgotten in my hand, flashed blindingly brilliant.

The kid eyed the sword. He marked the runes edging the blood channel, the satiny steel. Then he looked at me. Lifted his head with a slight aggressive tilt. Anger was in his eyes.

I stared right into them. "Is there a mark on you? A birthing mark?"

A muscle leaped in his jaw.

"Show me."

He stood very still before me, clad in only a dhoti and sandals. Stubble was turning into beard, just as my own was. I saw nothing of me in his face, nor anything of the woman he claimed was his mother. But it had been twenty-three years. It was true I had slept with many over the years, and most of them I couldn't remember.

That woman, I did. Sula had been my first, followed by others in the Salset; I was a slave; I did what I was told. But only one woman had been my first as a free man. A headman's daughter in a tiny village on my way to Alimat.

"Show me."

Abruptly he hooked thumbs into the top of his dhoti and jerked it down, displaying his lower abdomen, the thin line of dark hair vertically bisecting paler flesh. And the small, purplish mark the Stessoi called keraka, the god's caress. I'd seen it on Herakleio; Del had seen it on me.

I nodded once.

Nayyib pulled his dhoti back up. The anger simmered.

He wanted something. Acknowledgment. Confirmation. But I was empty of all emotions save overpowering disbelief, despite the presence of the keraka. Nothing in my life had ever prepared me for this. I had never even *imagined* it.

He stood waiting, every fiber in his body tensed with increasing anger. I had not responded to his announcement, had given him no clue to what I was thinking.

Inane, incongruous laughter bubbled up. I blurted the first thing that came into my head. "What did you expect?" I asked. "That I would fall at your feet and praise the gods?"

His eyes flickered. Those liquid, melting, honey-brown eyes, set beneath mobile eyebrows. "I don't know what I expected."

"Oh, I think maybe you do."

He met the challenge. "All right. I dared to hope, once or twice, that you might be pleased."

I was completely, tactlessly honest with him. "I'm not certain that's possible at this particular moment."

It shocked him. Shook him. Then he put on a mask, hiding his feelings. "Now what?"

"Now you go back to Mehmet's little village."

"What about you?"

"Oh, I'm going to go sit in the dark for a while and think about things."

He opened his mouth. Then shut it. No doubt there were all manner of things he wish to say, of questions he wished to ask, but he had the sense to realize now was not after all the best of times to say or ask any of them.

He turned to go.

Went.

I walked unsteadily back into darkness, gripping my *jivatma*.

When I came down from what remained of Beit al'Shahar, Del was waiting. She sat beside the stream on the far side, watching idly as I made my way across the stepping stones. By the time I got there, arms outstretched for balance, she was standing.

She smiled, lifting her voice over the rushing of the water. "You look as if someone hit you over the head with a cantina stool."

Since she had seen me be the victim of that very occurence, she knew what she was talking about. "Someone did."

She looked more closely. "Are you all right?"

"For someone who's been hit over the head with a cantina stool." I was still trying to reconcile emotions. "I just can't make my brain understand it. It heard the words, even understands

them, but refuses to acknowledge that they apply to me. I mean,
I know he told me the truth—"

"Do you?"

I looked at her. "Yes."

"*Do* you?"

I released a long breath. "Yes."

"But you didn't feel inclined to fall at his feet and praise the
gods."

I winced. "He told you."

"I believe he got hit with the same cantina stool."

"Hoolies, Del, I didn't mean it to come out like that. But he
wanted me to say I was pleased, and how could I? I'm too confused
to be pleased!"

"Are you *dis*pleased?"

"No! I'm too confused to be anything." I stared at her plead-
ingly. "Don't you understand? It's not something I ever contemplated. Not once."

Her chin lifted. "Nor ever wanted?"

I flung out a hand. "Look at what happened to me! I was born
as my mother lay dying in the middle of the Punja. I survived only
because the Salset came along—and they made me a slave! Salset
slaves don't have children. They may sire some, or bear some, but
they aren't allowed to keep them. Then for twenty-three years
I've been a sword-dancer, never sticking anywhere. It's no kind of
life for a woman—" I saw the flicker in her eyes but didn't retreat.
"—who wants to have her man nearby, and a family. I can't be
that kind of a man for that kind of a woman. So I never thought
about it, until that foolish foreign kid with the axes went around
telling everyone he was mine, knowing full well he wasn't."

"Neesha isn't that foolish foreign kid. He *is* your son."

"I know. I know." I shook my head. "I just can't think, bascha.
There's too much in my head. I need time to work through all of
it."

"Why? You don't have to *raise* him. He's a grown man. All
you have to do is acknowledge him."

That stung. "I didn't say he wasn't my son!"

"But you told him you weren't pleased."

"Because I wasn't! I wasn't anything. Hoolies, I was lucky I could find the words to say anything at all."

Del smiled faintly. "The Sandtiger—speechless. Truly a miracle."

I had to make her understand. "There is nothing, *nothing* in this world that could have stunned me more than what that kid told me. I don't know how else I could have reacted under the circumstances. I did the best I could. Maybe it wasn't enough, maybe it wasn't what he wanted, but it was all I had in me right then." I shook my head, still lacking words. "I've never claimed to be a perfect man, and I sure as hoolies wouldn't claim to be a perfect father. Especially when I didn't know I was a father at all."

I must have made some headway; her tone was kinder. "I did warn him not to have expectations."

"Well, I think he did!"

"Hopes, perhaps. How could he not? He has known since childhood you were his father. He's heard all the stories of the legendary Sandtiger. He has wanted to find you for all of those years. But he was afraid."

"Afraid?"

"That you would disbelieve."

"I did *not* tell him I disbelieved him."

"Nor did you welcome him." She put up a hand to halt more protestations. "It took him a very long time to find the courage to search for you. And even more to look into your eyes and tell you."

"He didn't 'tell' me. He yelled it at me."

"Sometimes yelling at you is the only way to get anything through your head. But that's not the point." Her eyes were sad. "He swore me to secrecy. I was not to say anything to you at all. It was *his* task."

"But you did threaten to tell me if he didn't get to it today."

Del nodded. "Because I knew what you were thinking."

"You did?"

"You were becoming more and more certain something was growing between Neesha and me."

"Ah, Del . . ." I planted my rump on the cool earth of the stream bank, rubbing hands through my hair. "He's twenty-three. He's a good-looking, smart kid with a head on his shoulders who's got his whole life ahead of him. What woman wouldn't be attracted?"

Del sat down next to me, left leg touching mine. "A woman who is content with what she has."

I didn't prevaricate. "*Why?*"

She leaned against me, put her head on my shoulder. "I can't define it. I just know it. Better than I know anything in this world."

I stared hard at the rushing stream, trying not to weep. "I don't deserve you."

"Probably not."

After a moment I smiled. "That time we talked about children wanting to know who they are, who their blood parents are—that was because of Neesha."

"That was part of it, yes."

"And as it turned out, I was searching for my mother. I just didn't know it at the time."

"But you knew how important it was that you find her."

"Yes."

Del nodded against my shoulder. "It was the same for Neesha."

I watched the water run. "You were so protective of him, so obsessed with his welfare. Always claiming we owed him a debt, insisting we rescue him from Umir. Because he was my son."

"And I *like* him, Tiger. There is that as well."

I sighed, nodded. "He's a good kid. I like him, too."

She lifted her head from my shoulder and leaned in to kiss my cheek. "Go tell him that."

I stared into water for a moment longer. Then pressed myself up from the earth, reaching down for Del. She rose as I pulled, and I wrapped her up in my arms. "Thank you, bascha."

After a moment she leaned away. Her smile was luminous. "He's out with the horses. They're picketed near the corral."

THIRTY-SIX

I DID NOT immediately go to find Neesha. I watched Del walk away, heading back toward Mehmet's house. Then I turned, stared pensively up at the broken chimney for a time, then into the rushing water.

I have a son.

Alien words. Alien concept.

I have a *son*.

I had believed it impossible. Not because I was incapable or infertile, but because at the core of my being a small, cold, piece of me remembered all too well how the Salset treated the get of chulas, if the women were unlucky enough to carry to full term when herbs didn't loosen the child. They were made slaves themselves, or sold to slave-dealers, or exposed out in the desert.

When you have lived among the Salset for sixteen years, you do not easily forge a new identity, a new view of yourself. I had spent far more years as a sword-dancer, but slavery had shaped me. A part of me would always be a chula in mind if not body.

I have a son.

Born into freedom, not slavery. Not sold. Not exposed.

Despite what I had told others, I had never *not* wanted children. I had simply never allowed myself to consider that I could.

I have a son.

I felt the kindling of a new emotion. Felt tears on my face.
Praise the gods.

As Del had said, I found Neesha near the corral, grooming and
talking quietly to the horses. It struck me yet again how good he
was with them. Firm but not heavy-handed; calm, soft-spoken,
yet clear on who was in charge. He had already groomed his horse
and Del's gelding; now he worked on the stud. More than a little
surprised by the stud's quietude, I watched without indicating I
was nearby.

But he knew. Whether it was the stud's pricked ears or just an
extra sense because of his background, he glanced over a shoulder
as he smoothed the brush around the healing wound on the
brown haunch.

It was too difficult to say what I wished to say. So I opened
with a compliment that was also the truth. "You are very good
with horses."

He looked away. "Is that your way of suggesting I should go
back to the farm?"

Oh, he was indeed in a mood. "It was my way of saying you're
very good with horses."

He ran the brush down to the stud's hock. "But you *think* I
should go back to the farm."

I told myself to be patient, that I had set up this scene by my
own reaction to his news. "If that was a question, I'll answer it: If
you want to. If it was an accusation, then I'm denying it."

"Maybe you don't care enough to have an opinion one way or
the other."

Anger flared; of course I cared. But how could he know if I
didn't tell him? Even if I had no idea how to begin.

I let the anger die. "Maybe I have an opinion but don't care
for people trying to put words in my mouth."

"I thought about leaving." He eased around the stud's rump,
moved to his head to brush the far side. "I thought about saddling

up and just going, with no word to anyone. But I decided that would be childish."

I smiled. "Well, yes."

"And besides, I really *did* come to ask you for lessons, and I really *do* want to be a sword-dancer."

Finally I had to ask it. "And when did you plan to tell me you were my son?"

He moved to the stud's withers and looked at me across his back. "When I felt I was good enough that you'd be proud of me."

That was a kick in the gut, if not a stool over the head. "So, you had not planned to tell me at any point during the ride here."

"No."

That hurt. "Then why did you? I know what Del told me; but she wouldn't have given you away. You could have kept your mouth shut."

He hitched a single shoulder in a self-conscious shrug. "When I got up there in the rocks and came face to face with you, I thought I couldn't. Decided not to. But then I brought your sword out, and I thought that would please you—"

"It did please me."

"—so I decided to take a chance. And then—I couldn't. I couldn't say it. And you got angry."

Dryly, I explained, "I hate it when people won't say what's on their mind. I tend to yell sometimes, or so Del tells me."

"And then it just came out. And you—didn't care. Didn't believe me, until I showed you the mark."

"And then you decided I wasn't pleased."

"Because you said—"

Hoolies, couldn't he see? "What I said was that it wasn't a good time to expect anything out of me. I had just had the shock of my life. There were too many thoughts in my head for me to make any sense at all of *any* of them, let alone to say anything worthwhile! Think of it as being so drunk you can barely remember your name . . . the gods only know what will come out of your mouth." I twisted mine. "For what it's worth, seeing the mark was only confirmation. I did believe you. But I wasn't remotely prepared for that kind of announcement. Hoolies, I was expecting you to say something entirely different! Had expected it for some time."

He had stopped brushing and stared at me, brows knit. "What were you expecting me to say?"

I drew in a breath. "That you wanted Del. And she wanted you."

His mouth dropped open. "*What?*"

"That's what I was expecting."

"I—but . . . but what—I mean . . ."

I laughed. "See? Sometimes you can't make your brain form a real sentence."

He got the point. Closed his mouth. Tried again. "Why would you think anything of the sort?"

"I saw how you looked at her. Today in the other canyon. And at other times."

He stared at me as if I had two heads. "Gods, she's breathtaking! She's what we all dream of. How could *any* man not stare at her?"

I could not keep the curtness from my tone. "Or not wonder what she'd be like in his bed?"

Color bloomed in his face. "You tell *me*, Sandtiger! You're the one who took my mother to his bed when she was barely sixteen!"

After a moment, I said, "You know how to pick your weapons."

"But it's true."

"Yes." I nodded, aware of a trace of shame. "Yes, I did take her to my bed. I was a scared, foolish kid drunk on freedom, dreaming of making himself someone of significance in the circles at Alimat. She was very pretty, and I couldn't understand how she might be attracted to me. But she made me feel special." I had to look away from him; couldn't face his eyes. "She made me feel like a *man* instead of a chula."

He too looked away for a long moment. Then met my eyes again. "She said you were kind."

My reply was heartfelt. "I hope I was. She deserved kindness."

"She said—" Abruptly his mouth jerked into a crooked smile. "She said I take after her father, the headman. That I have a little of your height but not your eyes. Or hers."

I smiled, remembering. "She had very dark eyes."

"My grandfather has Borderer blood in him. It shows in me."

"There's Skandic in you, too. But your grandfather, if he had those eyes, probably could have taken his pick of any woman on the border."

Neesha grinned. "Ah, that's right. You said I could make every woman spread her legs for me."

"A not inconsiderable feat."

"Except for Del." He shook his head. "Would I want to?— hoolies, I'm a man, not a fool! But she sees no one but you. That was quite clear when I tended her in the lean-to."

Unable to speak openly about something this important, I resorted to off-handedness. "Nah, she just wants me for all my vast riches." Then I grinned. "And now, let me say this: You are a good-looking, smart kid with a head on his shoulders. And I like you. But I have never been a father, nor ever expected to be. I don't know how."

With wide, melting eyes, Neesha told me, "It's not as if you'll need to change my diapers."

"And you've got a smart mouth on you, too."

He affected innocence. "My mother doesn't, nor the man she married. I must have gotten it from someone else."

I scowled. Pointed to the stud's immaculate left leg. "You missed a spot." Then I stalked away.

Later that night as we lay in Mehmet's bed feeling the effects of a large feast, Del asked, "Did you tell him?"

I had been just at the edge of sleep. "Tell him what?"

"That you like him."

I yawned widely. "Yes, I told him that I like him. I told him everything you told me to tell him, that I had told you."

I heard a breath of laughter. "What did he say?"

"That he must have inherited his smart mouth from me."

After a moment of startled silence, Del began to giggle against my chest. I went back to sleep.

When I awoke not long after dawn, I discovered Del was missing. No wonder the bed felt so empty. I dragged myself out of it, slipped into harness and sword, wandered through the front room to the dooryard and saw Neesha lying belly-down at the edge of the stream, staring into the water with one arm submerged beyond his elbow. He didn't move. Finally I went over asked asked what he was doing.

"I'm hoping to catch some fish."

"There are fish in there?"

"Del and I saw them yesterday, after you'd gone back. Quite a few up in the pool in the other canyon."

I decided to mention it. "You don't have a hook or line."

"No, I'm planning to tickle them."

"*Tickle* them? Fish?" I'd always considered tickling for women and children, not fish.

"If you tickle their bellies, they get a little sleepy. Or whatever fish do; I'm not sure. Maybe they just stop paying attention. But you can grab them and throw them on the bank."

I grunted skeptically. "I wasn't born yesterday, and you're not fooling me with such nonsense."

"It's not nonsense. I've done it many times."

"Where?"

"In the borderlands, close to the North. Lots of streams and creeks up there."

It still sounded unlikely to me, but I didn't know him well enough to be certain when he was joking. "Huh. I'll bet Mehmet has a hook and line."

"Probably, but I didn't want to disturb him. And I like doing it this way. Sometimes you need to know you're smarter than the fish."

Dryly, I observed, "I wouldn't think that'd be too hard."

Equally dry, he told me I'd be surprised.

I observed him a moment longer, marveling. *This is my son.*

Then I reached over with a foot and bumped his leg. "Come on. It's time for your first lesson."

He was startled. "Now?"

"Why not? I like to believe I'm better company than the fish."

Neesha shot me an elaborately assessive glance.

I smiled, baring teeth, and unsheathed my *jivatma*. After that he didn't look at anything else. "Come on, Nayyib-Neesha. This is just the beginning of a long and painful process."

He stood up from the bank. Eyed me again, this time seriously. And sighed. "Yes, I suspect it will be."

THIRTY-SEVEN

I BROKE through Neesha's guard six times in a row. By then he was frustrated and humiliated. He'd wanted very badly to show me he had some grasp of the essentials, when what he felt he'd shown me were weaknesses. Of course, that's what I'd expected; but I'd also anticipated that maybe, just maybe he could do to me what I'd done to Abbu so many years before, if I wasn't careful. And while that no doubt would have pleased Neesha, it might also have gotten me hurt.

So I was careful.

And I am, after all, the legendary Sandtiger, seventh-level sword-dancer out of Alimat . . . besides, if I was to shape a new legend, he needed to understand he had to be better than good.

Sweat ran down his face, bathed his chest. He was quick, graceful, focused. He was also angry with himself. So I told him we were done.

He lowered his sword. "Already?"

"Already."

"We've barely begun!"

"And we're finished. For now. We'll go again tomorrow." I jerked a thumb over my shoulder. "Go wash off in the stream. Cool down."

He wanted to say more. But he shut his mouth on it, put his sword back in his harness, and stalked past me.

"And kid . . ." I waited until he turned around. "It will be a long ten years—or seven, or six—if you get this frustrated every time."

His mouth was a grim line. "I wanted to be *good*."

I grinned. "Good doesn't happen overnight—or even after four lessons with Abbu Bensir." I bent, grabbed up my own harness, sheathed the *jivatma*. "Tomorrow. In the meantime, I'm going to track down Del."

"She told me she was going up to the other canyon."

I shook my head in resignation. "Seems like Del tells you more than she tells me."

An odd look passed across Neesha's face. Then abruptly he turned on his heel and headed for the stream.

By the time I hiked up around the elbow and through the passageway, the morning chill had faded. The sun now stood above the rim of the canyon walls, slanting blankets of light down the tree-clad mountain slopes. I heard birds calling and the chittering of something in the bushes, probably warning of my coming. The rush and gurgle of water underscored everything.

Del was where I expected her to be, up near the natural pool. At first I almost missed her as she lay on her back in thick meadowgrass. High overhead the eagle circled again against brilliant skies, accompanied by his mate.

I paused long enough to strip my sandals off, tie them together and sling them over a shoulder, then took pleasure in feeling the grass and cool soil under my feet. Remarkably different from Punja sand. My callused feet liked it very much.

I strode along the stream bank. "Catch any fish?"

I saw Del's hands go to her cheeks, wiping them hastily. Then she sat up. Her hair, worn loose, tumbled down her back. She smiled as she saw sandals dangling from my shoulder. Hers were lying near the water, along with her harness and sword.

Good idea. I dropped my sandals, got out of the harness, set it and *jivatma* in the grass. "All right," I said, "I may be male, but I'm not completely heartless. Tell me why you were crying."

Her eyes widened slightly, and then she laughed self-con-sciously. "Because it's so beautiful here."

This explanation seemed incongruous. *"That's* why you're crying?"

"Tiger—" She stood up abruptly, grabbed my hand, tugged me along the bank. Her free hand gestured broadly. *"Look* at it, Tiger! The trees are leafing out, the bushes are setting fruit, there are flowers in the grass, sweet water in plenty—"

"And fish that apparently like to be tickled."

In full spate, she disregarded the comment. "—and eagles in the sky, game on the slopes, a far more benevolent sun than any-where else in the South—*no* searing heat, *no* Punja, *no* sword-dancers hunting you . . ." She released my hand and dropped to her knees, plunging fingers into the ground and bringing up clods. "Look at this soil! So much would grow here . . ." She tossed the clumps aside and rose, grabbing my hand again. "Come here." She led me away from the water. "Do you see? There against the canyon walls? We could build a good house. Smaller houses—just rooms, really—could go across the stream against *that* canyon wall. And here, *here* there is room for multiple circles." Her ges-ture was all encompassing. "As many circles as you need in a school. And Julah isn't far for when we need supplies. Or if you and the students wanted to go in to the cantina for wine-girls and aqivi."

Ah. Now I knew where she was heading. And it apparently wasn't Alimat, if she had anything to do with it. "This is why you're crying?"

Color stained her face. "Because it's beautiful, yes. Because it offers us everything we could want. Because it gives us a future different from anything we've known, something we can build to-gether, starting over again."

Carefully I noted, "That's what I'd planned to do at Alimat."

"In the *sun.* In the *heat.* In the *sand.* Where, if there's water, it's always warm. Where I have to paint my horse's eyes and hang tassels off his browband so he doesn't go blind."

"Hey, that was your idea! I told you to get another horse, remember?"

"He's got the softest walk I've ever ridden. Probably softer than any *you've* ridden, you with that stubborn, nasty-tempered, jug-headed demon—"

"Now, let's not get personal about my horse!"

"—who'd just as soon throw you as carry you a yard—"

"All right!" My hand was in the air, silencing her. "We've established that your gelding has a better walk than my horse. Go on."

Del glared. "Because for the first time in more years than I can remember, I can let down all my walls. I thought I had forgotten how. My song is sung, Tiger. I found my brother and lost him again. I avenged my family by killing Ajani. I've proven to you I can dance with all the skill and honor of male sword-dancers—"

"With *more* skill and honor."

"—and defeat them as well." She was as fierce in her focus as I had ever heard her. "I have accomplished all that I set out to do, that day along the border when Ajani and his men killed my family, abducted my brother, and raped me. And I have given up a daughter, killed my *an-kaidin*, blooded—and broken—my *jivatma*, and have been exiled forever from my homeland." Her tone was sere as desert sand. "You asked me once what kind of man I dreamed of finding, and I told you I had stopped thinking of that the day Ajani came. I gave up all my dreams, all my hopes, all my *humanity* to become the weapon needed to kill Ajani. I even made a pact with the gods to keep me from conceiving again, so another child would not delay my plans as Kalle did." Her face was stark with pain. "So I would not have to give yet another child up."

"Del—"

"Two things, two things only, existed in my life: finding my brother and finding Ajani. I did both. My song is ended."

"Del—"

"And I was crying because this place is so beautiful it hurts my heart and because I know you won't want to stay here because there's Alimat, always Alimat—" She broke it off, drew a tight, rasping breath, began again. "And I even understand that because it's *your* song, *your* goal, *your* need, the way making myself into a weapon was mine. I understand it, and I hate it. I hate the sun and the sand and the heat, and the men who refuse to see a woman's true worth is in being something other than a vessel to bear babies and keep houses—" Now the tone was angry. "—and I hate it that you made yourself an outcast for my sake, breaking all your oaths and sentencing yourself to death by declaring *elaii-ali-ma* in front of all the others *and* Abbu Bensir—"

I raised a hand. "Del—"

Her voice tightened. "—and I hate it that you don't want children, because I'm going to have one and you'll want to leave."

Standing there suspended in disbelief, I discovered that once again I lacked the ability to find words, any words at all that began to address the situation in a calm, rational, sensible manner. Or, for that matter, that even approached coherency.

"And I hate it because I want this one to have a mother and a father of its blood—" She was running out of breath and intensity. "—and to keep it, to *keep* it, instead of giving it away as I gave away Kalle, to be a mother, a true mother, even though I know you'll want no part of this child or this life."

Empty of everything save sluggish shock and a wish to end a pain I could not begin to comprehend—and thus would lessen by any attempt—I walked away from her on unsteady legs and stood at the stream's edge, staring into rushing water. Lost myself in the sound, the tumult, the motion that required no words, no decisions, no compromises.

The cantina stool was getting harder all the time.

I squatted, leaned, scooped up and drank water. Sluiced it over my face and through my hair. Considered falling face-first into the stream and drowning myself, just so I never had to find myself yet again so utterly, completely, incoherently stunned.

Too much. All of it, too much. And Del knew it. Expected my reaction. Because I had told her what I'd told everyone: no children for me.

Go? Oh no. I had sworn oaths to Del, though she was un-aware. And these I would not break.

And then I thought, *I'll be dead in twelve years.*

I would never see the child as an adult, like Neesha. Another good-looking, smart kid with a head on his shoulders—or a girl with all the glorious beauty and strength of her mother.

But twelve years, ten years, were better than none.

It seemed, after all, there was no decision to make. No reluc-tance to forcibly sublimate. There was merely comprehension—and a little fear.

Then I remembered the dream. Me, alone, as everyone I knew—and some I didn't—walked away from me. That is what my life could be like. Me, refusing to accept responsibility for my own actions. Even for my children. And deserted because of it.

I'd survived hoolies all alone among the Salset. I wouldn't—couldn't—do it again.

I pressed myself up from the ground and went to Del. I cradled her jaw, smoothed back her hair, kissed her on the forehead, then took her into my arms.

Her body was stiff, her voice tight and bitter. "And here I was prodding Neesha to tell you *his* secret, when I've been keeping my own."

Into her ear I said, "I think I'd have figured it out one of these days even if you never said anything."

She pulled back. Walked away from me. Stood staring at something I couldn't see and probably never would. Her tone was oddly detached. "Don't worry, I don't expect you to stay."

It hurt. Badly. But I had done it to her. Had done it to myself.

She turned. The angles of her cheekbones were sharp as glass. Her eyes were ice. "I will not force a man to stay who has no wish to. I have been alone in much of what I've done since my family died; I can be alone in this."

I drew in a shaking breath that filled my head with light. "Well, it's not an entirely new idea, this being a father. I've had all of, oh, about a day to adjust to the idea of Neesha being mine."

Her tone was scathing. "Neesha is not a *child.*"

"But it's a start. I mean, you're not going to drop this kid tonight or tomorrow." I paused. "When *is* it due?"

"Around six months from now."

I shrugged off-handedly, keeping it light. It was what she was accustomed to. "I figure if I can get used to having Neesha around, I can get used to a baby."

Del was not in the mood to be amused. "Babies are considerably more trouble than a twenty-three year-old man."

"Bascha . . ." I wanted to go to her, to take her into my arms once again. But I had learned to read her over the years, and that was not what she wished me to do. So I stayed where I was and told her the truth. "I knew when I stepped out of Sabra's circle and declared *elaii-ali-ma* that the life I'd known was over. I knew when Sahdri chopped off my fingers that the life I'd known was over. There on that island, with you lying next to me in the sand, I decided to build a school and become a shodo. Whether it's here or at Alimat isn't important; what matters is that I'd *already* made the decision to stick in one spot. Knowing there's to be a baby doesn't alter that." I paused. "Though I confess I'm not exactly sure how this has happened, since you made that pact with the gods. But then, I don't have much to do with gods—except when I curse—so what do *I* know?"

Her mouth compressed. "It happened because my song is over. Being gods, they knew it."

"Your song isn't over."

"That part of it is. I vowed to find my brother and kill Ajani." Her tone chilled. "Apparently they decided the pact no longer applied."

"Then make a new song. You're a sword-singer, after all."

Pain warped her words. "A sword-singer without a *jivatma*."

"Well, I've got one of those. And a terrible voice, as you've pointed out—you can sing *for* me."

It did not set her at ease. "This is not a casual decision, Tiger. This is a song that lasts a lifetime. Kalle I gave up. At the time it was all I could see, were I to achieve the goal I set myself, the goal that allowed me to survive. It wasn't a wrong choice; it was the *only* choice. But I am older now. I am different now. I have killed and will undoubtedly kill again; I know I will dance again. That is what I am; no child changes that."

"No," I agreed.

"But this time, I wish to preserve life. I have no goals beyond that, no song to sing, save I wish to make a new beginning with a new life." She said her walls had come down. I could hear in her voice the attempt to rebuild them, should it be necessary. "I will ask no man to do what he cannot do."

"Then don't ask me. Just tell me what you need. Now—or after the baby's born. If Alric can do it, I can."

One pale brow arched. "Do you really believe so?"

I needed badly to knock down the nascent walls. "Well, maybe only until the first time it spits up on me."

Her mouth twitched in a faint smile. "You missed all that with Neesha."

I feigned wide-eyed hope. "I don't suppose you could arrange for it to be born as a twenty-three-year-old?"

"Twenty-three-year-olds spit up. *You* spit up. That's what happens when you drink too much."

"As you found out."

Del sighed. The tension began to seep out of her shoulders. "As I found out."

"Look, bascha, what I said yesterday was the truth. I've never claimed to be a perfect man, and I won't ever claim to be a perfect father. And getting hit over the head with a cantina stool two days in a row is more than a little tough to take in! But if you'll give me the chance to do it—*and* forgive my lapses—I'll never say anything rude about how big you look when you're about ready to drop the kid."

"You don't drop a baby, Tiger; it isn't a foal. You *have* a baby. And you will too make rude comments."

"Well, all right, yes, I probably will. Some things I just can't change." I glanced around. "But I guess I can change where I'd planned to start a sword-dancing school. This place *is* beautiful.

Alimat had its shodo and became a legend. This is Beit al'Shahar, and we can found a new one."

She hadn't yet relaxed. "A child is not a stray kitten, or a puppy with a broken leg, or even an orphan sandtiger cub. A child is for life. Make no promises you cannot keep."

"As I made to my shodo?"

From that, she flinched. "I didn't mean it so."

"Then let me make this promise: I will try."

She lifted her chin. "Are you certain?"

"Hoolies, no! But I don't know that I'd be any more certain if we were at Alimat just now." I smiled crookedly. "I never really planned to become a teacher. I never thought beyond dancing. I expected to die in the circle, to meet an honorable death. But that song for me is ended just as yours is for you. It's time I began another."

Her eyes searched my own. "Can you do that?"

I lifted my hands. Displayed them. "I knew I would have to that day atop the spire in ioSkandi. A child played no role in that decision."

"It does now."

Softly I said, "Give me a chance, bascha."

She closed her eyes a moment, as if praying. Then she opened them. "No wine-girls for you when you go into town."

I sucked in a dramatically stricken breath. Then, "Aqivi? At the very least?"

She considered it. "If you'll have Neesha tie you on the stud when you're too drunk to ride, and bring you home safely."

"If we're tying me on horses when I'm too drunk to ride, can I borrow your gelding?"

"Hah. I *knew* you liked his walk."

"And I'm thinking I'll invite Alric to pack up Lena and the girls—and maybe a boy, now—and come down here to live. I'll send Neesha to Rusali to ask. Lena could tend the baby while you're tending sword-dancers."

She didn't say anything for several moments. Then she took the steps necessary to put herself into my arms.

I cradled her head against my shoulder. "Are you crying again?"

"No."

"You are, too."

"Maybe a little."

"What's your excuse this time?"

She drew her head back and looked me in the eyes. "Not excuse. Truth: I may have stopped dreaming about the kind of man I wanted long ago, but I found him anyway."

I grinned. "You're just trying to sweet-talk me into your bed."

She took my hand, drew it down to her belly. "I think this baby proves you've already been there."

I laughed. "Well, yes."

Her hand, without excess fanfare, shifted from her belly to mine. And slipped lower, sliding suggestively between dhoti and skin. Which quivered.

"Uh, bascha . . ."

Her other hand was working at the tie-strings. "Hmmm?"

"What if Neesha comes?"

"Neesha knows better."

"What if Mehmet comes, or some of his people?"

"Then they'll all simply discover that their beloved jhihadi is also a man."

Self-control was on the verge of departing. "What about the baby?"

Del laughed. "The baby won't mind. The baby won't even notice."

I caught the hem of her tunic, slipped it up above her hips. "Are you sure?"

Her smile was glorious. "I'm sure."

"Well, if you're *sure* you're sure . . ."

Her mouth was against mine. "*Shut up*, Tiger."

Tiger shut up.

EPILOGUE

ALRIC DRAGGED me out of the house. "Come on, Tiger."

"I'm not going—Alric, let go . . ." I tried to free my arm. "This is my own house, you know!"

He didn't give up. "Yes, I know that. I helped you build it. Now, come on."

Another harsh, half-throttled cry came from the bedroom where Del was in labor. Lena was there and one of Mehmet's aketni, an old woman who'd borne many children herself. Alric's children were off being tended by another of Mehmet's aketni, to get them out from under our feet.

I planted mine. "Alric—"

"We're going." He practically jerked me off my feet. "Trust me, there is nothing we can do except get in the way. Lena told me that with the birth of every baby. Now that it's you in my sandals, I understand why."

He'd gotten me as far as the dooryard. The panoply of the canyon opened before us, a spectacular fall day with trees ablaze, but I was in no mood for scenery. "How can you expect me to wait out here? She's been in labor since last night. She could die from this!"

He shoved me toward the stream. "Yes, she could, but I doubt it. Del is strong, and she's had a baby. Now, go sit down with your feet in the water."

"She had that baby nine years ago!"

"Tiger, she's young enough to have ten or twelve more after this one."

Hoolies, what an image! I stomped down to the stream, swearing all the way. Alric followed me, likely making sure I didn't try to go back to the low-roofed house built of mudbrick hauled in from elswhere, since the soil here was better fit for crops. It's what Mehmet and his aketni had done.

I stood on the streambank and listened for Del's cries over the sound of the water. I didn't hear anything, which was probably Alric's intent.

Something occurred to me: absence. "Where's Neesha?"

Alric sat down in the grass, then leaned back on elbows. "He and Ahriman climbed up to the chimney earlier. Your new student is very eager to learn everything he can about his shodo."

I grimaced. "Ahriman won't make it past the second level."

"No, probably not. But he's a paying student for the time being."

One student in six months. Two if you counted Neesha, but I didn't expect him to pay; I figured a father owes his son that much, especially when he's been absent for almost twenty-four years of his life.

I smiled. "Neesha will make it past the second level."

Alric laughed. "*Oh* yes."

"He wants very badly to achieve seven levels faster than I did."

"Of course. He's your son. But he's hungrier than you were."

I glared at Alric. "You weren't there. How do you know he's hungrier than I was? He's certainly had an easier life than I did!"

"It's a different kind of hunger, Tiger. Your ambitions were to escape slavery in body and mind. Neesha wants to live up to the legend he's held in his mind since childhood *and* to make you proud of him."

"I *am* proud of him!"

Alric shrugged. "He has to discover it in his own way."

But my mind turned from Neesha and back to Del. Unable to stand still or sit, I began to pace. "Hoolies, I'd rather be in the midst of a death-dance than this. How can you stand the waiting, Alric?"

"Well, I've done it four times, so I have experience. And will likely do it again a few more times." His smile was content. "Four healthy daughters."

I stopped pacing. "Del says men make their wives keep having babies until they get a son, even if their wives don't want to."

"That may be true of some men," Alric agreed equably, "but I'll have sons enough when my daughters marry."

If I had a daughter . . . if I had a daughter, men would think of her as they did of all women. Even as *I* had, before Del trained me out of it.

Well, mostly.

"I'll kill them," I said.

Alric's brows ran up beneath the fair hair hanging over his forehead. "Kill who?"

"The men who try to get my daughter into bed."

The big Northerner laughed. "She's not even born yet, Tiger—and she may be a *he*!"

"I need to think about it, though. What I might face. Because, you know, if it is a girl, and she looks like Del . . ."

"Let's hope so. I'd rather a daughter look like Del than a big, slow danjac such as her father."

"I can't do this," I said abruptly. "I can't just wait out here. What if Del wants me with her?"

"Trust me, Tiger, Del doesn't want you with her. Best you stay out here—unless you *like* having her curse you."

"I'm going." I started toward the house, taking huge, long strides to get me there the faster. Then Lena appeared in the doorway and I began to run. "Is she all right? Is she all right?"

Lena was smiling as I arrived. "She's well, Tiger. So is the baby."

I stopped dead. "The baby? It's here?"

"Yes, the baby is here. Go in, Tiger. You've been waiting long enough."

But suddenly I couldn't make myself move. "Maybe I shouldn't. Del will be tired. She'll want to rest."

Lena laughed. "Go on, Tiger."

I felt a hand come down on my shoulder. Alric's. "She won't curse you now. They never do once the baby's born."

I took a deep, steadying breath, then a second one. And I went in to see what the Northern bascha and I had wrought.

The old woman of Mehmet's aketni was helping Del drink a cup of something that smelled slightly astringent. When she saw me come into the bedroom, she smiled, set the cup down, and waved me in. Staring at Del, I didn't notice her departure.

I couldn't see any baby. Just Del, lying beneath the covers. She was propped up against pillows. Lines of exhaustion were in her face, but there was also a contentment that outshone everything else.

I lingered in the doorway until she saw me. Her hair, wet with perspiration, was pulled back, braided out of the way. Her smile was weary, but happy.

"Where is it?" I asked.

"Where is *she*, Tiger. A baby is not an it."

Ah, good. She sounded normal.

Then it struck me. "It's a girl?"

"That's what 'she' usually means. And she's right here."

I saw then that they had wrapped the baby in so many layers that she looked more like a lump of bedclothes than a person. Del lifted that lump from beside her. I heard a muffled noise that sounded suspiciously like a sandconey warning of predators.

"Come see your daughter."

I didn't move. "You don't want to do this again, do you? Ten or twelve more times?"

Del looked horrified. "No! Why do you ask me such a thing?"

"Alric said you could have ten or twelve more . . . and he and Lena are already headed in that direction."

She laughed. "Tiger, stop putting it off and come and see your daughter."

When I reached the bed, Del put up a hand and urged me to sit. I did, very carefully. And then she peeled back the wrappings and I saw the face.

I was aghast. "What's wrong with her?"

"There's nothing wrong with her."

"She's all red and wrinkled! And she has no hair!"

Del's smile bloomed. "The red will fade, the wrinkles will go, and the hair will grow. But she does have *some* hair, Tiger. It's baby fuzz. See?"

To please Del, I said that yes, I could see the wisps of something that approximated hair. But if that's all she was going to have the rest of her life, I wouldn't have to worry about what men might think.

"Hold her, Tiger. She's yours, too."

I recoiled. "I'd drop her!"

"You won't drop her. Have you ever dropped a sword?"

I refused. "You can hold her. I'll just look at her."

"I'm very tired," Del said. "I'm very weak. I need you to hold her."

I cocked an eyebrow at her. "You aren't any better at lying now than you were before she was born."

Del was aggrieved. "I *am* tired, Tiger."

She was. Some of the animation in her face had faded. "Are you all right? I mean, *will* you be all right?"

"I will be fine just as soon as you hold your daughter."

I scowled. She always did drive a hard bargain. "All right. What do I do?"

"Just take her in your arms and cradle her. Put her head in the crook of your elbow."

"What if she cries?"

"Just hold her."

"What if she's hungry?"

"Then give her back to me."

I leaned forward, grasped the lump, lifted. Discovered she weighed nearly nothing.

Del's tone was appalled. "Don't just clutch her in midair, Tiger! Hold her against your chest."

Apparently I got it sorted out, because Del quit giving me advice. She lay there smiling at us both.

I ventured, "Does she have any arms and legs, or is she just a lump with a head attached?"

Del sighed. "I should have known you wouldn't appreciate the moment."

I grinned. "It's not a moment, bascha. It's a *baby*."

She reached out a hand and stroked the wrappings. "I thought maybe we could call her Sula."

It shocked me. I could think of nothing to say.

"That woman gave you your freedom," Del said. "As much as there was to be found in the Salset. Not enough, I know—but more than you might have had otherwise."

After a moment, when I had my emotions under control, I nodded. "Take her," I said. "Bascha—take her."

She heard the tone in my voice. "What is it? What's wrong?"

"Nothing's wrong. Nothing, bascha." I leaned forward, steadied the little bundle as she was taken from me, then bent down and kissed Del's forehead. "Rest. I'll come back later."

I waited until she had settled the baby beside her. As her eyes drifted closed, I left the room.

Alric saw my face as I came out of the house. "What's wrong?"

"Nothing's wrong."

"You look—odd."

"I'm fine."

"Then why are you in harness?"

"There's something I need to do."

"Tiger—something's wrong."

"Nothing's wrong," I repeated. "There's just something I need to do." I paused. "Alone."

Alric was troubled. He and Lena were sitting outside the

house on the wooden bench I'd built. The chickens Mehmet had
given us darted around the dooryard, and the half-grown gray
tabby cat was chasing an insect. We had, in six months, accumu-
lated all the trappings of a regular family: a house, chickens,
mouser, two goats.

And now a daughter.

"I have to, Alric. I'll be back later."

He nodded and let me go.

I met up with Neesha and Ahriman at the passageway into
the upper canyon. Ahriman was a short, compact Southroner
with black hair and eyes. He was several years younger than
Neesha and rather shy in my presence. Which made it difficult to
get him to actually attack me in the schooling circle. He did better with Neesha, whom he did not hold in awe.

"How's Del?" Neesha asked at once.

"She's fine. So's the baby."

"She had it?"

"Her. She had 'her.' " I nodded. "A little while ago."

Neesha was studying me. "What's wrong?"

"Nothing's wrong."

"Tiger—"

I stopped him with a raised hand. "Nothing is wrong. Go on
up and see Del and the baby—she's your half-sister, after all. I'll
be back."

Neesha didn't look any less concerned than Alric. But I had
no time for them.

No time for much of anything.

The climb up to the broken chimney was easier now than when
I'd made it six months before. Not only did I know where I was
going, but I was utterly focused on my goal. When I reached the
tunnel, I didn't think twice about the darkness. I ducked my head,
went inside, followed it back to the slot near the boulders blocking the rest of the passageway. There I took off the harness,
dropped it to the dirt floor, and pulled the stopper from the little
pot I'd collected on the way out of the house. I smeared grease on

my abdomen and spine, tossed the empty pot away, unsheathed the *jivatma*. I left the harness where it lay.

It wasn't easy getting through the slot. Neesha had been right about leaving layers of skin on the rock. But the grease served me well, and at last I scraped myself into the chimney.

The chamber was small, about one-quarter the size of the original circle. Sunlight worked its way down through cracks, illuminating the area, but the chimney wasn't a chimney anymore. Mostly it was a pile of rocks and sections of ribbed wall. But the floor was still the pale Punja sand Del and I had discovered before.

I glanced around. Found what I expected: Del's *jivatma*. Boreal lay in two pieces. I didn't touch them. I set down my sword and bent to unlace my sandals. When that was done, I stripped out of my dhoti. I collected my sword, moved to the center of what remained of the chimney chamber, and sat down cross-legged with the *jivatma* across my thighs.

In fractured light, I looked at my hands. Two thumbs, three fingers on each. The stubs were no less obvious than before, but I hadn't really noticed them for a while. The training I'd done on the island near Haziz still served me. Since settling in the canyon, I had spent every day working through the forms, keeping myself fit. Sparring matches with Neesha and Alric—I had refused to fight Del once I knew she was pregnant, which irritated her to no end—maintained my speed, strength, and technique. In fact, Alric said I was better than before.

If that were true, it was because something inside me, some facet of the magic, lent me an edge. When I danced, I felt four fingers on the hilt. Not three. My grip was the grip it had been before losing them. And I had no explanation. Only gratitude.

I closed my hands lightly over the sword. Went into my head. Dug into my soul. Peeled the flesh off the bones, shed muscle and viscera, until I found the magic buried so deep inside.

It wasn't a flame, but a coal. It burned steadily, unceasingly, using me as the fuel. It would kill me one day, merely because it existed. Because my mother was of the Stessoi, one of the gods-descended Eleven Families of Skandi, and those gods had been

capricious enough to set their mark on me even as my mother,
and I, lay dying in the Punja near my father's body. Because I was
ioSkandic, a mage of Meteiera, meant to leap from the spire to
merge with the gods when the madness overcame me.

In ten years. Twelve.

I had a son. A daughter. I had Delilah.

I wanted to live forever.

Or at least as long as I possibly could as man, not mage, without the interference of a magic I never wanted. Even though I'd
used it.

"*Find me,*" she had said, "*and take up the sword.*"

My mother had died giving birth to me. But she had served
me nonetheless by setting me on the road to this place. To this
moment. To this decision.

No other was possible.

I found the coal inside. Took it up. Blew gently upon it. Felt
the heat rise; saw the flame leap. I coddled it. Cradled it. Nursed
it into being. Kept it alive. Bade it serve me.

Made it serve me.

Once I had had a sorcerer inside me. And in my *jivatma*.

It was time to put the mage that was me in the *jivatma*. The
power, if not the man.

For the first time since I'd been reborn atop the spire in Meteiera, I thanked the priest-mages who had altered mind and body.
Because in doing so they had given me the key.

Discipline.

"Mother," I said aloud; and discovered how odd it was to use
the word as an address. A title. "Mother, you bred me for this.
Bred it *in* me, bequeathing me something else of your people besides height, coloring, even keraka. Magic, magery, is not a gift I
desire, or require. I wanted freedom—and won it because of Stes-
sor magic. I wanted to be a sword-dancer—and became one because of Skandic strength, the heritage of you, my father, and
everyone before us. But now comes the time for me to look forward instead of backward. To, as Del would say, make a new song.
To do that, I must make a new man. One who wishes to live for

the children *he* has made, children who are of Stessoi flesh and bone even as I am. But also of the North, and of the South. If to do that I must cut away a part of me that you gifted me, so be it. I have made the choice."

There was no answer. I had no bone to fuel the dream-walk. But I had clarity of purpose, and the certainty to fuel that.

It took time. It nearly took me. But I felt the flame of the power become conflagration, feasting on my flesh. I poured it into and through my arms, down into the sword. Into Samiel, whose song I sang in a broken, shaking voice.

Discipline.

And when it was done, when the magic that had, at age sixteen, won me my freedom, resided in the sword, I stood up from the sand. Walked to the chimney wall. Found a crevice. I thrust the *jivatma* blade into the stone as deeply as I could.

And then I broke it.

I was a sword-dancer. It was all the magic I needed.

I smiled even as I wept. Even as I placed the two halves of the broken *jivatma* with Del's. Even as I shakily put on dhoti and sandals and went back through the slot, leaving layers of grease and skin.

In the tunnel, I collected my empty harness.

When I walked up the canyon I was thinking about Del. Not about circles, or sword-dancers, or *elaii-ali-ma*. Not about challenges. Not about dancing. Not about the price for breaking lifelong oaths.

Certainly not about Abbu Bensir. But he was there. And I understood why. On this day of all days, we had finally arrived at the moment we both had known would come: the dance that would define us both.

He stepped out of the doorway of my house as I approached. He wore only a dhoti and held a sword. "You were hard to find," he told me, "but then I heard about Alric and his family heading down here with a kid who'd been seen with you and Del, and I knew."

I said nothing. I waited.

His tone changed. "Sandtiger," he said, "by the rite of *elaii-ali-ma* I am not required to challenge you or to meet you in the circle. I am required only to kill you. But I have not forgotten the ignorant boy who, all unknowing, taught me a lesson before others at Alimat, even before the shodo. For that, I will offer you the honor of meeting me in the circle."

Very slowly, I unbuckled my harness. Dropped it to the ground. Spread my hands. I had no sword; I could not accept.

Abbu Bensir smiled. "The boy has said he will lend you his."

The boy. My son. Who had once been taught by the man before me.

"Where are they?" I asked.

Abbu stepped out of the doorway into the yard. Neesha came out. And Alric.

The big Northerner said, "Lena's with Del. She's fine."

"Does she know?"

Something spasmed briefly in Alric's face. "She's asleep."

Ah. Well, probably for the best.

Abbu nodded. "I have asked the boy to start the dance for us. Shall we waste no more time?"

"The boy," I said, "has a name."

"Nayyib. I know. I met him some years ago, apparently, though I confess I don't recall." He flicked a glance at Neesha, standing white-faced in the dooryard. "Give him your sword."

We had met several times, Abbu and I. That first time at Alimat, when I nearly crushed his throat. His voice still bore the scars. Once or twice after that, merely to spar because we ran into each other in a distant desert town with no other entertainment. Then for years, nothing. The South is a large place, and we ranged it freely. We were to meet again at Iskandar during the contest, but I'd been kicked in the head by the stud and was in no shape to dance. More recently, we had met at Sabra's palace, where I had aborted the dance by declaring *elaii-ali-ma*.

To this day neither of us knew which was the better man.

I walked over to Neesha and looked him in the eye. "I thank you for the honor of the use of your sword."

He wanted to speak. Didn't. Just unsheathed and gave me his sword.

I led Abbu to one of the sparring circles and waited. He studied it, walking the perimeter, noting how the turf was incised and marked with small pegs denoting the circle, so the grass wouldn't cover it. Inside, the meadowgrass was beaten down, crushed by feet. He walked there, too, to learn the footing. In a strange place, we would not have done so; but this was my home, and Abbu was due the chance to learn what its circle was like. He set his sword in the center, then walked away. I did the same. We faced one another from opposite sides.

He was older than I, smaller, lighter. But he'd always been fleet of foot. Age lay on him more heavily than the last time we'd met, but he was as fit as ever.

"I hear you danced against Musa."

So, he knew him. Or knew *of* him. "Umir's idea. But yes. I did."

"I hear you killed him."

"He insisted."

"Ah." Abbu nodded. "Musa was a proud boy. I did warn him it would get him killed one day, if he didn't quench it. I didn't believe it would be this soon."

"How well did you know him?"

"I taught him. Oh, not as the shodo taught us. He didn't stay with me for years, learning the forms. He came to me with a natural skill honed by other instructors: the sword-dancers he'd already defeated. He wished to defeat them all and desired my help. When I saw how he danced, I gave it to him." His creased face tautened briefly. "I did not believe you could defeat him."

I nodded. "Neither did Musa."

Dark eyes flicked to Neesha. "Now."

Neesha stood two paces away. Alric had moved to stand behind me, well out of the way.

I looked at my son and nodded.

His jaw clenched. "Dance."

It was a fast-moving, vicious fight, unlike anything Abbu and I had engaged in before. But then, though not friends, we had been friendly rivals, more interested in the challenge. We had never fought to the death. Even before Sabra, he had retained the honor I'd always seen in him, doing his best to respect the honor codes despite Sabra's desire for me to die.

He respected those codes now. But this time he wanted me dead.

Within four engagements each of us had drawn blood. I had a slash across one thigh and a cut along my ribs, matching the one Musa had given me on the other side. Blood dripped from the inside of Abbu's right arm, but it wasn't a mortal wound. We were a long way from dying.

And I had discovered that the ritual I performed to rid myself of the magic had also tired me. I felt as if a part of me were missing; and maybe it was. The fingers were. No more was there the odd conviction that they were still attached. My hands were as Sahdri had made them: a thumb and three fingers, no more. The stumps were sore. My grip was weakened. As Abbu engaged my blade again, the sword twisted in my hands.

Abbu Bensir was not as young as Musa, but he was far wiser. He would not make the mistake Musa had.

And I could die for it.

My world closed down. My mind registered all of the factors that affected a dance, such as footing, footwork; how the light lay; the reach of blades and arms; the rhythm of my breathing and his; even the blood running down my flesh. The canyon was filled with the belling of blades, the screech of steel on steel.

Yet again his blade touched me, slashing high across one hip. I broke away, stumbled, felt more blood running, saw the light in Abbu's eyes. He came in, blade raised and moving. I blocked it, held it, spun away. Felt the pain in my hip. Felt the sudden tilt of the world.

I took a step forward. Went down. Caught myself with both hands splayed against the ground. The hilt of Neesha's sword remained beneath my right hand, but I couldn't grasp it properly. The stump banged against leather grip, sending fire through my arm.

Abbu came on. I grabbed the fallen blade, stayed on my knees, brought the hilt up. I planted the pommel in his belly even as his sword sang down on the diagonal, slicing straight into the meat up my upper arm. I felt the steel grate on bone.

But Abbu had lost the impetus of his blow when I jabbed the sword hilt into his abdomen. He fell back, gasping, slightly hunched. I got to my feet, aware that the wound was a bad one. The arm didn't want to work. I wavered, nearly fell down, caught my balance with effort. Blinked as sweat ran into my eyes.

Abbu went to one knee. He cradled his lower belly with his left arm. His face was gray.

I was one-armed now. I stayed on my feet with effort, aware of the roaring in my ears. And then, as it so often did, time slowed for me. I had no magic, but I had skill and the odd accuity that always served me.

Abbu got up. He winced as he straightened, then wrapped both hands around his sword hilt. He came across the circle.

Slowly. So slowly.

I saw the blade rise. Saw my blood on it.

As he came on, I let go of the sword—Neesha's sword—in midair and caught it upside down as it hung there at the apex. I held it overhand now, the pommel exiting above my thumb. I pulled it and my arm back across my body, elbow bent; as Abbu closed, I snapped my arm toward him in a backhanded, punching thrust, keeping the power close to my body. The desperate maneuver allowed Abbu inside, to make contact with my body, but by then my blade had been shoved straight through his body. I heard his outcry, felt the warmth of his breath on my face, took his weight on my right shoulder as he fell forward.

With the last bit of my strength, I thrust him away from me

with my right arm, letting him take Neesha's sword. He fell hard, full-length, his head smacking dully against the ground. The sword stood up from his body.

They were with me then, Neesha and Alric. I felt hands on me, holding me upright, supporting my left arm. Someone tied something around my upper arm to try to slow the bleeding. But I pushed them away, staggered to Abbu. Saw the blood on his lips. Before I could say a word, before I could speak the ritual blessing for a seventh-level sword-dancer at the edge of death, he was gone.

Over.

Ended.

The first of the shodo's greatest lay dead in the circle.

This time I didn't fight them as Alric and Neesha gathered me up, kept me on my feet, aimed me toward the house. We were nearly there when I saw Del in the doorway. Hollows lay like bruises under her eyes, and her lips were pale. One hand clutched the doorjamb; the other lay across her mouth, as if to physically restrain the fear that she would not confess.

But a smile of relief began behind the hand, and she lifted her fingers away. She reached out, closed that hand on the back of my neck, shakily pulled me close. Her robes were immediately soaked with my blood. "Come inside."

Alric and Neesha got me there. Del directed them to the bed in the other room. I protested weakly. "What about the baby?"

"She's in the cradle," Del told me. "She missed her father proving once and for all that he *is* the greatest sword-dancer in the South."

"Well," I gasped, "she'll probably see it again."

Alric and Neesha helped me to sit on the bed. Unconsciousness crowded in. I was aware of people moving around, bandaging me, of words exchanged about a heating knife; but none of it made any sense. Everything felt distant.

"What about you?" I asked Del, even as they made me lie down.

She had moved around to the other side of the bed. She sat down, caught her breath, then took my right hand. "I'm here."

I wanted to tell her she had no business sitting up in bed hanging onto me so I could hang onto her, but then Alric thrust a twist of cloth between my teeth, told Neesha to hold my arm, and pressed the red-hot knife blade against the wound in my upper arm.

I woke the baby up. Del said something about having *two* screaming infants in her house, and then she very suddenly lay down next to me.

Ridding my mouth of cloth, I croaked, "You all right?"

Her head moved against mine in a weak nod.

I glanced at Alric, who was dropping the knife into a wooden bowl. "You enjoyed that. Making me yell."

He grinned. "So I did."

Now I looked at Neesha. "Still want to be a sword-dancer, after seeing that?"

He drew in a breath. "After seeing that, I want to be nothing else."

Guess it was in the kid's blood after all. I smiled faintly to tell him I approved, then rolled my head toward Del. I heard the sounds of Neesha and Alric leaving. The baby had gone back to sleep. I thought her mother was on the verge herself. "You awake?"

Her voice was a breath of sound. "Barely."

"I have a question."

She was fading fast. So was I. "What?"

"Who's really the best? You or me?"

Del lifted her head enough to stare at me in wide-eyed, rigid disbelief. Then dropped it back down again. "I guess we'll just have to have a dance to find out."

"All right. Tomorrow?"

"Fine," she murmured.

I turned my head enough to feel her hair against my face. Opened my mouth to tell her we'd have to be vigilant about the men who lusted after our daughter—and then exhaustion hit me over the head with a cantina stool.

A woman. A son. A daughter.

Was this what I had expected?

No.

But it was what I had dared to dream, at night among the Salset.

Author's Note

It has been eighteen years since I first conceived a book about a male chauvinist pig of a Southron sword-dancer who has his consciousness raised by a very independent Northern woman in the same line of work. Though envisioned as a novel with a subtext about how sexism can hinder a gender from achieving freedom of mind and body, I also intended it to be entertaining, a fast and fun romp through the South with Tiger as a guide. It was to be a single book; but by the time I finished writing *Sword-Dancer*, I knew I wanted to write more about Tiger and Del. They were just too much fun to play with.

A question I have already been asked is whether there will be more Sword-Dancer books. I must be honest: I have no plans to continue Tiger's and Del's story. Maybe it's time for another generation, or another universe full of different characters.

That being said, I would like to express my appreciation for the readers who have written me over the years to comment on the books. Tiger and Del have reached many people, and I am particularly proud of the male readers who've written to say that the books have altered their views of women. The point of these books was always to present women as *humans*, not individuals defined solely by gender. If I have made anyone think about the role of sexism in society, I've accomplished a goal. By the same token, I don't intend polemic to get in the way of a good story, and I hope readers have enjoyed their visit to the world of Tiger and Del regardless of the subtext.

Two specific questions are the most often asked in e-mail and at personal appearances. The first is, why did I, a woman, choose to write the books from Tiger's point of view?

The answer is simple: It's the way the opening scene in *Sword-Dancer* presented itself. I "heard" Tiger's voice in my head one night, odd as that sounds, while taking a break from the Cheysuli series back in 1983. Once I sat down and wrote the opening line, *Sword-Dancer* was off and running.

The other question deals with point of view, or *pee-oh-vee*, as we writers call it. Most fantasy novels are written from what's known as the third person, when the story is told *about* characters. Many readers don't care for the first-person POV, preferring books that approach the story from a greater distance or from multiple points of view. I understand this; I recall when I was in high school putting first-person books back on the shelves rather than checking them out. But as a writer, I discovered that "personage" allows the author a great deal of flexibility. Some stories need to be told from a broader perspective. But for some reason, Tiger was very insistent about telling his own story.

That story, now, is ended. I would like to thank all the readers who kept "T&D" alive through so many exploits. Over eighteen years, my own life has undergone nearly as many convolutions as Tiger's: single when I wrote *Sword-Dancer*, then married, then divorced. I lost the two people closest to me—the people who raised me, who taught me to love books—in my grandfather and mother, eighteen months apart, in '97 and '99. And I moved from the Big City to rural acreage in the shadow of pine-clad mountains.

In the meantime, there are others stories to be told. I hope readers will enjoy them with me.

—J.R.
Flagstaff, Arizona
November, 2001

About the Author

Jennifer Roberson has published 22 novels, including historicals *Lady of the Forest* and *Lady of Sherwood*, both reinterpretations of the Robin Hood legend emphasizing Marian's role; and *Lady of the Glen*, a retelling of the historically documented Massacre of Glencoe in 1692. Her primary emphasis is fantasy, and she has to date published eight novels in the *Chronicles of the Cheysuli*; six volumes in the *Sword-Dancer* saga; and a media novel set in TV's *Highlander* universe; and she has collaborated with Melanie Rawn and Kate Elliott on historical fantasy *The Golden Key*, short-listed for the World Fantasy Award in 1997. She has edited three fantasy anthologies: *Return to Avalon, Out of Avalon, Highwaymen: Robbers and Rogues*, and has contributed to collections, anthologies, and magazines. Her works have been translated into many foreign languages.

Jennifer Roberson has a BS in journalism, and is preparing to pursue a Master's in Liberal Studies. She lives in Northern Arizona, where she breeds and exhibits Cardigan Welsh Corgis in conformation, agility, and obedience. At last count her household numbered six Cardigans, two Labradors, three cats, and a Lipizzan gelding, but that is always subject to change.

The author may be reached via her website at: *www.cheysuli.com*